also by dc palter

Fiction

To Kill a Unicorn

Non-fiction

Colloquial Kansai Japanese: The Dialects and Culture of the Kansai Region

countdown to decryption

DC Palter

SüprDüpr Publications

SüprDüpr Publications
Copyright © 2025 by DC Palter. All rights reserved.
Countdown To Decryption

Second Edition
Softcover ISBN: 978-1-968784-02-7
eBook ISBN: 978-1-968784-03-4

First edition published in 2024 by Pandamoon Publishing.

Jacket design and illustrations ©Pandamoon Publishing
Art Direction by Elgon Williams: Pandamoon Publishing
Editing by Rachel Schoenbauer and Tylee Ertel: Pandamoon Publishing
Back cover image by Image by rorozoa on Freepik

All rights reserved under International and Pan-American Copyright Conventions. Library of Congress Cataloging-in-Publication Data is on file at the Library of Congress, Washington, DC

contents

To my princess, from your frog.

one
kill joy

The door rattled open and Sumire walked into my apartment as if she already lived here. "It's terrible," she cried from the doorway.

I had no idea what she meant. When she left her boots lying on the floor instead of lining them up against the wall, I should have realized something was wrong and rushed over to her. But I was in the middle of a Zoom with one of the biggest, baddest venture capital firms in Silicon Valley excited about funding my startup and hardly glanced in her direction.

While I was trying to convince the neckties to hand me millions of dollars to get my programming schools off the ground, Sumire strode across the carpet to where I sat at the computer, the smell of chamomile trailing in her wake. Ignoring the dead-fish eyes following her from the other side of the screen, she buried her head in my shoulder and started sobbing.

In a panic, I switched off the camera to wipe away her tears and told her I'd be finished as soon as I'd closed the investment. I expected her to retreat to the sofa to wait, but she only squeezed me tighter. By the time I turned the camera back on, half the neckties had dropped off the call. The bald necktie in the middle of the screen cleared his throat before informing me they were passing on this opportunity.

"Wait!" I begged as the remaining squares popped away, leaving only my own frustrated face staring out from the empty meeting room. I banged the keyboard to kill the video. "What is it?" I snapped.

She pulled away, tear-filled eyes burning into my forehead. "Ted Hara! You didn't read my message!"

I'd DND'ed my phone for the call with the moneymen, I pleaded in my own defense. That brought me no sympathy from judge or jury—there was no excuse for ignoring her messages no matter what the emergency. I picked up my phone and scrolled through the alerts until I found her text.

"joy murdered."

That's all it said. That's all it needed to say. Joy was one of her best friends, a classmate from Berkeley Law. We'd been to Joy's birthday party only a week ago. How could she be dead?

"Oh, Bunny, I'm sorry," I said, feeling like a jerk. I wrapped my arms around her and held her tight. Her body shuddered against me, her breath ragged, as tears pooled on my skin.

When she finally let go, I offered to make tea, my mother's cure for everything wrong with the world. She sniffled and headed into the bathroom, slamming the door behind her. I put on the kettle anyway and checked the news while waiting for the water to simmer and Sumire to simmer down.

At the top of the San Jose Mercury site, a serious, thin-lipped woman in a mortarboard, yellow tassel hanging over her face, stared out as if she were still alive. The headline read: "Daughter of Congressman Killed."

The article didn't have many details, and what it had wasn't enlightening. "Joy Miyazaki, 24, of San Jose, was fatally shot in a suspected home invasion robbery at 6:30 a.m. this morning." It described Joy as a prominent human rights lawyer and the daughter of Congressman George "Jiji" Miyazaki. Though the police claimed to be pursuing multiple leads, no arrests had been made. At the bottom of the page was a shot of the crime scene, yellow caution tape blocking the wooden stairway leading up to her second-floor apartment. The same stairway Sumire and I had climbed a week ago.

While San Jose had its share of drugs and homelessness, our town was hardly San Francisco or Oakland—more suburban sprawl over a high-tech hub of office parks than downtown urban decay. Even Amazon deliveries were safe from the scourge of porch pirates in the old Greek neighborhood behind the Tamien train station where Joy lived.

A home invasion robbery made no sense—the criminals would've had to climb the staircase on the side of her two-story apartment building in full view of the other six apartments looped around the driveway. Joy must've been targeted for some reason. While the water ran in the bathroom sink, I continued scanning the news to find out why.

On the website of a local TV channel was a clip of an interview with a neighbor shocked at the murder of such a sweet and quiet young woman. She'd clearly never met the strident, abrasive Joy. The new police chief vowed swift justice for the perpetrators and asked the public to call the tip line if they had any information. In other words, they didn't have a clue. Other sites had nothing other than the same wire story until I landed on the Patriot News Network.

I usually avoided the alt-right conspiracy page—their obsession with Washington politics had little relevance to me. But with Joy's father a Democratic congressman, they were frothing over her murder. They claimed anonymous police sources had divulged that Joy was a known drug kingpin, perhaps the biggest in San Jose, who used her illicit earnings to fund her father's election. Her murder was no home invasion robbery— this was a hit from the gathering forces of Q, the opening shot of The Storm when the swamp rats surrounding her father would be purged by the patriotic forces loyal to the once and future president. Despite my over- whelming gag reflex, I couldn't click away.

When Sumire stepped out of the bathroom looking sad but composed again, she caught me stuffing my phone in my pocket. I told her it was nothing, but she held out her hand demanding to see it anyway.

After reading the headline, she muttered to herself, "Filthy lies," repeating it like a mantra as she scrolled down the page. At least she wasn't crying—now she was furious.

Fists clenched, she bit her lower lip. "You know she wasn't a drug dealer, Ted. And her murder can't be random." I nodded. Her wide, dark eyes bored into me from behind black frame glasses. "Can you do me a favor?"

"Anything," I said, wary of what she'd get me into.

"Can you find out about Joy?"

I didn't know what she wanted. "Find out what?"

"Anything suspicious. An argument with a neighbor. BiteCoin transac- tions. Someone stalking her. You know, stuff like that."

That sounded like a job for the police rather than a mathematician. I'd only met Joy once and knew nothing about her. Which didn't matter to Sumire.

"Teddybear?" The tips of her ears stuck out from the curtain of shoulder-length raven hair like a cartoon rabbit.

"Yes, Bunny?"

Without saying anything, she pointed her chin towards my computer.

"You want me to hack into her account?"

As a lawyer, she couldn't ask me to commit a felony. Instead, she brought my hands to her lips and kissed my fingers. "Can you see what you can find?"

I was pretty sure the police wouldn't appreciate me snooping in the personal data of a murdered woman during an active investigation. Only four months ago, the cops had thrown the ebook at me for hacking. Sumire had gotten me off with a warning, but they'd threatened to charge me with unauthorized computer access, wire fraud, and aggravated identity theft if I ever did it again. Still, it didn't take an advanced degree in mathematics to know there was only one correct answer. "Sure thing, Bunny," I said with as much enthusiasm as I could muster.

It would be easy enough to snoop around the underground sites and see what turned up. If her murder really had anything to do with an alt-right conspiracy, it would be plastered all over Truth Social and promoted by the Russian troll groups on Facebook. More likely, though, I'd find nothing but the same stupid muskrats hurling the same invective at Joy's daily X posts demanding social justice. Despite Patriot News' breathless claims, I doubted her politics had anything to do with her murder. I was unlikely to find out who killed Joy or why, but at least I'd keep Sumire content while the police went door-to-door searching for videos showing faces and license plates, the real way to uncover the murderer. Then I could return to what I needed to be doing—finding new investors for my startup after the venture capitalists who'd committed to funding my Teddybear Coding School ditched me the moment the economy hit a speedbump. Fortunately, Sumire had kept her job at the law firm until we were up and running, but I was in a pinch, begging the stooges of scrooges for money to keep my plan alive.

She kissed me on the lips, electricity zapping down my spine. "Thanks, Ted," she said, satisfied with my half-hearted promise. "Call me if you find anything." She threw her bag over her shoulder, preparing to leave. "I'll see you tomorrow, okay?"

I thought she'd come to me for sympathy and companionship, not just a tour guide into the dark web. "Are you sure you want to be alone tonight?"

"Higgs will keep me company," she said as she slipped into her pea coat. "I wish I could stay longer, but I need to get home to walk him."

I put my hands around her waist and pulled her close. "Bring him here," I offered, though I knew that would be a disaster—the ugly chihuahua liked me even less than I liked him. "You can both stay here tonight." The offer wasn't entirely altruistic. I wanted to be more a part of her life, but she still kept me at a distance, afraid I'd hurt her again.

She glanced around the musty apartment, rolling her eyes at the old couch where I slept. "Not tonight," she said through a sad smile, crooked tooth sticking out, and pecked me on the cheek before walking out of the apartment, the door rattling closed behind her.

🔒 🔒 🔒

The cold air oozed through the gaps in the window frame as I watched Sumire hike up the sidewalk. The sun was a dim glow low on the horizon behind leaden clouds rolling in over the mountains. Prime time in Japantown, commuters were racing down Jackson Street, swerving past the Ubers and DoorDashers double-parked in the middle of the road.

Sumire navigated around the locals lined up outside the old tonkatsu restaurant and pushed through the crowd of drunk frat boys in front of the rock 'n' roll sushi abomination to reach her lemon-colored Prius. Backing out of the parking spot, she nearly sideswiped a speeding BMW before rolling away. After her taillights disappeared into the distance, I flopped down onto the couch.

My eyes closed, I pictured Joy as I remembered her from the party: short black hair curled around a long, elegant neck; sharp jaw with prominent cheekbones; narrow eyes exuding a keen intelligence. But her severe expression never lightened even as we regaled her with Happy Birthday and brought out the candle-covered cake. She had none of Sumire's warmth, none of her compassion. No twinkle in those black eyes, only righteousness; no smile on her thin lips, only indignation. A true killjoy. Unlike my mother who hid her resentment behind the mask of a *tatemae* smile, Joy made no attempt to disguise her disdain for anyone who disagreed with her. I had a hunch her unyielding attitude had something to do with her murder.

My attempt at small talk with the birthday girl had ended when she declared anime for children and video games worse than porn. While I hung out with the other appendages in the back room in a Battle for Centaurus shootout, she gave Sumire unsolicited advice that she could do better than a geek who'd never accomplish anything. That I could forgive, but not her attempting to set up Sumire with her friend. The kind of friend who spoke five languages, played lacrosse instead of video games, and drove a Tesla rather than a rumbling 1960's Mustang.

The truth was I didn't like Joy. I doubted I was alone. She collected enemies as easily as Sumire gathered friends. Had she made someone angry, someone who nursed a grudge and knew what to do with a gun in real life instead of just in video games? If so, was there a trail I could follow to find the gunman? If nothing else, that would make Sumire happy while proving Joy wrong about me. Finding the killer of the woman who thought I was useless would be too ironic to bear.

I rolled off the couch, popped a pod into the Keurig clone, and sat down at the computer to work. This was the kind of work I enjoyed, the kind of work I was good at, the kind of work I'd quit cold turkey when the police had caught me hacking a few months ago.

I cracked my knuckles before digging up everything about Joy I could find. The undergrad degree in Poly Sci from Harvard and the law degree from Berkeley looked like a well-worn path into politics. But instead of joining a prestigious law firm after graduation, she'd taken a position at a non-profit, Lawyers on the Frontier, and marched off to Turkey to assist Afghani refugees applying for asylum. Had she done something to anger the Syrian warlords smuggling heroin into the country? Or gotten mixed up in a personal dispute between people who resolved their arguments with AK-47s?

Her daily screeds on X and Insta were all about politics and not very politic: demands to free dissidents in Russia, Hong Kong, Burma, and other countries I couldn't pin on a map; demands that the President allow more refugees across the border; demands that the Democrats block passage of a New Patriot Act to protect our privacy. It wasn't clear if anyone was listening to her demands other than the trolls who spewed hateful invective in response.

The mention, though, of the New Patriot Act made my stomach churn. Although nobody else would make the connection, it was I, Ted Hara, a lowly hacker in Silicon Valley, who'd set the President, FBI, Attorney General, and police forces all over the country begging Congress to pass a law to guarantee them unfettered access to everyone's personal data. And Joy's father, the representative from San Jose, who was leading the resistance in Congress.

A few months ago, I'd helped Sumire search for her missing brother by hacking into his MeCan account. When details of how I'd broken into the servers of the ubiquitous purveyor of cheap phones and free email filtered through the hacker grapevine and onto the pages of a prominent New York newspaper, MeCan's CEO was hauled before Congress for a grilling. This time, they couldn't plaster over the security hole with empty promises to enhance user privacy. Instead, MeCan reengineered their entire infrastructure to encrypt all user data and keep it secret from everyone, including themselves. Google was shamed into following suit while Apple reminded everyone they'd been feuding with the FBI over user privacy since releasing IOS 9 in 2015.

Now if I hacked into Joy's account, instead of being able to download all her emails, photos, and GPS data, I'd see nothing but page after page of hex code. Without her password, MeCan couldn't read anything in her account, and neither could a hacker. And neither could the police, the FBI, or the spies at the NSA. Even a subpoena was useless. And that was the problem.

With warnings of impending doom from law enforcement that could no longer tap anyone's phones and email, the only people happy with the new security were those who understood that if the cops had a way to peek into everyone's bank statements, nude photos, and porn downloads, so did the North Koreans, Russians, Chinese, and every script kiddie in the world.

But that hoisted me on my own petard. The only way I could read Joy's email, follow her location, or ogle her photos was with her password. And unless she'd stuck that password on a Post-it hanging from her monitor, the police had no way of getting in. They were screwed.

There was no way I could guess her password, and MeCan would shut down a brute force attack before it could get started. But most people used the same password across multiple sites. It was bad security practice but remembering different passwords for a thousand different sites was impossible. All I had to do was find the passwords Joy had used elsewhere and hope she'd used the same one for her MeCan account.

Fortunately, obtaining hacked passwords was simple—the Password Pirate Emporium, the supersite for stolen passwords, had twenty billion of them for sale. I set up a VPN through Bulgaria before opening a Tor browser to dive into the depths of the dark web, navigating straight for the pirate's cove.

The cyber buccaneers did not disappoint. They had a baker's dozen of passwords on offer for Joy's personal email. The passwords weren't cheap—the pirates demanded more than a thousand dollars for the booty. They might as well have asked for a treasure chest filled with gold and pearls. As the sole employee of an unfunded startup, the only thing keeping my bank account from negative territory was the amount reserved for this month's student loan payment. I couldn't ask Sumire to front the cash since that would only prove Joy right about me. There was no choice—the government would have to survive another month without my contribution. I converted everything I had left into BiteCoin and transferred it to my crypto wallet.

As soon as I executed the blockchain contract, the Bites disappeared from my account and a text file took its place. I held my breath as I opened it, knowing there'd be nobody to complain to if the file was filled with nothing but lol emojis.

Fortunately, the password pirates were honest thieves; the file contained the promised thirteen logins to hotel sites, insurance providers, delivery apps, even a medical center. I was heartened to see that most of the passwords consisted of "IdesOfMarch"—Joy's birthday—with minor variations. There was a chance she'd used the same password for her MeCan account. Joy must have done well enough on her SATs to get into Harvard, but when it came to computer security, she was an idiot.

I copied the first password into the MeCan login. I wasn't surprised it failed. But below the red box around the password field was an error message reminding me that MeCan required a capital letter, a lowercase letter, a number, and a special character. The only one that met the criteria was "!des0fMarch"—her Red Cross password hacked in 2022.

I pasted that password into the login box while saying a prayer to Ebisu, the Japanese god of luck and fortune. Still, I was stunned when the error disappeared, and the page opened to her account dashboard. I was in! I thanked Ebisu, promising to buy him a beer.

"Welcome, Joy!" said Tangy, the annoying tangerine-shaped assistant hopping around on stick legs at the bottom of the screen. "What do YOU want to do today?"

I wanted to track Joy's whereabouts for the past week to see if anything looked sketchy. Sure enough, her location history was sus city—her phone had moved this morning. I checked the time—7:22 a.m.—less than an hour after her murder. Had the killer taken the phone with him, broadcasting his whereabouts every second? That would be incredibly stupid, but even here in the tech capital of the world where everyone had an advanced degree in something, there weren't many criminals who had a Ph.D. in Murder & Mayhem or even a basic A.A. in Nefarious Studies.

All I had to do was pinpoint the location then tell the cops to roll up in a cruiser and nab the perp. I imagined the headlines in tomorrow's Mercury —Miyazaki Murder Solved by Local Hero. There was even a $10,000 reward for information leading to the arrest. That would cover my student loans and rent for the next two months while I looked for funding for the startup.

I superimposed the phone's GPS coordinates onto a MeCan map. The blue pin popped up close to downtown San Jose—no surprise as that was the center of drugs and crime in the city. As I zoomed in, though, the pin turned out not to be in the blighted area around City Hall, but a mile to the northeast, near the Guadalupe River. How stupid, I realized. My daydream of superhero hacker exploded into bits. Joy's phone wasn't hidden in the crib of a drug lord who had hired the hit on Joy; it was sitting on a detective's desk at police headquarters, the last drops of battery juice draining away, nobody daring to power it down and put the dead woman to rest.

Tracking her movements before her murder showed only how boring Joy's life had been—every morning she followed the same trapezoidal path on a jog around the neighborhood, ate at five restaurants in the past week, shopped at Safeway on Monday and Thursday, and stopped at the dry cleaners on Tuesday. The only time she'd left the neighborhood was to take the train up to San Francisco. No midnight trips to Oakland, no lurking around the port at 3 a.m. Despite what news for crazies claimed, Joy was no drug dealer.

Next, I dove into her photos. Would I find naked body parts, men in bondage, or some other weird fetish that had gotten her in trouble? Nope. Food, food, food, and more food. Her photo archive looked like Food-PornHub Central.

The dinners often included two main dishes together with a tableful of appetizers—far too much food for a woman who weighed under a hundred pounds. Then I glimpsed a pair of slender fingers touching the plate in one photo, found a shot of a full hand in another. A hand with hairy knuckles. A man's hand. I scrolled through bowls of tom yum kung, plates of pesto gnocchi, and a hundred kinds of curry until I found his face reflected in a mirror.

His hooded gray eyes were set deep in their sockets behind a beaked nose, his narrow chin covered with thick, dark stubble. Definitely not Japanese. I remembered seeing him at Joy's party acting haughty and imperious. One more Tesla-driving lawyer I'd assumed. He and Joy made a perfectly joyless couple.

Scrolling further, the food porn stopped suddenly, giving way to a dusty landscape of barbed wire fences and gray metal cannons sticking up from a row of mud-splattered tanks—a refugee camp. In the dim light of what had to be a medical tent, people pointed at burns covering their bodies, limbs bent at impossible angles. I wanted to click away from the horrific injuries, the pain and misery on every face, but forced myself to keep scrolling until I landed on a shot of a doctor suturing wounds. He had the same hooded eyes and sunken cheeks as the man at the restaurant, the man at Joy's party—her boyfriend behind the blue mask and blood-stained gown. Not another lawyer. A doctor.

Once I knew Joy's bf was a surgeon who'd worked in the Syrian refugee camps, it was easy to find Dr. Nasir Khan on the staff page of Regional Medical Center, a big hospital a couple miles east on Jackson Street, across from the Chinese garden. His profile said he spoke Pashto and Dari—which meant he was Afghani. That was no surprise. So many Afghani immigrants had moved to the South Bay that a section of Fremont had become known as Little Kabul.

Clicking onto Joy's email, I found her inbox overflowing with offers from Nordstrom, Bloomindales, and Saks Fifth Avenue, a steady barrage of newsletters on refugees and climate change, appeals for donations from Harvard and Berkeley. All were unopened.

I scrolled down the page until I found the last email Joy had opened. It'd landed in her inbox at 6:24 a.m., only minutes before her murder. The subject: "Urgent message from Afghanistan" from someone named Mohammed Abdul.

I would've marked the message as spam and sent it straight into the bit bucket, but Joy was a human rights lawyer working with refugees from the country and had opened it. The message was only three lines. No exclamation points, no all caps, no widows of Uganda oil ministers asking for help transferring ill-gotten gains. It looked legit. It was the scariest thing I'd ever seen.

"Joy. You helped me find my brother in Kandahar and now I want to return the favor. Daesh is planning an attack that will kill many innocent people. Their plan is in the attached file. Use the password you gave me to open it. You must warn everyone. It is a matter of life and death."

I stared at the screen, my mind in a panic, goosebumps crawling up my arms. Who was Daesh? A quick lookup made me gasp—the Arabic name for ISIS.

No way it was a coincidence that a warning from Islamic terrorists had landed in Joy's inbox only minutes before she was murdered. Twelve hours had passed since then. My heart started racing. How much time did we have left before the explosions began?

jiji the jijii

S UMIRE GASPED when I read her the message. "You have to call the police right now!" In the background, the brown-nosed chihuahua barked his agreement.

"There's a little problem," I said, wishing it were that simple.

The details of the attack were in an attached file, a Word document, "Daeshplan.docx." A document that was password protected. Using a different password. A special password Joy had given the sender. Before calling Sumire, I'd hit a dead end trying to open the file. And if I couldn't open it, the local police wouldn't have a clue. I needed to get it to the people who knew what to do with an encrypted file—the FBI. But that meant navigating layers of forms and flunkies that would take weeks before it reached the right hands. And then there was the little matter of hacking into a murdered woman's email. Though the FBI tip line was supposed to be anonymous, there was no way they wouldn't be able to trace it back to me. "Can you get me immunity or something?"

"There's no time for that, Ted!"

"Then what?"

"How about Joy's father?"

Right. I should have thought of that—a congressman could dial up the mucketies at the FBI and get someone on the line. "You got his number?

"I'll call her mother."

A minute later, my phone buzzed with an address in Almaden. *"meet me there rn."*

🔒 🔒 🔒

The McQueen-green '69 Mustang galloped down Highway 87, weaving through evening traffic. I followed the chain of twinkling lights up the mountainside, climbing past the darkened country club and into the narrow streets through the woods. The higher I went, the bigger the houses grew. Down below, San Jose was a glowing grid of white and red lights covering the valley floor.

When MapLady chirped that my destination was ahead on the right, I swerved around a hairpin curve, then had to slam on the brakes to avoid smashing into a news van stopped in the middle of the street. I pulled to the curb and waited until the lemon wedge rolled to a stop behind me. When I opened her door to help her out, she groaned, "You came dressed like that?"

I was wearing an MIT sweatshirt against the chill, the Asahi baseball cap pulled down low on my forehead. She'd changed into a gray one-piece over a white blouse, already dressed for the funeral. "You look beautiful, too," I said, draping the black shawl over her shoulders. She rolled her eyes and grabbed the baseball cap off my head, tossing it into the car.

We hiked up the steep pavement and past a convoy of satellite trucks until we reached the fence in front of the house where a KPIX reporter was live on the air, spotlights rendering her a shimmering ghost in the darkness. At the gated driveway, two hulking rentacops stared straight ahead, stone-faced against our pleas to pass.

After Sumire messaged Mrs. Miyazaki, one of the guards melted into a submissive lump, yes ma'aming into his earpiece. The wrought iron gates swung open like a parting of the Red Sea and Moses led us up the driveway.

At the door, a maid stood holding slippers waiting for us. We followed her down the hall, across the inlaid wood of a wide, ornate ballroom, and through a pair of double doors into a paneled trophy room. "Wait here for the missus," she said, closing the doors behind her.

We waited for the missus in front of the fireplace where the crackling logs cast a flickering orange glow and warmed our hands. Behind us, framed photos covered an entire wall, displaying the congressman's life story: a short, pugnacious boy on a high school football team; a sailor aboard a battleship; a local politician in a Hawaiian shirt leading the Japantown festival; a congressman shaking hands with presidents and prime ministers. In the final photo, he stood beside Evgeni, the CEO of MeCan, at the groundbreaking of their Tangerine Tower headquarters where I worked until I was fired for hacking. I spotted Satoshi Nakamoto, the reclusive inventor of the original Bitcoin and the new and improved BiteCoin and my mother's tea ceremony student, hiding behind the row of VIPs.

"Come take a look at this, Ted," Sumire said pointing at a sepia photograph, the same picture hanging in every shop and restaurant in Japantown —Asahi emblazoned in cursive letters across the chests of a baseball team lined up in front of a rickety grandstand. On the far left was my great-grandfather, the team's third baseman. I wondered why the photo was hanging here amidst the Miyazaki family portraits. The congressman's family had landed in California from Hawaii after the war, after the internment, after my great-grandfather and almost everyone else in the photo had died fighting in Germany.

While I examined the photo for the millionth time, a middle-aged woman, bare arms as thin as tree branches, slipped into the room. Though her eyes were red and puffy, she carried an air of elegance and trailed the scent of sandalwood. "I see you found my grandfather," she said through a sad smile. "The right fielder," she added, pointing to the man standing behind my great-grandfather.

I wished Sumire hadn't ditched my Asahi cap in the car. Joy's family and mine had once been joined on the baseball diamond. San Jose had been a small place then, filled with prune and apricot orchards farmed by Japanese immigrants. Though the town had blossomed into the third largest city in California and the center of Silicon Valley, the Japanese community felt even smaller now. We were all connected somehow.

Sumire turned to Mrs. Miyazaki and bowed deeply, apologizing for our intrusion. Instead of bowing in reply, Mrs. Miyazaki pulled Sumire to her breast. "Oh, Suzie, thank you so much for coming," she said through a sniffle. "You've been such a wonderful friend to Joy. I know you're hurting, too."

They hugged forever while I stood there not knowing what to do. When they finally parted, Mrs. Miyazaki held Sumire's hand as she looked me over, making me even more uncomfortable. "Is this your new boyfriend?" She sounded as gushy as the nosy aunts my mother had always avoided.

I bowed, introduced myself, and stammered out the words of condolence: *goshusho-sama desu*.

She grabbed my arm, her grip surprisingly tight. "Ted Hara? Don't tell me you're little Tatsu-kun? Hanae-sensei's son? And still playing with Suzie-chan? Oh, how wonderful! You remember me, don't you? Of course you do—I came to your house for tea ceremony classes with your mother. You were such a precious little boy."

I remembered now the middle-aged woman wearing bangles and strong perfume who'd come to the makeshift *chashitsu* in our living room where neither jewelry nor scents were allowed. After only two lessons, my mother had kicked her out for injecting politics into the harmony of the tea room. If Mrs. Miyazaki held a grudge many years later, she was enough of a politician not to show it. But was that the real reason her daughter had hated me?

"Oh, here's Jiji," she said as Mr. Miyazaki stepped into the room, the ice in his whiskey clinking against his tumbler. A garish, green Hawaiian tie hung askew from his open collar. With a wrinkled face and bald spot that covered most of his head, he was known throughout Japantown as Jiji the *Jijii* since he reminded everyone of their goofy uncle. But the smile that plastered every billboard in town before each election was nowhere to be seen now. He looked up from his glass to glare at Sumire and growled, "Who the fuck are you?"

"Jiji!" Mrs. Miyazaki snapped. "This is Suzie. Joy's friend from Cal."

"That so?" he grunted. He gave Sumire a lecherous once over while downing a big gulp of whiskey. I pulled her towards me. He pressed himself into my face, close enough to smell his alcohol breath. "What the fuck do you want?" He thrust the glass against my sternum, the condensation sending spikes of cold through my chest.

"Jiji!" his wife chided again. "Be nice to the kids. That's Tatsu-kun."

"Who?"

"Hanae Hara's son. You remember her. She was Joy's calligraphy teacher over at Betsuin Temple."

"Hara? You mean that crazy bitch who threw herself off a mountain? After her fuck-up of a husband smashed his car?"

Yup, that was me. And I'd heard enough. "We gotta dip." I pulled

Sumire's arm to go. I'd have to figure out some other way to contact the FBI. Maybe I could hack into their tip database and put myself at the top of the queue.

But Sumire didn't budge. "I'm not going anywhere until you show Mr. Miyazaki what you found."

"And Jiji, dear," his wife warned, "you're going to keep your mouth shut for once and listen."

The congressman gulped down a slug of whiskey, his face beet red, but stayed silent while I pulled out my phone to log into Joy's account and scroll down to the last opened email.

"What the fuck are you doing?"

"Trying to help?"

"Trying to help?" he spat. "By fucking up the investigation? What are you—a perv? Looking for nude photos? No, you're worse than that— you're one of those fuckwads trying to sell shit to the press." He downed the last of the whiskey and stared at the ice swirling at the bottom of the glass. "I'm calling the cops. Ilene—you got that number for Captain Dixon? Never mind, I've got it. Get those security guards in here now and make sure this piece of shit doesn't try anything."

Sumire pushed herself between the congressman and me. "You have to see what Ted found in Joy's email," she told him. "It's a message from ISIS."

Joy's mother gasped.

But Jiji didn't care. "ISIS?" he roared. "What kind of bullshit is that? Go home young lady and keep your cute little nose out of where it doesn't belong."

"Jiji!" his wife yelled.

"What?" he said, not backing down. "I just flew back from Washington to deal with my daughter's murder. The last thing I need are these two amateur Nancy Drews telling me my daughter is involved in some terrorist conspiracy. I get enough of that shit all day in Washington. The right-wing crazies are pushing some inane story about how Joy's a drug dealer financing my campaign. I've got armed protestors outside my office. And now this fuckwad is telling me Joy's a terrorist. Enough! I can deal with all the phone calls and emails, the hate mail, the death threats. That's Washington. But don't bring that shit into our home."

I didn't need this shit either. "I'm leaving."

"Theodore Tatsu Hara! You're not going anywhere." Sumire ripped the tumbler out of Mr. Miyazaki's hand and banged it down on the bookshelf. "And you—you listen to me. Joy was my friend. I don't know what she was mixed up in, but lives are in danger. Understand? We're not leaving here until you take ten seconds to see what Ted found."

Jiji barked at the rentacop walking in. "Escort these two back to their car."

"Yes, sir," Moses of the Gate said as he reached out to grab the hood of my hoodie.

Mrs. Miyazaki sighed. "Hold your horses, Martin." She took the phone from my hand. "Show me," she said. I pulled away from the guard's grasp and scrolled the page for her. Her eyes grew wide. "You need to take a look at this, Jiji." She pressed the phone into his palm.

Despite grumbles, he pulled a pair of half-moon reading glasses out of his pocket. His eyes scanned back and forth over the three lines of the email multiple times.

"Are you sure it's not a virus?"

"It's not," I said. "I checked the source code and the metadata. There's nothing embedded other than the attached file."

He poked the link to the attachment with a fat finger, and when nothing happened, he poked it five more times. "What's in the file?" he asked.

I shook my head. "No idea. It's encrypted. You can't open it without the password that only Joy and the sender knew. Which is why it can't be a virus."

"Then what do you want from me?"

"Call the FBI," Sumire said.

"They should be able to open it," I added.

He handed me back my phone. "Yeah, whatever. Forward me a copy. I'll get my staff to liaise with the pukes over there."

I forwarded the email to Sumire and asked her to send it to Jiji.

"Are we done?" He grabbed his glass off the bookshelf and chomped on a last sliver of ice. "If you'll excuse me, I'm in need of a refill." He hollered to the maid to bring out more ice.

"One more thing," I said.

"What now?"

"Can you not mention me when you tell the FBI about the file?"

"Yeah, sure," he grunted and sauntered out in search of a fresh bottle.

🔒 🔒 🔒

The hulking guard escorted us back to Sumire's car and stood in the middle of the street. I wrapped my arms around her, pulling her tight against me.

"Goodnight, Ted," she said after a quick peck on the lips.

The guard tapped his shoe impatiently. I leaned into Sumire. "Are you sure you're okay?"

"I'm fine."

"You don't need to be alone tonight. Stay with me."

"I'm fine, Ted."

"I can come to your place if you want."

She put a hand on my cheek. "Goodnight, Teddybear."

As I stood in the street watching the lemon wedge roll away, the guard chuckled. "Take it from me, son," he said, breaking his mute surveillance, "you're better off by yourself. Do what you want, don't have to answer to nobody. When you feel lonely, hit the bars. Those women don't want nothing from you but a good time. And looking at your sorry ass, it's obvious the one thing you need is a good time."

I thanked him for his concern and headed back to the pony.

He followed me to the car. "Nice wheels," he said. "Bet that's a serious chick magnet."

It was my father's car that he'd plowed into a lamp post after a few too many Johnnies. I'd put it back together again like Humpty Dumpty, a complete restoration from scratch; the only thing missing was my father. It might have been a babe magnet back in the security guard's day, but now if you weren't electric, you were a planet killer, worse than clubbing baby seals. But I loved the feel of the cracked vinyl bucket seats, the smell of oil, the burble of the badass engine. I squealed the tires as I peeled away and zoomed down the hill. I considered stopping at a bar—I needed a drink more than anything else in the world—but if there were any single women there, their idea of a good time wasn't discussing Fermat's Last Theorem with a short geek.

Instead, I headed back to my humble apartment, resigned to spending another night alone, not even a frosty blue bottle of Mu for company. Flopping down on the couch, I stared up and counted the spots of mold on the ceiling like stars in the Milky Way. I'd done what I could, I told myself, gone above and beyond the call of duty. Now it was up to Jiji and the FBI to take over and do their jobs.

But what if Jiji didn't call the FBI despite his reluctant, half-drunken promise? Or his urgent message got lost in the bureaucracy? If an airplane smashed into the Tangerine Tower tomorrow and killed all my former co-workers, would I feel guilty? I'd done everything I should have and more, I reminded myself, but had I done everything I could? Not really.

I threw off the blanket and returned to the computer. The room was dark, the world silent, the blue glow of the monitor lighting the room. Opening Joy's account again, I stared at the mysterious email. "Daesh is planning a big attack that will kill many people. The information is in the attached file." By the time the FBI decrypted the file, it might be too late. I had to find a way to open it right away.

I looked over the source code of the email again for clues. The email was received from a MeCan SMTP server in Dubai. I couldn't trace it any further than that. Was the sender, Mohammed Abdul, in Dubai or logged in from Iran or Turkey? Impossible to tell. He could be using a VPN to connect from anywhere.

Joy's in-box showed she'd opened the email, the last one she'd read. Unfortunately, she hadn't forwarded it to anyone—not the FBI, not her bosses at Lawyers on the Frontier. A search through her email archive found messages from people named Mohammed or Abdul, but none named Mohammed Abdul or included a password.

There was no choice but to try again to open the document. A small box popped up on the screen: *Enter password to open file.* I tried each of Joy's passwords I'd bought from the pirates, but they all dinged with the same error message: *The password is incorrect. Word cannot open the document.* I wrote a script to try a few more variations on IdesOfMarch, but none of them worked any better.

The email implied Joy had given the sender, Mohammed Abdul, a password to use. If she hadn't emailed or messaged it to him, it had to be something easy to remember, like 123456, passw0rd, or iloveu. I found a list of the thousand most common passwords and wrote a script to try them all. A thousand error messages filled the screen. None of them opened the file. I set a dictionary attack running using a million variants on common words and phrases with no better success. My attempt to guess what words Joy would use as a password failed miserably. It was time to change tack. There had to be another way to open the file.

I expected the security on a Word document would be trivial to crack, like opening luggage locks with a paperclip, deterring the clueless rather than stopping a determined hacker. Microsoft wasn't exactly known for rock-solid security. But a little checking changed my opinion. Earlier versions of Word were indeed trivial to hack, but the current version was a serious upgrade to military-grade 256-bit AES encryption. It was impossible to break into a bank vault with a paperclip, even a heavy-duty one. I'd have to try something else.

I reached out my arm for the glass of sake that wasn't there. Though I hadn't had a drop of alcohol in more than three months, if there was ever a time I needed to get the brain juices flowing, this was it. But there was no alcohol in the apartment; I'd promised Sumire that. No Johnny hiding above the fridge, no gin floozies cavorting with the cleaning tonics under the sink, not even cheap cooking sake to nip in a pinch. All I had was coffee. To prepare myself, I dispensed with the coffee dispenser and spooned the grounds straight from a k-pod, using the remaining grit on the bottom to draw a line of warpaint under my eyes. Now I was ready.

I searched the hacker boards for exploits to break into a Word document. I found none. When I posted an anonymous question on one board, the redditors responded with lols and animated GIFs of laughing cats. There had to be vulnerabilities, this was Microsoft after all, but hackers didn't care about hacking Word documents. It wasn't good sport like taking over Elon's own X account to declare that X was being re-renamed Twitter. And the money was in raiding movie studios and hospitals and holding their databases hostage. Word documents weren't filled with millions of credit card numbers or government secrets, so they were worthless to amateurs and pros alike. In fact, though every business in the world used Microsoft Word, nobody used the document encryption feature, except terrorists, apparently.

It looked like the only way in was a brute force attack, running through every possible combination of letters and numbers. Fortunately, my computer had an Nvidia 30-series RTX graphics card with ten thousand cores, table stakes for anyone who took gaming seriously. Just like the Bite-

Coin miners who'd turned Nvidia graphics cards into electronic gold mining, I could use each core as a separate CPU to attack the file with the power of ten thousand computers at once.

Though there were hundreds of password hacking tools, most helped parents break into their kids' computers, designed for ease-of-use rather than raw processing speed. I needed the software the pros used—the open-source application, *pw_hack*. With reviews like, "Best crack s/w in whole universe, you try now," it was impossible to tell if it came from Russian hackers or a parody of them, and I worried the app was filled with trojans that hackers used to hack other hackers. But since the software did exactly what I needed, that was a risk I'd have to take. Still, I backed up everything and installed the app in a sandbox, just in case. Then I set about rewriting the source code to run in parallel on ten thousand cores.

When I was done, it was already after 4:00 a.m. My head throbbed, my fingers ached, my chest felt like I'd run a marathon. I compiled the code one last time and sicced it on the encrypted document. The fans whirred up to full speed as the CPUs started crunching large polynomials. While waiting for the password to pop out, I laid down on the couch and fell into a deep slumber.

In a dream, I was standing on the pitcher's mound at MeCan Park before a Giants game. With Sumire beside me beaming, Mr. Miyazaki pinned a Congressional Medal of Honor on my T-shirt for preventing a terrorist attack. The entire stadium erupted in cheers, stomping and shouting my name. The chanting grew louder and louder until my eyes fluttered open to find my room bathed in the soft, pale light of morning.

"Hara!" yelled a voice I wished I didn't recognize from the other side of the door. I pulled the blanket over my head, willing the banging to stop.

"Open up, Hara!" the banging continued, making it impossible to return to sleep.

"Not home," I grunted.

"Now!" came a second voice I wanted to hear even less.

My head throbbing, a hangover without even drinking, I rolled off the couch, threw on the sweatshirt and stumbled to the door. In the dim hall-way, two cops stood in starched blue uniforms, peaked caps down to their unibrows. Mike Mayeda, the Japanese-Hawaiian cop who bullied me in high school, was flanked by his blond, muscle-bound partner, a hulking Viking.

"Let's go, shrimp," Mayeda said, grabbing my arm. "Got orders to take you in."

"What for?" I grumbled.

The Viking grabbed my other wrist and squeezed tighter than handcuffs. "New chief wants a word."

three
the fourth degree

Sumire and I were locked inside a narrow, airless confession room that reeked of stale coffee and fresh testosterone, her hand caressing my shoulder. When the door banged open and the new chief of police sauntered in, I was relieved that instead of the uniformed thug who'd previously held the position, this chief was dressed in a sharp suit that cost as much as his BMW. With a bright blue tie and Bally shoes, he looked more like a McKinsey consultant than the head honcho of the fourth largest police force in California.

Trailing in the wake of the chief's musky cologne was a rumpled man in a rumpled sports jacket followed by a bureaucrat with an American flag pinned to his pinstripe suit. Despite the concrete walls and battleship-gray metal furniture, this felt more like a pitch session with a bottom-tier venture capital firm than an interrogation by the cops. Or whatever this was.

I could only assume they'd dragged me in to ask about the file. Despite his promise, Jiji must have ratted me out. But charging me with hacking would be a job for flunkies. The only reason the chief would want to meet me in person was to thank me for the tip. Still, given my history with the Saint Josey cops and the way Mayeda and the Viking had tittered like schoolgirls the entire ride to the station, I couldn't help feeling nervous.

Fortunately, Sumire had arrived quicker than I'd thought possible in a Prius. Without her make-up, she somehow looked even more radiant than usual. And calm. Having her beside me in her lawyer's uniform of pantsuit and pearls settled the insects crawling in my stomach.

When I jumped to my feet to hail the chief, he seemed surprised to be looking down on a short, scrawny geek with wire-frame glasses and shaggy hair instead of the usual toughs and criminals. I was glad the sleeve of my MIT hoodie covered my cartoon elephant tattoo. Still, he eyed me warily, like a scorpion—potentially lethal despite the size. I could see the gears turning beneath the perfectly coiffed hair trying to figure out how a mathematician could've caused the downfall of his predecessor, unsure whether to thank me or lock me up.

The rumpled cop behind him banged the door shut and set his coffee on the table, combing the few remaining strands of hair over the top of his wrinkled head. Flagpin dragged a chair to the back corner to observe the action from as far away as he could get.

The chief remained standing by the door, arms folded over his chest. "Thank you for coming in today, Mr. Hara," he said, as if I'd had a choice. At least he wasn't rolling up his cufflinked sleeves to punch me like his predecessor, who'd given me the third degree, then the fourth and the fifth. My ribs still ached from my last visit to this room where the previous chief had conferred a master's degree on me in police interrogation.

"It's an honor to be of service," I mumbled.

"Let me do the talking," Sumire whispered. That was fine by me.

The chief motioned for us to sit, though he remained standing.

"What are you charging my client with?" Sumire asked. The three men grinned at each other.

"We wanted to have a little chat with you regarding the Joy Miyazaki murder," he said to me, ignoring my attorney. "Starting with the file you purportedly found in the victim's email."

"Of course," I said, wary now. There was nothing purported in what I'd found.

Sumire tapped my leg with her shoe, a warning to be quiet. "My client—"

"Let me stop you right there, young lady," the chief said, holding up a hand. "If I were you, I'd be very careful." He pointed at Flagpin in the back corner. "Let me introduce Deputy Assistant Director Harris who's observing this interview."

Flagpin flashed a badge, the big, blue letters—FBI—visible across the length of the room. "San Francisco Field Office," he announced. "San Jose Satellite Office."

"And Senior Detective Kapoor, who's heading the Miyazaki investigation."

Combover slurped at his cup of coffee, cutting bite marks into the styrofoam.

"We were contacted this morning by Director Harris about a tip they received overnight. An email was purportedly discovered on the victim's computer pertaining to a terrorist plot. Did I get that right, Mr. Hara?"

Before I could answer, Sumire tapped my leg again. "How does this pertain to my client?" she asked the chief.

"We were hoping Mr. Hara could enlighten us on the contents of that file."

Were they asking my help to open it? "I have a password cracker running—"

Sumire tapped my leg again, harder this time, reminding me to be quiet.

The chief pointed at Combover. He set his coffee on the table and glanced at me with sleepy eyes. "This file you planted, Mr. Hara—it has nothing to do with a terrorist attack, does it?"

"I didn't plant it," I said.

Sumire stepped on my foot. "Quiet, Ted."

"Tell us what's in it."

I had to make them understand. "I didn't—"

She stepped on me harder. "Shut up, Ted!" I was lucky she'd worn flats today instead of her usual heels.

Combover stared at Sumire. She pushed her glasses higher on her nose and stared right back at him. He turned to me. "See, we've got a bit of a problem here, Mr. Hara. It appears the victim's account was penetrated. Her email was accessed. I don't know what you'd call that, but around here we call that evidence tampering. Understand what I'm saying?"

Sumire didn't have to kick me this time to stop me from answering.

"It appears you have quite the record." He flipped through a thick folder and pulled out a printout, reading off the sheet. "Unauthorized computer access, aggravated identity theft, trafficking in passwords. Care to explain?"

Yes, I did want to explain. I hadn't broken into the MeCan servers this time or wormed through their firewalls. I'd logged into Joy's account using her own password and that was completely different. "I didn't—"

Sumire slapped her hand over my mouth. "My client doesn't need to answer."

A grin crept across Combover's face. "That so, miss? Do I understand you're his defense counsel?"

"Yes, sir," she answered, sounding self-assured despite being a first-year associate in intellectual property; her only experience with criminal law was defending me.

Combover chuckled. "Can't say I'm surprised Mr. Hara is back to hacking. Or that he planted a file on the victim's computer."

"I didn't plant the file!"

Sumire kicked me, hard, causing me to yelp. The police weren't breaking my ribs this time, but my attorney was breaking my leg.

"What I really find surprising is that the informant who notified the FBI of Mr. Hara's illicit activity was someone named Suzie Yamashita. That wouldn't be you, would it, missy?"

I jumped to my feet. Nobody called her *missy*. I stood there trying to look menacing; Combover only chuckled. "Sit down, Ted," she said, pulling my arm. I didn't resist.

"Yes, I'm his attorney," she said, less self-assured than before. "Kind of—"

This time I tapped her leg under the table. She ignored me. "I informed Congressman Miyazaki about a suspicious file on Joy's computer."

"The file that Mr. Hara planted? Let me be the first to commend you for ratting out your client."

"I didn't plant that file!"

"I found that file," Sumire declared to everyone's surprise.

The cops glanced at each other and laughed. Which made Sumire angry. "I found that file!" she insisted. "Me. Not my client. Joy gave me her password when we were working on a class project together. That means I had permission to access her account."

Sumire was protecting me. Again. In high school, she'd broken Mayeda's nose to stop him from bullying me. Now she was lying to a roomful of cops to save my butt. Half of me hated her protecting me as if I were a helpless boy. The other half wanted to kiss her.

Combover scratched a note on a small pad of paper like in an old detective show. I wondered if there was a Cops-R-Us somewhere nearby where the detectives bought their spiral notepads. When he finished writing, he looked up at Sumire. "You realize, missy, making a false statement to the police could get you disbarred?"

"Yes, sir," she replied, jaw set, eyes blazing in anger. "And you'll address me as *Ms. Yamashita*. Or *counsel*, if you so prefer."

Combover leaned back in his chair looking satisfied, his melon belly peeking out from under his shirt. I didn't understand why he was grinning. There was nothing more he could do to prosecute me for breaking into Joy's account. I thought we were done. As soon I confirmed that the FBI was working on opening the file, Sumire and I could head out for pancakes before she had to go into the office.

But no, we weren't done. Combover took one last slurp of coffee and tossed the cup in the trash. "Be that as it may, *Ms. Yamashita*," he resumed, "your client is in serious trouble."

"For hacking? I told you—"

"No, young lady. I don't give two shits about hacking. In case you haven't noticed, this is a murder investigation. We don't have time to waste on petty hacking charges." He turned to me and bared his yellowed teeth. "So how about we cut to the chase, Hara, and you tell us everything you know about that file?"

"Give him immunity," Sumire said.

Combover glanced over at the chief, who shook his coiffed head, not a hair out of place.

"Here's your choices, young lady: your client can tell us why he planted that file. Or we charge him with conspiracy to commit murder."

"I didn't plant that file!"

Sumire kicked me again. "Mr. Hara had no involvement with the murder. Unless you have evidence otherwise, I'll assume he's free to leave."

Combover turned to the FBI agent in the back corner. "Harris, what did your boys come up with?"

Flagpin looked up from his phone. "We haven't been able to open the file yet. But I'm confident our boys at Quantico will decrypt it soon."

That was bad news if the FBI hadn't figured out how to open it.

"That may not be necessary," Combover said. "We have a hunch it wasn't from Middle Eastern terrorists but planted locally."

"It came from Dubai," I insisted.

"Could've been routed through a VPN," Flagpin stated. He wasn't as clueless as he seemed.

Combover ignored both of us. "Either way, I think we can all agree the murder was no home invasion. We're confident the perp was someone who knew her. Somebody like Mr. Hara."

"Me?" I blurted out. "I didn't know her." Sumire kicked me again. "It had to be her boyfriend."

Why couldn't they see the obvious? Five minutes with Wikipedia was all it took to know that the ISIS affiliate in Afghanistan was at war with both the Taliban government and the West. They'd killed two hundred Americans and Afghans during the evacuation of Kabul. Now they were planning a fresh attack. When Joy had received the email, her Afghani boyfriend reading over her shoulder had stopped her from getting the warning out with extreme prejudice. The murder was solved; the terrorist threat was urgent.

Combover banged his fist on the table. "We've got witnesses, Hara. Witnesses who'll testify you were present with the victim on March 15."

March 15? A week and a half ago. "Her birthday party?" I said before Sumire could stop me. "I barely said hi to her."

"That's not what our witnesses tell us. They say the two of you hit it off —you and the Miyazaki woman—didn't you? And I'm not surprised— you've got a lot in common."

I wondered who these witnesses were and why they were fingering me. "I have a girlfriend," I said. A girlfriend who was shushing me, trying to get me to shut up.

"No matter. Sometimes the person you come with isn't the one you leave with. Isn't that right?" He turned to the FBI agent. "The two of them are a perfect match, aren't they Harris?"

"The Myers-Briggs assessment shows a high degree of compatibility."

Wait—the FBI had profiled me? I didn't know whether to be honored or terrified.

"This is love like you've never experienced before, isn't that right, Hara? You're over the moon. You're so happy you can't breathe. Until one morning when you pop over to her apartment. And what do you see? Another man leaving her apartment. You burst in to confront her. She lied to you. She humiliated you. She's a cunt, isn't she, Hara? You're angry. Angry like you've never been before. So you point a gun at her. You want to scare her, make her understand how furious you are. You expect her to plead for forgiveness. But no, not Joy Miyazaki. Uh-uh, not her. Instead of cowering, she tries to grab the gun away. And that's a big mistake. Because the gun goes off. Maybe it was reflexes, maybe she squeezed your hand, maybe you don't even know what happened. All you know is she's lying in a pool of blood with her guts spattered all over the room. You didn't intend to kill her, but she's as dead as a duck in Peking. And you...you're in deep shit. So what do you do? You make it look like a robbery by stealing her computer. But you're a smart guy, aren't you, Hara? It doesn't take you long to realize we'll find witnesses who saw a runt like you running out of her apartment. We'll find security video showing a runt like you driving away. You need to do something. You can't spend the next twenty years in prison for an accident that wasn't your fault. You figure the first person we'll suspect is the boyfriend. And you're in luck—he's Afghani. The perfect suspect. Everyone thinks they're a bunch of terrorists. So you cook up a story about ISIS and plant a file on her laptop to scare the bejesus out of everyone and send the police on a goose chase searching for terrorists instead of a pathetic, scorned lover boy. Isn't that right, Hara?"

I didn't know where to start. "No."

"No?"

Sumire kicked me. "Don't say anything, Ted."

"That's not what happened."

"Then what did happen?"

"I don't know. Not that. I don't own a gun."

"Why did you steal her laptop?"

"Ted, don't say anything."

"I didn't steal her computer."

"Then how did you find the file?"

Idiots. Didn't they have a clue how the cloud worked? "Everything's online."

"Ted!!!"

Combover broke into a wide grin. "Ah, the truth comes out. If the files are online, why did you steal her laptop?"

"I didn't steal her laptop. I wasn't even there."

"Prove it," Combover demanded.

He clearly hadn't majored in logic. "How do I prove I wasn't there?"

From the corner of the room, the chief spoke like the voice of God. "Show us your location history."

"Ted, wait, don't—"

But I wasn't waiting. I didn't kill Joy, and I wanted that to be clear quickly so we could get back to what was important: decrypting the file and stopping the terrorist attack. I pulled up my location history and scrolled to the time of the murder. "See," I said, holding up my phone, "I was at home. Asleep."

Combover reached out a hand. "Give it here."

"Ted, don't."

I pulled it away. "March 24, 6:30 a.m." I read off the GPS coordinates. "What more do you need?"

"We need to do a full analysis," Combover said.

"Not without a warrant," Sumire replied.

"Analysis of what?" I asked.

"Of everything. We need your password, too."

"For what?"

"Come on, Hara," Combover yelled. "What are you hiding?"

"Ted, stop!"

"Nothing," I mumbled. I had secrets, of course, the same as everyone. I didn't want the hairy trolls in the I.T. dungeon snickering over my Pornhub search terms of tall girls in stiletto heels. But I could live with that. I was more worried the FBI would find out I was responsible for the Sword of Muramasa fiasco. Still, hacking was better than murder, and if the gaming company sued me for damages, all they'd recover was the extensive collection of vacuums I'd inherited from my mother.

Flagpin joined Combover, both of them leaning over the table, teeth bared, coffee breath blowing over my face. "Because of your antics," Combover said, "we no longer have access to the information we need to conduct a proper investigation. Now we're reduced to begging scumballs like you to hand over their evidence. Which gives us no choice but to throw you in jail until you agree."

He had a point. I was kind of responsible for the police not being able to get my coordinates directly from MeCan. I grasped my phone. "You won't look at anything else, will you?"

"Can't promise that, kid."

Sumire grabbed my arm. "Don't do anything until we get you a real lawyer."

"I didn't do it."

"Doesn't matter."

I pulled the phone away.

Combover looked over at the big boss still standing beside the door. "What do you want to do with him, Chief?"

"Book him," the head honcho said. "Unless he cooperates."

Combover sneered at me. "What's it gonna be, Hara?

A bomb was about to go off somewhere while these guys screwed around with me. I had no choice. I handed over my phone.

The cops filed out, locking us inside the room. I banged my head against the concrete wall behind me. Sumire put her hands on my shoulders to stop me. "Don't worry, Ted. They'll see you had nothing to do with it. It'll be okay."

"I didn't do anything!" I yelled towards the ceiling where the microphones were hidden.

"Next time, listen to me, okay?"

I leaned forward to rest my forehead against hers. We sat there together for what felt like forever. "Bunny?" I whispered.

"Yes, Ted?"

"You know everything they said about me and Joy was absurd?"

"I was wondering..."

"I didn't even like Joy."

"But the two of you are so compatible."

"I love you. Not her."

She took my hands in hers. Short fingers with a strong grip from years of aikido, nails painted opalescent pearl with a hint of pink. I lifted her hands to my lips and kissed each finger, ignoring her half-hearted pleas to stop. I leaned forward to kiss her lips, our glasses getting in the way.

"Teddybear," she said.

I took off my glasses, turning the world into a blur. "Yes, Bunny?"

"Not here."

I kissed the tip of her ear that stuck out through the curtain of black hair. "Why not?"

"It's not professional."

"So?" I nibbled her earlobe, the thin down tickling my tongue, hoping the cops were watching over the cameras. Sumire was my girlfriend; I had no interest in Joy.

"I'm supposed to be your lawyer."

I kissed the smooth skin of her neck. She pushed me away. "How can you think about that now?"

"Beats thinking about being charged with murder." I pressed my lips against hers until the resistance faded, her lips parted, and I tasted her hot breath. Then the door banged open and Combover marched inside.

"You kids still in high school? I'd tell you to get a room, but you won't like the ones we've got." He laughed at his own joke while we scrambled to sit upright. Sumire swiped a strand of hair from her forehead and adjusted her glasses. Her face flushed, she looked even more beautiful than ever.

Combover held my phone in the air. "Looks like you left this at home when you went to Miyazaki's apartment to kill her. Proves premeditation. Murder 1 instead of Murder 2."

Sumire put a hand over my mouth to stop me from answering. "You didn't find any evidence, did you?" she asked the cops.

Combover grumbled as he handed the phone back to me.

"Is my client free to go?"

Combover shook his head. "Not yet."

We sat in silence waiting for the door to bang open again. The ancient deputy chief wobbled in wearing a dusty herringbone sports jacket. He grinned when he saw me. "Good to see you've been keeping yourself out of trouble, son."

Combover thrust a printout into Herringbone's gnarled hands. "Chief says charge this asswipe with unauthorized computer access."

Herringbone read the sheet, then looked up at me and sighed. "Can't say I didn't warn you."

🔒 🔒 🔒

It was already evening by the time I made bail and birded the ten blocks back to Japantown, wanting nothing more than a shower to scrub away all the muck that had been thrown at me. As I scooted down Jackson, I was surprised to see a row of satellite trucks parked in front of my apartment.

When I skidded to a stop at the corner, a dozen microphones rushed at me like a pack of hyenas.

"Theodore Hara!" they brayed. "Can we get a comment?"

Had the FBI decrypted the file and arrested the terrorists while I'd been stuck at police headquarters?

Microphones jostled at my face. "Why did the police name you a person of interest?" a blonde reporter asked.

That had to be a mistake. "I had nothing to do with the murder," I told them. "I was only charged with hacking." I thought that would send them scurrying away. Instead, it sent them into a frenzy.

"Why were you arrested for hacking?"

"Why did you steal the woman's computer?"

"Who killed the woman?"

"Why did you kill Joy Miyazaki?"

"When will you be charged with murder?"

I fought through the crowd and slipped inside the lobby, snapping the front door shut. Trudging up the stairs, I was ready to DND myself for the night, but when I reached the third floor, I found my door unlocked.

Inside, the room had been ransacked—a week of dirty laundry was strewn across the carpet, my mother's tea ceremony implements buried under a layer of trash. I thought I'd been robbed until I noticed the folded sheet of paper on the desk—a search warrant. Underneath, the monitor cable was hanging loose, connected to nothing. My computers were gone— the cops had confiscated everything.

four
the dandy lion

Before I could shut the blinds to hide from the world, I caught a glimpse of the peaked cap and blue uniform of Mayeda on the sidewalk below chatting with the reporters camped in front of my building. The man who'd bullied me in high school. The man who was still in love with my girlfriend. The last man I wanted to talk to, but the only man who might tell me what was going on.

I threw on a Giants hoodie and cinched it tight around my face. A surgical mask and sunglasses completed the simple disguise to get past the reporters. I climbed down the rickety stairs and pushed through the emergency exit to the back alley.

Glancing around, my head ducked low, the alley was safe—no camera lights shining in my eyes, no reporters hiding in the rancid dumpsters behind the sushi restaurant. A block away, I cut back to Jackson Street. The dentist offices, hair salons, and krapknack shops were already shuttered, the cute girls who manned the Shiseido store gone to meet their boyfriends. I hid in the optometrist's darkened entranceway to ambush Mayeda.

"Heya, shrimp," he said when he noticed me, a stupid grin on his face. "Aren't you supposed to be in jail?"

An offensive lineman on our high school football team, Mayeda was still offensive. Sauntering over to where I was standing, he towered over me, a couple heads taller and twice as wide. Despite the old Japanese family name, he was more Hawaiian than Japanese. I hated him calling me shrimp or *chibi* or quarter-pint back in high school when he'd bullied short, scrawny kids like me. Now that he was a cop with a gun and a crush on my girlfriend, I hated him even more. The fact that he'd saved my life made it even worse. And now I needed his help again. I swallowed my pride and pointed up the street to the Dandy Lion. "Want to grab some noodles?"

Mayeda cocked his head, suspicious of any invitation from me. "Sorry, shrimp, on patrol."

The street was quiet except for the drunk frat boys outside the rock 'n' roll sushi abomination. No drugs, no gangs, no encampments in the alleys. Nobody jaywalked in J-town. Not a speck of litter anywhere, not a single cigarette butt on the ground. Nothing for a cop to do except warn dog walkers not to leave poo on the strips of grass alongside the sidewalk. "Can't you spare a few minutes to prevent a terrorist attack?"

He shook his head. "I don't know nothing about that."

"How about a cup of sake? The good stuff Kenta keeps hidden. I owe you that at least." No way he'd refuse an offer like that.

"Sorry, shrimp, I'll have to take a rain check."

How could I convince him to talk to me? "It's about Sumire."

That got him to radio the dispatcher to say he was going off duty. He followed me up the sidewalk, his gun, taser, and handcuffs jangling with every thump of his jackboots. When we reached the faded wooden sign with carved dandelions swaying in the wind, I rolled the door open on its metal rail and slipped through the narrow entrance. Enveloped in the Dandy Lion's sauna-like warmth, the smell of frying pork and garlic felt like home.

The dinner rush was in full swing, nearly all the tables taken. The ramen joint buzzed with the chatter of diners, the clatter of dishes, the sizzle and pop of gyoza frying behind the counter. Overhead, the TV blared the Giants game though it was only preseason. The golf farts camped out in the back corner were well into their Johnnie Ices, regaling each other with the same stories I'd heard years ago from my father.

"*Oi, Tatsu-kun,*" Kenta greeted me from behind the counter, using my Japanese name. Every head swiveled to stare in my direction. The restaurant fell silent other than the cheers of the baseball game on TV. Someone whispered, "That's the guy who murdered Joy." I realized then that Einstein was wrong: within the confines of Japantown, information traveled faster than light.

Yukiko hurried over to seat us at an empty table by the door. She unclipped the pen from her apron and stood waiting for our orders. Mayeda declared, "Bring us a bottle of your finest sake!" If I was buying, he was enjoying to the max.

Yukiko didn't even try to hide her scowl. She turned to me and asked, "Dassai or Kubota?" She and Sumire had grown up together and though it was ancient history, she still blamed me for breaking Sumire's heart when, after my father's accident, I'd left her for a bottle of whiskey. Yukiko was less than thrilled that we were together again and considered it her responsibility to protect her friend from me. As soon as I took a single sip of sake, a shaky snapshot taken from behind the counter would pop up on Sumire's phone. No matter what excuse I offered, that would be the end. "How about a nice warm Sho Chiku Bai for my friend," I said. "And a mugicha for me."

She hardly disguised her disappointment as she left to get the sake and barley tea. "What's this 'show chick' stuff?" Mayeda asked.

"You'll like it," I assured him. "A man's sake. Bold flavors. Nice and hot to warm you up after being out in the cold all day." In truth, it was total crap, the cheapest stuff they had. Still, I expected Mayeda would appreciate its alcoholic bite more than the subtle notes of a fruity *daiginjo*.

Yukiko set the ceramic flask on the table in front of Mayeda and handed me a glass of iced barley tea. I reached across the table to pour the steaming sake into Mayeda's cup. "Very nice," he said after taking a sip. "You're not having any?"

I shook my head. "Stopped drinking."

Mayeda gasped. "Sue Mary got you whipped!"

"Sumire," I corrected him, "Sue-me-ray." For someone in love with my girlfriend, he couldn't even pronounce her name.

He gulped down the rest of the cup. "So what's this about? Sumire ready for that date she promised me?"

I took a deep breath, unclenched my fists, and refilled his cup. "We're pals, aren't we, Mikey?"

"Sure, shrimp, whatever you say."

"You know what happened after you brought me in today?"

He chuckled. "Heard you had a rough time. Surprised they let you go." He slid the flask across the table. "Bet you could use a drink."

The sweet fumes of alcohol wafted into my nose. It was tempting. But it would take more than bad sake to quench the dumpster fire burning in my gut. I refilled his cup and left the flask as far across the table as I could reach.

"Who tipped off the press?" I asked.

"Like I said, pal, I'm a beat cop. Patrol the neighborhood. Stop the tourists from tossing cigarettes butts on the sidewalk before Mrs. Konishi makes a citizen's arrest."

I told him about the message I'd found warning of a terrorist attack. "Joy was murdered minutes after opening the email."

Mayeda shrugged. He already knew.

"I spent all day proving to your bosses I had nothing to do with the murder. So why did you guys come back and take my computers?"

"You're barking up the wrong tree, shrimp. Nobody tells me shit."

He was lying. He may not have been on the case, but the cops gossiped in the locker room worse than high school girls on TikTok. If there was news about me, Mayeda's buddies would've filled him in. "What about Joy's boyfriend—the Afghani doctor? Why aren't you interrogating him?"

He pulled at the collar of his uniform "Where's our ramen? I don't have much time."

He knew something. I filled his cup again. Instead of drinking, he checked the clock on the wall.

What would make me Mayeda's BFF? The cheap sake wasn't doing it. 'Niners tickets? The season was six months away. Video game weapons? He had a real gun on his belt. What did he want? Other than the obvious— Sumire. The one thing I couldn't give him. Too bad all her friends went to liberal Berkeley—a cop was an automatic swipe left.

But that gave me an idea. "Let me check on the ramen."

Behind the counter, Kenta wore a green apron over an undershirt and smelled of grease and fried pork. "Bruh!" I said, bumping fists, then pointing towards the stockroom.

Yukiko eyed us suspiciously as we headed to the back together. After closing the door, he punched me on the arm. "What the ef, bruh? Every-one's saying you murdered Joy."

Jeez—even Kenta. He was the biggest gossip in Japantown, a better source of news than the free weekly paper. But he knew everyone in town and everything going on and that's what I needed now. "The police are fucking with me," I said. "Mayeda knows why. Can you help me get him to talk?"

"Anything, bruh. What do you need?"

At least I could count on Kenta. "A girl. Someone who kind of looks like Sumire. Know anybody?"

"If she finds out—"

"Not for me. For Mayeda. I want to set him up."

"Oh. Gotcha. Hmm. What about Kristi—you know, the Shiseido girl?"

The model with shiny hair and glowing skin who left a trail of men drooling whenever she sauntered out of the cosmetics shop in her tight miniskirt. "Isn't she dating some rich surfer dude?" Not that Mayeda would have a chance, or anyone else who lived in Japantown instead of Atherton or Los Altos Hills.

"Hmm. How about Runa-chan?"

I was pretty sure she was a lesbian. For someone who knew everything going on in town, Kenta didn't know much.

"Really? That explains a lot. Hold on, let me get Yukiko."

I didn't want to explain to Yukiko what I was doing. But when he returned with her in tow, I didn't have a choice. She stood in the door-way, hands on her hips. "What stupidity are you getting my Kenny into now?"

I ignored her surliness. "Know anyone interested in dating a cop? My friend is kind of lonely."

"Friend? Hah. I know you, Ted. You're up to something."

"I want him to be happy."

"Yeah, right," she snapped. "Mikey's okay, though. Unlike you. What about Emi?"

"Emi!" Kenta clapped. "She's perfect."

I had no idea who Emi was. Yukiko found a snap she'd taken of a flock of nurses in pink scrubs eating ramen together. "Her," she said, zooming in on a woman with green-streaked hair and a tattoo of a hypodermic on her wrist. Strong enough to wrestle anyone to the ground who refused to get their shots. She looked absolutely nothing like Sumire. But a better match for Mayeda. Yukiko shot me a copy of the photo as I marched back to the table.

"There's someone who wants to meet you," I said, holding the phone up to show him.

He glanced at the screen and shook his head before I could even point out Emi. "Um, I'm not really...there's kinda someone else..."

Yeah, he still had a thing for Sumire. I had to find him a girlfriend so he could stop mooning over mine. "She saw you here last week and asked Yukiko about you." He wasn't interested. "She loves football," I tried. "Huge 'Niners fan."

"I'm kinda into the Steelers."

You can lead a horse to water. But you still have to kick him in the balls. "Just look," I said. I ditched the photo of the nurses and scanned through Insta until I found Kristi the Shiseido goddess preening in a bikini. "If you're really not interested..." I shoved the phone in his face.

His eyes bulged, his saliva glands went turbo. "She...she wants to meet me?"

"Told you she's got a thing for cops. And football players. But I don't know...the Steelers? Sounds like a deal breaker."

He quickly changed his lifelong loyalties for a polka-dotted bikini and a glimpse of photoshopped skin. "The 'Niners are okay, too, local team and all. And now that Polamalu and Roethlisberger are retired..."

"Great. I'll tell Yukiko to set it up." I knew I'd be in trouble when Emi showed up for the date, but I'd figure something out before then. Nobody looked like their Insta profile anyway. In the end he'd thank me. But now he'd better start talking if he wanted to meet Emi.

"Why did you guys name me a person of interest?"

Mayeda shrugged.

"What are your detectives doing about that file I found on Joy's computer?"

He gulped down his sake. "Hey, this is great shit."

It was just shit. I topped up his cup and asked the question again.

"I really don't know anything."

"Emi's not interested in dating a cop who doesn't know anything."

"It's just rumors."

"Spill it."

He leaned across the table and whispered, "The FBI can't open the file. They're hoping it's fake. And leaning on us to get the password."

"Is that why they're searching my computers? And made me give up my own password?"

Mayeda smirked at me. "Whaddya think?"

"They're not going to find anything other than my password cracking software."

"They're pretty sure the file came from either you or the doc."

"It wasn't me." I raised my hand in a fake oath. "That means it must've been the doc. Why aren't you interrogating him?"

"Had him in all afternoon. Picked him up right after you."

"But you let him go?"

"No evidence," Mayeda claimed.

"What about the laptop?"

"What laptop?"

"Joy's laptop. It's missing. Your guys said it was stolen to make the murder look like a robbery."

Mayeda shrugged. "Don't know about no laptop."

"What about witnesses? Security cameras? Don't you guys have video?"

"I'm sure somebody's out canvassing the neighborhood, but that's not me," he said. "All I heard is Dr. Khan's phone showed him leaving Joy's apartment before 6:30 and the 9-1-1 call didn't come in until 6:40."

"But that's only ten minutes later."

"Yeah, but the neighbor who called 9-1-1 swears there's no way the shots could've been fired even three minutes earlier."

That didn't seem like much of a difference, especially without exact timestamps. "So you know the doctor did it, but you don't have any evidence other than some confused guy who heard shots and lost track of time? That about sum it up?"

Mayeda stared at me. "I told you, shrimp, I'm not a detective. They don't tell me shit."

"But you know he did it."

"Well...sure, statistically the husband or boyfriend is always the likely perp." He sounded like he was auditioning for a role as a TV detective.

"Then why call me a person of interest?"

Mayeda laughed. "Gotta finger someone. Who better than the hacker who broke into a dead woman's computer and claimed her murder has something to do with terrorists? At least we know you're guilty of something."

"But I had nothing to do with the murder!"

"Can't finger the doc."

"Why not?"

"'Cause he's Afghani. If it turns out he didn't do it, we'll have protests all over town, start that 'defund the police' shit all over again."

"So you finger me instead?"

"Sure. Fingering you is like eating two chickens with one fork."

"What the hell does that mean?"

"Chief gets the press off his back, and he settles a score at the same time."

"What score? I didn't do anything to the new chief."

"You don't get it, do you, shrimp?"

"Get what?"

Mayeda slurped down the last drops of the shit sake as if it were the greatest ambrosia. "Nobody on the force likes you. The last chief came up through the force. He got us raises, more officers, new equipment. And you got him fired because he owned a few shares of stock in a startup. Now all we got is a political hack who doesn't know nothing. And you pissed him off, too, going to the FBI and claiming there's a terrorism connection with *our* murder case. Now he's got the Feds on one side trying to take the case away and Judge Jeanine on the other screaming we gotta arrest someone today. Person of interest? Ha! That's the least of your worries, shrimp. If I was you, I'd watch my back. And my front, too."

five
ososhiki

My eyes fluttered open to a hazy image of a huge black crow with wings stretched wide. Instead of cawing, it spoke with a woman's voice, a voice I recognized. A voice that sounded like a layer of silk covering steel rebar. "Why aren't you ready?" the crow squawked, sounding like Sumire.

My tongue stuck to the roof of my mouth, my teeth covered with film, I fumbled around for my glasses. "Ready for what?" I mumbled.

"The funeral!"

Still half-sleep, my brain decaffeinated, I felt like I'd been punched in the gut. Then kicked in the ribs. Then had an anvil dropped on my head.

As I slipped on the wireframes, Sumire came into focus, holding up a garment bag in each hand. Dressed in a somber black dress and a double strand of pearls, the white pancake makeup and crimson lipstick made her look too much like my mother. I pulled the blanket over my head. "You don't expect me to go, do you?"

She lay the garment bags over the edge of the sofa and yanked the blanket away, exposing the morning hard-on sticking out of my *jinbei* pajamas. She groaned and threw the blanket back over me. "Get up, sleepyhead," she said. "The funeral is at ten."

"Everyone thinks I killed her."

"When have you cared what other people think?"

I didn't care about the twits on X and Insta, but everyone in Japantown would be at Joy's funeral. This was my community, my refuge from the world. The stinkeyes shooting at me from every direction, the buzz of gossip following me around the room, would make me an outcast in my home. Besides, with two parents dead and cremated, I'd already filled my lifetime quota of funerals. "Don't I get a pass?" I tried. "I didn't even know her."

"Get dressed," she answered.

Time to play my trump card. "I need to buy a new computer this morning and get back to seeing what happened to Joy." I pointed at the square outlines on the carpet where my confiscated computers belonged. With the FBI stuck opening the file and the cops fingering me for the crime, I needed to do something other than praying to Buddha. "Isn't finding Joy's murderer more important than going to her funeral?"

"Theodore Hara!" she answered, trumping me back with my own name.

"I don't have anything to wear." If I showed up in a black hoodie again, all the *obachans* and *ojisans* would be convinced I was a criminal.

"Hah!" She unzipped a garment bag adorned with a Bloomingdale's logo and pulled out a black suit jacket. The fabric was silky, unlike the scratchy wool suit I'd worn to my father's funeral and my mother's memorial. It felt expensive. I searched for the price to see how many months of college loans I'd owe Sumire, but the tag had been snipped away.

"No returnsies," she said, tossing the slacks over my shoulder. Inside the second bag was a crisp white shirt, already ironed, and a black funeral tie.

"Socks?"

She handed me a brown paper bag with a pair of lace-up dress shoes instead of a bottle of whiskey, a pair of socks at the bottom. I dropped them on the floor in horror.

"Hurry," she said. "We're already late."

We had plenty of time to arrive before the start of the ceremony, but we'd have to head out soon to arrive early. I grumbled but tossed the blanket aside and carried the garment bags into the bathroom. Scrubbing away the residue of the night, I frowned at what I saw—a wide nose holding up geeky glasses, shaggy hair hanging low over my eyes.

On the other side of the door, Sumire paced the hallway, impatient to leave, but I wasn't ready. As I buzzed away the dots of stubble with an electric razor, I wondered if this was how married life would be—comfortable and confining in equal measure. Growing up together, the little sister of my best friend, Sumire and I already knew each other better than most married couples. I wondered if we knew each other too well. When I slipped into the clothes she'd bought me, they fit perfectly, better than if I'd picked them myself. Somehow, even the dress shoes fit me like Cinderella.

The necktie, though, was a different matter. It took five tries before I completed a lopsided knot that didn't hang down to my knees. When I poked my head out of the bathroom to show her, Sumire clapped, then pushed me back into the bathroom and stood behind me in front of the mirror.

"See how handsome you look?" she gushed.

Handsome—me? Two words rarely heard together. Smart—yes; best MMORPG gamer in town—the rankings didn't lie. Sharpest coder in Silicon Valley—certainly high on the list. But short and scrawny, I hardly set women's hearts racing. Did Sumire really think I was handsome? I looked at her face, a hint of the smile she kept hidden behind thin, pink lips, afraid to show the crooked front teeth that made her look like a rabbit. Cuter than hell and smarter than anyone I knew, including my Nobel laureate professors, she was stern but kind and couldn't resist a hopeless case like me. I realized how much I loved her. Even if she was lying when she said I was handsome. Especially if she was lying. The warm glow from her eyes made me feel a foot taller.

She put her hands around me and laughed, rouged dimples shining on her cheeks. "Didn't anyone teach you how to put on a tie?" With nimble fingers and a few waves of her arms like a magician, a perfect knot took shape around my neck. Then she helped me into the suit jacket that made my shoulders broader. As if by magic, I was transformed from a boy into a man. No longer a minnow, I'd become a shark. Maybe dressing up wasn't so awful. Except for the tie choking my throat. I pulled the knot loose. Sumire tightened it again, patting the lapels. "You need a haircut."

🔒 🔒 🔒

Arm-in-arm, we walked the three blocks towards Betsuin, my stiff dress shoes rubbing off a layer of skin with every step. The sun was bright in the cloudless sky, the air calm and warm. A perfect day for just about anything except a funeral.

When we reached 5th Street, the road was packed with cars: gleaming black town cars and dusty white Prii, double-parked in the street. News vans lined the curb while squat men shouldered cameras in front of sculpted blondes wielding microphones.

Up ahead, Mayeda was on traffic duty. "Hi, Mikey!" Sumire called.

He waved to her, then yelled to me, "Did you set up my date yet?"

I ducked my head. "What's that about?" Sumire asked. I promised to explain later.

When the temple's red roof tiles emerged from behind the ugly concrete building next door, my heart started pounding and my stomach twisted into a knot. I'd been to Betsuin Temple hundreds of times, the summer *matsuri* that filled 5th Street with taiko drummers and *bon odori* dancers, the Japanese language classes every Saturday morning when I wanted to be out playing baseball. But it was the crowd in black milling in front that reminded me of my father's funeral. I had to stop until Sumire wrapped her arms around my waist and I was able to stand upright again. Then she took me by the hand and dragged me into the crowd.

I hated all crowds, not just funerals. Surrounded by taller people, it was impossible to see and difficult to move, leaving me feeling trapped. But today at least, I hoped nobody noticed me hidden in the sea of humanity.

As we weaved up the concrete path, a friend of Sumire's reached out to hug her. While they screeched and cried, another woman joined their huddle, and then another, leaving me alone on the sidewalk. To escape the river of people flowing towards the temple entrance, I stepped onto the lawn and leaned against a stone *toro* lantern that resembled a miniature spaceship.

I noticed a man and woman on the veranda of the temple who looked out of place. Not only were they two Caucasians in a sea of Japanese people, but they didn't resemble lawyers or politicians or the Valley types who spent all day sitting in front of a computer, either. The man had a salt-and-pepper buzz cut circling a white hole of baldness, and a rough face with a scooped jaw that resembled the business end of a bulldozer. The rest of him looked assembled by Caterpillar, too, with wide shoulders and a barrel chest straining against his suit jacket. Beside Bulldozer was a woman who looked ten years younger but even more ferocious. A ponytail of brown hair matched her horsey face and thin, bloodless lips. In a black shirt and black slacks with dark sneakers instead of dress shoes, she looked more like a waitress than a mourner. But it was her eyes that stood out from across the lawn; a blue that matched the cloudless sky, they were focused on me with the intensity of a high-power laser. Just the thought of getting paired against her in an Alien Hunter battle made me shiver. When she caught me staring back at her, she whispered to Bulldozer beside her, and pointed in my direction. He scanned the crowd until his eyes lit on me. I ducked behind a circle of Teslaturds comparing their lease terms. But through a gap between their heads, I saw Bulldozer and Laser-Eye watching me.

They had to be part of the security team, I realized, or maybe a Secret Service detail protecting the congressman. From this distance, it was impossible to make out the bulge of a Glock or a coiled earpiece that denoted government agents in every movie, but the pair looked the part. Unlike the rentacops guarding Jiji's house, I had no doubt these two would take a bullet to keep the congressman safe. To escape their stare, I turned my back and wedged myself into Sumire's circle of Berkeley friends. One threw me a stinkeye; the others pretended I didn't exist. When I looked back over my shoulder, I could feel the heat of the laser eyes focused on the center of my forehead.

After the women finished hugging each other, Sumire and I joined the line at the reception table where three matrons in formal attire were accepting the envelopes of *o-kōden* cash and recording the amounts in the guest registry. I hadn't brought the obligatory gift, I realized with a sickening feeling. "Let's go inside," I whispered, hoping we could sneak past the matrons.

Sumire opened her clutch and handed me an oblong envelope decorated with black and white ribbons, both of our names written in kanji outside, $500 in crisp, fresh benjis inside. My mother would have loved Sumire if she hadn't hated her so much.

When we reached the front, a matron bowed as she thanked us in English and Japanese. She slid the registry across the table together with a calligraphy brush. Sumire wrote her name in flowing script that reminded me of the manga she used to draw. I scribbled my own name in kanji, but instead of lines that cascaded from one stroke into another, the lopsided characters looked in danger of falling on their faces. If my mother had seen my woeful penmanship, she would have sat me down and forced me to practice writing my name a hundred times, then a hundred times again. Sumire only shook her head, resigned to yet another irredeemable flaw.

The matron reached out with two hands to accept the envelope from Sumire, raising her plucked eyebrows when she read my name. She coughed into her hand but marked the amount in the register and bowed again in thanks.

Climbing the tall steps to the veranda, a gauntlet of somber men in black *hakama* kimono stood on either side of the door. At the threshold, I was careful not to anger the gods by touching the wooden rail with impure feet when entering the dimly lit temple.

Inside, I was hit by a mélange of odors: the musty smell of dust and decay; the earthy scent of the sandalwood incense burning beside the casket; the medicinal smell of a thousand white lilies lying atop the coffin; the cloying scent of a hundred perfumes applied too liberally. A young girl, a Hello Kitty bow in her hair, thrust a program into my hands as if this were a baseball game. In the back corner, a cameraman stood behind a tripod, streaming the procession to friends and family around the world watching the funeral in their jammies.

At the altar, the dark wood of the coffin gleamed under bright spot-lights. Behind it, a poster-sized photo of Joy's unsmiling face looked down over her own dead body. A row of wreathes surrounded the coffin, donors' names written in perfect calligraphy. In the back, five golden Buddhas sat watching the mourners, smug in their knowledge that this world was but an illusion and life was nothing but suffering.

Sumire slipped into a pew in the back with her friends, motioning for me to squeeze in beside her. The *obachan* next to me gasped when she saw me and excused herself to find another seat. I bowed my head low and waited for the funeral to begin. When the *orin* bell rang out, the chatter quieted to a low murmur. Three monks in orange robes with shaven heads began chanting Buddhist sutras. Bulldozer and Laser-Eye shuffled in with the stragglers to sit in the last row behind me. Their eyes boring into the back of my neck made me uncomfortable.

When the attendants closed the heavy doors, the light of the outside world faded to the dim golden glow of the Buddhas. The monks continued chanting, oblivious to the shuffle of feet, the crinkle of candy wrappers, and the buzz of phones powering down, each line of sutra punctuated by the resonant chime of the bronze bell.

The minister walked up the first row where he hugged Mrs. Miyazaki and shook hands with Jiji. After offering condolences to the rest of the family, he stepped up to the dais. The bell rang a final time as the chanting sputtered to a halt and a hush fell over the room.

The minister led a series of prayers in English and Japanese, then Jiji delivered the eulogy. With a tear in his eye, he apologized to Joy for not protecting her from evil. To amens from the mourners, he promised to do everything in his power to make this country safer. Sniffles followed him back to his seat where he embraced his sobbing wife.

The eulogy over, I waited for the minister to resume the prayers. Instead, he introduced Joy's boyfriend, the doctor, his face covered with thick stubble. The doctor rose, shook hands with Jiji, kissed Joy's mother on the cheek, and stepped up to the podium.

"What's he doing?" I whispered to Sumire.

The *obachans* around me turned to give me the stinkeye. Sumire shushed me, even as she leaned away.

The doctor glanced over the audience, his expression imperious, before looking down to read the sheet of paper he set on the podium. He'd first met Joy in the refugee camps of Turkey when she'd burst into the tent where he was performing surgery. She'd demanded he get out of the way so she could document the patient's burns as evidence of a gas attack. He'd ordered her out of the tent; she'd refused to leave. She'd convinced him that the only way to stop the carnage was by showing the world the horrors. He'd continued operating while she shot photos of the patient. Then she'd stayed in the tent the rest of the day assisting him with surgery. After that, they'd been inseparable. Until now. Joy was gone. Taken from him. Taken from her parents. Taken from the world. Why? Why would someone murder this selfless woman who'd dedicated her life to justice? The doctor's haughtiness melted, his shoulders slouched. He wiped tears from his eyes. "I know this is Allah's will," he sobbed, "but I can't understand it."

The minister patted the doctor's shoulder. Jiji took him in a bear hug. Joy's mother pressed her face into his chest. I was sure he was faking.

The bronze bell chimed again, and the monks returned to chanting. Mourners lined up in front of the casket. Sumire and I sat in silence, listening to the droning monks, the sobs and sniffles, the growing chatter until the ushers motioned it was our turn to join the line. When we reached the front, Sumire and I stood side-by-side and bowed to Joy's photo.

Inside the coffin, Joy was laid out in a cream-colored kimono matched with a black *obi* belt, her sleeves decorated with embroidered cranes and chrysanthemums. Her face was painted with rouge on her cheeks and deep red lipstick that I doubted she ever wore in life.

We pinched the incense powder in the bronze bowl between thumb and index finger and lifted it to our foreheads, then sprinkled it over the candle's flame, repeating the motion three times. The smoke from the incense made me dizzy. Palms together in *gassho*, we bowed to Joy once more before returning to our pew.

When the last of the mourners took their seats, a final toll of the bell ended the chanting. The minister led the chorus in one last psalm before the service came to an end. As everyone stood, a dozen men in black kimonos gathered around the coffin. With a collective grunt, they lifted the casket off the pedestal and carried it up the aisle. The ushers threw open the doors; a beam of sunlight stretched into the room, setting the dust in the air aglow.

Starting in the front, one row at a time, the mourners followed the casket through the door where Joy's mother and father, three grandparents and an *obachan* waited in a reception line. The doctor stood awkwardly at the end, a breach of protocol since he wasn't family.

After a peck on the cheek from Joy's mother, Jiji and I faced each other. I was angry he'd broken his promise not to give me away to the cops. His disdain for me was clear without having to say anything. To avoid shaking hands we bowed to each other, more head bob than formal bow. I mumbled my condolences. He grumbled something that sounded like cocksucker. Rather than consoling the doctor like everyone else, I ducked out of line and escaped down the stairs to the lawn. Sumire shot me a stinkeye as she stayed with Joy's mother.

While waiting for Sumire, I stood on the grass away from the flow of the crowd. When Bulldozer and Laser-Eye exited the temple with the last of the mourners, they towered over everyone. But if they were security, why were they in the reception line instead of standing guard? A handful of cops were out in the street making sure the weird protestors waving American flags and Lock Him Up signs with Jiji's face stayed behind the barricades, but nobody seemed to be protecting the congressman from a gunman or terrorist bomb.

After passing the reception line, Bulldozer and Laser-Eye followed down the concrete path until Bulldozer suddenly stopped and turned in my direction. "Hey! Aren't you Ted Hara?"

I buried my head in my phone and pretended to be playing a game. He stomped across the grass to where I was standing. He must have decided that not only was I the murderer, but unlike all the other people here, he was going to do something about it. I considered running away, that was my only chance of surviving a fight I couldn't win, but with the entirety of Japantown watching, all I could do was stand there cringing as he pulled up in front of me.

"You're Mr. Hara, right?"

I folded my arms to protect my ribs against an attack. Instead of punching me, though, he asked, "Aren't you the guy who found that file on Miss Miyazaki's computer?"

I looked up at him surprised. How did he know about the file? It hadn't been mentioned on the news, not even on the conspiracy sites that claimed to have all the inside information. "Um, yeah?"

He waved Laser-Eye over to join us. "See Liz, I told you that was him." He reached out to shake my hand. "Frank Key," he introduced himself. He squeezed my hand so tight I almost yelped in pain. He nudged Laser-Eye towards me. "This is Elizabeth Ross," he said with a wink, like he was trying to set us up.

"Call me Liz," she said, her face expressionless, watching me with cold laser eyes.

"You guys security?" I asked.

Bulldozer chuckled. "No, sir! You think this little lady is going to stop anybody?"

The "little lady" looked like she could stop a runaway train by shooting out the brake lines from a quarter mile away. But she only smiled demurely and took a half-step back behind Bulldozer.

"We worked with Ms. Miyazaki. Pretty crazy what happened. You a friend?"

I pointed up at the veranda where Sumire was still chatting with Joy's mother. "Friend of a friend."

The pair hadn't been at Joy's birthday party. I wasn't good at remembering faces, but no way would I have forgotten these two. And they didn't look like the human rights activists milling around in shiny dress shoes instead of muddy combat boots. "Lawyers?" I asked.

"No, sir. I.T. staff."

They didn't resemble the I.T. trolls I'd worked with—men with pale, blotchy skin who hadn't seen the sun for years.

"Heard the file you found was encrypted," Bulldozer added. Noticing my surprise, he laughed. "Got friends on the force." He pointed at the cops in the street. It was easy to imagine Bulldozer and the Viking hanging out in the gym together lifting weights. "They decrypt that file yet?"

I shook my head. "Not as far as I know."

He nodded. "Yeah, that's what I figured. They don't know shit about cracking passwords, do they?"

"Nope."

"Somebody needs to do something, don't you think? Before it's too fucking late."

"Yup," I agreed. I hoped the FBI was taking the threat seriously because there was nothing more I could do. Though if this pair were part of Joy's I.T. team, it was possible they knew the passwords the lawyers gave out to informants and dissidents to send them secret documents. But when I asked, Bulldozer pointed at the doctor walking with Jiji towards the hearse. "He's the one that knows the password. Why hasn't that piece of shit been arrested yet?"

I shrugged. "Maybe he has an alibi?"

"Fucking Afghani," he hissed. "Even looks like a terrorist."

I took a step back from Bulldozer, wondering if my own certainty that the doctor was responsible for Joy's murder was his nationality, religion, or stubble. But no, it was the fact that he was in Joy's apartment a few minutes before her murder that made me sure he was the killer.

"If that was a home invasion," Bulldozer said, stepping closer to me again, "Why did they steal a laptop?"

I shrugged, trying to hide my surprise at how much he knew about the investigation.

"At least it ought to be easy to find. Wanna bet it turns up in that scum's apartment?"

More likely, it was smashed to bits and buried in the trash. "I hope the police find it," I said, glad to see Sumire finally heading down the path towards me. I waved my arms until she noticed me behind Bulldozer's hulking presence. "Nice meeting you," I said to be polite, then tried to squeeze around him.

He blocked my way. "You think the police know how to track a laptop, Mr. Hara?"

"Sorry," I repeated, "My girlfriend's waiting."

He didn't take the hint. "You work for MeCan, don't you?"

I was surprised he knew where I used to work. "Not anymore," I answered, making a mental note to update my LinkedIn profile.

"I know those guys," he said, pointing at the cops on the street. "They couldn't track a laptop if it bit 'em on the ass. But I'm sure you MeCan whizzes know what to do. How much you want to bet that scum has it hidden away somewhere? All it takes is someone to find it and put him away where he belongs."

Unlike a phone which was easy to locate with GPS, there wasn't any way I knew of to track a missing laptop. But there was no point in explaining that. "I'll give it a try," I said as I darted around Bulldozer.

"You do that," he said, letting me pass.

But before I could get back to Sumire, Laser-Eye stepped in front of me. "Someone needs to do something, Mr. Hara," she said. "And I reckon you're the man to do it. I hope you find that laptop." She reached out to shake my hand, smiling as she crunched my bones even worse than Bulldozer. "Everyone is counting on you."

"Uh...sure," I said as I hurried away.

"Who's she?" Sumire asked, eyes narrowed.

Though her jealousy gave me a little thrill, siren assassins weren't my type. I told her the pair were I.T. trolls who worked with Joy. "They're convinced the doc killed her."

She glared at me. "Naz didn't do it," she said, certain as always.

"How do you know?"

"Because I know him. Joy loved him. And he loved her. Aren't you paying attention? Just look at him. He's not some crazy terrorist."

I wasn't convinced. "If it wasn't him, then who?"

She huffed and walked away.

I raced after her, dress shoes cutting fresh blisters into my heels. But before I could catch up, someone called out, "Mr. Hara?"

I thought it was Laser-Eye again until I saw the reporter rushing towards me. She thrust a microphone in my face. "Mr. Hara? Why did you murder Joy Miyazaki?"

Sumire pulled me away before I could answer. But that brought the entire pack of reporters racing over, blocking the sidewalk, recorders shoved at me.

"How many other women did you kill?"

"Who helped you?"

"When will you be charged with murder?"

Sumire stepped in front, protecting me from the pack. "He has no comment," she said. But all of Japantown was watching now, everyone thinking I'd killed the beloved daughter. This was no time to stay silent. I had to defend myself.

"I had nothing to do with the murder," I insisted. "I discovered a suspicious email Joy received which I reported to the police."

Sumire yanked my arm. "Let's go, Ted."

But the reporters caught the whiff of a real story and closed in for the kill.

"What email?"

"How was the email connected to her murder?

"What did it say?"

Sumire tried to drag me away, but I didn't budge. I hummed a stanza of "I Fought the Law" out of tune. When I finished, every camera was trained on me. I opened my phone and read back the message from the informant: "'Daesh is planning a big attack that will kill many people. You must warn everyone. It is a matter of life and death.'"

The reporters stopped shouting; the street grew silent. A crow gawked from the top of a eucalyptus tree. Then pandemonium broke out. Questions assaulted me from every direction while a flock of birds squawked overhead. From the calm eye of the storm, I stared into the glowing red light atop the KRON-4 camera and declared, "The email included a file with details of an impending terrorist attack. The file is encrypted, and the police confiscated the computers I was using to open it. Please direct all questions to them." I pointed at the cops in their crisp uniforms standing in the street.

From the side of the hearse Jiji threw me a stinkeye. Joy's mother put her hand over her mouth. But Laser-Eye was smiling. She was right. Somebody needed to do something. And I was the man to do it.

big hero 6

AS SOON AS Sumire's lemon wedge rolled away to the cemetery, I dashed back to the apartment to change out of the monkey suit. Shirt and tie swapped for a Giants T-shirt, sandals replacing dress shoes, I jumped into the pony and galloped to the BadBuy to grab the biggest, baddest computer they sold. Walking down the aisle of big screen, bigger screen, and mega-screen TVs, the entire row was suddenly filled with giant images of my face humming out of tune. I ducked behind the wall of stainless-steel refrigerators before anyone noticed me.

News anchors described panic breaking out all over the country. Images of 9/11 played in the background while talking heads debated whether the email on Joy's computer was legit. Fortunately, nobody in the store was watching. I pulled the Asahi baseball cap low over my brow and slurked to the electronics aisle where I grabbed the first half-decent server and the fastest graphics card before escaping through the hissing doors.

By the time I got Qubes Linux—the secure operating system—installed on my new computer and Firefox pointed to the news, the military had been put on high alert. The National Guard was being dispatched to protect airports, power plants, and water treatment facilities. All flights from the Middle East were being diverted. NYPD was erecting barricades around the new World Trade Center. Disneyworld was shuttered until further notice, Mickey and Minnie hiding in their cartoon bunker. Talking heads on the left and right for once agreed on something—the terrorists had to be stopped. All eyes were on the President, asking what he would do. He was hunkered down with his advisors in a secret underground lair.

I pulled the source code of my password cracker from GitHub and rewrote it for the new Nvidia RTX graphics card. With twenty thousand cores and a shit-ton more RAM than the previous card, it could rip through passwords ten times faster. I held my breath and set the program running. The fans revved up to full speed, the computer sounding like a Boeing 787 taking off under the table. The counter for the number of passwords rolled over faster than the eye could follow. The cracker was working again, checking every combination of characters.

There was no way to know how long it would take for the password to pop out. Maybe a minute, maybe a day, maybe ten million years.

Was there something else I could do while I waited? After taking a break with a cup of tea, I realized I'd committed the cardinal sin of hacking —I'd let myself get tunnel visioned on breaking into the file instead of poking around at every wall until I found a crack to pry open.

What cracks could I find? Had Joy opened the terrorist's plan and saved a copy on the laptop's desktop? Was that why the doctor dashed off with it after murdering Joy? If so, there might be a copy in her MeCloud files since MeCan turned on automatic backup by default.

That meant logging into Joy's account again, something I'd sworn to the cops I wouldn't do. I didn't want to see Mayeda grinning beside the Viking as he kicked my door in, so I set up a doubly secure tunnel through Romania around a VPN from Switzerland. No way even the FBI could trace that back to me.

Fortunately, nobody had changed Joy's password or shut off access to the account. But with packets bouncing across the world, the connection was painfully slow. It took forever for Tangy to hop onto the screen and ask, "What do YOU want to do today, Joy?"

In not so polite language, I told the annoying fruit-flavored chatbot to get out of my way. Tangy hopped twice, waved, and poofed off the screen, leaving me in peace to search Joy's files. But I couldn't find a copy of the terrorist file, protected or unprotected. She'd never saved a copy, never forwarded it to anyone. It was impossible to tell if she'd ignored it, thinking it was a virus, or been murdered as soon as she opened it and showed her boyfriend.

I read the email message again: "Use the password you gave me to open it." What password would Joy have given out? And why wouldn't the I.T. staff at her employer know what that was? But when I'd asked the pair at the funeral, Bulldozer had suggested tracking the laptop instead, something an I.T. pro ought to know was impossible.

I ran a quick search for "find lost laptop" just to prove him wrong. Tangy popped up on the screen again. "Can I assist you?" she asked, her voice a couple of notches past cloying.

"How do I track a laptop?" I asked.

Instead of a nonsensical answer like Hansel and Gretel followed a trail of breadcrumbs, I was surprised when she offered, "Would you like to enable the FindMyLaptop feature on your account? 92.7% of users say this feature is useful."

Was Tangy hallucinating? AI chatbots were famous for making up nonsense when they didn't have an answer. I asked how it worked. Tangy quoted a dumbed-down feature description that was pretty slick. When turned on, every MeCan phone listened for the MAC address of the missing laptop's Wi-Fi interface. If it heard it, the phone sent the location and signal strength back to a MeCan server to triangulate the location.

That made Bulldozer right in principle, though completely wrong in real life. I couldn't understand how 92.7% of users could find this feature useful. It was great if the laptop was up and running, but lost or stolen computers weren't. Two days had already passed since the murder. If the laptop wasn't in a dumpster somewhere smashed into bits, it would've gone into sleep mode or run out of battery a long time ago.

"Would you like to enable the FindMyLaptop feature for the device named *Joy to the World*?" Tangy asked again.

"Sure, why not?" I answered. There was no harm in trying. At least it would send an alert with the location if the laptop was ever powered up again.

Tangy hopped twice and replied in a pleasant robotic voice, "OK! Finding your laptop now..." The dots dipped up and down in a wave for close to a minute. I was ready to give up when a map popped up on the screen with a blue pin for the laptop's location.

Either someone had recently turned the laptop on, or it was plugged into a power strip somewhere. Remembering my prior glee at tracking Joy's phone to police headquarters, this time I refused to get excited. The laptop had to be sitting on a detective's desk reunited with her phone. I zoomed in anyway and was surprised when this time, the map pointed to the opposite side of town, a residential neighborhood behind Prusch Farm, a couple of blocks from Target.

"Hey, Tangy, give me the coordinates." She hopped twice, happy to oblige. She even looked up the owner of the house for me, saving me loads of time. The single-story rancher had been purchased twenty years ago by a couple named Kumar.

The husband worked at IBM, the wife at Evergreen Valley College. The middle-aged couple hardly seemed the type to invade homes and murder residents. Was he having an affair with Joy that he had to hide from his wife? More likely, the couple's teenage son had picked up the laptop from one of the vendors at the flea market selling stolen crap. Or had the family AirBnB'ed their home to terrorists while they visited relatives in India? It wasn't obvious why Joy's laptop was at their house. Or why the FBI hadn't found it already.

I considered calling the cops to give them the location, but that would mean admitting I'd hacked into Joy's account again. And it was possible the whole thing was nothing but a Tangy hallucination. I decided to check it out myself—the address wasn't far.

Instead of driving over in the pony that someone might recognize, I hopped on a Bird and zipped the four miles down residential streets, ignoring the stop signs and traffic lights, until I reached the East San Jose neighborhood known as Cinderella. The street in front of the Kumar residence was packed with Hondas, Toyotas, and Hyundais; the other side of the street was empty—it was street sweeping day.

I skidded to a stop at the Kumar's house. The lawn was trim and neat; the grass was freshly cut. Yellow roses ran the length of the white picket fence along the sidewalk.

I plugged the coordinates into my phone, accurate to three meters. Instead of directing me inside the house, it pointed at the curb. I walked in a circle to make sure I'd found the exact spot—inside a silver BMW 5-series parked beneath an oak tree. That didn't make sense but there was no doubt Joy's laptop was inside the car and turned on. It couldn't have been here very long, and probably wouldn't be here much longer.

I shot a photo of the license plate, then called Mayeda.

"Heya, pal!" Mayeda answered. "When's the date with Emi?" Not even hello.

"I need a favor," I mumbled.

He groaned. "Not what I wanna hear."

"I'm texting you a license plate. Can you check who owns it?"

"No way. Not for a civ. That's privileged info."

"Joy's computer is inside," I told him.

"What computer?"

"Her laptop. The one the murderer took."

"How do you know it's inside the car?"

"Can't tell you," I said. "Privileged info."

"Where's the car at?"

I wasn't giving that info away so easily. "You gotta tell me who owns it first."

"Why the secrecy?"

"If the car belongs to who I think it does, that changes everything."

"Who do you think owns it?"

"Just call it in already," I pleaded.

Mayeda grumbled but put me on hold. When the line crackled again, he was no longer surly. "How do you know the victim's laptop is inside the vehicle?"

"Can't tell you."

"You gonna tell me the location, or do I have to put out an APB on you?"

"Who's the owner?" I asked.

"Who do you think?"

"He have a medical degree?"

"Yeah."

That's all I needed to hear. I'd already confirmed that a Dr. Nasir Khan lived with two older Khans—almost certainly his parents—the next block over. He'd moved his fancy Beemer for street cleaning. I DM'ed Mayeda the address. "Get someone over here right away to search it."

"Can't do that," he said. "Gotta have probable cause."

It had to suck being a cop, knowing who the perp was and not being able to do anything about it. "Didn't you overhear him at the funeral saying he'd hid Joy's laptop in his car?"

"Nope. Didn't hear anything like that."

Jeez, an honest cop. Where were the thugs in blue who'd tried to railroad me? "You found it yourself. On your own initiative. You tracked the computer here."

"I don't hack into people's computers. I'm not like you."

He made it sound dirty, like I was some kind of Peeping Tom. "It's not hacking. You went into Joy's account and asked Tangy to locate the laptop. Easy-peasy. Even your grandmother could do it."

"I don't know her password."

"Joy gave Sumire her password. She told you."

"But she didn't."

I messaged Sumire, asking her to DM Mayeda the text: "!des0fMarch." When his phone buzzed, I said, "Now you've got her password."

"But it's still illegal."

"Look, Mayeda. Terrorists are about to crash an airplane into the World Trade Center, and you've got the key to stop them. You. All you need to do is get someone to search the car. That's it. This is your chance to be the hero. They'll give you a medal. They'll make you detective."

A long silence. "I'll think about it."

"There's no time for thinking. Just do it."

Mayeda grumbled, as close as I'd get to a yes.

"And Mayeda?"

"Yeah, shrimp?"

"You can't tell anyone I had anything to do with this."

deep thoughts

ONCE I HEARD the sirens screaming towards the doc's vehicle, I birded back to my apartment and opened a dozen tabs in Firefox to monitor the full spectrum of news, from left-wing libtard through right-wing nutjob and deep into the infrared insane. I waited to hear the news about the doctor being arrested. And waited. What was taking so long?

While waiting, I dove into the logs to see how my password cracking software was progressing. I wasn't surprised it hadn't found the password yet, but it was a punch to the gut when I saw it was still churning through four-character combinations. Something was broken. So far, all it had checked were trivial one, two, and three-character passwords. I'd accomplished nothing.

The worldwide agglomeration of know-it-alls on Reddit claimed that any decent laptop could run through a hundred million password attempts per second. If they were right, my homemade supercomputer with twenty thousand GPUs ought to be checking a trillion passwords with every tick of the clock. A six-character password had 590 billion permutations, which meant I should be able to check all possible combinations of six characters or less in under a single second. So why after more than an hour was I still stuck on four-character passwords?

I reviewed the code line-by-line but couldn't find anything wrong. It wasn't until I ran a performance profiler that the problem smacked my face. There was nothing janky about my code itself, but the way it was checking passwords was a disaster. It wasn't comparing password hashes, a simple operation that required only a few CPU cycles; instead, it opened Microsoft Word for every password attempt to try to decrypt the entire file.

Unfortunately, there wasn't a better solution; opening an encrypted Microsoft file was fundamentally different from breaking into a website. Even after porting the software from the Linux emulator to native Windoze and minimizing memory swaps and cache misses to improve efficiency, the best I could do was 200,000 password attempts per second. A six-character password—a throwaway—would take thirty-five days to check every permutation. A half-decent eight-character password would need 851 years.

As I banged my head against the table in frustration, the browser dinged with an alert, then another and another. The FBI was holding an important press conference that all the news sites were streaming live. I lifted my head off the keyboard to watch Louis Willimont, the Director of the FBI, standing in front of the beige concrete of the butt-ugly Hoover Building. A messy mixture of sleet and snow was falling from slate-gray skies over the nation's capital, as if the entire country was crying. That hardly cheered me up as I waited anxiously, hoping to hear that after his arrest, the doc had divulged the password and the terrorists had been thwarted.

But instead of triumphant, the Director's countenance was downcast, his face stern, his body hunched by the gravity of the situation as he stared deep into the camera. In a low, sonorous voice, he declared international terrorists a grave threat to the safety of all Americans. He assured the public the FBI was doing everything in its power to prevent an attack. But he admitted that the FBI was struggling to open the file discovered on Joy Miyazaki's computer.

The director stood up straight behind the podium and pointed a finger at the cameras. "For the safety of all Americans, there is only one solution. Congress must pass a bill giving us the tools we need to open this file and others like it. Make no mistake, we face a grave danger that can only be met by restoring the tools law enforcement depends upon to stop terrorists and murderers. We call on Congress and the Administration to pass legislation without further delay."

Ignoring the braying pack of reporters, the director turned and walked through the glass doors into the building and was gone. Nothing about Joy's laptop. Nothing about a BMW owner who was in Joy's apartment moments before her murder. Just a ton of bullshit. Not letting a good crisis go to waste, they were taking advantage of this emergency to get what they'd always wanted—complete access to everyone's private data. It made me angry.

Even if Microsoft added a backdoor to Word documents, it wouldn't do anything about the file on Joy's computer that needed to be opened now. Worse, giving the FBI access to all our emails, phone calls, texts, and location data required adding a backdoor to every app. Even the noobiest programmer knew the problem with that: if the cops had a way in, so did the bogons in Bulgaria. Requiring a warrant from a secret court might prevent abuse by the FBI, but it wouldn't stop the Russians. Or the North Koreans. Or freelance Romanian hackers. And it wouldn't stop terrorists who'd simply switch to a secure app like Telegram, run from secret servers in Dubai where the short arm of American law couldn't reach.

The FBI had been pushing for a similar law for years, every time there was a murder they couldn't solve, or child pornography popped out of the gutter. They'd been blocked in Congress by a strange alliance of Democrats, led by Jiji, protecting personal privacy, and Republicans convinced the FBI had been weaponized in a conspiracy against them. When I'd worked at MeCan, we'd laughed about the FBI's periodic attempts to require us to turn over the keys to our digital kingdom, but this was no longer a joke.

I was about to close the browser when they cut to Jiji in his black funeral suit. He was standing in front of a wrought iron fence under a cerulean sky, tombstones of the old Japanese cemetery lined up behind him. Jiji was angry, his mouth distorted, one eye twitching, squinting into the cameras as he announced his full support for the FBI. He was co-sponsoring the New Patriot Act and called on his colleagues to pass the legislation in an emergency session of Congress.

I couldn't watch. If the FBI said the only way they could stop terrorists was to scan all of our private messages and ogle our nude photos, I'd have to prove them wrong. I'd have to find a way to open the file and show it could be done. But how? My single graphics card wasn't close to having the horsepower to do the job. Scotty, we need more power.

Where did everyone get more power? Not dilithium crystals, but the nearly infinite computing power of Deep Thought, MeCan's network of forty-two data centers stretched across the globe, each the size of a city block, built in remote locations like the fjords of Norway to take advantage of free energy, free cooling, and free taxes. Much cheaper than AWS, Azure, or Google Cloud, every startup in the world, from side hustles to unicorns, ran on Deep, as everyone called it. To handle its insane growth, MeCan was constantly adding newer and faster servers; at any time, less than half its capacity was actually in use. Which meant there was the equivalent of twenty-one datacenters sitting idle, waiting for instructions. My little server cranking away under the table was nothing more than a bacterium in a world of tyrannosaurs. Unleashing that power would take serious coin, billions of dollars for the electricity alone. Even a year of student loan payments would only buy a few nanoseconds. I'd have to convince MeCan to donate their unused resources for the good of the country and their users' privacy.

At MeCan, a decision of any magnitude flowed up the tower to Evgeni, MeCan's founder and CEO, the top turtle of the forty-four floors of turtles where I'd worked until recently. He must've had a last name on his passport, but to the entire world he was known only as Evgeni, like Newton, Einstein, and Rihanna. One of the most powerful men in the world, there was no way he'd answer a call from a grunt like me. Which meant I'd have to be someone else.

I dialed the company's switchboard and asked to speak to Evgeni. In a gruff voice, I said I was Congressman Jiji Miyazaki and demanded to speak with Evgeni. That got me to an intern in the company's department of governmental affairs. She forwarded me to Evgeni's personal assistant. The phone rang and rang until it went to voicemail but now I had a name. I called once more and shouted at the operator, trying to sound like Jiji. "This is a goddamn fucking national emergency. Get me Britney McPherson right now!" I was uncomfortable playing the jerk, but since I was no longer on the company's Slack, this was the only way to get anyone at MeCan to pick up a phone.

When Evgeni's PA answered, I yelled at her, too, as nicely as I could. But I was still surprised when the phone rang through to Evgeni. In his much-lampooned Russian accent, he said, "To what do I owe this honor, Congressman?"

"Hello, Evgeni," I said. "Are you ready to help your nation?"

"Of course, sir! What can a humble businessman like me do to assist our great nation?"

"We urgently need to crack an encrypted file. I assume you've seen the news? We want to use all of Deep's available compute resources in a parallel brute force—"

Evgeni was suddenly suspicious. "Who is this?"

As the congressional representative for San Jose and the CEO of its largest employer, Jiji and Evgeni would have met many times, probably chatted regularly. There was no way I could pull off impersonating Jiji. "This is Ted Hara from Congressman Miyazaki's office—"

"Hara?" he interrupted. "Why's that name familiar?"

I felt a tinge of pride that the CEO of the biggest tech company in the world remembered me. "I used to work at MeCan," I said to my former boss' boss' boss' boss' boss' boss' manager.

"Ted Hara?" he spat. "That Ted Hara? The Ted Hara we fired for adding back doors to our code?"

I hadn't added a back door, I protested. I'd taken advantage of a minor bug to peek into a friend's account.

Evgeni hung up on me.

eight
bad reception

I'D HAVE to convince Jiji to call Evgeni himself. But how could I get Jiji to listen to my plan? This was way too complicated to relay through Sumire and Joy's mother. Then I remembered the reception Sumire was going to after the funeral.

The humiliation of the funeral was bad enough; the reception would be ten times worse. But this would be the only way to corner Jiji today. Tomorrow might be too late.

My name wouldn't be on the list of friends and family, and even wearing a suit, I doubted I could convince the guards I was a major campaign donor. I messaged Sumire hoping she hadn't already left. *"can I go to the reception with u?"*

My phone dinged back, *"yes! ty! pick u up in 5."*

She was already on the way. I hurried to change back into the monkey suit. Even following MeTube videos, though, I couldn't get the tie into a decent knot. I finally gave up and stuffed it into my pocket as I headed out to the street.

While waiting for Sumire to pull up in the lemon wedge, I checked the news again. The same blonde reporter who'd accosted me after the funeral was live in front of the police station, blue and red lights of police cars strobing the street like a disco. "You can see the situation unfolding here in San Jose," she said, hair whipping across her face. "Nasir Khan, a surgeon at nearby Regional Hospital, was taken into custody this afternoon after the police uncovered evidence linking him to the murder of Joy Miyazaki."

I breathed a sigh of relief—the doctor was finally arrested. I dialed Mayeda, my new BEF.

"Thanks for the tip, pal," he said. "Can't talk now, gotta run. Gotta get to the reception. You gonna be there?"

Mayeda was neither friend nor family. "What are you doing there?"

"Chief told me to come."

"For what?"

"Dunno. Security, I guess."

"Don't tell him about me, okay?"

Mayeda chuckled. "Yeah, don't worry about that."

He was about to hang up. "Wait! Did the doctor give up the password?"

"Gotta run, Hara. Maybe I'll see you there."

"Come on, Mayeda. You owe me." No answer. But he didn't red-button me, either. "Please?" I tried, surprised it had any effect.

"Nah, nothing yet."

Damn. If there was ever a time to torture prisoners, this was it. The previous police chief wouldn't have hesitated; my ribs were testament to that. But the new chief played by the rules. As usual, the cops were useless for anything other than guarding coffee shops and making my life miserable.

When the lemon wedge rolled to the curb, I leaned across the seat to kiss Sumire. Her eyes were bloodshot, eyeliner streaked, mascara smeared. Her impregnable mask of calm composure had been melted away by tears. Burying her friend must've been rough. I'd been so focused on the terrorist threat that I'd forgotten about her pain. "Sorry I didn't go out to the cemetery with you," I said as she merged the car into traffic.

Her shrug said little but cut me deeper than any words. She didn't expect anything more from me. I gripped her hand and kissed it. "Are you okay?" I asked, sounding as sympathetic as I could.

"I'll be fine," she said, her face brightening a little. "Thanks for coming with me to the reception."

I decided not to mention why I was coming. At least the stares would be off me now, the buzz all about the doctor. I told her what I'd just heard from Mayeda. She slammed on the brakes, nearly causing a pileup behind us. Another driver screamed at her before zooming off in anger.

"Why was Naz arrested?" she asked, staring straight ahead, the car stopped in the middle of the street.

"The cops discovered Joy's laptop in the doctor's car," I told her, leaving out my involvement in that discovery.

"So what? There're a million reasons the laptop could've been in his car. Maybe she left it there. Maybe he was taking it in for repair."

I loved Sumire for wanting to protect everyone, but this time she wasn't thinking straight. "Then why didn't he tell the cops it was in his car when they questioned him?" They'd as much as accused me of stealing it, and I hadn't been in her apartment minutes before her murder.

"If Naz really killed her, do you think he'd be stupid enough to leave evidence lying around like that? Besides, the police surely searched the car yesterday and didn't find it then."

She had a good point. But I didn't trust the cops to find anything they didn't want to see. Or else he'd hid it in the car this morning in case the cops showed up with a search warrant for his home. "Why else would Joy's laptop be in his car?"

"Why else, Ted? Because he was framed! Whoever killed Joy planted the laptop there knowing he'd be the obvious suspect."

I told her she sounded like a lawyer trying to find any excuse for a client caught red-handed.

She glared at me, growing angry. "No way," she said. "Not Naz."

"How do you know?"

"I know, Ted. He's a doctor. He cares about people."

I should've kept my mouth shut. I should've agreed with her. Instead, I blurted out that the previous leader of Al-Qaeda had been a surgeon, too.

She stared straight ahead, her eyes tearing up. I felt like a heel again. "I'm sorry," I said.

"Just shut up, Ted."

This time I knew better than to ignore her advice. Despite the honking behind us, I undid my seatbelt and leaned over to hug her. She pushed me away. I stayed firm until her resistance melted and she set her head on my shoulder and began sobbing. With her arms wrapped around me, I steered the car to the side of the road where we stayed until she sniffled, wiped her eyes with the side of her hand, and put her hands back on the wheel. "Naz didn't murder Joy," she said, the resolute Sumire again. "We need to help him."

I was more concerned about stopping a terrorist attack. But this wasn't the time to argue. "How?" I asked, worried what Sumire would get me into next.

"I don't know," she said. "We'll figure that out at the reception."

🔒 🔒 🔒

We parked the car down the hill from Jiji's house and stepped out into the chill. Sumire looked at me and shook her head. "Where's your tie?" she asked.

Nobody would care if I wore a tie, not even to a funeral reception. Nobody except Sumire. But if there was ever a time to argue with her, I knew this wasn't it. I pulled the tie from my pocket and placed it in her hand. She stood behind me in the car mirror and knotted it around my throat. Tight. She didn't say I was handsome this time, only a final tug before grabbing my arm. "Let's go," she said, pulling me up the hill.

As we approached the gauntlet of cameras lined up in front of the mansion, I braced for the onslaught of microphones, rehearsing what I'd say when the reporters accosted me. This time, though, they ignored me, as if I wasn't the biggest story of the century only a few hours ago. Rather than relief, I felt lonely. The only thing worse than the torment of villain-hood was the humiliation of being a nobody.

At the gate, they were taking security seriously. We had to line up to check in with the guards including a weapons search with a wand like we were going to a concert. There was some consternation when I announced myself to the guards but after a series of phone calls and an especially intrusive pat down, the waters parted, and they let me through to join Sumire on the driveway. As we headed towards the door, we heard a commotion on the street. I turned to see the pack of reporters jostling around a poop-brown Crown Vic pulling up at the curb. The chief stepped out of the passenger door and unfolded to his full six-foot-six height. Mayeda hopped out the back, hair slicked, looking spiffy in a starched uniform.

Standing beside Sumire, I was forced to watch as the chief spoke to the cameras, lauding my rival for her affection as a hero for his smart thinking and decisive action. Why did that bug me when he'd done exactly what I'd asked?

"That's great for Mikey," Sumire said. "I'm so proud of him. I hope he makes detective."

I should've kept my mouth shut but I couldn't let that pass. "How much you want to bet Mayeda didn't find that laptop himself?"

She turned and stared at me. "Ted?"

"Yes?"

"Spill it."

I cleared my throat. "Are you my lawyer?"

"I'm your girlfriend, Ted."

"Girlfriends don't get attorney-client privilege."

"You haven't signed my retainer agreement. And you haven't paid for legal services rendered. So technically, I'm not your attorney. If we were married, there'd be spousal privilege…"

Married? Panic hammered my chest, running down my bones all the way to the blisters on my feet. Why was she talking about marriage?

She noticed my alarm and laughed. "Don't worry, Ted. As your non-lawyer, I'm simply advising you of your legal options. That's all. But as your girlfriend, I'd advise to you fess up. Right now."

I took a deep breath before answering. "I told Mayeda how to find Joy's laptop."

"I know," she said as if that were the most obvious thing in the world.

"How?"

"You had me send him Joy's password. I knew you were up to something. I'm proud of you for letting Mikey take the credit." Her expression lightened. I thought I was off the hook. I should've known better. "But you listen to me, Ted Hara—Naz did not kill Joy. Now that you helped him get arrested, you're going to help me get him released. Understand?"

I nodded, though I didn't understand at all.

At the doorway, I slipped off my shoes, leaving them in the jumble of identical men's lace-ups. Sumire picked them up and set them in a row beside her own strappy heels. In our socks, we slipped across the polished wooden floor all the way into the formal ballroom. Soothing orchestral music rained down from the ceiling, covering the buzz of chatter. Bursts of laughter exploded like hand grenades all around us. Everyone was dressed in formal black, every hand filled with a glass of wine or whiskey. Tuxedoed waiters glided through the room balancing platters of sushi. This felt more like a black-tie political fundraiser than my father's funeral reception. Missing were the wailing mourners, the screaming between my mother and my aunties while I hid in the garage staring at the empty space where the crumpled Mustang belonged to finish off my father's last bottle of Johnnie alone. When a waiter floated by with a tray of drinks, Sumire pushed a glass of sparkling water into my outstretched hand.

As we walked through the hall, she was enveloped into a circle of friends. I left to loop through the living room in search of Jiji. I passed the temptation of the open bar and slipped through the French doors to the patio where Joy's mother was holding court with a flock of elegant women. Circling through the beehive of activity in the kitchen and out to the dining room, I spotted the FBI's mope, Flagpin, next to Detective Combover in a circle of grayhairs, a glass of whiskey in every hand. As I turned to escape, I caught the gruff voice of the salty seadog congressman inside the whiskey circle.

"Jiji-san," I called. The entire circle turned to stare at me, none of them friendly. Combover bellied up in front of me, the watermelon of his gut pushing against my chest. I tried to squeeze past him. He grabbed my collar. "Who thinks we ought to throw this weasel in jail?" The group laughed their approval.

Flagpin moseyed up beside Combover, blocking me from Jiji. Standing on tiptoes, I waved my arms. "Jiji-san, I need to talk to you."

From behind the wall of law enforcement, I heard Jiji grunt, "No need to talk to you." More laughter followed.

"It's important," I pleaded. "It's about the file on Joy's computer."

"You can talk to the FBI right here."

"I need to talk to *you*. Alone. I promise it'll only take a minute."

I ripped my collar out of Combover's grasp and dashed around to reach Jiji like a game of duck, duck, goose. "I figured out how to crack the file," I said, "but I need your help. Just give me one minute to explain."

Jiji swallowed a gulp of whiskey, then pointed down the darkened hallway with the glass in his hand.

"I'm going with you," Flagpin said, fortifying himself for this suicide mission with a fresh whiskey from a passing tray. Exactly the person I didn't want with us, but at least it was only him.

Halfway down the hallway, Jiji opened a bedroom door. A dozen perfumes drifted out to assault my nose. Flipping on the light illuminated a young girl's room of peach-colored walls and white furniture. The narrow bed was covered with piles of expensive coats.

Jiji set his empty glass on the desk. "Talk," he ordered. "You've got one minute." He pointed at his Rolex.

"I figured out a way to crack the file," I said.

Behind me, Flagpin snorted. "We got a team of Ph.D.'s in D.C. saying that's impossible in our lifetime."

Winning over Jiji alone wouldn't be easy; convincing Flagpin to support me, too, would be harder than cracking the file. But I had to try. "What if what takes the FBI a year could be done in three seconds?"

Flagpin rolled his eyes. "You got a magic wand?"

"I don't, but MeCan does."

He gasped. "They have a quantum computer?"

Unfortunately not. New computers based on quantum physics were promising miracles of decryption not possible with regular CPUs, but despite the billions that had been thrown at them, so far, they couldn't keep up with the calculator feature of an iWatch. "We can attack the file with all the unused capacity of Deep Thought."

Flagpin made a sour face. "No budget for outside services."

How much was a life worth? How much did the World Trade Center towers cost and the war in Afghanistan? Would the government have paid a billion dollars to prevent that attack? Apparently not. "MeCan will do it for free," I offered on their behalf.

"How nice of them," Flagpin said. "And why would MeCan put billions of their own money into decrypting a file?"

"Because that'll cost less than implementing the New Patriot Act."

Allowing the cops access to all their users' data while keeping hackers out would be an operational nightmare of unimaginable—and expensive— proportions. Telling the Chinese government they couldn't have the same access to their own citizens' data would get MeCan booted out of China. That alone would cost them $100 billion. Running some cracking software for a few hours on servers sitting idle anyway was a tradeoff Evgeni would make any day. If the government asked him.

But Flagpin wasn't convinced. "You want *me* to withdraw the legislation in return for MeCan's help decrypting the file?"

"They'll help you stop the terrorists. Isn't that what you want?"

"You're missing my point, kid. I don't have the authority to make that kind of deal."

"Then who does?"

"A decision like that would have to come from the Director himself. Maybe even the AG."

"Then get him on the line."

Flagpin practically spat. "The FBI doesn't take orders from punks like you. If the Director wanted to talk to you, he'd have a Deputy Director call you himself. Your minute's up. Let's go, Congressman. I hear a scotch and soda calling."

Flagpin opened the door. But Jiji didn't follow. "You know, Harris, I think the kid might be onto something. In fact, I like his idea better than co-sponsoring your legislation."

"Do you? Well, Congressman, I can't stop you from doing whatever you want. But let me warn you—Evgeni is a Russian national. There's no way of collaborating on a national security effort if he's involved in any way. Nor the other twenty-five thousand foreign nationals on their staff."

It was true that MeCan employed as many H-1B visa workers as the government would let them hire, mostly from India and China, and even set up a research office in Shanghai to appease the Chinese government. But I didn't see how that got in the way of stopping terrorists. "What's that have to do with cracking the file?"

"Stay here," Jiji ordered, as if I were a dog. He marched out, slamming the door behind him. Flagpin shot me a nasty look and marched out after him, slamming it even harder.

Joy's room had been frozen in amber since she'd left for college. Tennis trophies atop the dresser, framed spelling bee ribbons pinned to the wall. Photos of a young girl in a Cinderella dress reaching up to shake hands with presidents and world leaders. A bookshelf filled with dusty history books and boring Russian novels. But the bottom shelf was packed with the bright blues and neon reds of the twenty-eight volumes of Red River manga. I was surprised such a serious woman read manga alongside Tolstoy and Dostoyevsky, but I shouldn't have been. Both were full of dashing princes and beautiful countesses. Sumire had loved them, too. I pulled out

Issue 1 and thumbed through it. Unlike the hundred volumes of One Piece manga that filled my own bookshelf, her pages were pristine—no dogears, doodles, or sheets stuck together with crumbs and soda spills.

Flipping through the book brought back memories of the basic story—a teen girl named Yuri, the same as Joy's Japanese name, was a time traveler to ancient Turkey. She had to escape from an evil warlord planning to use her as a human sacrifice. It didn't sound much different than current-day Syria or Afghanistan. Had this manga rattling through her subconscious been the inspiration to rush off to troubled lands to aid refugees? Was Naz the prince who would rescue her so they could liberate a benighted civilization together? Instead, she was dead, while the warlords were preparing to attack us.

I was engrossed in the manga when the door swung open. "What the hell are you doing?"

I looked up at Jiji glaring at me. "Reading?"

"Those are Joy's."

"Sorry," I said, replacing the volume on the shelf. I braced myself to be castigated. I had plenty of training at that. But instead of laying into me, Jiji ordered me to sit on the bed. He turned the small wooden chair to face me and sat. His head hung low, not a congressman, just another old man, the cloying smell of alcohol on his breath, no different from my father.

"My daughter's dead," he said, eyes welling up.

I had no idea how to handle the tears of a congressman. Was I supposed to hug him? I wished Sumire was here with me. She'd know what to do.

"We buried her today," he said, choking up. "Out at Colma. Ever been there?"

I nodded. The old Japanese cemetery. The ashes of my parents who hated each other side-by-side for eternity among the four generations of the Hara family that my mother couldn't stand.

"Never imagined I'd see my little girl buried before me. And for what? I served in the Navy, saw friends die in Iraq. But at least they died protecting our country. Securing prosperity. Stopping a murderous dictator. But Joy's death—for what?"

I couldn't mouth the platitudes that it was God's will, or Buddha's plan, or that she was in a better place. I was tempted to tell him the truth that it was for nothing, because in the end we all die. "I'm sorry for your loss," I said, the best I could choke out.

Jiji coughed twice and stared at the floor. "Thank you."

"I'd better go," I said, standing up from the edge of the bed.

"You're not going anywhere, Hara. I told that FBI dufus to get the Director on the line. Now. If he wants my support. I sure hope you know what you're doing because you're going to tell the head of the FBI how to do their own fucking job."

nine
federal bureau of idiots

Jiji led me to the end of the hallway where a spare bedroom had been converted into a congressional field office. After opening the steel-lined door locked with an industrial deadbolt, he ushered me into the room and dug a phone out of the top drawer of a file cabinet secured with a padlock. An ancient Blackberry would have been an upgrade from this stale snickers-phone, but at least it was secure—even the Russians wouldn't be able to hack into this candy bar. Jiji clicked on the tinny speakerphone to make the call.

Disembodied voices gave their names and titles: director of this, deputy director of that, executive assistant director of something completely different that sounded exactly the same. It was impossible to tell which people were the top-floor turtles and which were the basement grunts. Nobody on the call seemed to be in charge of I.T. or cryptography or information security; they all sounded like bureaucrats with law degrees who wouldn't know the difference between Java and JavaScript and thought Go was a Japanese game.

In the background, a door clicked shut. "Sorry I'm late," said a deep, booming voice. "Just wrapped up briefing POTUS on the situation."

"That's Willimont," Jiji whispered to me. I recognized the voice from the news—the Director of the FBI.

"Perfect timing, Lou," a director of something said. "We're just getting started."

"Who's on the call?"

"Congressman Miyazaki and a staffer," said the Assistant Director of Introductions.

"I have an intern for technical affairs on the call with me," Jiji said. "Ted Hara."

When did I become an intern? I wasn't interested in Monica Lewinsky's old job. "Consultant," I corrected the record.

But nobody heard me over the groans. "Hara?" gasped the Deputy Director of Derision. "That Hara? The Hara who keeps mucking up our investigation? Who authorized that fuckhead to be in on this call?"

I was glad to learn I was so well loved at the highest echelons of law enforcement. I'd thought it was only the local police who hated me.

"I authorized him," Jiji said. "And the only thing he did to muck up your investigation is to do your fucking job for you."

Go Jiji! I suddenly loved the crispy old seabird. This was the first time a boss had ever stuck up for me instead of taking credit for my ideas while blaming me for his failures.

Static over the speakerphone. A cough. Papers rustling. Then the Director of Directors asked, "What's his clearance level?"

"None," Jiji said. "But he found that file that's got you guys stumped. He's doing more than all of you combined to find out what the hell's inside, so I want you to hear his idea for how to crack this fucker already."

The one woman on the call spoke up. "With all due respect, Congressman, we can't—"

"He's in or I'm leaving."

"But sir—"

"And I'm going straight to the CNN crew camped in front of my house to tell them I'm opposing your New Patriot Act."

I had to cough to avoid laughing out loud. I hadn't enjoyed myself this much since...maybe never. I was ready to volunteer for Jiji's re-election campaign and tell the whole world how Jiji was a bureaucrat slayer.

After a lot of whispering, the line suddenly cut to the dulcet tones of violins playing Motown. Then just as abruptly, Motown was gone and the Director of Directors declared, "Alright, Congressman, we'll do it your way. The Deputy Director of Protocol has made an excellent suggestion. Jim?"

"Congressman—all of us here would like to express our sincere condolences on the passing of your daughter. To honor her courage, we'd like to rename the New Patriot Act as the Joy Miyazaki Act."

Instead of melting from the decoration of his daughter, Jiji banged his fist on the desk. "I don't give a shit what you fucktards want to call it. Have you found a way to decrypt the file yet?"

"Well, sir..."

"Yes or no?"

"We're working on it, sir."

"In other words, no."

"You have to understand, these things take time."

"How long?"

"Impossible to say. We're running many different angles of attack. Devon, can you brief the congressman on the efforts underway?"

The Director of Opaque Transparency read from a briefing sheet full of words he didn't understand. They were trying a number of different cracking tools whose names they weren't at liberty to disclose. They were contracting every security company that claimed to have a solution. They even had Microsoft hunting through the Word source code searching for a zero-day to bypass the password. "I assure you, Congressman, no stone is being left unturned. Make no mistake, we will open that file."

"In other words," Jiji said, "you've struck out. Hara thinks he has a way to open the file now. I want you to listen to what he has to say."

Polite chuckling around the table. "Did he find a decoder ring in a box of cereal?" snarked the Deputy Director of Institutional Snarkery.

I didn't appreciate the crack from someone with a degree in political science who couldn't factor a polynomial if his promotion depended on it.

"Let's hear him out," said the Bureaucrat of Bureaucrats. More groans around the table.

Suddenly I was on the spot—the entire upper echelon of the FBI was listening to my advice, which consisted of urging them to call Evgeni and have MeCan get them out of their jam.

"It was MeCan that got us into this mess when they changed their security protocol," whined the Assistant Director of Whining.

"Cooperating with MeCan would hinder the President's plan to pursue anti-trust against them," mumbled the Manager of Mumbling.

"It's absolutely the wrong optics," protested the Executive Director of Optics.

"This is a national emergency!" Jiji yelled. "Nobody cares about your fucking optics."

The Bureaucrat of Bureaucrats attempted to diffuse the Jiji bomb. "Here's what I can do, Congressman," he said in a soothing baritone. "We'll take Mr. Hara's suggestion under advisement and see what the Attorney General has to say."

Even a noob who'd been an unpaid congressional intern for less than five minutes recognized this was how a bureaucrat said no when he couldn't say no.

"Thank you for your time, Congressman," said the Director of Directors, about to hang up. Jiji's finger headed towards the silvered buttons on the snickersphone's antique keypad.

"Wait!" I yelled. I was surprised when they actually waited. But I didn't know what to say next. If they wouldn't work with MeCan, where else could we get the CPU resources we needed?

I thought of the computer on the floor of my apartment, cranking through 200,000 passwords every second. How many video cards did Nvidia sell each year—it had to be in the millions. What if we could combine all that unused computing power together? Plus the millions of computers in people's homes and offices, their CPUs idle 99% of the time. And the four billion cell phones sporting quad core CPUs with built-in AI engines. Even the millions of Xboxes and PlayStations with killer GPUs. If we could harness even a tiny fraction of all those computers, gaming consoles, and phones, that would be orders of magnitude more power than even Deep Thought. But how could we get a hundred million people to lend us their spare computing cycles? "What if we offered a reward?" I suggested. "Something that will get the entire country working on cracking the password."

"No budget for it."

"That would require explicit authorization from Congress."

"We don't have the resources to run a public-facing operation."

When the bureaucrats finished grumbling, the Director of Directors proclaimed, "Sorry, Congressman, I'm afraid that's outside our purview."

"Fuck you guys," Jiji said. "I'll offer a reward myself. One million dollars."

I was thinking more of a hundred-million-dollar Powerball jackpot than a basic scratch and sniff card. But the Director of Directors squashed even that small reward. "Congressman, I'm afraid you don't understand—"

"No, Lou, it's you who's not understanding. I'm putting up the reward. One million dollars. You can either support me, or I'll do it on my own. But don't expect me to sponsor your bill. Understand now, Lou?"

"But Congressman—"

"No buts."

"We'd have to clear this with DoJ."

"Fine. You've got an hour."

Jiji wanted to slam down the phone, but all he could do with the old candy bar was jab at the silver buttons. "Fuckers," he grunted as he tossed the phone back in the drawer. "Okay, Hara, you've got your reward. Now it's up to you."

"That's not much money," I mumbled. "Or much time."

"Too fucking bad. That's what you've got."

Jiji snapped the padlock on the cabinet shut. "What the hell are you waiting for—get to work!" He pointed toward the hallway. "You've got an hour to get your thing working."

the long dark
tea ceremony of the soul

I RETURNED to the ballroom to the scene I least wanted to see—Sumire chatting with a beaming, spiffed-up Mayeda. When I inched up from behind and slipped my hands around her waist, she turned around to shake a finger at me. "Where have you been? You left me here all alone."

She hadn't been alone long before another suitor had come to her rescue, I wanted to argue. "I'll explain in the car," I said instead. I needed to get home in a hurry.

"I'm busy talking to Mikey."

"Heya, pal," he said with a smirk. He didn't ask about the date with Emi I owed him.

"We gotta dip," I told Sumire. "It's an emergency."

"I need to find out what's happening with Naz," she said, throwing me a stinkeye. "And you promised to help."

I was caught in a pinch, the weight of the FBI, Jiji, and a terrorist attack on one side, helping Sumire with a lost cause on the other. It wasn't a fair fight. Either way, the loser was me in the middle. I pulled her aside and told her about the deadline Jiji had given me. She wasn't happy but pecked me on the cheek and left me to head home in an Uber.

Back at the apartment, I hoped for a miracle from the cracking software running on my computer. But miracles only happen for holy men and athletes; mere mortals are subject to the immutable laws of statistics. The software had tested more than a billion passwords while I'd been gone, but that was a miniscule fraction of all the possible permutation of characters. I'd have to get the software running on hundreds of millions more computers.

To do that, I'd need a way to distribute blocks of passwords to all those millions of devices to check and keep track of the results. But as I started thinking through how the system would work, the enormity of it hit me. It wouldn't be ready in an hour. The architecture alone would take a day to sketch out. The routines would take months to write. And that was just for the Linux version. Porting the code to MeOS, MacOS, Windows, and mobile phones and creating a front end that grannies on their old iPads could manage would take at least a year. There had to be a better way. But I was stuck. I needed inspiration.

In the kitchen, I rummaged through the cabinets searching for what I knew wasn't there—a bottle of sake or a bullet of whiskey, a secret flask of gin. I'd binned them all, even the Robitussin. From the distant shoals of the Nijiya refrigerator case, I heard the sirens of sake calling. I closed my ears and recalled my vow to Sumire, my promise to myself. I pictured my father sipping his Johnnie in silence while my mother insisted the only path to truth was over the Way of Tea. Perhaps a thousand years of matcha-sipping monks weren't entirely wrong. But a tea ceremony ran for four hours; I didn't have that kind of time. This would have to be the fastest ceremony in the entire history of tea.

The antique *chado* cabinet my mother had brought with her from Kyoto sat in the back corner of the room. She'd inherited it from her grandmother and bequeathed it to me by default when she'd thrown herself off the mountain. Paulownia frame with interlocking dovetail joints, not a nail or hinge anywhere; cabinet doors of dark *keyaki* wood, dark stain highlighting the grain. When I opened the cabinet for the first time in months, the empty top shelf made me sad. The tea bowls that had filled the space, each with a story of the craftsman who'd made it, were gone, returned to the dirt from which they'd been molded, to join my mother's ashes. In her absence, a layer of dust had settled onto the shelf, the dust she'd led an army of vacuums into battle against every day. I grabbed the pink vacuum, her favorite, from the closet and went to war on her behalf.

When all the bamboo whisks and lacquered tea caddies were clean again, I set an iron pot on an electric burner atop a thin *goza* mat on the floor. Not exactly the proper tatami mats of a proper tea room, but as Senno-Rikyu, the saint of tea, once said, the only thing that matters in a tea house is a roof to keep guests dry.

While the water heated, I began the purification process, running a folded silk square over the *chashaku*—the long, thin bamboo tea scoop—and the *hishaku*—the water ladle—focusing on the intricate hand movements of the ceremony. Kneeling on the mat to face the cast iron pot, when the water started to hiss, I ladled steaming water into a tea bowl to warm the sides, then poured it out again. Using the *chashaku,* I dropped the first scoop of matcha powder into the bowl to bring me wisdom, then added the second scoop for strength. Then I broke the sacrosanct laws of tea and dumped in a third scoop and a fourth—a fuck you to all the stupid rules I hated.

After ladling hot water over the powder, I used the *chasen* to whisk the slurry to a seething froth. With the bowl in the palm of my left hand, I turned the front to face me. A first sip of the jade liquid filled my mouth with warmth. I tried to clear my head. A question bubbled up out of the tea—was there still a way to convince MeCan to volunteer their resources? Stop. Don't think, I reminded myself. Breathe deep. Drink.

A second sip sat sweet on the tip of my tongue, then went down with a chalky bitterness. Why couldn't the FBI crack the file themselves? Stop. Empty the mind, I told myself.

I finished the bowl with a slurp of the thick dregs. How could I build the infrastructure to coordinate a billion devices in concert? Stop. Clear my head. Appreciate the moment.

I stared deep into the porcelain tea bowl, cobalt blue above the unglazed clay base grading to white at the lip, like waves rising up from the deep blue sea of the famous Hokusai woodblock print, fingers of white foam grasping at the humans cowering in the dinghy below. My mind wandered off into that angry sea, waves crashing down around me, while far off in the distance, the gods atop Mt. Fuji watched impassively.

My eyes fixed on the perfect cone of Fuji-san, reminding me of something. But what? Its jagged edges, the flattened top—it hit me out of the cobalt blue sky behind it—a chart of the price of BiteCoin: exponential growth until it hit a long plateau and was now on a downward slope back to *terra firma*. And that's when the winds stopped and the ocean calmed, the waves retreated, and the grasping fingers of foam dissolved into the sea. I wouldn't have to build the infrastructure myself—BiteCoin had already done it. Its mining algorithm coordinated responses from millions of servers around the world operating independently; its software was optimized to scavenge available CPU cycles on any operating system. Best of all, it already used decryption for its proof of work algorithm. It would be easy to switch the code from mining for Bites to mining for the missing password.

I set the bowl down and bowed to the missing tea host, reciting the words of thanks to my mother. Would she be proud of me for doing this ceremony? No, she'd itemize everything I'd done wrong, from the color of my socks to the height I'd held the bowl to the angle I'd bent my elbow. The mindedness of tea ceremony came from years of practice until its motions became as precise as an equation. I'd been too impatient to appreciate its beauty when I was young, but perhaps I could try again now that I was older. But first, I had a password to crack. And that meant finding Satoshi —a man who didn't want to be found.

countdown to decryption

SATOSHI NAKAMOTO, the inventor of cryptocurrency, the creator of the original Bitcoin, the founder and CEO of its successor—BiteCoin, and the seventh richest man in the world, had gone into seclusion after his side hustle as lead investor in his girlfriend's startup had imploded into indictments for mass murder. Somehow, he'd not only convinced the world he no longer existed, but that he'd never existed at all. I knew better.

Satoshi had been my mother's tea ceremony student for years while I was growing up. Every Thursday, he'd come to our home to learn tranquility through the process of making a cup of tea according to complex rules that took years of study to master. He'd become her devoted disciple, helping her run her classes on Sundays at Hakone Gardens in the hills of Saratoga, finding inner peace and outer humility by cleaning cups and utensils. Despite being wealthier than the Emperor of Japan and the Queen of England combined, he bowed deeply to each guest who paid $25 to enter the tea house, presenting them with a cup of matcha and a *higashi* candy before fading into the woodwork.

Thwarted in his attempt to purchase the historic Zen gardens for my mother after my father's death, he'd spent a billion dollars acquiring the entire mountainside behind it, building a palace in the woods overlooking the splendor of the garden's cherry blossoms in spring, the wisteria arbor in summer, and the *momiji* maples in autumn. But when my mother threw herself off a mountain in Kyoto, Satoshi retreated to the palace to direct his blockchain empire in solitude.

Alone, that is, until he became entangled with Katie Deauville, the glamourous young founder of SüprDüpr and the worst mass murderer in California history. When she disappeared to a small island in the Caribbean with white sand beaches and no extradition treaty, everyone assumed she'd killed Satoshi, too. He faded from view aided by stories planted in newspapers and tech journals claiming to have discovered the real inventors of Bite-Coin. Satoshi's Wiki page was updated to declare him the pseudonym of a person or persons unknown. Every photo of Satoshi on the internet somehow disappeared.

There was only one person who'd want to eliminate every trace of Satoshi's existence—Satoshi himself. The fact that he didn't exist was proof that he was still alive. A recluse at heart, he'd succeeded at making himself invisible. Fortunately, I knew where to find him—at his palace in the hills overlooking Hakone gardens. Unfortunately, I had no idea how to convince him to let me in.

I tried messaging Satoshi using the phone number he'd once given me. A response buzzed back immediately: *not a valid number*. I tried calling; the robotic voice confirmed the subscriber's number was no longer in service. A DM rocketed into the void and disappeared into the bitbucket where blocked DMs go to die. An email went out in search of the DM and was never heard from again. There was no other way to get in contact with him—I'd have to show up unannounced.

But not empty-handed. The ghost of my mother would've boxed my ear if I went anywhere without bringing a gift, a *faux pas* worse than wearing shoes inside their house. She'd always brought *manju* sweets or fresh fruit from our garden, but that would be strange for a man. I dashed across the street to the krapknack shop to grab a tin of matcha. But not the cheap crap for tourists—Satoshi would know the difference. I had to get the good stuff—the ceremonial-grade matcha from Uji—that cost more than a bottle of *junmai daiginjo* sake.

Setting coordinates for Hakone Gardens, I let MapLady lead the way. The pony galloped towards the mountains that divided Silicon Valley from the sea. After passing the small sign for the garden, I caught a glimpse of Satoshi's palace at the summit of the mountain. But I couldn't find the entrance. There was no break in the stone wall that paralleled the street for miles. No driveway anywhere. How did Satoshi get in and out? How did he get his mail? Then I remembered the secret passage he'd used to meet me in the garden.

The last time I'd seen Satoshi in person, I'd caught a glimpse of him sneaking through a hole in the floor of the tea house to return to his own mansion. So that's how I'd have to get in. I doubled back to a small sign on the side of the road adorned with ceramic *kawara* roof tiles and turned up the steep, twisting road that wound through the forest of scrub oaks and eucalyptus trees until it reached the garden. Late in the afternoon on a windy weekday in March, the parking lot was empty except for a couple of dusty Prii and a mud-splattered maintenance truck.

At the front gate, the ticket lady behind the window who'd sat in the same folding chair for all eternity wanted to reminisce about my childhood visits to the park. I was in a hurry. I slid the entrance fee through the opening, then pushed through the ancient green turnstile into another world.

On the other side of the gate was the serenity of an Edo-era Japanese garden. But I had no time to enjoy the views of the humped vermillion bridge over the pond or the flashes of orange in the murky water of the koi that Satoshi and I once fed together. I hurried up the asphalt path to the tea house.

At the wooden pavilion, the sliding doors were shut, a sign across the front marked *Authorized Personnel Only*. Looking around to make sure the lone security guard was elsewhere, I declared myself authorized and slipped under the chain. After hiding my sandals in a corner, I slid open the door on its wooden rail and bowed low as I entered.

The air inside the tea house was heavy with the grassy smell of fresh tatami. There was no hanging scroll or flower arrangement in the *tokonoma* —no guests were expected today. The floor consisted of five and a half tatami mats, each two inches thick, in an interlocking pattern surrounding the sunken hearth for the kettle. Though the woven straw surface of the tatami had yet to fade from green to brown, the brocade around the edge of the half-sized mat in the middle was already frayed. I wedged my fingers between the heavy mats, but without a crowbar, I struggled to pry it up.

Beneath the tatami was a concrete floor with a cylindrical hole drilled into the ground. Even with the phone's flashlight shining inside, I couldn't see the bottom. I reached my arm down into the hole, trying not to imagine an *oni* leaping out to attack me. Feeling around, my fingers touched cold metal—a ladder bolted onto the side. Holding my breath, I set one foot onto the top bar. Then the other foot. The hole was narrow, barely wide enough for a scrawny person like me to squeeze through. There was no way the big security guard could follow. Lowering myself into the hole, I stepped down one rung at a time.

As my head dropped below floor level and I sunk into the darkness of the earth, the hole felt like it was growing narrower. Terrified of getting stuck, my heart started beating faster and I broke into a cold sweat. I closed my eyes and stepped down another rung, and then another and another, until my foot hit solid ground where the tunnel turned sideways and headed straight into the mountain.

I crawled forward on my knees, the top of my head scraping the jagged rock above, dirt spilling over my face and sticking to my glasses. The flashlight showed nothing but empty space in front, no light at the end of the tunnel. My heart pounding, the damp smell of mud in my nose, I pushed forward because there was no way back. The tunnel felt like it was sloping uphill, but that could have been an illusion. I crawled and crawled for what felt like forever until my head smacked into something solid.

The flashlight hunted for the opening, but all it found was earth. This was the end of the tunnel. Above my head was a circle of wood. A door. Kind of. No knob, no doorbell, no RingyDing video, nothing but a small keyhole.

I banged on the door, heard it echo on the other side, but there was no response. I pounded harder, shouted louder, yelled Satoshi's name. No reply, no sound of footsteps, no voices on the other side. No way in. I banged with my fists, thumped with my forearm, kicked it with my feet. The solid door didn't budge. No way to break it down. I banged and screamed until I nearly blacked out, then lay on my back breathing heavily. There was nothing to do but turn around and crawl back out again.

When I stuck my head out of the tunnel, even the reddening light of a March evening nearly blinded me. Once my eyes adjusted, I pulled myself out and curled up on the tatami. I felt like I'd escaped from prison. But what could I do now? I still needed to find a way into Satoshi's castle. If only I had a key.

I dashed back to the entrance gate and asked the ticket lady if the garden kept a key for Satoshi. She stared at me as if I were speaking in tongues. "Do you have a way to call him?" That got the same response as if I'd switched to an obscure dialect of tongues.

"Please, please, please," I begged. "It's a national emergency."

"He's gone," she said. "Poof. No more Satoshi."

I was sure she was lying but there was nothing I could do. How else could I break in? All I needed was a key. Like the time my mother had changed the locks when father didn't come home one night. He'd called a locksmith to let him in, though when he walked through the door, my mother was waiting on the other side gripping her favorite santoku knife.

I called every locksmith within a ten-mile radius until I found one who weighed under a hundred pounds and wasn't claustrophobic. When she arrived, I showed her the tunnel. She laughed and said, "Sure, no problem. But that'll cost an extra hundred. You got I.D.?"

I held up my driver's license. She looked at it, then looked at me. "This not your address."

"It's my father's place."

She snickered. "How come your name not Nakamoto?"

Damn. She knew this was Satoshi's place. Everyone in the neighborhood knew who'd paid a billion dollars to acquire this swath of parkland.

"He's my step-father," I lied. I wasn't sure if that was my mother's fantasy or mine. But he almost married my mother. Maybe. The truth was I had no idea what happened between Satoshi and my mother after my father died and I ran away to college. I suspected Satoshi had something to do with her throwing herself off a mountain in Kyoto, but even her ghost wouldn't divulge those secrets.

The locksmith didn't believe me. I pulled up a photo taken in this tea house of Satoshi and my mother clad in formal kimonos surrounded by a group of guests. Easy to mistake for a Japanese wedding by someone who'd never seen a tea ceremony.

"Hmm," she said, looking closely at the photo. "Satoshi is billionaire. You're son-in-law, yes?" I saw the gold glinting in her eyes.

"I'll throw in an extra thousand," I offered. "You take BiteCoin?"

She smiled. "Two thousand. Cash only. Payment in advance."

I Venmo'ed the money to her personal account.

"See you in a jiffy," she said and disappeared down the hole. Thirty minutes later, she climbed back out and declared the door open. "Cheap lock," she scoffed. "Could've opened yourself with paperclip." She handed me a business card along with the receipt. "Tell billionaire stepfather I install better lock if he wants to stay safe from son-in-law."

After she left humming to herself, I crawled once more through the dark tunnel to Satoshi's mansion. This time, the door was hanging open, a ladder lowered into the hole from overhead. I climbed the ladder into Satoshi's home where I found myself in a basement storeroom of wall-to-wall shelves, all of them bare. Down the hallway, the first door opened to a cavernous garage filled with a dozen Lamborghinis and Ferraris, a real McLaren F1 race car, and vehicles from manufacturers long gone on display like in a museum. In the center was the *pièce de résistance*—the Batmobile—the real Batmobile, the black one with orange striping from the old TV show.

Did the recluse ever take his cars out for a spin? There had to be an exit somewhere, but I couldn't see it. In the back, though, was a car that didn't belong—a white Prius coated in a thick layer of dust, a BiteCoin King sticker affixed to the back bumper. That had to be Satoshi's car, the real one he drove. His car was here, so he had to be here, too, somewhere in this sprawling palace.

I passed a glassed-off machine room filled with winking LEDs, and at the end of the hallway, found the concrete steps that led up to the main floor and into a living room as large as an airport terminal. The house was built into the side of the mountain, held up with steel pillars. It had twenty-foot ceilings and an entire wall of windows looking out over the forest of oak and eucalyptus. Down below, the sculptured beauty of the Zen gardens shimmered in the last of the fading light. In the distance, the flats of Silicon Valley were laid out on a grid all the way to the Diablo Mountains on the other side of the bay.

"Satoshi?" I called. No answer. No butler, no maid, no kitchen staff, no security guard to kick me out. The house was silent except for the metronomic thunk of an old grandfather clock in the corner. "Satoshi?" I hollered. Only the grandfather clock replied with its tick-tock.

I walked down the hallway to a long row of bedrooms in the back. The first room was filled with Norwegian furniture, the next room built as a shrine, a third was decorated with Hello Kitty everything. I counted four-teen bedrooms, each with a different theme, until the hallway ended at a steam-filled room with cedar walls and a hot-springs bath open to the outdoors. No Satoshi anywhere. Maybe he really had left to join his fugitive girlfriend and help the Caribbean island nation convert their economy to BiteCoin.

Doubling back, I found the bedroom that had to be Satoshi's: a dark, narrow room with tatami floors, a hard pillow filled with buckwheat chaff, and a simple futon folded neatly on a shelf. "Satoshi?" I called, but the room was empty.

Back at the airport terminal room, I stepped out onto the sun deck, but there was no Satoshi sunning on the beach chairs or napping in the cabana. Looking around the terminal, I noticed empty cardboard cartons strewn over the dining table. Stepping over the rug to investigate, I nearly tripped over the body on the floor.

Wedged awkwardly against a white leather sofa, neck bent, legs akimbo, I thought he was dead. Then I noticed a slow rise and fall of the chest, a barely audible whistling through the nose. Satoshi was passed out. Brown smudges covered his face, chest, and hands. Dozens of foil wrappers were scattered all around him. Had he been smoking heroin? With so many foils, it was a miracle he was still alive. I prodded his chest. "Wake up," I said. "We need to get you to a hospital." His head wobbled, then fell back again.

I picked up a foil. No burn marks. I held it to my nose. A cloyingly sweet smell, a faint hint of alcohol. The writing on the cardboard boxes was in Japanese. Inside were cartons of vibrant reds and blues, a picture of a bottle on the front of each and a Kit Kat logo. Not the matcha Kit Kats they sold at Nijiya, these were sake flavored. Imported directly from Japan, each box was made from a different sake from around the country. Alcohol content 0.4%. Satoshi was passed out in an alcoholic stupor. The matcha-totaling mahatma was addicted to sake chocolate bars.

I ripped open a fresh package and took a bite. Chocolate plus sake, the two greatest flavors in the world. Mixed together, they were disgusting. Too sweet. Too bitter. Too everything. And not enough sake. I spat it out. I grabbed him by the shoulders and shook him until his eyelids fluttered open.

His eyes looked like black holes as he struggled to focus. "What's the rate?" he mumbled, his head lolling side-to-side.

With one hand, I held him upright; with the other I checked my phone. The panic of terrorism had been joined at the top of the news feed with breathless articles about BiteCoin. "Just cracked fifty thousand dollars per

Bite," I said. Overnight, Satoshi's net worth had increased by three billion dollars. I thought he'd be thrilled. "Not dollars," he croaked. "Eth."

I checked the ETH-BITE exchange rate. When I told him it was just under ten, he looked like I'd stabbed him in the chest. He pulled himself up into a sitting position, his back resting against the sofa. "Have to do something," he muttered. "Can't let them catch up."

Though the price of BiteCoin piled absurdity atop insanity, Satoshi couldn't stand that in the recent downturn Ethereum had made up ground while Diem, Dogecoin, and the other shitcoins continued shooting towards the moon.

Helping him up onto the sofa, my hands brushed the white leather. It was amazingly soft. Buttery beyond comprehension. I rested my head against a cushion, wanting nothing more than to lie down on this couch and sleep forever.

Satoshi's eyes started to focus, recognition dawning. "Tatsu-kun? What are you doing here?"

"I need your help."

"Help? This is your fault!" He pointed around a room filled with furniture that cost more than most countries made in a year.

He was blaming me for the mess with Katie and her failed startup, but all I'd done was expose her crimes. "It's your own damn fault," I said. "If you'd married my mother, you wouldn't be in this mess. She would've kept you in line. Doesn't matter if you're a billionaire, you have to wash your hands. Both sides. With soap. And don't splatter water on the floor."

It was easy to imitate my mother—she'd yelled at me every day to wash my hands properly. I marched the seventh richest man in the world into the bathroom and forced him to clean himself up. Then I led him stumbling down the hallway to the hot springs room where I stood in the doorway, hands on my hips, ordering him to scrub away every trace of grime under the shower before stepping into the steaming bath.

If he'd married my mother, I'd be soaking in that tub every day. While sipping hot sake. And sleeping on the couch of clouds. And driving the Batmobile. And Satoshi would've gotten the discipline he so clearly needed instead of his nebulous solitary existence. The life of a billionaire didn't suit him. Unlike Bezos' snarky smile, Musk's hyperkinetic blathering, and Gate's philanthropic glow, Satoshi just looked old. The hair he used to shave like a Buddhist monk had grown back in a weird horseshoe pattern with a patch of turf in the front. The placid eyes that had once reflected Nirvana were now rimmed in red. I'm sure he would have been happier as an anonymous Stanford mathematics professor than central banker to the crypto world.

But my job wasn't to make him happy; it was to get him sobered up. When he stepped out of the bath, skin glowing lobster red, I handed him a fluffy robe and led him back to the airport terminal room where I sat him down at the table. In the kitchen, I boiled water on the stove and spooned in half the tin of matcha. After slurping down a cup that contained twice the caffeine of a Starbucks double venti, Satoshi jerked alert. I explained my plan to use the BiteCoin mining infrastructure to find the password to the terrorist's plan.

He cocked his head, confused. "How does that help me beat Ethereum?"

"It doesn't. But you're going to do it anyway."

"Why?"

"Because it's the right thing to do. Because you owe me. Because you owe the world."

Satoshi didn't agree. "We would have to shut down BiteCoin mining. Cost $73 million dollars a day."

That was a lot of coin. But a drop in the bathtub for Satoshi. It was time to get tough. Time to channel my inner Jiji. I rose up to my full five-foot-five and put the fear of Buddha in him. "You're doing this, Nakamoto," I ordered, "because if you don't, I'll explain to Congress how the Russians are using BiteCoin to finance their war with Ukraine. I'll show the FBI how BiteCoin is enabling child porn. I'll help the ATF bust all the drug deals made with BiteCoin. And I'll convince the SEC you're as bad as Sam Bankman-Fried."

He looked like I'd punched him in the face. Then kicked him in the balls. He nodded meekly, reminding me of my father. It was sad to see. But there was no time to worry about the hurt feelings of a billionaire. It was time to get the file decrypted so we could stop a terrorist attack.

I sat beside Satoshi as he called an emergency zoom of the BiteCoin management team, Satoshi's face algorithmically altered to match his new identity as an old white codger with a mustache named Edgar Codd. He explained to the group what we needed to build. Satoshi anointed me leader of a new project codenamed OpenSesame and declared it Priority 0, the same level as the most fatal security hole.

Once we finished outlining the architecture and dividing up the work, I called Jiji. Instead of being pleased at my progress, he growled, "It damn well better work," and hung up. I texted him the link to the new website and asked him to tell the FBI it was ready to announce to the public.

I brewed a strong cup of matcha for myself, then borrowing one of Satoshi's stash of laptops he used for testing, I cracked my knuckles and dove into writing code. As the sun slipped behind the mountains, the world narrowed to the glowing rectangle in front of me, my fingers flying over the keyboard, building routines faster than at a hackathon competition. I was hardly aware of anything around me when Satoshi interrupted me to show me the news.

The Director of Directors was standing behind a podium. After announcing the file decryption challenge with Jiji's million-dollar prize, he introduced the Associate Deputy Director of Community Outreach, a slim woman with a too-bright smile and too-perfect skin. She took to the microphone to implore every American to fight against terror by joining Project OpenSesame, pointing to a poster behind her with the address of our website.

Fortunately, we'd already created a signup form on the project site. The internal stats showed more than seventy-thousand people signing up in the first minute. When I hit refresh, the number was over two hundred thousand. The good news was the whole world was signing up for OpenSesame, exactly what we needed to crack the file quickly. The bad news was the whole world was signing up for OpenSesame, and we weren't prepared for that kind of flood.

I slacked the infrastructure team to warn them to get ready for millions of users. It would be a long night. I needed coffee. And pizza. All Satoshi had was sake-flavored Kit Kats. What did he eat every day? His professional kitchen had no professionals, but it was hard to imagine him cooking. Did he live off DoorDash like everyone else I knew? If so, where did they deliver?

I offered to drive over to the nearest In-N-Out to pick up a bunch of burgers. How cool would it be to hit the INO drive-through in the Batmobile? Satoshi shook his head. "Meat is bad for the environment. Big carbon footprint," he said. "Bad for your health, too." A diet of sake-flavored Kit

Kats for breakfast, lunch, and dinner hardly seemed a silver bullet for global warming or high blood pressure.

Inside the walk-in pantry was an entire shelf of squat white jars labeled Slurry. "Better than Soylent," he said, comparing it to the undrinkable protein powder that had once been the default food for gamers and coders. "All natural. Made from yeast. Like liquid sourdough bread."

I told him I'd prefer real tacos made on a real taco truck.

"I was a seed investor in Slurry," he said. He unscrewed the cap and handed me a jar. The gray powder smelled faintly of bananas. And onions. I handed it back. No wonder he'd gone on a Kit Kat bender. "No pizza flavor?"

Satoshi laughed, the first time I'd ever seen him break through his stoic stare. His front teeth were brown. He had crow's feet around his eyes. He pulled out his phone and sent a text. It buzzed back within seconds.

"CEO says pizza flavor coming next year. He thanks you for the suggestion." He showed me a message from someone named Robin. I wondered if he wore a yellow cape and rode beside Satoshi in the Batmobile.

Satoshi heaped Slurry powder into a tea bowl and whisked it with a bamboo *chasen*, then passed the frothy white slurry to me with a bow as if this were a formal tea ceremony.

"Got anything else?" I asked.

He pointed to the stack of cardboard boxes filled with Kit Kats. I'd have to survive on Slurry. I added two scoops of matcha powder into the bowl and took a sip. It tasted like gritty tea. It wasn't good, but at least I could feel the overdose of caffeine and cholesterol recharging my brain.

We coded all evening and into the night, cat herding the team of a thousand developers modifying the BiteCoin code to meet our needs, downing one bowl of matcha Slurry after another to keep ourselves awake. By the time the mountains outside the window shaded gray and the sun poked through the gap, we had the software ready. The final piece in the thousand-piece puzzle, I dropped the encrypted terrorist plan, DaeshPlan.docx, into the source code tree and started the compilation. Within minutes, the OpenSesame executable was built and posted to the website for download.

At the top of the page, I added counters showing the password length currently being tested and the total number of passwords checked so far. I labeled it "Countdown to Decryption," but since it was impossible to know whether the password was eight characters or eighty, I added a countdown to the number of passwords left to check before starting over with a longer password.

After Jiji made a formal press announcement, we opened the floodgates to the two million people who'd signed up already. The biggest distributed computing project in history had begun.

In the blink of an eye, the password length reached seven characters, the number of passwords checked spun through millions to billions to trillions. In less than a minute, it started churning through eight-character passwords. OpenSesame was working just as I'd hoped. The countdown to decryption showed five quadrillion combinations to check before starting over with nine-character passwords. For the first time since I'd found the file in Joy's email two days ago, I breathed a sigh of relief. By morning, we'd find the password, decrypt the file, and stop the terrorist attack.

My fingers cramped from too much typing, my eyes unable to focus, my heart beating erratically from too much caffeine, it was time for sleep. Satoshi led me down the hall to a guest bedroom with a Viking theme, a reindeer head and wooden swords mounted on the wall over the bed. I closed the blinds, stripped off my T-shirt and jeans, and flopped down onto the enormous bed that filled the room. It had been years since I'd slept on an actual bed instead of my old sofa. Under the heavy fur blankets on a soft memory foam mattress, I felt like I was being hugged, the hug of a batty aunty who squeezed too hard and didn't know when to let go. Unable to move, I was trapped beneath the covers. No matter how many reindeer heads I counted, I couldn't fall asleep. I wished I was sleeping on the soft couch in the living room instead of in Valhalla.

I picked up the fur blanket and carried it back to the airport terminal room where I curled up atop the buttery couch, pulling the blanket over my head to block out the brightening light outside. Within seconds, I was deep asleep.

But as I dreamt of floating in the clouds, Satoshi shook me awake. He pointed at the laptop still open on the table where a string of messages was scrolling up the screen. OpenSesame had crashed.

twelve

orange is the new funeral suit

The press was in a tizzy, all of X atwitter, and Jiji was demanding to know what the hell was going on. The countdown was stopped at forty quadrillion passwords.

I slacked the project team to find out what had gone wrong. The infrastructure group assured me it was a simple matter of an overloaded router they'd have back up in minutes. But as soon as they upgraded the router, traffic flooded in and the blockchain ground to a crawl.

The engine crew fingered a problem with the gas allocation. The gas guys said it was a limit of the network bandwidth. The network team claimed the app was broken. The application devs said the socket calls were getting backed up by the blockchain engine. Around we went in a circle of blame. The usual clusterfuck that I had to get unfucked in a hurry.

The largest group I'd ever led was a three-person hackathon team. Now I had a thousand people waiting for me to tell them what to do. I'd always hated my know-nothing bosses who instead of solving anything themselves, ordered us to fix it. Now that boss was me. I told the entire crew to rewrite the code and upgrade the infrastructure to handle a load ten thousand times larger than they'd ever seen. If this was a MeCan project, we would've allocated a month for planning, six months for coding, and two weeks for QA; I gave them an hour.

When the hour was up, we watched the system spin up and hand out blocks of passwords to more than two million users. A giant emoji storm of confetti and claps erupted over Slack. Then it crashed again.

We spent the entire day playing whack-a-mole, swatting bugs only for the problem to pop up elsewhere. We pushed out an update every hour, even faster for critical fixes. As the day progressed, the app stayed up longer and the bugs grew less severe. By the end of the day, we were humming again, finished with the eight-character passwords and working on nine. On every news program, my decryption countdown replaced the stock ticker. Some reporter posted an exposé claiming OpenSesame was burning 250 gigawatts of electricity—the equivalent of five hundred power plants—and spewing more than 200,000 tons of carbon dioxide into the atmosphere. I prayed to Ebisu, the god of probability and statistics, that we'd find the password before we melted the ice caps.

By the time Satoshi and I took a break for a midnight matcha Slurry dinner, OpenSesame had finishing checking all 541 quadrillion nine-character passwords and started on the fifty-two quintillion combinations of ten characters. I was disappointed it hadn't decrypted the file yet but at least it was making progress. When the skies lightened to morning gray, the countdown reached zero again and reset for eleven-character passwords. Five sextillion was a lot of combinations to check, but with more and more people from all over the world joining every second, I was sure the password would pop out at any second.

My body buzzing with caffeine, my brain fuzzy from a lack of sleep, I laid down on the couch and curled up under the fur blanket, hoping we'd find the password before I woke up again. As I floated away, the phone started buzzing. I was sure it was the President calling to thank me for cracking the file and saving hundreds of lives. I was confused when a woman's voice said, "Good morning." A dog growled behind her.

My head fell back on the pillow. I drifted back into the clouds.

"Ted!"

"Uh..."

"Wake up!"

"Uh..."

"You have to come to the courthouse."

"Sleeping..."

"Now!"

It took all my willpower to slide out from under the warmth of the fur blanket and the loving embrace of the oh-so-soft cloud sofa. I dragged myself into the bathroom to splash cold water on my face and slap myself awake. Breakfast was a stack of Kit Kat bars followed by a Slurry chaser. The countdown showed OpenSesame making progress, but the password hadn't been found.

My T-shirt and jeans were caked in sweat, my underwear worse for wear. Satoshi offered me one of his white buttondowns but they were three sizes too big. He returned with a kid's BiteCoin King T-shirt that fit me perfectly. If only I didn't have to squeeze out the tunnel to get back to my car.

🔒 🔒 🔒

Sumire was standing beside the lemon wedge in her navy lawyer's uniform, a string of pearls around her neck. After hugging me, she waved a hand in front of her face. "When was the last time you showered?"

Time had lost all meaning. How many days had it been since I'd broken into Satoshi's place? And what had I done before that? I couldn't remember.

We slipped through the crowd milling outside and into the courtroom where the hearing was already in session. The judge, a gray-haired woman, was addressing a lawyer while a man in an ill-fitting suit stood behind a table scratching his tattooed neck.

"Why are we here?" I whispered to Sumire. She motioned for me to be quiet.

I DM'ed her a confuse-y face, causing her phone to buzz. The judge looked up over narrow glasses. Sumire lowered her head in shame. After she apologized to the judge and muted her phone, I messaged her a gif of a sorry dog bowing.

"*hes next*" she shot back.

"*who?*"

"*Naz!*"

I sent her three more confuse-y faces. Why had she dragged me here at the ungodly hour of 9:00 a.m. if not for my own case?

The judge read out a docket number and the crowd filed in from the lobby. Through the side door, a bailiff led the doctor into the courtroom. Though he was dressed in the black suit he'd worn to the funeral, he looked tired, his hair disheveled, the stubble on his chin grown into a scraggly beard. But even with his arms shackled, the doctor sneered with disdain. He faced forward, his body erect, while the judge read a single charge of conspiracy to commit murder. "How do you plead?"

"Not. Guilty."

His lawyer requested that as a respected member of the local community with no criminal history, he be released on his own recognizance. "We ask that Dr. Khan be allowed to return to his critical work saving lives as an emergency room surgeon."

The judge nodded in sympathy. She turned to the pair of prosecutors dressed in cheap suits behind the opposite table. "Does the State have any objection?"

The female prosecutor stood. "Your Honor, not only is the defendant a flight risk, but he has remained wholly uncooperative in the government's efforts to prevent a terrorist attack. It would be a grievous error to allow the defendant to remain free to assist in carrying out this heinous plan. We strongly urge the court to find that the defendant must be held without bail until trial."

The judge glanced over the case notes, then looked up at the crowd. A hush settled over the room. "Bail denied," she declared, punctuated by a bang of the gavel.

"Please, Your Honor—" he shouted.

"Defendant may apply for rehearing in two weeks if he cooperates with the investigation, including turning over the password immediately."

"I don't know the password!"

The judge banged her gavel once more and called the next case. The bailiff yanked the doctor towards the side door.

"We have to do something," Sumire said, her eyes narrowed, snorting like a very small bull. I struggled to follow behind as she pushed her way through the crowd and hurried down the staircase. Outside, instead of heading back to the parking lot, she stormed down the walkway towards the county jail in back.

At what passed for a reception deck, a pasty-faced guard leered at Sumire from behind a wall of plexiglass and pushed a form through the slot. When she filled it out and pushed it back, he scanned down the page and grunted, "You that creep's lawyer?"

"Yes," she lied without even her usual smile.

"The chair's too good for him. You ask me, we oughta tar and feather terrorists like that."

"Nobody's asking you."

He pointed a stubby finger at me. "Who's he?"

"My paralegal."

"He got I.D.?"

I pushed my driver's license through the opening. He held it up to the light, then ordered me to fill out a visitor form, too.

After confiscating our phones, another guard led us down a dingy hallway and into a meeting room. We sat on the metal chairs until a guard led Naz, dressed in an orange prison jumpsuit, into the room. "You got thirty minutes," the guard said before banging the door shut behind him.

The doctor stared at me, deep-set eyes set to kill. I had to turn away from the heat of his glare. I felt sorry for Joy if that was the last thing she'd seen before she was killed. When Sumire hugged him, his expression softened.

"What's *he* doing here?" the doctor said, pointing at me.

"The two of you need to talk."

"We have nothing to talk about." Naz turned towards the door.

"Sit down!" She grabbed his arm and sat him across the table from me.

"Why are you helping him?" I said to Sumire. "He killed your friend."

"Stop lying already," the doctor yelled. "You know I didn't kill anyone. You framed me and put me here."

"All I did was find Joy's computer in *your* car."

"Where *you* put it and called the cops."

"I never touched her computer."

"Then how did it get into my car?"

"You hid it there."

"I did not."

Sumire whistled, nearly piercing my ears. "Boys!" she shouted. "Stop it!"

If the doctor didn't hide the laptop in his car, who did—the cops? That made no sense. If the cops wanted to frame him, they'd plant the murder weapon or smear her blood on his clothes, not hide a laptop in his car and wait for me to find it. Nobody else would even think of leaving her computer there, which meant he had to be lying. Even if he didn't pull the trigger that murdered Joy himself, he had to know something about it.

Sumire sat beside him and put her hand on top of his, as if I wasn't on the other side of the table, growing angrier by the second.

"Thanks for seeing me, Naz," she said.

He glanced at me before turning back to Sumire. "Why did you come here?"

"Do you have a lawyer?"

"The court appointed someone."

"Get a good lawyer," she said. "Maybe Joy's friends can help find someone."

"Doubtful. Seeing how they all think I murdered her."

"I'll ask around."

"Thanks." He didn't look very thankful.

"Listen, Naz, it's not my place to say this, but I think you'd help yourself by giving the police access to everything."

He banged his fist on the table, startling both of us. "I did!"

"What do you mean?"

"I gave them my password," he shouted. "To all my accounts. There's nothing there."

Sumire cocked her head. "Then why are they saying you're not cooperating?"

"They want the password to that stupid document someone sent Joy."

"And you won't give it to them?"

"I didn't send that document! Don't you understand? I don't know the password because I had nothing to do with it. The police keep demanding the password, but I don't know it. I'll bet *he* sent it!" Naz pointed straight at me. "Why don't you ask *him* for the password?"

"You know I didn't plant the file," I said.

He stabbed a finger at me. "Then how did you find it?"

"I hacked into her account."

"That's impossible."

"Easy-peasy," I said. "She used her MeCan password on a Red Cross website."

"No way."

"No way what?"

"No way Joy would ever do that."

"Do what?"

He turned to Sumire. "You know Joy—she's nothing if not meticulous.

And security conscious. Everyone at LoF is. They have to be. They're supporting dissidents of regimes that will murder anyone who speaks up against them. Joy used a password manager to create a new password for every account. She'd never use the same password. Never. LoF would fire her if she did."

"Maybe she was careful with her LoF email," I conceded, "but not her personal MeCan account."

"Same thing," the doctor insisted. "She used the MeCan account with dissidents since anyone caught even talking to LoF could get shot. She'd never create an account with anything other than a fully secure password."

"Then how come I was able to get in with 'IdesofMarch'?"

"Because that's not her password."

"Then what is?"

"I don't know. But not that."

The doctor had to be lying. The proof was in the password. "If 'IdesofMarch' wasn't her password, then how did I log into her account?"

"You're a hacker. You found a way to break in. That's what you do, isn't it?"

"Why would I do that?"

"How should I know? You're the one who killed her."

"Boys!" Sumire shouted.

Naz scratched at his beard. "Look Suzie, all I want is to get out of here. Everyone thinks I'm a terrorist. Even the serial killers here spit in my face. The guards assault me every chance they get. Look at this." He opened his jumpsuit to show her deep bruises covering his shoulders and back.

"That's not right," she said, shaking her head. "I'll get you out on bail somehow. I'll find a way." Her eyes glowed with determination. "And Ted is going to figure out how you ended up here in the first place."

I started to protest.

"Aren't you, Ted?"

"Um—"

"Say yes, Ted."

"Yes," I said. I'd find whatever evidence I could, which would probably end up being more proof that he'd killed Joy.

The door swung open, and the guard returned. "Time's up."

Naz hugged Sumire. "Thank you."

"You can count on us," she promised. She stepped over to the guard and stood on tiptoes to thrust a finger in his face. "You'd better see to it your prisoner is cared for or I'm coming after you."

He backed away from Sumire to let us out the door.

🔒 🔒 🔒

Outside, the morning sky was cloudless and the air warm, a perfect San Jose spring day. Sumire took my arm and pulled me tight against her. "Thank you for coming with me," she said. As if I'd had a choice. "You believe me now?"

"Believe what?"

"Naz didn't do it. Someone framed him."

"Who?" I asked. "And why?"

She didn't have an answer.

"His story makes no sense. He's saying someone broke into Joy's account and changed the password so I could hack in. Then the person stole Joy's computer and hid it in Naz's car so I'd find it."

"Exactly. And you're going to prove it."

"How?"

"That's what you're going to figure out, aren't you, Teddybear?"

thirteen
frontier lawyers

From the parking lot, Sumire called around trying to find an experienced attorney willing to defend a suspected terrorist. Leaning against the pony, I considered what Naz had said. He'd sworn Joy had used a unique password for everything under orders from her employer. To prevent exactly what I had done—leveraging a password stolen from one hacked site to break into everything else. Basic hacker tradecraft.

Even more than the military, LoF needed to keep their network secure. But I knew from personal experience it was impossible to tell lawyers what to do. If everyone at LoF was like Joy, their I.T. department had to be the worst job in the world. Rather than outsourcing to India like everyone else, LoF needed I.T. hardasses who'd put a bullet through your hard drive if you ever reused a password. Hardasses even Joy wouldn't ignore. Hardasses like Bulldozer and Laser-Eye.

If Joy was using a password manager as Naz claimed, that pair would know the details. They might even have an uber-password to the password manager to abracadabra everything. And they'd certainly be able to access her corporate email and her database of contacts which might include whoever sent the file.

The police ought to be investigating themselves, but since the LoF Bay Area office was in San Francisco, outside their jurisdiction, it might take weeks for them to get through the paperwork. In the meantime, I could head up there myself and have an informal chat with Bulldozer. He seemed to like me, even if he was scary intense. He'd be happy to find out his suggestion had been the key to finding Joy's laptop in the doctor's car.

But I didn't have his contact information and couldn't remember his name. Fortunately, Sumire knew many of the other lawyers at LoF as friends of Joy's.

When another law firm told her they were too busy to take the case, I opened the passenger door. "Hop in," I said. "We have to go up to the LoF office in San Francisco. You can continue calling while I drive."

She stepped away from my old muscle car in horror. "Uh-uh. I'll drive."

The Prius rolled up 101. Slowly. Passed by semis, construction equipment, even food trucks trailing the scent of grilled meat. My stomach gurgled. I hadn't eaten anything other than Slurry and Kit Kats for what felt like an eternity. I pointed at a tacomobile exiting towards San Mateo. "Follow that truck!"

Sumire gagged and continued on the highway.

"What's wrong with tacos?"

Sumire rolled her eyes. "No time."

If she was in a hurry, her driving didn't show it. As the spiky skyline of San Francisco filled the windshield, she slowed even further. When we hit the city streets, she pulled over to check in with the dogwalker taking care of Higgs, cooing to the mutt before setting off again. She navigated around the potholes and pedestrians clogging the Financial District until I spotted the slate-gray high-rise in the shadow of the Transamerica pyramid.

After parking in the underground garage that cost more than a tin of matcha, we rode the elevator to the fourth floor where we found the glass nameplate of Lawyers on the Frontier in gold lettering affixed to a solid oak door.

Sumire pressed the buzzer and introduced us as friends of Joy. When the door buzzed open, the woman at the reception desk threw us a practiced smile and told us Brandi, the branch manager, would see us shortly. She pointed at a row of chairs in the corner to wait.

"I want to name my first daughter Brandi," I joked. "And my second Sherry."

Sumire wasn't amused. "Not with me, you aren't."

"Why aren't boys named Beer or Whiskey?" I pressed. She buried her nose in the Chronicle and ignored me until Brandi came out to greet us.

She was a tall, curvaceous woman with long, blonde hair dressed in a too-tight pantsuit. When she shook my hand, it was bigger than mine. Stronger, too. In fact, everything about her was powerful, from her broad shoulders to her tattooed biceps. It took me a moment to realize she was non-binary. She hugged Sumire, folding her into her body. "It's horrible what happened," Brandi cried. "Everyone here's in total shock."

Following Brandi through the office, I looked around for Bulldozer and Laser-Eye. But the only people I saw were a pair of button-downs at the kombucha cooler. The lawyers were probably working from home, but where was the support staff?

The walls of the meeting room were covered with photographs of refugee camps and prisons, closeups of police in riot gear, views of tear gas spreading over broken bodies, blow-ups of blood oozing into the ground. The room felt as airless as the police confession room, though at least it smelled better. And had coffee.

"What brings you all the way up here?"

She pointed at me. "Ted had some questions about Joy's computer."

Brandi stared at me, eyebrows arched in disdain.

"I'm working for Congressman Miyazaki," I said, hoping that would lend me some cred.

She looked me over, from the Crypto King T-shirt to my sandaled feet, and turned back to Sumire. "He shitting me?"

"Programmer," Sumire said, summing me up with a single word. Though I really was a mathematician only working as a coder. Unfortunately, nobody knew what a mathematician was, not even mathematicians.

Brandi crinkled her nose against the stench of programmers. I felt like a sheep in a zoo.

"Ted found the file on Joy's computer," she explained, like she was describing how much wool I could produce.

"Him?"

I fought the urge to leave and took control of the convo. "Did Joy ever report being contacted by anyone connected to ISIS?"

"No," Brandi answered.

"What would she do if that happened?"

"Notify our response team in Washington."

"Did she do that?" I asked.

"No."

"Do you know if she was in contact with someone named Mohammed Abdul?"

She looked about to lay into me, but through clenched teeth, only answered, "No."

"Has anyone checked her work email?"

"Of course."

"And?"

"The FBI went through it thoroughly," she said. "There was nothing there."

"Do you know what password she'd tell dissidents to use to send her sensitive information?"

"That's not how we operate."

"How do you operate?"

"We use Telegram for anything sensitive."

Of course they'd use an encrypted messaging app. I wouldn't trust email, either. "What did the FBI say about that?"

Brandi held her throat, pretending to gag. "They made some comments I can't repeat in polite company. Warned us that once the New Patriot Act is passed, Telegram will be illegal."

"They're renaming it the Joy Miyazaki Act."

"Joy would've been appalled. She called it the Police State Act. It lets the government spy on anyone for any reason."

"They'd need a court order," I countered.

"You know how many warrant requests the FISA security court rejects?"

I shook my head.

"Exactly. We don't know. Because it's a secret. And now they want to eliminate oversight completely. We've seen this story before. Fascism gets invited in on the best of intensions."

I thought that was a bit extreme, but we were in San Francisco, the capital of extreme. Though we were only an hour from San Jose, this was a different planet. As Brandi launched into a rant about politics, I interrupted her. "Is there any way to access Joy's Telegram account?"

"You'll have to talk to I.T." She wrinkled her nose against the stench of I.T., even worse than programmers.

I peered through the window of the conference room into the open office. Another buttondown had joined the pair yakking at the kombucha cooler. I didn't see Bulldozer or Laser-Eye. "Are they here?"

She scribbled a note and handed it to me. "You can call them yourself."

It was a 202 area code. I had no idea where that was other than it wasn't anywhere in the Bay Area.

"What about your I.T. staff here?"

"I.T. is handled out of D.C."

Would a pair of I.T. staffers have come all the way from Washington for Joy's funeral? Seemed unlikely. Unless they were here to help clean up Joy's accounts. "Did they come into the office yesterday?"

"Who?"

"The pair from your I.T. group."

Brandi didn't understand. So I described the sprinkling of gray in Bulldozer's buzzcut, puffed myself up to imitate his buff body. Brandi shook her head. I described Laser-Eye, the piercing blue eyes with the unswerving focus, trim body poised to spring like a cat.

Brandi made a sour face like I was doing Vogon performance art. She pointed at the phone number. "You'll have to call the I.T. office."

Sumire pulled out a pen and started sketching, reminding me of our days in high school sitting on the banks of the Guadalupe River, my head resting in her lap while she drew manga of the stories I made up to amuse her. When she was finished, she showed the drawing to Brandi. It captured Bulldozer and Laser-Eye perfectly, down to the intensity of their expressions.

"No idea who they are," Brandi said. "But I assure you I've never seen them."

fourteen

o say can you see a funeral crasher?

BACK AT MY OWN APARTMENT, after showering, changing into fresh clothes, and scarfing down a bento from Nijiya, I sat at the desk and set out to find the pair. But no matter how hard I squeezed my brain, I couldn't remember their names. The only hope of finding the mysterious duo was with an image search. Though Sumire's drawing captured them perfectly, it was useless for facial recognition software. I'd need a real photo.

I rewound my memory, trying to recall anyone taking pictures at the funeral. Maybe not during the funeral itself but outside before or after. The memory banks were hazy, though—I hadn't been paying attention. Then I remembered the livestream of the ceremony.

Through a post on a scary neo-Nazi Facebook group, I found an alt-right conspiracy site with a copy of the video helpfully annotated by crazies. It pointed out the congressman, the drug dealers, the election fixers, the pedophiles, and the murderer (me). It made me sad that the video had millions of views and tens of thousands of likes. The comments made me angry, asking why the funeral hadn't been bombed in payback for Pearl Harbor. I'd never seen so many idiots in a single place. Dangerous idiots. For a moment, I wondered if one of them had murdered Joy in some convoluted white supremacist attack. But no, these idiots were too stupid to pull off anything that required planning.

I muted the snide remarks about my height and fast-forwarded through the video until I found the pair in the queue to pay respects to Joy.

Towering two heads over anyone else, Bulldozer's buzzcut was easy to follow as he trudged forward, Laser-Eye beside him, until suddenly she jumped in surprise. I rolled back to see what was up, zooming into the grainy video to watch Bulldozer slide his hand down Laser-Eye's back to squeeze her butt.

I expected her to slap him, or at least throw him a glare cold enough to freeze his face into ice. But no. She looked up at him with a thin smile, then stood on tiptoes to kiss him on the lips.

I took a screenshot and blew it up to fill the entire monitor. The image was pixelated, the lighting in the temple dim, his deep-set eyes hard to see. But the chin was unmistakably Bulldozer. Who was he and what was he doing at Joy's funeral? And why was he watching me?

An app ran its magic to fill in the graininess. The scooped jaw became as sharp as a knife; his clear brown eyes stared outwards. An image search on MeCan, Google, Bing, and Yandex returned fourteen million hits. Fourteen million men with close-cropped hair and lantern jaws. None of them Bulldozer.

The only way to convert a face to a name was with facial recognition software tied to an immense database. If I still worked at MeCan, I would've elevatored up the gilded heights of the thirty-first floor to ask the AI image processing team to run a match against their billions of subscriber photos. But I was *persona au gratin* there, personally cheesed over by Evgeni. After toiling for two years in the sweatshop of the fourteenth floor, did I have any friends left who would help me? It was depressing to realize the answer was no. My cubiclemates and I had tolerated each other only through the magic of sound-cancelling headphones. My manager had been happy to see the back of me, even though I'd saved his butt at every deadline. Which meant I'd have to convince someone it was in their own interest to help me.

Fortunately, the entire MeCan AI team was on LinkedIn to make it easy for headhunters to make them offers they couldn't refuse. None had been at the company for more than a year, and most wouldn't be there much longer. The majority were academics with PhD's; they wouldn't break the rules to help out someone like me. But one goof listed his biggest accomplishment as winning a Call of Duty tournament. Call of Duty was a stupid game for stupid people who enjoyed shooting without blinking for hours. This CoDfish was my way in. To get his attention, I challenged him to a CoD duel over Twitch. He replied within seconds.

"*hara-boi?!?!?! cnt w8 2 tl mah crew u legend here man u ass fired from this shiathoe wahaha wat up u?*"

Every bit the annoying CoDfish I'd expected. Exactly the kind of person I needed. But I had to play him like a gamer, talk a little trash. I messaged back: "*building new startup using artificial intelligence for facial recognition. bet it blows away your artificial stupidity.*"

"*u and 50k others!!! got funding?*" Of course he had to follow that with five screaming cat emojis.

Was he a jerk or just an idiot looking for a new gig? Either way, I saw my opening. "*bruh! closing $5M seed from a16z.*" Name dropping the venture firm that funded the biggest unicorns in Silicon Valley would get his attention.

"*gr8!!! y u txt m3.*"

"*hiring CTO need expert in face recog.*"

"*what % u offering?*"

Nobody cared about salaries. Or health insurance. Or even the free kale and tempeh gluten-free pizza in the 24-hour cafes that dotted the MeCan campus. Not anymore. The only thing that mattered was stock options, and how many billions they'd be worth when the startup went IPO. I had no idea what an overconfident snapperhead like him would find tempting. But it wasn't like I had anything to give him. "*rite ur own ticket.*"

"*count m3 in I rote the m3cn algo.*"

I couldn't help laughing at his claim to have written MeCan's facial recognition algorithm. He was one of hundreds of programmers who'd worked on different parts of the code. As a noob, there was no chance he'd done anything more than grunt work. But humility and modesty got you nowhere when they handed out the stock options that catapulted goofs like him from cockroach to TEDx speaker. It was time to rope him in. "*how good is your algo w/o context???*"

It was easy to match a face when you could narrow down the choices to a hundred Facebook friends; it was a billion times more difficult comparing against all humanity.

"*fn best in fn world*" he boasted.

"*bet u can't match this*" I tossed the photo of Bulldozer at him like a grenade in Call of Duty.

"ha! gimme 1 usec"

Three dots appeared next to his message, an annoying dink dink dink burbling as I waited. And waited. And waited. Until an attachment dropped into the chat, followed by *"ha!!!!!!"*

I held my breath as I opened the jpeg. It wasn't the headshot of Bulldozer in front of fake puffy clouds I was expecting, or a snapshot of him swilling beer with friends posted to an ancient Facebook timeline. Instead, it was a group of kids and parents inside the Lucky Charms pastel world of an elementary school, holding up crayon drawings that displayed their dreams for world peace. At the end of the row was a small boy with sandy hair and freckles who'd drawn a man in a turban with a machine gun shaking hands with a soldier waving an American flag. Standing next to the boy was a man with a bulldozer jaw wearing a Baltimore Ravens football jersey. Bulldozer. On the other side was a woman with short-cropped blonde hair, unmistakably not Laser-Eye.

"u da goat!!!" I shot back, adding a gif of a goat drinking beer.

"400K base + 20% stock if u want m3"

I almost hated to break the news that I wasn't hiring yet. A string of expletives followed until I x'ed the browser closed. Despite being an annoying CoDfish, I felt a little bad for scamming him into helping me. I tracked his address to an apartment in Hayward and Postmated him a Gianni's XXL pizza. With a side salad. And a six-pack of Red Bull. And for good measure, threw in a $100 gift card. It wasn't a billion dollars in stock options in my non-existent AI startup, but it would take care of his crew of CoDfish friends for a full night of shooting at each other.

Now that I had a photo, it was easy to find its source: an elementary school in a town I'd never heard of—Columbia, Maryland—halfway between Baltimore and Washington. It sounded quaint. And boring. But I'd hit the jackpot: the photo was from a PTA newsletter with the kids' names in the article. Charlie Henderson was the boy who'd drawn the confab with insurgents inside the tent. His mother, Alysia Henderson, popped up in a previous issue with a recipe for blackberry pie. That made it as easy as pie to find her address, and with her address the name of her husband—also named Charles Henderson but known as Chuck. Though I couldn't remember the name he'd used to introduce himself after the funeral, it wasn't Chuck Henderson.

I looked up his address on MeView to see a split-level house with white shingles and red brick, on a street of identical houses that differed only in the color of the shutters. With wide lawns of brown grass and snow piled up along the curb, it looked very East Coast, though newer and neater than Boston where I'd survived six years of college. There were no liquor stores within walking distance, nor a Bird to scoot the 2.3 miles to the closest slice of pizza. Not a taco truck in sight. I couldn't imagine anyone wanting to live in a boring suburb of Baltimore. With the photo already over a year old, perhaps Bulldozer had gotten divorced and was living in the Bay Area now. That would explain why he wasn't wearing a wedding ring and was pinching Laser-Eye's ass.

I dialed the number Brandi had given me but wasn't surprised to be told there was nobody named Charles Henderson in the I.T. department. If he didn't work at LoF, wasn't a friend of Joy's, and lived three thousand miles away in Maryland, why was he at Joy's funeral?

Even with his name, it wasn't easy to track him. There were more than a hundred Charles Hendersons on LinkedIn in Baltimore and Washington alone. I went through every one of them, but none had a shovel for a chin. I couldn't find him on Instagram, either, nor did he have a Facebook page.

Using his address in Maryland, I tried to buy his social security number which along with fifty-five dollars, would get me his credit history. But I couldn't find it anywhere, not on the sketchy lookup sites, nor down in the depths of the dark web. That was consistent, at least, with his claim to be an I.T. nerd who understood security, even if he didn't look the part.

Fortunately, his wife, or ex-wife, was much less of a cypher. Alysia Henderson popped up as a nursing administrator on the staff page of a Maryland hospital. Her bio said she'd served in the Army's medical corps seeing duty in Iraq and Afghanistan. I wondered if that's where she'd met Chuck.

Her social security number and credit history were easy enough to acquire. I could see how much she spent at Macy's each month and the lease on her Ford Explorer. Though she paid her mortgage on time, her credit card bill grew dangerously large every January. There was nothing in the credit report about a divorce or a recent name change. Nor was there any record of a divorce in the Howard County court records. I'd have to dig deeper.

I dialed the hospital where Alysia worked and hit zero enough times that the auto-attendant gave up and passed me to a human. I said I needed to talk to Alysia Henderson and insisted it was urgent.

"Yes?" a woman answered.

"Sorry to bother you at work," I started, "but Chuck told me to call you."

I waited to hear whether she was annoyed to hear Chuck's name. All I got was a drawn out, "Okaaay."

I knew how to talk to a CoDfish but didn't know what to say to a nurse. "I work at your son's school."

That made her worried. "Is Charles okay?"

I tried to sound like a teaching assistant. "Oh, yes, we love having him in class. I'm just putting together a list of emergency contacts." Not a great cover story, but the best I could come up with on the fly.

"You've got our contact info already," she said, her guard up. "Who is this?"

I told her I was Camus Murakami, the alias I used when I was goofing on a new game and didn't want to dishonor my reputation.

"Then who's Theodore Hara?"

Damn. I'd forgotten to turn off caller ID. I red-buttoned the call immediately. But before I could figure out what to do next, my phone buzzed. Unknown caller. Normally, I'd let it go straight to voicemail, but on the chance it was Alysia calling back, I green-buttoned it.

"Don't you fucking dare call my wife again," a voice shouted at me, "or I'll fucking kill you, you twerp!"

It wasn't Alysia but a voice I recognized—her husband. Bulldozer. No doubt. Not as friendly this time as when he pulled me aside after the funeral. He probably thought I was calling to tell his wife about Laser-Eye.

Unfortunately, he hung up as soon as he delivered his message, leaving me no way to trace his call. But he'd called back within minutes, so it was clear he wasn't divorced or separated. Which meant he was living in Maryland in a brick split-level with a wife and a Mini-Chuck. It didn't explain why he was at Joy's funeral two days ago, and who Laser-Eye was other than someone whose butt he wasn't supposed to be pinching.

Now I knew where he lived. But I needed to know where he worked. I was three thousand miles too far away to follow his car to the office. I could try asking Jiji to have one of his interns in Washington do it once he returned from California, or call the cops, but they'd only scoff. I'd have to figure out a way to do it myself from here.

Expanding the MeView image of his house, I imagined Bulldozer behind the faded brown front door. If only the view was live instead of a photo from a year ago. Then I noticed the doorbell mounted next to the door, a RingyDing video camera that recorded everything. Exactly what I needed. But how could I get into his account? If Bulldozer was sophisticated enough to hide his credit history, there's no way he'd leave his doorbell camera set to the default password like everyone else.

Taking a virtual tour of the street, Bulldozer's house wasn't alone—almost everyone had a RingyDing, a Ding Dong or an Alexa Bell affixed to their door. Hacking into Bulldozer's account would be difficult, but probably not his neighbors'. I only needed to find one with a view facing outward to Bulldozer's home. The house across the street had a RingyDing and was owned by a couple in their late sixties. Best of all, the husband still used an AOL address—three letters that guaranteed hackability. I went straight to the Password Pirate site and bought all his passwords. No surprise the same password he used for his Target, car finance, and Yahoo! accounts got me into his RingyDing.

The RingyDing page had a recording of every postman and postmate who'd trudged to their door in the past thirty days, but I needed to see who came and went from the house across the street. There were no recordings of that, of course, but I could turn on his camera and watch a live view.

Three hours ahead of us, flurries were falling from heavy clouds that filled the late afternoon sky. A salt-streaked car zipped down the street every minute or two. Two boys in pastel helmets bicycled past, bookbags slung over shoulders. Nothing was happening at Chucky's house, and I couldn't sit forever on a virtual stake out. I wrote a script to pipe the video to my hard drive so I could zip through it later.

That done, I set about trying to find Laser-Eye, shooting a close-up of her horsey face from the funeral video to CoDfish, hoping he'd be my bestie after the pizza arrived.

"im vegan u slime" he replied, unhappy with the pepperoni, followed by emojis of eggplant and knives. Idiot. I was glad I didn't hire him for the job I didn't have. But how could I find Laser-Eye without his facial recognition software?

I shot the photo over to Sumire. *"anybody know her?"*

"no" she texted back a few minutes later. Another dead end. I was trying to figure out how I could hack into Facebook's facial recognition software when my phone buzzed from Sumire telling me to meet her at the Miyazaki's home right away.

🔒 🔒 🔒

I played the video of Bulldozer and Laser-Eye shuffling down the aisle.

"Never seen them before," Jiji said.

Mrs. Miyazaki closed her eyes, tears smearing her mascara. Sumire grabbed the phone out of my hand to shut off the funeral. I should've realized watching it would upset her, but I never thought about those things. "I'm sorry," I said. "I should go now." Another waste of time.

Mrs. Miyazaki squeezed my arm. "Wait a second," she said before heading out of the room. She returned with a Trader Joe's bag that she held out to me. I thought she was handing me a present—oranges or mikan from their garden or leftovers from the reception, expecting her to push it at me and insist I take it home. Instead, she pulled out four identical notebooks, black with gold trim—the guest registries from the funeral—and a big stack of sympathy cards and envelopes previously filled with cash.

She distributed one book to each of us. We scanned through them looking for Charles Henderson. He wasn't there.

"Maybe they didn't sign in," I said.

Joy's mother stared at the books with a faraway look in her eyes. "Nakamura-san would never have let them past."

We went through the books again, one guest at a time, reading them aloud, until Sumire called out the name, Francis S. Key.

"That's him!" I shouted. He'd introduced himself as Frank Key, I suddenly remembered.

Sumire looked at me cockeyed. Jiji mumbled *bakatare*, an ancient Japanese insult for a dolt.

I glanced over Sumire's shoulder to look at Bulldozer's alias written in small, tightly drawn letters. The ink was smudged—a leftie. My mother thought lefties were evil. This time, she might have been right.

Underneath his name was a woman's neat cursive, the tail at the end of Ross looping around to the beginning of Elizabeth. Now I remembered Bulldozer's wink as he introduced me to his girlfriend—Liz Ross.

Sumire rolled her eyes. Jiji repeated the insult, louder this time. Mrs. Miyazaki patted my arm. I had no idea why. A quick search for Elizabeth Ross pulled up a Wikipedia page. Was Laser-Eye famous?

No. I really was *bakatare*, I realized after reading the first line. Elizabeth Ross was Betsy Ross, the seamstress of the American flag. And Frank Key was Francis Scott Key, writer of the national anthem. O say, can you see a pair of aliases? Frank Key was Chuck Henderson, but I had no idea how to find the real name of Liz Ross.

I handed the guest book back to Mrs. Miyazaki and apologized for wasting their time.

She put on her glasses to peer at the entry. "No *o-koden*," she pointed out. All the other names had numbers penciled in beside them—a hundred dollars or fifty dollars—the funeral gift. One big-time donor had given ten thousand. I was glad Sumire had put $500 in the envelope, the most generous of her friends. Bulldozer and Laser-Eye had given no funeral gift, not even a card, nor left an address to send the thank you note.

Sumire and I stood to leave. Jiji gulped his whiskey. "Enough of amateur hour," he said. "You got the photos?"

I forwarded him my screen capture of the pair. He dialed the San Jose Police and ordered Chief Patterson to check it.

"I'll have the case team take a look," the chief promised. "They should be able to run it through the system first thing in the morning."

Jiji yelled into the phone, "Find someone there to do it right fucking now!"

The new chief of police knew where his toast was buttered. He promised to find someone who knew how to operate the system and would get back to Jiji as soon as he could.

"I'll stay here on the fucking line until you get me an answer."

The speakerphone filled with the tinny sound of hold music repeating forever. Until it stopped abruptly. Papers rustled. The chief cleared his throat. "Representative Miyazaki," he started, surprisingly formal for someone who'd been backslapping Jiji over whiskey at the funeral reception. Was someone else listening in?

"Who are those two assholes who crashed my daughter's funeral?"

"Well...I need to know where you got that photo."

Jiji eyeballed me. I waited for him to finger me and offer to have his security guard hold me until a squad car arrived. Instead, he yelled into the phone, "Me! I took the photo of those two assholes at the funeral. I want to know who the hell was at my daughter's funeral."

"Uh, sir?" said a younger detective, sounding nervous. "Look, sir, I'm sorry to inform you that those identities are classified. Even we don't have access."

"Then who does?"

Whispers on the other side until the detective spoke again. "Uh, sir? I believe that would be the FBI."

"Then I suggest you get the fucking FBI on the horn and get yourself access. This is a murder investigation. Of a congressman's daughter. Do you understand?"

The detective stuttered until the chief took over. "Look, Jiji, I'm sorry. It's out of our hands. The FBI demanded to know who ordered the lookup when we put your photo into the system."

"Fuck it all to hell." He turned to me and ordered, "Don't you go anywhere," before storming out of the room. At the other end of the house, a door slammed.

While Sumire chatted with Joy's mother, I scanned the Wikipedia entry on Francis Scott Key, a lawyer who represented the owners of runaway slaves to help them regain their property. An amateur poet who wrote his paean to the Stars and Stripes after watching a battle with the British. A battle at Fort McHenry, in Maryland—a recurring theme. I could read the notes on the sheet music now, but I still couldn't follow the tune.

When Jiji stomped back into the room, his face was bright red. His wife pried the phone from his fingers and rested a hand on his shoulder. He pulled a handkerchief from his pocket to wipe the sweat from his face. "I gotta get back to Washington tomorrow."

Mrs. Miyazaki sighed. "It's too soon, Jiji. I need you here."

"No choice. The local FBI guy, what's his name—Harris—he's fucking useless. Gave me the runaround, wouldn't tell me a thing. I'm meeting the Director of the FBI first thing tomorrow to get to the bottom of this. I've got to take the redeye back to National."

"Can't you do a zoom or something? I really wish you wouldn't go."

"Yeah, me, too." He took her hand and kissed it tenderly. Then he turned to me. "You let me handle this, Hara, understand? Don't go off half-cocked."

I nodded. I understood. I told him everything I knew about the funeral crashers, Frank Key and Liz Ross. It wasn't much. When I described Bull-dozer attending Joy's funeral with Laser-Eye while his wife and kid waited back in Maryland, I got trapped in a stinkeye sandwich between Sumire and Mrs. Miyazaki. Jiji ripped into me, too, saying Bulldozer's personal life wasn't pertinent to his daughter's murder investigation and I had no right to be hacking into people's accounts or spying on anyone. He ordered me to leave the investigating to the police and the FBI without even a word of thanks.

Fine, I thought, I was happy to be done. OpenSesame was humming along without me, counting down the number of eleven-character pass-words remaining to check. Jiji could get the FBI to look into Bulldozer and Laser-Eye themselves. At least Sumire thanked me as we walked back to our cars for trying to find out what happened to her friend, sharing a kiss as we parted and promising to drop by after work the next evening.

But when I returned to my apartment, the video from the doorbell across the street from Bulldozer's home was waiting. Jiji had ordered me not to go off half-cocked. But after watching Chucky Henderson, a.k.a. Frank Key, pulling into his driveway in a hulking orange Ram TRX pickup, I was fully cocked to find out who Bulldozer was.

fifteen
ellicott city

Though I couldn't see Bulldozer's face through the glass, I could sense his hulking presence inside the orange truck rumbling up the street, headlights piercing the darkness. When he parked in the driveway, I zoomed to max resolution, but the license plate was too grainy to read, the bumper stickers on the back nothing more than a smear of purple.

At the front door, his wife greeted him with a kiss. The Mini-Chuck wrapped himself around his father's leg, and a German Shepherd bounded out the door and ran in circles in the snow until Bulldozer whistled for him to return. A few minutes later, the front door opened again, and the dog bolted out to the sidewalk, pulling Bulldozer behind him by the leash. There was no question the whole happy family lived here in Ellicott City, but how could I find out where Bulldozer worked?

Sliding the video back in time, I watched as the truck came into view through the four-way stop on the corner. Had he just returned from California? Since he didn't have a suitcase, he must've come back yesterday or the day before, right after I'd met him at the funeral.

Either way, I was sure that in the morning, I'd see him head back out through the same intersection. How could I track him from there? Breaking into video doorbells one block at a time all the way to the office wasn't practical, especially if he took the highway. What I needed were highway cameras. And Howard County had a network of traffic cams to monitor the major thoroughfares.

Unfortunately, the ones available to the public were low-res with a one frame per second refresh rate, making them useless for following a vehicle, even a big-ass orange pick-up. I needed the original videos in all their 1080 HD glory that the police used to track suspects.

I cracked my knuckles and ran a port scan on the county's Dept. of Transportation website only to have it blocked. I tried hitting the firewall directly, but it was up to date with all the current security patches. I'd need a more elaborate plan to get in.

Watching the snow falling in front of Bulldozer's house gave me an idea. After negotiating a spam list vendor in India down from $1000 to $50 for the email addresses of a thousand employees at the Howard County Dept. of Transportation, I crafted a message from their HR department regarding an expected snow emergency in the morning. Sprinkled with heretofores and consequentlys to sound like a bureaucrat, I urged the staff to check the website throughout the night for updates, and helpfully included a link. Not to the real website, of course, but a mirror image of howardcountymd.gov that I created at howardcounty.md using the .md domain I bought from the republic of Moldova. I only needed one person to click on the fake link and install a trojan on their computer.

After blasting out the email, I checked in on the progress of OpenSesame. I was disappointed to see it hadn't cracked the file yet. With more than a hundred million people all over the world lending us their CPUs, we'd finished testing every possible combination of eleven characters and were working on twelve, a common password length. I was confident we'd decrypt the file by morning at the latest. But the press was growing restless, with talking heads claiming the attack should have happened already. Attention seekers on every social media platform from X to Threads to Truth Social were gloating, calling us the biggest failure in the history of computing. And the Director of the FBI was once again begging Congress to pass the Joy Miyazaki Act before it was too late. I clicked off the news and returned to my phishing project.

Within minutes, a handful of people installed my trojan; one had remote access software running on his computer, exactly what I needed. That let me use his VPN to get through the firewall. Once logged into the servers with his admin credentials, it didn't take long to find the recordings of traffic cams all over the county.

Starting with the camera at the main intersection closest to his home, I set the video playing from a few minutes before he returned home. I was soon rewarded with a glimpse of a burnt-orange TRX with a menacing black grill turning off the main road onto the slush-covered residential streets.

From there, I followed him back to Route 29 where the pickup had been heading south on the eight-lane highway. Before that, he'd been traveling westbound on the Baltimore National Pike. But as the suburban parkway rolled past car dealers, bowling alleys, gas stations, and a Papa John's, the orange truck was nowhere to be seen.

Had Bulldozer been on his way home from the airport? No, this was not the route he'd take to get back from BWI. Nor from central Baltimore or Washington. The only reason he'd be on the Baltimore National Pike was if he was picking up a pizza at Papa John's or returning from Ellicott City. Though Bulldozer seemed like a Papa John's kind of guy, I was betting on Ellicott City.

The street view showed a small town of stone and mortar buildings that resembled a movie set for a Revolutionary War movie. The blacksmith, saloon, and general store that two hundred fifty years ago had lined the three blocks of Main Street had been replaced with restaurants, bars, and coffee shops inside the historic buildings. Beside the red, white, and blue of the Betsy Ross flag flapping above every doorway was the purple and black banner of Baltimore Ravens football. A tourist trap. There was even a Japanese krapknack shop across from the old train station, its window filled with Pocky and Hello Kitty goods. At least I knew where to find good quality matcha if I ever found myself in Maryland.

There weren't any traffic cams along the narrow road that curved down the hill to the river, but most of the shops had security cameras mounted over their entrances. The password for the free Wi-Fi of a wine bar helpfully included in their Yelp review got me into their security system. It didn't take long before I caught the orange pickup rolling past the door of the bar, Bulldozer's face staring out through the windshield. I was closing in.

From the camera of another restaurant, I hit the jackpot—the truck pulling out of the empty lot where he'd parked. I had him now. Sliding back a few minutes, I watched Bulldozer emerge from the side of a darkened electronics shop in a building of roughhewn granite.

I rolled the video back to watch him arrive in the morning. Instead of entering through the front door of the shop, he went around to the side, tapped a badge to a card reader and leaned into the camera. Was that a retina scan? That would be super crazy security for an old electronics store. When he stepped through the entrance, I caught a glimpse of his heavy boots stomping up a staircase before the door snapped shut behind him. Not the electronics store downstairs—he was headed to the second floor.

Next door to the electronics shop was a dentist's office. Together, they filled the ground floor of the building. Bronze numbers were screwed into matching garnet-colored doors. Above the shops were two floors of windows trimmed with white shutters. Did Bulldozer work in an office there? Or was it Laser-Eye's apartment? There was no directory pointing to businesses upstairs nor a buzzbox for residents. The tinted windows made it impossible to see what was inside.

Three more people arrived soon after Bulldozer, tapped their badges, scanned their retinas, and headed up the stairs. They were all dressed in heavy coats and hats, making it hard to tell from across the street who they were. As the time approached 8:00 a.m., people continued trickling in. Then I saw it. She wore a brown wool coat cinched tight at the waist, hiking boots, and a yellow knit cap. When she turned her head, even from across the street, there was no mistaking the laser focus. I pushed the cursor back to watch her climb out of a white F-150 pickup she parked beside Bulldozer's orange monster.

This had to be the office where the pair worked. But what kind of business would be located above an electronics shop and dentist office in the tourist trap of Ellicott City? It was exactly the kind of fake-authentic atmosphere that drew startups to San Francisco. But why would a startup require retina scans to enter through a blast-resistant door and send its employees across the country to the funeral of a murdered human rights lawyer? It was hard to tell much from a handful of people tramping through a door, but the vibe seemed more nine-to-five than the chaos of a startup.

Sure enough, skipping back to the evening, eleven people streamed out the door at exactly two minutes after 5:00 p.m. Definitely not a startup, nor any tech company. Bulldozer in a leather jacket led a cluster of men through the falling snow while Laser-Eye in her yellow cap chatted with another woman a few steps behind them. At the parking lot, the group split up and drove away, except Bulldozer and Laser-Eye who remained beside the doors of their trucks, waving to their departing colleagues. Once the others were gone and the lot empty, Bulldozer stepped around his pickup to join Laser-Eye at hers. They glanced about to make sure nobody was watching, then embraced, arms folded through heavy coats, faces mashed together. When they drew apart again, Laser-Eye hopped into her pick-up and kissed him once more through the window. Bulldozer stood watching as Laser-Eye rolled into the street. Then he climbed into his own truck and drove off in the opposite direction, back home to his wife and kid, and a German Shepherd that needed walking.

Who were these people in a high-security office on Main Street in Ellicott City? An article in the Post profiled the electronics shop that had been in the same location for two decades, a kind of mini-Fry's (god rest its geeky soul) where otaku from all over Washington flocked to buy Nvidia cards and PC cooling enclosures for serious gaming and BiteCoin mining. My kind of place, though I wondered how a dusty shop in a tourist trap in suburban Maryland could compete with Newegg and Amazon. Although the Yelp reviews for the unclaimed business raved about Aaron, the proprietor and only employee, saying he could repair any computer, disinfect any virus, and recover any hard drive, the shop didn't have a website much less a slick e-commerce operation. Just an old geek with a bunch of components he probably bought off eBay.

The dentist beside him, Dr. Charles Brown, D.D.S., didn't have a website either. Nor a Facebook page. Or an Insta following. I couldn't find a single review of Dr. Brown—not on Yelp nor any of the clickbait sites ranking dentists. If a dentist wasn't on Google, did he actually exist? It was like peering into a world from fifty years ago, or Revolutionary War times. I hoped he used an electric drill and Novocain instead of pliers. I scanned the video to see what kind of patients showed up for teeth cleaning by a dentist named Charlie Brown, but not a single person passed through the darkened door all day.

The Ellicott City business listings, the local Chamber of Commerce, and the free local rag all told me nothing about the businesses inside this building. Costar and LoopNet had rental listings for most of the buildings on Main Street, but not this one.

Fortunately, Howard County had an online system to look up property records. It only took a few minutes and a few dollars to pop out a report that listed the owner of the building as an organization called the General Services Administration. I laughed. It would be hard to come up with a more sketchy sounding name. I was sure that had to be scammers, but the GSA turned out to be a federal agency that owned 8,700 government buildings across the country worth a half trillion dollars. Including this one in Ellicott City purchased in late 2001. Which made no sense. Why did the feds own an old building in Ellicott City leased to an otaku electronics shop and a dentist with no patients? And had a secure facility on the second floor where Bulldozer, Laser-Eye, and a dozen other people worked?

After flopping onto my couch to think, I must've fallen asleep. Because when I heard the trilling of Sumire's ringtone, the room was filled with the soft light of morning.

I punched on the speakerphone. Sumire's voice was loud and shrill, not her usual soothing calm. "Did you see the news?" she shouted.

I jerked awake. Had we found the password? Broken into the file? Stopped the attack? Arrested the terrorists? "What news?"

"The terrorist attack!"

I navigated to CNN where a red alert scrolled across the top: "150 Killed in Islamabad."

Shit. There was no article yet, just the headline. But the trending hashtag #PakistanAttack showed horrific photos of the scene.

Oh shit. Shit. Shit.

sixteen
wdoml

THE DEATH TOLL climbed from 150 to 300 to over 500 as news reports filtered in. People were buried under rubble. Thousands more were injured. Three sites around Islamabad had been hit: a hospital, a government ministry, and a popular park, all crowded with people in the early evening. The suicide bombers had arrived in ambulances packed with explosives and nails. Islamic State of Iraq and the Levant claimed credit for the outrage. With every update on CNN, every photo of the dead and wounded reposted on X, the enormity of my failure to decrypt the file made me want to throw up again. On the corner of the screen, my countdown to decryption ticker continued rolling down the number of twelve-character passwords left to check, as if it still mattered, as the death toll ticker rolled up. This was the worst day of my life.

Jiji called me for no other reason than to berate me. "You fucked me, kid, you fucked me, bad. You said you were going to crack that fucking file. Instead, you made me look like a fool. I'm dead meat, you ass, and it's all your fault."

When the death toll rose yet again, I felt so miserable, I messaged Sumire, "*wdoml*".

She shot back a hug and promised to drop by in the evening after work. I had a whole day with nothing to do. A whole life that lost all meaning. There's no way anyone would invest in my startup now. Or hire me for anything.

Still the news kept pouring in, filling my screen with pictures of mutilated arms, bleeding people crying for help, wailing mothers in misery. I couldn't wait until Sumire arrived. I needed comfort now. I escaped my apartment and wandered the streets, trying to clear my head.

My feet carried me past the Nijiya market, the rock 'n' roll sushi abomination, the Dandy Lion. Though the shops were overflowing with the lunchtime crowd, the sight of food made me sick. I passed the doctors, the dentists, the optometrists, didn't stop for a manju at Shuei-Do or a tin of tea at Kogura. I kept going until I found myself standing on the corner in front of Kelly's. I told myself not to go in. Then the bell jangled as I pushed through the door into the musty liquor store.

The Indian man, the son of the owner, his face dark with stubble, smiled at me like a long-lost friend. "Where you been, Hara? Haven't seen you in dog's years."

"Need some comfort," I said, plunking a Jackson on the counter and pointing at the Southern Comfort on the shelf behind him. He put the bottle into a black plastic bag and handed me the change. I took the bottle out and told him to keep the bag and the change.

With the bells jingling my exit, I cracked the cap and took a swig. A sad, old man with dirty clothes leaned against the stucco wall, watching me with thirsty eyes. The crap whiskey bit the back of my throat while the weird taste, sweet and tart, made me gag. It was hard to imagine anything more disgusting. I handed the bottle to the thankful homeless guy and went back in for a Johnnie Red.

I took my first shot as soon as I stepped out of the shop again. And my next at the stoplight. Another when I reached the front of my apartment building. And one more after I stumbled through the door. I curled up on the couch downing shot after shot until I was numb from the waist up. The more I drank, the more I shrank until I disappeared into the cracks between the cushions to join the coins and crumbs.

When a Slack alert awakened me from a nightmare of bloody hands chasing me through the wreckage of Islamabad, the light had dimmed. I'd been asleep for hours. While I was passed out, a million slacks had beeped at me—the password had been cracked. The BiteCoin team was celebrating. Someone had found the password and won Jiji's million-dollar reward. The countdown to decryption had stopped on 166 sextillion passwords checked before finding the right one. Now that it no longer mattered. If that was supposed to cheer me up, it only rubbed salt into the wound.

The twelve-character password turned out to be a simple variation of her name: "JoyMiyazaky!" Take away one of the characters and we would've decrypted the file yesterday in time to prevent the attack. The exclamation point at the end was like a dagger stabbing my heart. I'd even tried a hundred variations on her name, but it never occurred to me to change the final "i" to a "y". I took a fresh shot of Johnnie.

Now that the password had been cracked, the contents of the decrypted document were being dissected by every talking head on the news. The five-pages listed everything: locations of the bombings with timing precise to the second, turn-by-turn instructions for the routes so all three explosive-laden ambulances would arrive at their targets simultaneously. If Joy hadn't been murdered, she would have passed the document to people who could've stopped the bombing. If I'd been able to decrypt the file even a few hours earlier, I could've prevented the carnage. The death toll was now over seven hundred. I felt like shit. I hugged the Johnnie tight against my chest and breathed in the smell of my father.

At the end of the document was a final instruction that made me retch. The last task in the terrorists' plan to be carried out precisely fifteen minutes after the blasts: "N Khan to contact Al Jazeera tip line to claim responsibility for ISIS." *N Khan.*

Naz. Joy's boyfriend. The doctor who supposedly loved her. There was no question now why Joy had been killed. And who'd killed her. I started to call Sumire to tell her she was wrong about Naz, wrong, wrong, wrong, but that would accomplish nothing. I red-buttoned the call before it started ringing and took another shot to celebrate being right all along. But instead of bringing me joy, it made me throw up again. After rinsing my mouth, I took a mulligan, toasting Joy's fiancé, the love of her life, a terrorist and murderer, headed for Guantanamo. Or lethal injection.

Checking the news again to see what would happen to the doctor, the Director of Directors was already holding a press conference. Standing at the podium with the FBI logo behind him, he expressed regret for not being able to stop the horrific attack. "We call on Congress to give us the tools to prevent an atrocity like this from ever happening again," he thundered at the cameras. "Pass the Joy Miyazaki Act immediately! There's no more time to waste."

All I could do was salute the director with another shot of Johnny.

Beside the Director of Directors at the podium was a woman with a dazzling smile. He introduced her as the Associate Deputy Director of Community Outreach. She called on an elderly couple, the Amramsons, to join her on stage.

Once the dumpy, white-haired couple had hobbled to the front, she declared them the winner of Jiji's reward. A smattering of applause broke out around the room. Someone in the back yelled, "Yay, mom!"

The husband was grinning despite the deaths. I couldn't blame him—he'd won a million dollars. The wife, though, looked stern and angry.

The Associate Deputy Director read a statement describing the wife as a beloved second grade teacher while the husband ran a small business setting up computers for local businesses.

The grinning husband leaned into the microphone and said his heart went out to the families of all the people killed in today's attack. The stern wife grabbed the microphone to demand Congress put an end to Islamic terrorists. "We're donating this prize to defeat any congressman who fails to act immediately," she declared, "starting with Congressman George Miyazaki. He's been blocking the New Patriot Act in Congress for years, putting our boys in the army in danger." She didn't mention that the prize she was using to kick Jiji out of Congress was coming straight out of his own lunch money. The world was cruel in its irony.

When the presser was done, I couldn't take any more of the sad commentary on CNN. Switching to Patriot News, I found the anchors in full spitting rage, inveighing against the liberals putting the rights of terrorists over American citizens. They were traitors who ought to be shot or hanged, starting with Jiji. I took a swig and switched to the relative sanity of X.

But there was no shelter there where #RememberJoy was trending. The President posted a demand to put the Joy Miyazaki Act on his desk by tomorrow. Even the most progressive progressives conceded the Constitution said nothing about protecting the privacy of terrorists and child pornographers. Evgeni, too, backpedaled, posting that MeCan would roll back the changes to its privacy policy, effective immediately. User passwords would again be available to law enforcement. I took another slug of Johnnie and *pkill*'ed the browser.

After mindlessly flipping through the news about the couple who'd won the reward, I couldn't resist checking the internals of OpenSesame to see the details of the password. The logs confirmed it was discovered by username am.amramson@mecan.me—that had to be Grinning Amramson. He'd been one of the first people to sign up for OpenSesame as soon as the FBI had announced it. Though the old guy looked like a Microsoftie, he was running the OpenSesame software on Linux. Probably a retired Cobol programmer making extra coin setting up computers for neighbors. I ran a traceroute on his IP address and followed the packets across the country. They took the usual path from San Jose to Chicago and down to Washington until reaching a router labeled "elcymdel." A database of internet routers showed the node as Verizon's hub in Ellicott City, Md.

Ellicott City. No way that could be a coincidence. Ellicott City wasn't a big place and certainly not a hotbed of programmers. Looking up the old guy's address pointed to a house in Laurel, Maryland—a town seven miles due south of Columbia, twelve miles from Ellicott City. Hmmm. Something stank of onions.

But Grinning Amramson had discovered the password, of that there was no question. Was he a random grinner who'd gotten lucky and won the lottery? The fact that he was in Ellicott City near Bulldozer couldn't be anything other than an amazing coincidence. As long as the password he'd found worked, it had to be legit. I typed "JoyMiyazaky!" into the password box just to be sure.

But instead of opening, the computer dinged with the same error message I'd seen a million times: "*The password is incorrect. Word cannot open the document.*"

Strange. I took another hit of Johnnie before trying again, this time copying the password and pasting it into the box so there could be no typing error. The result was the same. Very strange.

This wasn't possible. The OpenSesame software had verified that the password opened the document. But it didn't. I had to be doing something wrong.

Pacing over the threadbare carpet, I couldn't think of any reason the verified password wouldn't open my copy of the file. Had Grinning Amramson somehow hacked the software to declare himself the winner? No, the file had been decrypted, its contents displayed on the news. The password had opened the file in the OpenSesame software, but not my copy —the original.

Which could only mean one thing: if the password didn't open my copy and it couldn't be the wrong password, then it had to be opening the wrong file. But how was that possible? And what file did it open?

I logged into GitHub and downloaded the version of DaeshPlan.docx that the software had cracked. Sure enough, the password opened that document to display five pages of terrorist instructions in twelve-point Times New Roman.

So why didn't the password work on my copy of DaeshPlan—the version I'd forwarded directly from Joy's email? My stomach sank when I compared the two copies and confirmed my worst fear—though they were both titled DaeshPlan.docx, they were not the same document. Confused, I took another hit of Johnnie.

Had I screwed up somehow? Used the wrong document when I created the hacking project? Written over the original file by mistake?

Scrolling through the source code revision history, I found the file used in v1.0. That was identical to my copy. The file must've gotten changed at some point. But when, why, and how?

I pawed through the hundreds of change entries for bug fixes and performance optimizations until I found an update to the file that had no reason to ever be changed. DaeshPlan.docx had been swapped in v2.33 of the software this morning. That was the final version because the password was discovered less than an hour later. Something was wrong. Very wrong. I took another hit of Johnnie to kill the stink of onions.

The log showed the file had been replaced by username *smartgrrl*. The change had been approved by Satoshi.

I slacked Satoshi. "*who is smartgrrl? why did she change the doc?*"

He slacked back, "*idk*"

"*does she work at bitecoin?*"

"*idk*"

I slacked the project managers who were supposed to be managing code changes. They didn't know either. "*The file was your responsibility*" one replied. That made me angry, mostly because he was right. But I hadn't authorized the change.

"*Why did you APPROVE THE change???*" I slack-hollered at Satoshi.

No reply.

"*why???*" I tried again, less txt-gressive this time.

"*idk*"

"what do u mean u dont know?"

"i pressed button. no time to check everything."

The logs showed Smartgrrl had swapped the files at 7:48 a.m., twelve minutes after the bombing. Satoshi had approved the change immediately. At 8:00, an automated job had compiled the latest version and pushed the new rev to users.

At 8:19, Grinning Amramson discovered the password to open the file. Not the original file—the one I'd copied from Joy's email—but Smartgrrl's version that had been swapped in a few minutes earlier. After the terrorists had already killed hundreds. After it no longer mattered. The stench of onions was overwhelming.

seventeen
wingwoman

Open-source projects were always chaotic, but getting the OpenSesame software written, debugged, optimized, and ported to multiple operating systems within a day guaranteed more chaos than usual. All that had been required to join the team was a GitHub account. No programming tests, no reputation checks. If the code worked, it went in.

The project included thousands of volunteers together with Satoshi's BiteCoin employees. A few were wizards famous throughout the open-source world, but most were college students or young grunts excited to be working on something more important than adding features to corporate software.

Smartgrrl's GitHub profile was blank—no photo, no description, no X account. No phone number or email. Time zone set to EST, so she might be living on the East Coast, or just as easily working in Bangalore or Manila on U.S. hours. She'd been an active participant from the very beginning, contributing to the MacOS version. Her code was solid C++. Elegant. Easy to follow. I was impressed. Not the usual spaghetti crap.

I posted a message to her GitHub board: "Fantastic work! Thanks for helping out. What's your email—I'm sending you an Amazon gift card as thanks for your contribution." Silence. Nobody ever turned down an Amazon gift card. I took another hit of Johnnie.

Next, I examined the document she'd added to the project. I'd seen the contents on the news but had never looked at the metadata. The properties tab showed the document was last modified at 10:44 a.m. today. East Coast time. Four minutes before she'd uploaded it to the project. Created on a computer named NSB-SRVR-34. IP address 10.88.127.3. That sounded more like corporate I.T. than a terrorist in a cave in Tora Bora. The IP address wasn't traceable—a big datacenter somewhere. While searching GitHub for any other files created on the same computer, I heard the doorknob rattle.

I jumped up in panic and stuffed the Johnnie under the couch. It didn't matter. When the door swung open, Sumire took one whiff and stared straight at me, eyes set to kill. Without saying anything, she turned around and slammed the door behind her.

I buried the bottle at the bottom of the trash and took off after her. "Sumire!" I yelled from the top of the stairs as she pushed through the door to the sidewalk. She didn't even glance back. I raced down the steps to catch her. When I banged through the exit, a gust of cold slapped my face.

She was waiting for the light to change at the corner, tapping her foot impatiently. Grateful for once that she'd never cross the street when the signal flashed *don't walk*, I jumped in front of her, arms outstretched, blocking her way across the street. She turned around and started back in the other direction. I dashed around and grabbed her. "Don't touch me!" she screamed as she pushed me away.

"I'm sorry," I said, my head bowed.

She crossed her arms. "How many times, Ted?"

"Just this once. I swear."

She scoffed.

"This was the only time," I insisted. "Just a few sips." I flapped my arms and touched my nose to prove I was somewhat sober. "See?"

"You can barely stand up, Ted."

Ignoring me, she crossed the street and marched up the sidewalk. I skipped backwards beside her, imploring her to stop until I hit a crack in the concrete and landed on my butt.

"Go home," she yelled, "before you hurt yourself!"

I knew it was over between us when she didn't even offer to help me up. Always ready to lend a hand to anyone in need, this time she left me sprawled on the sidewalk and marched off alone towards her car.

I clambered to my feet and dashed the half block to the lemon wedge parked in a neat diagonal at a meter. I leaned against the car as she stomped to the door and tried to elbow me aside. I didn't budge.

"Move," she ordered.

I stood my ground.

"Go home, Ted. Go back to your bottle. Leave me alone."

"Give me a second chance."

"I gave you a second chance. And a third. I gave you so many chances I've lost count. Now I'm done with you."

"I'm not done with you, Bunny."

She sighed. "What do you want from me?"

What did I want? Love? Sex? Companionship? A soulmate to share my life? Yes to all of the above. Was I getting any of that? Not completely. Maybe she was right. Maybe it was time to cut my losses and go back to being alone. Nobody to tell me what to do, nobody to tell me what I couldn't drink. Until I met someone who shared my interests. Someone to be my wingwoman. Someone who'd celebrate kicking major butt at the latest video game with a frosty bottle of Mu. Someone who'd enjoy spending a day with me at Oracle Park watching the Giants destroy the Dodgers. Someone who loved Taco Tuesdays and celebrated Pi Day and May the Fourth every year. Someone to share living to the max instead of telling me what I couldn't do.

I stepped aside and opened the door to usher her inside. I waited for her to strap on her seatbelt before pushing the door closed. The hybrid booted up with a whine that sounded more like a pool pump than a car. The brake lights flashed as she backed away from the curb. I watched the front wheels turn, Sumire staring straight ahead through the windshield. The pretty face, the soft features that belied the intensity and intelligence inside. The rabbit ears I loved sticking out from the curtain of shiny, black hair. It felt like a rope was tied around my guts, the other end attached to her bumper. Even the tiny electric motor would rip me in half as soon as the Prius started forward.

I jumped in front of the car, counting on her to drive slowly. She slammed on the brakes. Waved at me to get out of the way. I stood in the middle of the street, arms outstretched in front of the car. A BMW pulled up behind her, honking long and loud before swerving across the double yellow lines to zoom past.

She lowered the window to order me to get out of the street. "It's dangerous!" she shouted. I didn't move. "You're being stupid, Ted." I told her I agreed. I stood in front of the car in a standoff. If she was determined to leave, all she had to do was follow the BMW across the yellow lines, or back up and drive off in the opposite direction. Or start forward in a game of chicken knowing I'd have to move. But would I? I wasn't sure. If she left, there'd be no purpose to my life, no one to miss me when I was gone. Still, being crushed under the 15" tires of a bright yellow hybrid at 3 MPH was too ridiculous a way to die. She waited in the middle of Jackson Street for me to move out of the way. Waited, even as traffic backed up behind her. Waited for me. As long as she waited, there was hope. As long as I stayed right here in the street, she could never leave me.

But how long could I stand here? How could I convince her to park the car and stay? I'd have to turn on the charm. Unfortunately, I didn't have any. My out-of-tune singing always brought a smile to her thin lips that exposed the crooked tooth in front, but if I broke into song now, it would only prove I was drunk. I stepped around to her door, holding up a hand as if that could magically prevent her from driving off, then motioned for her to roll the window down again. I was surprised when she did.

"What do you want, Ted?"

Should I tell her I loved her; tell her I needed her; tell her I couldn't live without her? Or ask her to untie the rope around my guts and set me free? I had no idea what to say. She sighed and rolled the window up. I jammed my arm through the opening before it could shut.

"Please listen to what happened today."

"Go home, Ted."

"I'm not going home until you hear everything that happened."

"You're drunk."

"I'm sad. And angry. And frustrated. I need someone to talk to."

She stared at me, still furious, but she couldn't say no. "That's all?" She sounded skeptical.

"I promise."

"Then get your arm out of my window."

I pulled my hand away, half expecting her to drive off, but she put the hybrid in reverse and returned to the parking space. I waited for her to step out of the car. She sat inside, arms folded over her chest. I waved for her to join me on the sidewalk. She motioned for me to get inside.

The car enveloped me in the scent of chamomile and vanilla, a hint of coconut shampoo. The cramped little space was like a private heaven, being wrapped inside Sumire. The fake leather seat enfolded my body in warmth, more comfortable than Satoshi's couch. I sat there, smiling at Sumire.

"Talk," she said.

So I talked. And talked. More than I'd ever talked before. Because as soon as I stopped talking, it would be time to say goodbye. I told her about waking up to find hundreds of people dead because I hadn't been smart enough to crack the file faster. I told her about the call from Jiji, his career ruined because he'd trusted me. I told her I'd been right about Naz, but that only made me sick. Or maybe I wasn't right about Naz because the file didn't match, which made no sense. It was my fault for not locking the file so it couldn't be changed, my fault the file decryption project—the most important thing I'd ever do—was nothing but the biggest waste of electricity the world had ever seen. And now I was stuck with no idea what to do next, no job, and no way anyone would hire me. I'd bought the bottle for comfort. That was a mistake. But ice cream and Cheetos only went so far. I was sorry I was a terrible boyfriend and a terrible person and she'd be better off without me. And that was all I had to say.

We both stared straight ahead at the windshield, not looking at each other. People strolled past on the sidewalk oblivious as they went about their lives. Finally, she broke the silence. "Tell me, Ted, what is it you want from me?"

"A hug?"

She undid her seatbelt and reached across the center console to wrap her arms around me. I felt the heat of her shoulders through her silky blouse. She kissed me on the cheek. I pressed the side of my face against hers.

"You reek of alcohol."

There was nothing I could say other than sorry.

We stared ahead in silence until she switched on the ignition, or whatever it's called on a hybrid. A mechanical thunk reverberated through the cabin as the door locks snapped open, signaling my time was up. She cleared her throat. "Ted?" she said. I knew what was coming. I put my hand on the latch.

"You don't know how much I need you," I said under my breath, as much to myself as to her, my voice so low I wasn't sure she heard.

"Yes, Ted," she said, sounding angry. "I do know. That's the problem. It's you who doesn't know."

"Sorry," I said.

"Sorry's not good enough."

"What is?" I asked. I didn't expect an answer.

Traffic rushed past. The Chinese hostess in front of the rock 'n' roll sushi abomination shouted, "*Irasshaimase*" to a group walking in.

"Have you ever once asked what I need?"

I thought back through the million times I did exactly what she wanted —found a restaurant with salads instead of a pizza or ramen, didn't bother her when she was busy lawyering, watched a sappy movie with her when I wanted to enjoy the stupidity of Fast & Furious, even took her to karaoke. Sober. And sang with her. Badly. Most of all, I'd stopped drinking. Except this one time. But no, I'd never asked. Because I thought I knew what she needed. Maybe I didn't.

It was too late now, but I asked anyway, "Bunny-chan, what do you need most in this world?"

It made me sad to realize the answer wasn't me. Because the one thing I needed most was her.

"Thank you, Ted," she said, as if the car were a courtroom. "I'll bet you think it's for you to stop drinking. Or stop getting arrested. Or start acting like an adult."

"No," I said, though I kind of thought it was.

She scoffed. "Then what is it, Ted? You tell me. Tell me the one thing you think I need most."

I didn't have an answer. So I hummed. Badly. She looked at me cockeyed. I half sang, half spoke the chorus to her favorite Taylor Swift song.

That didn't get me a smile. Not even an indulgent half-smile. Not even a one-tenth hint of a dimpled non-frown. It was hopeless.

"Let me tell you, Ted—you think it's all about you. And sometimes, just once in a while, it needs to be about me. What I need. Inside. And you have no idea what that is. It's not a boyfriend who doesn't drink. It's not a friend who makes me laugh. It's not a lover who makes me smile. You know what it is, Ted? It's someone I can trust. Absolutely. Who'll stand with me through anything. No matter what. Because being with someone I can't trust is so much worse than being alone. And yet, stupid me, I keep falling for untrustworthy men. A married man. I should have known better than to trust anything he had to say. And Alex. Wow. He was like a god. Tall and handsome. Princeton MBA. A real cliché. He said he loved me, said he wanted to spend his life with me. Until the day he said he loved someone else more, wanted to spend his life with her. Which would have been kind of okay if he hadn't been facetiming her the entire summer we were traveling through Europe together."

I wanted to punch the waspy BMW-driving jerk who'd broken Sumire's heart. "White dude, right?"

"Really, Ted? Is that all you think of? Let me tell you, asshole comes in all flavors. For example, you know who the worst asshole of all time is?"

"Me?" I said, readying my protest that yes, I might've had a few drinks, and yes, as hard as I tried, I'd been inconsiderate. And yes, to everything else. But that hardly made me a GOAT in asshole-land.

Sumire closed her eyes. "My father," she said. "My father who hit my mother when he was drunk, or angry, or lost a client. My father who swore he'd change. Who said he'd stop drinking. Who promised to go to anger management. Every time. Until the day he left us. Which frankly was a relief." She wiped away the tears welling in her eyes. "And you, Ted. You burned me once, too. I thought maybe you'd changed. But people don't change, do they?"

How was I supposed to answer that? An old David Bowie song from my father's collection of vinyl started playing in my head. But it felt wrong, like the record was skipping. This wasn't the time for humming. I remembered the last time she'd bared her soul after her brother's disappearance. What she'd needed then was someone to hold her and tell her she wasn't alone, that I was here to share the weight and help her carry the tune. I reached out to put my arms around her.

She pushed me away. "Don't touch me!"

It was hopeless. I ought to leave. It was the easiest thing to do. Open the latch, step out of the car, walk home, and finish the bottle. Navigating Sumire was more difficult than finding the secret treasure in the Pirate's Cove. More difficult than hacking into the FBI, without the thrill of defeating their defenses. Because winning meant losing. And losing meant losing, too. And yet, I couldn't go. She was in pain. And it was my fault. I couldn't leave her here. Even if she wasn't my girlfriend any longer, she was still my friend. The one friend I could trust, even if she couldn't trust me.

There was only one medicine that could dissolve the pain inside. A magic powder Japanese had used for half a millennium to strengthen the bonds of friendship. My mother's answer to life, the universe, and everything, and maybe Sumire, too. "Bunny-chan?" I said softly. "Would you join me for a cup of tea?"

No answer. Eyes closed. Then a hint of white teeth like the sun peeking through dark clouds. "That would be nice," she said.

We trudged up the sidewalk, side-by-side, not holding hands. When she stepped into the apartment, she took one whiff and stopped in the doorway. "Where is it?"

I felt like I was being asked to rat out a friend. "Under the sofa," I said with a sigh. It didn't matter, I told myself—I wouldn't be drinking again. Besides, Johnnie Red was the crappiest, lowest, meanest Walker brother who ever walked the earth. And anyway, the bottle was nearly empty.

While I retrieved the tea bowls from the *chado* cabinet, Sumire recovered the bottle, covered with a layer of dust. "An entire bottle?" she said, incredulous, holding it up to the jury.

There was no denying the evidence. "*Nolo contendere,*" I pleaded.

She dumped the dregs into the sink and washed out the bottle before dumping it in the blue bin. She rummaged through the rest of the refuse searching for any of Red's more decorous brothers sheltering beneath the empty Keurig boxes.

"There's nothing else," I said.

She looked as if I'd caught her hunting through my phone for texts from other women. "Where are they hidden?"

I ladled matcha powder into two bowls. "That's it. That all I've had to drink for four months."

She didn't believe me. How could I convince her? I poured hot water and whisked the tea into a thick green goop, handing Sumire a bowl. "I swear on my mother's grave. My father's, too. May they haunt me forever if I'm lying."

She looked surprised, but I think that convinced her. Even though my mother would haunt me forever anyway.

I took a sip of the tea and felt the warmth flowing down my throat. As she sipped with me, the day's disaster wasn't undone but somehow put into perspective—one day in a lifetime, one life out of billions on one planet in an infinite universe. It was humbling. But liberating. There was nothing to do but sit back, relax, and hold on for the brief roller coaster ride. As we took a second sip, I watched the anger melt away from Sumire's features—her jaw unclench, the fire raging behind her glasses dial back to a simmer. Her shoulders relaxed as she let down her guard. I put my hand on her back and massaged. A soft purr escaped from deep inside. "I'm sorry," I said. "I really am. I didn't mean to hurt you. It's just...I was feeling totally shitty and there was no one to turn to."

She put her hand on mine. "That's what I'm here for, Ted."

But she hadn't been here. "I was all alone."

"If it's an emergency, Ted, tell me. I'll find a way to get here."

"You could lose your job."

"I was top of my class at Berkeley Law. I can find another."

I leaned in to kiss her. She turned away, fanning the air with her hand. "You reek of alcohol."

I hugged her, pulling her body tight against mine, feeling the lithe muscles of an aikido 3-dan. We stared at each other saying nothing until she broke the spell by kissing me on the cheek. "I realized I never said thank you for everything you've done. I'm sorry I got you into this mess asking you to hack into Joy's email. I don't know what I expected to happen, but it wasn't this. It's my fault the police are hounding you now. And my responsibility to get you out of this mess."

Did this mean I'd been reinstated? I wasn't sure. At least we were a team again and I felt tethered once more. "Our responsibility to find out what really happened," I said.

She sipped the last drops of tea, turned the bowl around, and handed it back to me. "Naz is innocent, isn't he?" she said, more a statement than a question.

"Maybe," I admitted.

"If the file was fake, someone is framing him."

I showed her the decrypted version of the document with five pages of attack plans that mentioned N. Khan by name. Then I showed her the original version that we still couldn't open.

"Can you find the real password so we can prove the original had nothing to do with him?"

The project was over, the winners found, Satoshi and his blockchain crew returned to mining BiteCoins. There was no way to get hundreds of millions of people to rev up their CPUs again because we'd cracked the wrong file. I shook my head in shame. "Too late."

"It only took sixteen minutes for that guy to find the password for this file. Why can't we do the same thing with the real file?"

"It's a lot easier to find the password when you already know what it is."

"But why?"

"I can give you a million reasons."

"So he's Smartgrrl?"

"Maybe his wife is a lot smarter than she looks on TV."

"How did they do it?"

Swapping out the document wasn't enough. If they wanted the reward, they had to "find" the password. But our software was handing out lists of passwords to millions of computers to check. How could the old grinning guy have worked it so he'd been assigned the right one?

I pulled up the system logs and found the digital equivalent of "bingo!" when Grinning Amramson's computer declared it'd discovered the password. But digging into the details, the password, "JoyMiyazaky!", had never been assigned to any computer to check. The software had stopped running once Grinning Amramson yelled bingo and identified the password that opened the file. We were searching twelve-character passwords at the time but were only up to ones that started with uppercase letter H. It would have been a few more minutes before we got to J and that particular string of characters would have been assigned to someone. The software shouldn't have allowed Grinning Amramson to call bingo on a password he wasn't assigned. Except we'd never added a check for that. Anyone who returned the password that opened the file got the prize.

We'd been pwned. Now that I saw how they'd done it, the hack wasn't difficult—replace the real file with a fake one for which they knew the password. Then at the right time, claim they found the password. I should've realized that wasn't Joy's real password—no Japanese person would think of writing her name as Miyazaky instead of Miyazaki.

A million dollars scammed from Jiji. Not bad for a couple days of work. I'd been stupid. As a hacker myself, I should've expected every hacker in the world to be looking for ways to grab the reward.

I explained it all to Sumire. It took a while. I knew she got it when she gasped. "See? I told you!" she couldn't help telling me. "Naz didn't do it."

It was strange that Grinning Amramson and his sidekick, Smartgrrl, had gone through the effort to create a document with the precise details of the attack. It would've been faster and easier to reuse some old document. Nobody would know the difference. And if they were only after the million-dollar reward, why frame Naz? Even stranger, the metadata showed the fake file had been created two weeks ago. Long before any reward. Even before Joy had been murdered and anyone knew about a file in her email. This didn't add up.

They'd been bold. Or maybe just stupid. They went on TV. A press conference in front of the world. The hack was clear to see, the fraud simple to prove, the pair easy to throw into jail. They weren't Russians or North Koreans who'd never be extradited. We knew exactly who they were and where they lived.

"You gotta find them, Ted," she said. I was already on it.

"What do you need?" she asked.

"You," I answered without looking up from the screen.

She chuckled, not taking me seriously. "What else?"

"Coffee pods. A lot of them. And food." I hadn't eaten all day. I grabbed my hoodie and reached for my Asahi cap to head out to the Nijiya market with her.

"You get started," she said. "I'll pick up supplies. I got you into this mess. It's the least I can do to help get you out. What do you want?"

It would be a long night and my body only ran on only two kinds of fuel. "Tacos," I said, "from the truck out on 4th Street." They had the best Korean beef tacos in Japantown, even if it wasn't Taco Tuesday. "Otherwise, we can Postmates a Gianni's pizza."

She gagged. "I'll pick up a couple salads." She grabbed my hat—my remembrance cap—and pulled it down over her ears. I cracked my knuckles and got back to work. I had to find Grinning Amramson and Smartgrrl and figure out what they were up to.

pirates of the japan sea

I STARTED with the Amramson family of Laurel, Maryland. After winning the jackpot, articles about the couple popped up like mushrooms. In an interview on Patriot News, the wife again demanded that Congress pass the Joy Miyazaki Act to save the country from terrorists and criminals. Her strident tone contrasted with her second-grade students burbling that she was the funnest teacher ever. A customer of Grinning Amramson said he was the best computer guy in Maryland; anyone who needed his computer fixed should come down to his shop. The camera pulled back to frame an electronics store in a gray stone building on Main Street in Ellicott City.

Grinning Amramson was the owner of the electronics shop beneath Bulldozer and Laser-Eye's office. No way that could be a coincidence. Nor could it be a scheme to steal the million-dollar reward. The pair had traveled across the country to attend Joy's funeral before anyone other than the FBI, the local cops, and I knew of the encrypted file. Before we started the password search. Before Jiji had offered the million-dollar reward for Grinning Amramson to steal. But if they hadn't hacked our project for money, what were they after?

Sumire returned with a box of coffee and a TJ's sack filled with food. The java from the new hipster joint down the street was worse than Starbucks but at least it was hot and strong—exactly what I needed. One sip cleared away the cobwebs that Johnnie had left behind. A second sip jolted me upright. A third sip sent me into orbit. I didn't understand what Sumire had against alcohol when this coffee was more potent than pure cocaine.

Sumire pulled a plastic bowl from the bag and handed it to me. When I opened the cover, the steam fogged my glasses. The smell hit me, the most wonderful smell in the world—pork fat and boiled bones, dashi and soy sauce and mirin, with just a touch of chili—Dandy Lion ramen! And a plate of fried rice.

While I scarfed the noodles, Sumire took the reins of the computer to dig into Ellie Amramson. If her job as an elementary school teacher was a cover for something, she hid it well. In 2001, she'd moved with her husband from Arizona to Maryland, taking a teaching job in Montgomery County. There she'd been named teacher of the year in 2003, 2008, and 2014. But a database of political contributions showed her supporting right-wing, conspiracy-mongering candidates all over the country. She seemed to be a nice old lady who'd fallen into the tar pit of QAnon.

Her husband, Aaron, was more of an enigma. Grinning Amramson had no LinkedIn profile, no Facebook page, no awards from the Rotary Club. Unlike his wife, he'd made no political donations. All I could find were hints from his wife's interviews that he'd been in the military, transferring to Maryland after 9/11.

His shop didn't advertise, either. No website, no X or Insta, not even an old school BBB profile. Just the unclaimed listing on Yelp. Maybe he had all the clients he wanted, or maybe he didn't want customers. Could the shop be a front for whatever was going on upstairs? The entire building was owned by the GSA. If Grinning Amramson was an employee of whatever was happening over his head, there had to be a way to find out.

It didn't take long to find the Chinese hackers who'd broken into the Office of Personnel Management and grabbed the employment records of 22 million US government employees. The hack was in 2015, ancient history now, but that would tell me why Grinning Amramson had moved after 9/11.

Despite how moldy the data was, the hacking crew were still charging a hefty premium for access—a fifth of a Bite per record, nearly $10,000 at the current exchange rate. Unlike password databases, which had a shelf life of a few months, or credit card numbers which became useless within days, the OPM records had social security numbers and fingerprints that a basic smash and grab would never include. They even had security clearance reports covering drug use, infidelity, and sexual peccadilloes, a treasure chest of blackmail goodies available for an unlucky few. But I didn't have ten grand to spare and didn't care if Amramson got aroused by being tickled by boys in clown costumes. I pleaded with the hackers for a discount.

You want or not? they replied in Chinglish. I wanted, but I didn't have the coin.

I tried calling Jiji to get him to pay the cost of recovering his million-dollar reward. The reward that I was responsible for losing. My calls went straight to voice mail. I asked Sumire to dial his wife instead.

"Bad idea, Ted. What would happen if the public found out a congressman was buying stolen data from Chinese hackers?"

"Who's going to find out?"

Sumire threw up her hands.

"So what do you want me to do? I don't have ten thousand dollars to spare."

"I'll pay for it," she offered.

I hated the idea of taking her money again. I already owed her a million dollars in restitution for the upkeep of a retired elephant. And I owed her far more in *giri* than money could ever repay.

"You have a better idea?" she asked. She knew I didn't. She held out her phone. "Show me how to buy the crypto."

She was the best girlfriend ever, or friend, or whatever we were now. I exchanged her dollars for Bites and downloaded the stolen data.

Aaron Amramson's personnel records only went until 2012, but they were a goldmine anyway. He'd held a TS/SCI clearance, whatever that was, continuously since 1993. For seven years from 1995 to 2001, he was a Chief Warrant Officer in the U.S. Army 9th Signal Command at somewhere called Ft. Huachuca. On a map, I found a huge army base in the desolation of the Arizona desert. In Oct. 2001, less than a month after 9/11, he was reassigned to Ft. Meade, Maryland, another army base, between Baltimore and Washington, the headquarters of the NSA. Only a few miles from his new home in Laurel, Maryland. And Columbia. And Ellicott City.

Six months later, Amramson was reassigned once more, this time to an organization called the National Security Bureau. The address of this government agency was on Main Street, Ellicott City. I wasn't surprised to find it was the same address as his electronics shop. Now I knew why the

GSA owned the building. The electronics shop was a front for whatever was going on upstairs. Dr. Charles Brown, DDS, if he existed, had to be part of the organization. A dentist's office was the perfect place to pull teeth, or fingernails, from Russian spies. But what did the National Security Bureau do?

A search turned up nothing but military intelligence organizations in Taiwan and Poland. Those had to be unrelated. The one I was looking for had no website and no Wikipedia page, nothing but the ravings of stupid tinhats who confused them with the NSA. This was the NSB.

But that did remind me that Smartgrrl's fake file had been created on a computer named NSB-SRVR-34. Not a coincidence. A National Security Bureau server, properly named and numbered. I loved government I.T. Even a secret computer at a secret spy agency had to be cataloged according to the rules. Now I was sure Smartgrrl worked in the same office with Grinning Amramson and Bulldozer. And so did Laser-Eye, as well as at least one other woman I'd seen on the video. Assuming Smartgrrl was actually female. These were spies, after all, masters of misdirection.

I needed to find everyone who worked at that address or was employed by the NSB. Which was a couple of simple queries if I could access the full OPM database. I messaged the Chinese hackers and asked if they could get me that set of records.

"*1.0 Bite*," they replied. Nearly $50,000. "*You want or no?*"

Yes, I wanted, but I didn't have that kind of coin to spend on a fishing expedition. If I told Sumire, I was afraid she'd insist on paying. Her family had money, she'd casually mention, trying not to remind me that mine didn't. I asked the Chinese for a discount. "*1.0 Bite*," they repeated. "*You want or no?*"

I asked if they'd take a quarter Bite instead. "*1.0 Bite*," they answered. "*You want or no?*" They didn't seem to understand how negotiations were supposed to work.

I'd have to find another way. Could I hack into the Office of Personnel Management the same way as the Chinese and get my own, up-to-date copy of the personnel and security records of every Federal employee? Researching how the Chinese hackers had gotten in, it was a complicated hack that took months to pull off. I didn't have that kind of time. Their stolen database was sitting there, tied to an automated ordering system, a kind of dark web Shopify. Could I hack into the hackers to steal their stolen goods? It reminded me of One Piece—my favorite manga—where honest teenage pirates battled malevolent adult pirates. All I needed was a pirate hat and a sword. I found an old *kamikaze* bandana and turned it into an eye patch. Sumire laughed and told me to be serious. I reminded her Japan had been battling China since 1274, when a divine *kamikaze* wind had saved Japan from the wrath of Kublai Khan. She pulled the bandana off my head and tossed it onto the overflowing pile of laundry.

As I probed the defenses of their dark web site, something didn't look right. Everything was rickety, like the site had been cobbled together. Not by kids who knew what they were doing, but by bureaucrats. More than anything else, it reminded me of the Howard County Department of Transportation. Not what I'd expect from a slick Chinese operation that infiltrated secure U.S. government sites and stole everything that wasn't nailed down.

In fact, why were they reselling their hard-earned booty to random people like me? It didn't make sense. Unlike the Russian hackers who were free agents, in it for money and adventure and sticking it to the West, the OPM hack had been done by a group in the Chinese military equivalent to our NSA. It's not like they needed an extra Bite or two to buy the latest warship. But if it wasn't the Chinese hackers selling Grinning Amramson's military records, who were these people and where had they gotten the data?

As soon as I peeked at the source code of their site, the answer was obvious. The metadata was in Hangul—they were Korean. North Korean. Government spies, yes, but with a difference. They'd pirated the database from the Chinese military, the rightful owners of the stolen booty. Desperate for cash to build more nuclear bombs, they were selling it to any and all comers.

Japan may have been battling China since the 13th century, but it was the Koreans we were at war with. Especially the North Koreans, who had a predilection for kidnapping Japanese kids off the beach and firing ballistic missiles over Hokkaido. There were few things I'd enjoy more than stealing their stolen booty.

Fortunately, the North Korean bureaucrats were sloppy programmers. No surprise since the country ran on pneumatic tubes and 8-bit processors. Instead of using the real Shopify to automate one of the biggest sites on the dark web, they'd rolled their own rickety e-commerce platform that had to be full of bugs. Still, I was surprised how easily a basic SQL injection crashed their server and let me in. Of all people, they should've known better.

As I began the download of the giant OPM database, my computer revved up to turbo, sounding like it was getting ready to take off under the table. *Htop* listed a bunch of sus-looking processes that had started running on my machine. I should've been more careful. While I was busy hacking the North Koreans, they'd been busy hacking me. While I was downloading gigabyte after gigabyte of the personnel database, they were trolling through my hard drive and installing a keylogger.

I grabbed the bandana and threw it over the webcam in case they were watching. While my download continued, I swatted every malicious process that popped up on the computer. "Come on, come on," I yelled at the download. It didn't go any faster. New processes popped up a dozen at a time, a challenge to *pkill* them all. Fortunately, I had nothing on the machine worth stealing. I closed all the browser tabs just in case. They wormed into my BiteCoin wallet anyway. Fortunately, there was hardly any cash left. I pictured their disappointment when they realized all their efforts had gotten them less than forty dollars.

"Come on, come on," I muttered again, as I *pkill*'ed yet more processes. The download was still less than 50% complete.

"My phone is rebooting," Sumire said, holding it up to show me.

Shit. She was using my Wi-Fi network. They'd found the phone on the network and hacked in. I pulled the battery out to shut it down. But they'd gotten into my phone, too. Double shit. "Come on, come on," I yelled again. The download ticked forward slowly.

The second the download was complete, I pulled the plug out of the internet router to airgap the computer. The one thing I needed—the OPM database—I loaded onto a thumb drive. Then I wiped the hard drive clean and rebuilt the operating system from scratch. When that was done, I still felt itchy, like bugs crawling under my skin. But at least I had what I needed.

Powering up Sumire's phone again, I held my breath. Instead of Tangy bouncing across the screen, white text on a blue background popped up demanding $50,000 to unlock the contents. They'd gotten it all, hers and my phone, and everything they were connected to—our emails, our photos, our contacts, our entire life history. "*1.0 Bite,*" they said. "*You want or no?*"

I swallowed my pride and told Sumire to add it to my tab. "I'll find a way to repay you."

"You're not getting it, Ted. We're in this together. This is the least I can do to help find out what happened to Joy." She wrapped her arms around my shoulders and rested her head against my neck.

"Does this mean you forgive me?"

"Consider yourself on probation," she said. I wondered how long my sentence would last.

Sumire bought the crypto and paid the North Koreans. Once we unransomed our lives and put the pieces back together, I got busy with the OPM database.

The first name I checked was Bulldozer's. I hit the jackpot. Charles Henderson had been receiving a federal paycheck twice a month since before I was in kindergarten. The addresses made it easy to follow his career. Tours of duty in Iraq and Afghanistan, a short stint at Ft. Gordon before transferring to Ft. Huachuca. He'd spent two years baking in the Arizona desert overlapping with Grinning Amramson. Then they'd both moved to Ft. Mead on the same day in October 2001 where they were both soon reassigned to the National Security Bureau.

A query of the entire database found only twenty-nine people who'd ever received paychecks from the NSB, all at the same address in Ellicott City. The entire agency was smaller than my group at MeCan. More than half had been transferred from Ft. Mead on the same day as Bulldozer and Grinning Amramson. Most had retired long ago. A few had joined later. By 2015 when the data ended, the group was down to fourteen employees.

Going through the names one-by-one told me nothing. Like Bulldozer and Grinning Amramson, none had LinkedIn pages or X account and were impossible to find on Facebook. Most lived in homes in Laurel or Columbia with white picket fences, a few further afield in Rockville or Chevy Chase, closer to Washington. Two had moved to Dallas and Knoxville after retiring. There were only three women in the group; two were in their fifties, the other over seventy. Clearly not Laser-Eye. Which meant she'd joined the NSB sometime after 2015. I was at a dead end once more.

The database listed all the names and phone numbers. Sumire tried calling the retired women. Despite her pleasant voice and innocuous request, as soon as she mentioned the NSB, even the chatty woman in

Knoxville clammed up and would divulge nothing, not even that the NSB existed, much less what they did. When Sumire called one of the men, he hung up abruptly as soon as the letters, NSB, left her mouth. I had the feeling our calls would be reported to someone; I wished I knew who.

While I stepped into the bathroom to splash cold water on my face, Sumire began typing furiously at the computer. "What's that?" I asked when I returned, looking over her shoulder at a site I'd never seen.

"Lexis-Nexis," she said. "It's a database of court cases to research legal precedent."

I wasn't sure what kind of legal precedent would find a secret government agency disguised as a dentist in Ellicott City. I was surprised when a lawsuit for wrongful termination of a whistleblower popped up.

Clicking on the case, almost everything except the judgment itself had been redacted. Even the plaintiff's name. It looked like another dead end. Sumire turned to me. "This is the guy you have to find."

no such bureau

By correlating the few bits of unredacted information with the personnel records, we were able to narrow the list of nineteen employees down to a single person named Jared Johnson.

We had his phone number, at least the one from 2015. But I didn't see how that helped us. "He'll hang up just like everyone else."

"Not if I do it right."

"Which is?"

"I'll say I'm a lawyer preparing another case against the NSB."

With Sumire fastidious about lawyer rules, I was surprised she'd make up a story. "Isn't that fraud or something?"

"Not if it's true."

"But it's not."

"Sure it is. The NSB stole a million-dollar reward from Jiji. I'm helping him recover it."

"You don't work for Jiji."

"You do. And you're going to be my client. I need a retainer to make it legit. Give me a dollar."

There wasn't any cash remaining in my wallet. I handed her four quarters from the stash atop the dresser. "I need that back before laundry day."

She sniffed my T-shirt. "Laundry day was a week ago. Isn't there a laundromat around here that takes crypto?" She dumped the quarters into her bag while I scribbled down Jared's phone number.

We held our breath while she dialed, but no surprise, the call went straight to voicemail. "Leave a message if you're so inclined," said the scratchy voice of an older man, a heavy smoker. I didn't get the sense he was the kind of person who called back lawyers fishing for classified information. In fact, I didn't get the sense he called back anyone at all.

Sumire left a message anyway. "Hello, Mr. Johnson," she said in a chipper voice that sounded more friendly than professional. "I'm an attorney with Wilson Rosati. My client is preparing a lawsuit against an organization I believe you're familiar with—the National Security Bureau. If you have a few minutes, I'd like to chat about hiring you to assist us. Our consulting rates are $375 per hour if you're interested."

At $375 per hour, he was interested enough to call back in less than forty-five seconds. I clicked on the speakerphone. Sumire motioned for me to keep my mouth zipped.

"I want you to know, ma'am," he started, his weird accent making "want" sound like "worn". "I love my country. Despite how my country treated me."

"May I ask what happened?" she asked, sounding sympathetic.

"That's the thing, ma'am. Judge says I can't say nothing."

"We'll find a way to work around your non-disclosure, Mr. Johnson."

"Non-disclosure? Naw, those fuckers put a gag order on me. Protect national security, they say. Ha! Only thing they's protecting is themselves."

"Why's that?"

"Yeah...that's the thing I can't talk about, in'it? Fuckers are probably listening in right now."

She raised her eyebrows. "You think your phone is tapped?"

"Phone tap? You for real, lady? They don't need phone taps. They got all of it. The metadata for every call in this country, nearly every call in the world. Who called, what time, how long, GPS coordinates. All of it going into a big-ass datacenter they just built in Nevada. And if you's on one of their secret lists, they record the call itself and throw that in their database, too."

A secret datacenter. I was willing to bet that's where Smartgrrl's file came from. Before I could interrupt to ask where the datacenter was, Sumire threw me a stinkeye and motioned for me to stay quiet.

"Don't they need a warrant to obtain call information?" she asked.

"Ha!" he coughed. "National. Fucking. Security. You got that? You know what *National Security* means? It means they can do whatever the hell they want. If we're gonna continue this call, how 'bout we switch to Telegram?"

Sumire turned to me, confused. I wrote down my Telegram username and she read it off to him. A few seconds later, my phone jingled with an encrypted call.

"Now, how's about you tell me what it is you're after, ma'am?"

She cleared her throat. "My client believes he was defrauded out of a million dollars by the NSB. He wants to recover."

"That so?"

"You sound skeptical, Mr. Johnson."

"Nah, not skeptical. Just that you're not gonna get anywhere. You got witnesses, they'll be forbidden to talk. You got evidence, they'll stamp it top secret. You try bringing it to court anyways, they'll toss your ass in jail for disclosing classified info. You want my advice? Give up. You're wasting your time."

Sumire looked confused. "But you sued them."

"Not successfully. You seen my case?"

"It was all redacted."

"That's exactly it, in'it, ma'am? They redact everything 'til you don't have a case left."

Sumire's shoulders slumped. She muted the microphone. "What do I do?"

I leaned over and tapped the speaker on. "Hello, Mr. Johnson," I said, trying to sound friendly.

"Who the hell are you?"

"He's the client," Sumire said.

"You sound like one of them."

I told him I was the person who found the encrypted file in Joy Miyazaki's email. If he had any connection to the NSB, I was sure I didn't need to introduce myself any further than that.

"Oh, you's that Chinese kid? I saw you on TV. Person of interest and all that. What's this got to do with you?"

I wasn't Chinese and I wasn't a kid, but I bit my tongue and told him I led the OpenSesame project to crack the password.

A chuckle. "So that's what this is about, huh? I thought you were working with the FBI. And that short congressman that looks like Yoda. What kind of scam you running?"

I didn't appreciate the dig at Jiji. Or short people in general. Even if Jiji did kind of look like Yoda when he scrunched his brow. "No scam," I said. "I found the file in Joy's email after she was murdered. Brute forcing was the only way to open it."

"How I know that's really you?"

"Did you sign up for OpenSesame?"

"Maybe..."

"Give me your username."

He spelled out an address that was clearly a throwaway account. But that's all I needed to find him in the user list. As soon as I saw the handshake data, I whistled in appreciation. "That's some serious horsepower."

"Latest Nvidia system," he said proudly. "Ah do a little gaming."

He was using a hundred-thousand-dollar artificial intelligence server for his "little gaming." Not even available to the public yet, I wondered how he got it. And who he was working for now, if it wasn't the NSB. "You were one of the first people to sign up."

He'd joined the project only a few minutes after Smartgrrl. Despite his dispute with the government, there was no guarantee he wasn't recording every word I said to forward to Bulldozer. I'd have to be careful.

"Just trying to do my part. I guess congratulations are in order. I saw you found your password, even if you was a little late."

"That's the problem," I said. "The password we found was for a different file, not the one we needed to open."

I thought he'd be confused. But before I could explain, he started laughing. And laughing. And wouldn't stop laughing. I felt like an idiot again. I bowed my head in shame. Sumire put a hand on my shoulder. It helped a little.

When he finished laughing, he spat out, "Ha!" Then started laughing all over again. I could almost hear the tears rolling down his cheeks. When he finally caught his breath, he said, "That's about the funniest thing I ever heard."

"I'm glad you find it amusing. Please don't tell anyone. Nobody knows about it yet."

"Oh, you don't gotta worry about that. Who'm I'm gonna tell—old Aaron?"

"Aaron Amramson?"

"Yeah, the old keypuncher. Damn near smashed my TV when I saw his shit-eating grin on the news. Him and that bat-shit wife of his. Could barely keep a straight face. Knew something fishy had to be going on. Pretty sure you was running a scam. No way old Aaron found that password himself. He's the front man of the operation. Always been the front man."

"The front of what?"

"The NSB. Ain't that what your gal called about?"

"What's the NSB?"

"Look kid, if you don't know about the NSB already, there ain't much I'm at liberty to say. There's a reason it's called No Such Bureau. Far as anybody knows, it don't exist."

Sumire broke in. "Isn't that the NSA?"

"You're not listening, ma'am. The NSA is 'No Such Agency.' Least it used to be. Now everyone knows who they are. Even got their own exit off the BW Parkway. Big sign, right there on the highway says, "National Security Agency Employee Entrance." Even gotta museum open to the public. Kinda hard to be a secret agency when you can walk right into their gift shop. That's why they had to create the NSB. Nobody knows about them. Not even the President, I'd hazard to guess—plausible deniability and all that."

"Why the secrecy?"

Jared laughed. "That's the whole point. There's a lot you can do when you don't exist. When nobody's watching your budget. When you don't have congressmen making you testify to their committees. When you don't get reporters demanding documents under the Freedom of Information Act. When you don't have to answer to nobody but yourselves."

"I think I met one of your colleagues."

"That so? I wouldn't know. Been a while since they fired my ass."

"Someone named Charles Henderson?"

"Chucky! Oh yeah, he's been there from the start. The NSB is his baby. Him and old Aaron. Their idea. He's real gung-ho, ain't he? Up for anything, whatever it takes. Chucky's the first guy you'd want on your squad when they send your ass to Afghanistan. And Chucky'd be the first to volunteer."

"Know anyone named Smartgrrl? Any idea who she is?"

"Naw. But they got a whole new crop in there now. Most of them contractors anyways. It's not like Chucky can put a help wanted ad in the Bawlmurr Sun."

Contractors. They didn't get a paycheck from the government, so they wouldn't be in the OPM database I'd stolen. I'd need another way to find out who the new people were. "Was there anyone there who used the name Liz Ross?"

"Naw, not that I know of."

I DM'ed him the best shot I had of Laser-Eye. "Ever seen her?"

"Nope."

"She seems to be Chucky's girlfriend."

"Oh, yeah? Must be a fresh one."

Sumire grabbed the phone. "Why do you say that?"

"Cause anyone who's been there long woulda known to stay clear of Chucky."

Sumire threw me a stinkeye. I raised my hands in surrender. I might have dumped her once and more recently, broken my promise not to drink, but I'd never cheated on her and never would. That didn't stop her from blaming me for Bulldozer's infidelity.

I leaned into the phone. "Do you have any idea why someone at the NSB would swap out the file we found and replace it with a fake one?"

Sumire added, "And why the fake one implicated Dr. Khan in the terrorist attack?"

"Sorry, ma'am. Can't help you. What little I know, I sure can't say."

We were at a dead end. I pointed at the red button, but Sumire pulled the phone away. "Mr. Johnson?" she said in a soft voice. "There's a *little* detail I may have neglected to mention."

"Yeah?" he said, his guard up.

"The woman who was murdered—Joy Miyazaki—she was my best friend. We went to law school together."

"I'm sorry to hear that, ma'am. But I really ought to go. Please forget everything I said. I don't think I can help you. Best of luck to ya."

"My friend was murdered, Mr. Johnson. Savagely. Then evidence was planted against her boyfriend—Naz Khan. Dr. Khan. You don't know Naz, but I do. I guarantee he's no more a terrorist than you or I. He's the nicest, most gentle person you'll ever meet. An emergency room doctor. Saving lives. He volunteers at refugee camps to help displaced people. Now he's likely to face the death penalty. It's pretty clear Naz was set up by this bureau that doesn't exist. For reasons we don't understand."

He said nothing. But he didn't hang up, either.

"You know why Naz was set up, Mr. Johnson, don't you?"

"So that's what this call is really about, in'it?"

"You were a whistleblower," she said, the core of steel rebar in her voice returned. "You were fired by the NSB rather than do something you knew was wrong. And they've continued doing things you know are wrong. Like framing an innocent doctor for a murder he didn't commit. If you don't help us now, Naz's life is on your head."

Silence. We waited. And waited. He sighed. "You're one big ball of trouble, aren't you, young lady?"

I couldn't help laughing.

"I'll take that as a compliment, Mr. Johnson."

"It wasn't intended that way."

"I'll work with whatever I can get. Anything you can tell us. Any hints you can give us to point us in the right direction."

"What you gotta understand, ma'am, is we're soldiers in a war. A war on terrorism ain't nothing like a regular war. There's no battle lines. There's no here or there. And you can't stop the enemy if you're hand-cuffed by civilian laws. The NSB was created after 9/11 to fight terrorism. Anywhere in the world. It's a military organization and it operates under military rules of engagement. Even on U.S. soil. Because the terrorists are here. Some of them are even citizens. Some of them are lawyers and doctors. My job was to stop them. And even if I had some problems with how things were operating, I'm damn proud to say I did what was needed to protect our country."

"Joy was not a terrorist," Sumire insisted. "She was a fighter for human rights. Naz is not a terrorist. He's a doctor helping refugees."

"Don't be so sure, young lady. I wish I could tell you some of the things I seen."

"Impossible."

"Have it your own way. Maybe it's collateral damage. No matter how careful you try to be, sometimes civilians get in the way. That's the nature of warfare. There's nothing you can do about it without putting your mission in danger. Understand?"

"Yes, but—"

"And one more thing before you get all sanctimonious on me—your friend's father, the Yoda dude, let me tell you, he puts this country in danger every day. For years, he's made it impossible to get the intel we needed. If we can't tell a terrorist from some regular joe who stuck his head where it don't belong, I put that squarely on the congressman. And as to your human rights friend, well, lawyers sometimes get in the way protecting people who shouldn't be protected. Civilians can't understand but I'm proud of everything I did, young lady."

Sumire's eyes blazed, her jaw set. "So you killed her?"

"Me? Nah."

"But the NSB did?"

"No idea. Wouldn't put anything past them if it furthered the mission."

"What mission?"

"That's the question, in'it?"

"How do we prove it?"

"You don't."

"We have to."

"No, ma'am. You can't. They'll make sure of that. One way or another. Because they're fighting a war and you're not."

Sumire grabbed my arm. This guy was scaring us.

"And ma'am?"

"Yes?"

"I believe you owe me $375."

collateral damage

"WHY DID they have to kill Joy?" Sumire cried. "Why did they have to frame Naz?"

I wished I had an answer as she leaned her forehead against mine.

"Hold me," she whispered. I wrapped my arms around her and held her tight. We sat that way forever, the warmth of her body blanketing me as the air around us chilled.

When she finally pulled away, tears were rolling down her cheek. She grabbed a tissue to wipe her eyes and tossed it on the carpet.

"Are you okay?" I asked.

She sniffled and wiped away fresh tears. "Ted?"

"Yes, Bunny?"

"I don't understand. What did he mean by 'the mission'? What mission?"

I had no idea. "Stopping terrorists?"

"Why murder Joy? What did that have to do with their mission?"

"It sounds like they didn't like her. They really hated Jiji."

"But that doesn't make any sense. She's one lawyer at a big NGO. And he's one congressman."

"He's the chair of the House Technology Committee. He's blocked the FBI's demands for changes to privacy laws for years."

"And now he's sponsoring the Joy Miyazaki Act."

We looked at each other. "That's it!"

Sumire gasped. "Oh my god."

"The FBI finally gets what they want—the right to see all our email and texts and the rest of our personal data."

"We have to tell Jiji."

"He's already in Washington. They're voting on the bill tomorrow."

Sumire took out her phone. "We have to call him."

"They might be listening. That's what Jared said."

"On my phone?"

"Or Jiji's."

"I can call Mrs. Miyazaki."

"Not safe." Nothing felt safe anymore. "We need a secure line."

"You're being paranoid."

"That doesn't mean they're not after us."

"So what do we do?"

"To start with, shut down our phones." Phones broadcasted their GPS coordinates continuously, making it easy to track us. I powered mine down, then turned off the computer. And unplugged the router, too. Then pulled the entire power strip out of the socket, just in case. And shut the blinds. "Let's go," I said. I threw on a hoodie against the cold and donned my Asahi cap.

"Where are we going?"

"Jiji's house. We can call him from there."

"We can't just show up."

"We don't have a choice."

She followed me out the door and down the steps to the garage. Sumire stopped at the doorway. I pointed at the green pony parked against the cinder block wall.

She shook her head. "I'm driving."

We didn't have time for this argument. "We're in a hurry, Bunny." With the three-hour time difference, it was already late in Washington.

She folded her arms over her chest. "I want to arrive alive."

"I drive safe."

"When was your last drink?"

"I'm completely sober."

"When, Ted?"

It was less than two hours since Sumire had walked in on my tryst with Johnnie. Already a different lifetime. But the feel of the thick smooth glass of the rectangular bottle was still fresh on my fingers. I let the door bang shut behind me as I followed her out to the street.

🔒 🔒 🔒

"Did they really kill Joy?" she asked as we rolled down 87 towards the hills of Almaden. "This is the U.S. government. It doesn't assassinate citizens."

It was the only thing that made sense now that the weirdly shaped puzzle pieces were starting to fit into place. It explained what the NSB employees—Bulldozer and Laser-Eye—were doing in San Jose. And why they'd come looking for me after the funeral to encourage me to find the laptop they'd planted in Naz's car.

Sumire wasn't convinced. "How did they know you'd find the file in Joy's mail? You only looked because I was suspicious."

"The police would've found the file. I just got there first."

But Sumire had a point. How could they be sure someone would break in to Joy's account so quickly? I'd only been able to get into her email because she'd used the same password as her Red Cross account. Something Naz swore she'd never do. Maybe that wasn't luck after all. Maybe Bulldozer had gotten her real password using a keylogger. Or a gun pointed at her head. Then after killing her, he'd changed the password to make it easy for the police, or me, to get in. Had Laser Eye sent the email while Bulldozer killed her? Or had she pulled the trigger? Either way, I was sure the pair had done it. "They murdered Joy," I said. "Then they planted the file and framed Naz for it."

"I told you." She couldn't help reminding me. "But why?"

"Because everyone's worried about terrorists. Now the FBI can push their law giving them access to everything. It all fits. Even the timing." It was probably no coincidence that MeCan had changed their security policy only a month ago, and Google, Microsoft, and Apple had been forced to follow. "They had to do something," I said. "And fast. The FBI and NSA couldn't get into everyone's email and messages anymore. Their spying network went dark. And that was all my fault."

"You?"

"My hack into your brother's MeCan account convinced MeCan to change their privacy policy. Once MeCan couldn't access users' accounts, neither could the FBI."

"Oh, God, Ted, you're lucky they didn't kill you."

"Killing me wouldn't further their mission."

"I can't believe it," she said.

"Me, neither."

"What about the terrorist attack? Did they do that, too—kill all those people just to pass their stupid law?"

"Is that any worse than killing the daughter of a U.S. congressman?"

"Hundreds of people dead! Is that collateral damage?"

I didn't have an answer.

"We have to stop them!"

"Us? Nobody will believe *us*."

"Jiji's our only chance. We'll have to get him to call a press conference and tell the world."

Sumire was right. But we were still miles from Jiji's home. "Can you drive any faster?"

🔒 🔒 🔒

Moses of the Gate was off this evening. A different guard stood stone-faced in front of the driveway, refusing to let us through. "We have to talk to Mrs. Miyazaki," I told him.

Stoneface's eyes stared over my head, his face expressionless.

"It's an emergency," I pleaded.

He didn't care. "No visitors," he grunted without looking at me.

Sumire elbowed me aside. "Sir? Would you let Mrs. Miyazaki know that Suzie Yamashita is here. She's expecting me." She smiled at Stoneface, the full dimple treatment.

It didn't help. "No visitors," he grunted.

"We need to see her."

Stoneface didn't answer.

Sumire stormed off to her car, leaving me with Stoneface, and reached inside for her bag. When I saw her take out her phone, I raced over, screaming, "No!" to stop her from turning it on.

Mistaking the phone for a weapon, Stoneface whipped his pistol from his side and pointed it at her. "Halt!" he ordered. "Or I'll shoot."

Without thinking, I jumped in front of Sumire, my arms raised, to shield her from Stoneface.

"Cool it, Ted," she said, unconcerned. She stepped around me. "It's a *phone*," she yelled to Stoneface, raising it up to show him. "See?"

Without expression, Stoneface holstered his pistol and returned to staring straight ahead.

"It's not just a phone," I insisted, my heart pounding hard in my chest. "When it's on, they can track us. They'll know we're talking to Jiji."

Sumire rolled her eyes and called Mrs. Miyazaki anyway. "Hi, Ilene? This is Suzie Yamashita. Sorry to bother you. ... Yes, I know. ... Ted and I need to talk to you. ... We're here—yes, right outside your gate. ... It's kind of an emergency. ... Okay, thanks."

We soon heard the clomping of wooden clogs down the concrete walkway. She waved to us and told Stoneface, "Hector, can you let them in?"

"Sorry, ma'am," he answered. "I'm under orders. No visitors."

"It's just Suzie-chan and Tatsu-kun."

"Your husband said no visitors. He was very explicit about that."

"Listen, Hector. This is my house. Not my husband's. And you work for me. So if you want me to sign your check this month, you'll open the gate right now."

"Yes, ma'am. Sorry, ma'am."

Stoneface didn't look sorry, though. He looked stone-faced as he pressed a button to buzz open the gate. He continued staring forward, hand gripping his gun in its holster as we skirted past him up the driveway.

Joy's mother was wearing a long green dress with a string of pearls that glowed pink under the streetlight. For someone receiving no visitors, she was awfully dressed up. I was embarrassed to be in a raggedy MIT sweatshirt and my Asahi baseball cap.

"Sorry for interrupting you," Sumire said.

Mrs. Miyazaki waved her off. "It's fine. Just another interview. One of those horrible news shows. Maybe after this stupid bill is passed tomorrow, Jiji and I can finally have some time alone." She led us inside and asked, "So, what's this emergency?"

"We need to talk to Mr. Miyazaki," Sumire said.

"Sorry, dear, Jiji already flew back to Washington."

"We need to call him."

"You could've saved yourself a trip. I'll give you his number."

"Ted says he needs a secure line."

"Men," she grumbled but headed down to Jiji's office, returning with the old snickersphone. I dialed Jiji's number. It went straight to voicemail.

"Can you tell Jiji to turn on his secure phone?" I asked Mrs. Miyazaki. "Just that. Nothing more."

She looked annoyed but called her husband anyway. "Tatsu-kun is here," she told him. "He says he has to talk to you urgently. I'm not supposed to tell you anything more than that."

I nearly screamed. If anyone was listening, they'd know we were talking to Jiji. Urgently. On a secure phone. Our cover was blown.

"Jiji's busy now," she said. "Why don't you try him again next week."

Sumire grabbed the phone away, shocking Mrs. Miyazaki. "Jiji!" she ordered. "Call us back on the secure line. Now!" She dropped the phone back in Mrs. Miyazaki's palm. "Sorry," she said with an apologetic smile.

When the snickersphone buzzed, Sumire answered. Even without the speakerphone, I could hear Jiji shouting insults at her. I took the phone and told him he was an asshole.

"What the hell do you want?" he yelled. "You got ten seconds before I hang up." The line went quiet. I stood frozen. "Well? Time's up."

I had no idea where to begin. "Umm..." I started. And stopped. Until Sumire nudged me, and it all came spilling out. The whole story. When I was finished, Jiji muttered a string of obscenities that would have made his shipmates proud. His wife stood, hand over her mouth, eyes bugged wide in horror.

Sumire took the phone from my hand. "You have to stop the vote tomorrow," she said.

"That ship's sailed already."

"You can't let the bill pass."

"I can't stop it either. Flip flopping at the last minute—I'll get skewered from now until the day of my obituary."

"Give me that," Mrs. Miyazaki said, taking the snickersphone from Sumire. I thought she was going to hang up and shoo us away. Instead, she raised it to her mouth and in a calm, cold voice, said, "Jiji?"

"Yes, dear?" He no longer sounded like a congressman, or an old sailor, just another terrified husband.

"Here's what you're going to do, Jiji. You're going to get your staff to check out everything Tatsu and Suzie said. And you're going to do that tonight. If there's even a shred of truth in it, tomorrow morning you're going to announce your opposition to the bill."

"But honey—"

"No buts, Jiji. Find out what the hell's going on."

"That'd be the end of my career."

"So be it. There's no way I'm allowing your legacy to be a spying law named for our murdered daughter. Understand?"

"Yes, dear."

"Good. You don't have much time, my love, so get your cute ass in gear."

🔒 🔒 🔒

Once we were back in the lemon wedge, Sumire caressed my arm. "That was really brave of you," she said. "Stupid, of course," she had to add, "but incredibly brave."

I appreciated the praise but didn't know what it was for. Other than the obscenities, talking to Jiji wasn't much different than dealing with my mother. "It was Mrs. Miyazaki who got Jiji to listen to us. Without her, he would've hung up."

Sumire laughed. "You jumped in front of the guard to protect me from a bullet. That was the bravest thing anyone has ever done."

"Oh," I said. I hadn't even thought about it.

"He could've shot you."

"I was just reacting."

"My hero," she said, taking my hand to kiss my fingers. "Sometimes you can be so sweet."

A warm glow enveloped me the entire ride back to Japantown, a feeling I never wanted to end. But when she pulled to the curb in front of my apartment and I invited her upstairs, she said she had to get home to take care of Higgs. I'd have to spend the anxious hours until Jiji made his announcement alone. All I could do was sneak back to Kelly's and pick up a bullet of Johnny to get me through the night. This time, I'd be more careful—Sumire would never find out. But when she rolled down the window to kiss me goodnight, I realized that would be the worst mistake I could make.

As she pulled away, I waved my arms. "Wait!" I called.

She stopped the car and cracked the window open, smiling up at me.

"You know how you said you'd be there if I needed you?"

"Of course," she said, sounding wary.

"I'm not ready to face the apartment alone."

She nodded, surprising me. "Me neither."

"Come up with me?" I suggested. I didn't know how we'd spend the hours before the sun greeted us again, but I had some good ideas.

She had different ideas. "Want to get dinner?"

Not what I had in mind, but better than saying goodbye. I suggested ramen at The Dandy Lion. She wrinkled her nose. "I was thinking of somewhere a little nicer."

She unlocked the door and motioned for me to hop in, then navigated through downtown San Jose until she pulled to the curb between a Lamborghini and an Aston Martin in front of Elyse—the most expensive restaurant in town.

"Here?" Dinner would cost another month of student loans. "How about that new salad place?" I blanked on the name of the salad shop she'd once mentioned wanting to try. "Or tacos?" I pointed at a taco truck a block away lit up like a fiesta with a crowd camped out around it.

She laughed away my suggestion as the valet rushed over to open her door. At the entrance, the maître d' looked down his nose at my sweatshirt and made me ditch the baseball cap before he'd give us a table.

In the quiet restaurant with its heavy ambiance, we ate in silence, lost in our thoughts, unsure what to say. I didn't dare suggest a bottle of wine or even order a beer, washing down the foo foo food with plain water. We lingered over coffee and picked at a slice of chocolate cake until Sumire declared it time to go. "It's getting late. And Higgs is waiting for me."

I hated that dog more than ever.

She didn't suggest coming back to her apartment and given everything else that had happened today, this didn't seem the time to push it. I paid what little of the bill I could, and Sumire paid the rest. Soon the lemon wedge was rolling back to Japantown, Spotify set on Mozart concertos, filling the car with notes.

We were rolling up 1st Street, almost back to Japantown, when we heard sirens. Sumire pulled to the side to let a cop car roar past. Then another cop car raced up the street, blue and red lights flashing, then another and another.

Once the cops were gone and we turned onto Jackson Street, only a few blocks from home, the phone buzzed. A message on the dashboard displayed, "Incoming call from Mikey M."

"Didn't you shut your phone down?"

"Sorry," she said, rolling her eyes.

"Your phone tells them exactly where we are," I reminded her.

Before I could grab the phone from her bag, Sumire pressed a button on the steering wheel to answer the call. "Hi, Mikey," she said in a cheerful voice.

"Hey, Sue Mary—do you know where Shrimp is at? He's not answering his phone."

I was about to lay into him for calling me shrimp when Sumire answered sweetly, "I have an idea where to find him."

"If he's at home, tell him to get out quick. There's a warrant for his arrest. Bunch of patrol cars heading over to nab him."

Another siren screamed past to join the crowd of flashing lights surrounding my apartment building.

"Turn around!"

"That you, Shrimp?"

The traffic light at the next intersection was red. "Go right!"

Sumire turned on her directional signal and pulled into the left lane to wait. I tapped my hand impatiently, willing the light to change. Another two cop cars zipped around us to join the party up ahead.

"Why are you guys arresting *me*?" I yelled at Mayeda.

"Sorry, pal, no idea. Just caught the dispatch. Thought you'd want to know."

The light finally turned green. "Go, go, go!"

Sumire waited for the traffic to clear before pulling a U-turn.

As we headed away, I thanked Mayeda. I was about to red-button the call when he said, "Hey pal, you set up that date with Emi yet?" I yanked the battery out of the phone.

"Go back to my place?" Sumire suggested, the words I'd been waiting to hear forever. Now, though, it was the second place the cops would look for me. It wasn't safe to go there. I had no idea where to go but I had to get away from my own apartment as fast as a lemon wedge could take me.

softest comforter ever

I BEGGED Sumire to step on the gas, or the electric, or the lemon juice, or whatever powered the hybrid to get away as fast as possible from the red and blue lights strobing in front of my apartment. She rolled up 4th Street at exactly the speed limit.

"Back to the motel?" she asked.

The last time the cops had been hunting for me, I'd hid out at a cheap motel down by cemetery row. This time it wasn't just the cops; I was hiding from the FBI and the NSB and probably Treadstone and a dozen other secret agencies nobody had ever heard of. With all their resources, it wouldn't be difficult to track me to a motel, especially since I needed to get online. There was only one place I knew where someone could hide out and convince the world he didn't exist. I set navigation coordinates for Saratoga.

When we arrived at the deserted parking lot of Hakone Gardens, moonlight shining over the sycamores, I pointed at the sign for the employee entrance and told her to drop me off there.

Sumire parked the car and powered down the motor. I jumped out of the car and dashed towards the gate. Instead of driving off, she stepped out and beeped the locks. "Where are you going?" she called.

I didn't have time to explain. "Satoshi," I said, fumbling for the key to the employee entrance that I'd swiped from the crypto king.

"Wait up. I'm coming with you."

"It's dangerous."

"That's why I'm coming with you."

I told her no a dozen ways. She ignored all of them. She followed behind as I navigated through the darkened gift shop into the park.

Under the silver light of the moon, the Japanese garden was spooky. Overhead, away from the lights of the city, the glowing eyes of a million stars watched us scuttle up the path. The wind whistled through the bare trees, reminding me of the Japanese ghost stories my mother had read to me as a child, mostly about the spirits of abandoned women seeking revenge on men who happened by. Was the howling I heard in the distance a warning from my mother whose own troubled spirit still haunted the tea house where she'd once been wronged? As I slid open the door to the *chashitsu*, I bowed to her spirit and wished her the peace in the other world that she'd never found in this one. I urged Sumire to do the same. I doubt it helped— my mother had never liked Sumire, always calling her *that girl* with a sneer, recognizing in Sumire a rival as soon as I'd abandoned video games in my room to sit on the banks of the Guadalupe River with her.

A cold blast of wind slapped at us, a reminder of my mother's jealousy. We slipped off our shoes and stepped into the tea house anyway.

In the darkness without the light of the phone, I groped along the floor for the half-sized tatami mat, then dug my fingers into the crack to pry it up. "This way," I whispered, pointing down into the hole.

Sumire gasped. "No way."

"No choice."

She swallowed hard, held her breath, and followed me down the ladder. She stopped halfway. "It's dark."

"At least there's no snakes."

That didn't reassure her. "It's not safe."

"Take my hand," I said, reaching up to hold her.

She followed as I crawled along the narrow shaft, the damp smell of mud in my nose. Every few feet she squealed in panic. I'd never seen Sumire scared before. Though this was the first time we'd been in a three-foot wide tube in perfect darkness together.

I put my own fear aside to lead Sumire along. One hand on the dirt wall, the other holding her arm behind me, I inched forward while chattering about Satoshi, about my mother, about anything to keep Sumire calm.

Halfway there, she stopped and would go no further. "We'll be trapped!" she shrieked, her voice shaky, her breathing shallow. Sharp nails dug into my hand, zapping pain up my arm. My attempt at logic, explaining we'd be just as trapped if we didn't move forward, had no effect.

Contorting my body, I turned around to face her. I put my hands on her shoulders, hoping that would calm her. She sat frozen, unable to move. I pulled her tight and leaned in to kiss her, her breath bitter, her breathing ragged. She didn't react. I pushed against her, kissing her deeply, tongue probing for the crooked tooth in front. Her tongue met mine then ducked away. A swelling grew inside my jeans, rubbing up against her.

She shoved me away. "How can you think about *that* now?"

And...she was back. I grabbed her hand to pull her along. In a couple of minutes, we reached the door where I fumbled around to find the keyhole. When the door swung open, we climbed inside and rolled on the floor, gasping like fish in the air.

We searched the mansion for Satoshi, calling his name, until we found him at the end of the hallway, stepping out of the hot springs bath. Water dripped from his naked, hairless body, leaving a trail of droplets soaking into the cedar floor. He smiled at Sumire while his private parts hung free. Instead of averting her eyes or ducking behind me, she laughed. "Get dressed!" she ordered the billionaire.

Chided, he turned around and grabbed a washcloth to hold over his mid-section. "Who's your friend?" he asked me, his eyes scanning Sumire, the bottom of his towel rising.

"She's my girlfriend," I said. I didn't want him near her. I regretted bringing her here—not that she'd given me a choice. He'd had some sort of relationship with my mother, building this palace for her, and after my mother had thrown herself off a mountain in Kyoto, had consoled himself by becoming the lover of my boss at SüprDüpr. Sumire was making googly eyes at him in a way she never looked at me. I hated billionaires. Especially tall ones with broad shoulders and tight abs who were desperately in need of a mother. He kissed Sumire on both cheeks, a very un-Japanese habit, as he lifted her hand to his lips and introduced himself as Edgar Codd. Sumire was too busy fawning to ask about the fake name he'd appropriated from the godfather of databases.

"The cops are hunting me," I said to take his attention from Sumire.

Her hand still in his, he looked sideways at me, eyebrows raised. "Again?"

"Can we stay here tonight?" I asked. "*Onegaishimasu*," I added with a bow.

"Of course," he said, licking his lips. He pointed down the corridor. "Tatsu-kun, you can use the sofa you enjoy so well." He gazed at Sumire, staring deep into her eyes. "What do *you* like, Miss Sumire? My billions are at your disposal."

Stupid show off. He'd been catapulted into becoming the seventh richest person in the world by accident, his BiteCoin invention nothing but a grad student's thesis until the drug dealers, ransomware pirates, and anti-establishment loonies turned crypto into the newest new-new thing. Once the police were finished hunting for me, I'd have to convince him to invest a few of those billions in my coding school startup. Or get Sumire to pitch him the investment since he couldn't stop staring at her.

Sumire followed his bare butt down the hallway until he stopped in front of a closed door. "I think you'll like this room," he said. He opened the door and ushered her inside. I rushed over to stand beside her.

"Quite romantic, don't you think?" he said, leering at her as if I wasn't there.

The bedroom was larger than my entire apartment, the walls a light peach color, the four-poster bed covered with matching silk sheets and a fluffy quilt. French doors opened to a wide balcony overlooking the redwood forest, the sculpted beauty of Hakone Gardens glinting in the moonlight below. An adjacent bathroom with marble floors and gleaming fixtures was stocked with high-end beauty creams and a million shades of rouge. The closet was a mirrored maze of alcoves filled with all kinds of shoes in every shape and color glowing under soft spotlights, another room of dresses sparkling in silver, green, and crimson from inside dry cleaner's plastic. I recognized an emerald dress with spaghetti straps from a city council meeting only a few months ago.

"You're welcome to use anything here," Satoshi offered.

Sumire laughed, the spell broken. Not only were the dresses too flashy for her but they were six sizes too tall. These were the clothes of his girl-friend, Katie, hanging here, waiting for her return. I wondered if Satoshi facetimed Katie in her hideout in the Caribbean. I knew what she'd say if she found out Sumire had even touched *her* shoes.

After thanking Satoshi profusely, Sumire took my hand and led me down the hallway. Satoshi ducked into his own bedroom and emerged dressed like a grandpa. Sumire and I grinned at each other. Nobody looked like a master of the universe in blue polyester pajamas and Ugg slippers.

Sumire borrowed Satoshi's phone to ask a neighbor to take care of Higgs. Then she headed to the hot springs bath while I returned to the living room where the laptop I'd borrowed from Satoshi was still open on the table. I searched the news, trying to find out why the cops had converged on my apartment. There was nothing on the usual sites; I'd have to dig deeper. By the time I had a VPN set up through the Romanian tech hub of Cluj-Napoca, Sumire returned from the bath, her makeup stripped away to glowing red skin, wearing nothing under a plush white cotton robe. "Your turn," she said.

I pointed at the screen. "Busy."

"Take a break. The bath is glorious. You'll feel refreshed."

It was nearing midnight. I was just getting started. "Later."

"Bath," she ordered. "Now!"

There was no arguing. She marched me down the hallway and gave me a little shove into the hot springs room and closed the door behind me.

The room was a full Japanese-style onsen: a row of showers to scrub myself clean, then outside into the cool night air to descend into the scalding water of a mineral bath carved into the rock. From here at the top of the mountain, the only hint of humanity was a view of the deserted street down below. I bathed under the silvery moonlight surrounded by sycamore trees while the rest of the world faded away.

Enfolded in the water's embrace, steam rising up all around me, my muscles relaxed and my mind unclenched; I saw what I needed to do. I'd have to hack into the police department somehow to find out where the arrest order came from.

I toweled myself off, donned a cotton robe from the pile, and headed back to the computer. As I padded down the hallway, a door cracked open. Katie's bedroom. Sumire peeked through the gap. "This bed is so comfortable," she whispered from the other side of the door. "It's like lying on air."

"The sofa is even better," I told her. "It's like sleeping on clouds."

"You won't believe how snuggly this comforter is, Ted." She opened the door wider to show me the inside. "It's the softest comforter ever."

I told her about the fur blanket I'd carried to the couch. "It's like sleeping with dogs and cats."

Sumire sighed. "How can you be so smart, Ted, and yet so completely stupid?"

She reached out a hand, grabbed the collar of my robe, and pulled me into the room. Her lips locked on mine, her breath hot, her body pushed against me.

"No idea," I said when I came up for air.

I wrapped my arms around her waist. She pulled me backwards to fall together into the depths of the softest comforter ever.

twenty-two
level up

Sunlight streamed through the windows, a cloudless cerulean sky as far as the eye could see. Birds chirped a joyous morning symphony to greet the fresh new day. With Sumire curled up beside me after the most relaxing sleep under the softest comforter ever, I was optimistic for what today would bring. Somehow, it would all be okay. I stretched my arms, careful not to wake Sumire. But when I rolled over to kiss my sleeping bunny, my lips found only a Sumire-sized indent in the feather pillow. I panicked, my hands groping unfamiliar territory until I found my glasses. Once the world came into focus, I noticed the doors to the veranda ajar.

I called to Sumire outside on the balcony. She slipped back into to the room, sipping a steaming cup of tea. "Morning, sleepyhead," she said, looking at me with a contented smile, a smile I would die for. A flash of smooth thigh under the loose cotton robe as she sashayed towards me reminded me of last night's adventures completing the first levels of our own game.

"Ready to try the next level?" I asked, lifting the blanket for her to slide back into bed.

She reached out and mussed my hair. "Get up. It's time for Jiji's press conference."

The press conference that would clear up everything. The press conference that would shine a spotlight on the roaches scuttling in the corners.

The press conference that would squash my arrest warrant so we could leave Satoshi's castle to find a café in town and gorge on blueberry pancakes. After we conquered the next level in the best game ever created. I reached out to pull her back into bed.

"Later," she said, wriggling out of my grasp. She wrapped the robe tighter, cinching the belt around her waist.

Later, she'd have to go home to take care of Higgs, then head into the office. This would be our last chance to enjoy the magical comforter in the most romantic bedroom in the world.

My own robe missing in action, I crawled out of bed naked, wrapped my arms around her waist and pulled her against me, kissing her deeply.

"Mmmmm," I said, my eyes still closed. "Time to move up to the next level?"

"Time to brush your teeth." When I tried to kiss her again, she turned her head away. "Want coffee?"

"I want you."

I planted small kisses on the smooth skin of her neck and nibbled the tip of her ear sticking out through tousled hair until she squirmed away from me.

"Stop it, Ted. We don't have time—the press conference is starting."

She tossed me my robe and took my hand to drag me back to the living room where the sleeping computer awaited, dreaming of its own games. When I woke it up and navigated online, I couldn't find the press conference. Confused, I searched for the link. "Did Jiji change the time?"

"Try his website," she suggested.

On the home page of the official website of Congressman George Miyazaki, a notice stated that the scheduled press conference had been cancelled. No explanation. No new date. No statement of opposition to the bill in Congress. Sumire and I looked at each other. Had he looked into my story and decided it was nothing but paranoid delusions? Or had someone convinced him to support the bill anyway? The committee vote was in less than an hour.

"Try his Twitter feed," Sumire said, still calling it by its true name.

On X, #GeorgeMiyazaki was trending, X'ers posting how wonderful Jiji was, how he'd served his country for decades. Trolls were calling him a traitor who'd sold out our country to tech billionaires and Jews. He must've announced his opposition to the bill, I thought, until I scrolled down the page.

"Nooooo!" Sumire screamed. She grabbed my arm and buried her head in my shoulder. "Oh my god, oh my god, oh my god."

I didn't understand what was wrong until I saw the post reporting Congressman Miyazaki's car had gone over an embankment on the highway the previous evening and he'd died in the accident. Oh shit.

As Sumire and I held each other, an official message from the President popped up in the feed:

All of America grieves for the tragic loss of our friend and compatriot @CongMiyazaki. On behalf of myself and my family, we extend our thoughts and prayers to his wife @IleneMiyazaki. 1/2

The best way for America to commemorate George's sacrifice to our country as @USNavy sailor, local leader, and long-serving congressman is to honor his final wish. On behalf of @CongMiyazaki, I appeal to Congress to pass the #JoyMiyazakiAct TODAY. 2/2

🔒 🔒 🔒

Sumire sobbed on my shoulder while I struggled to dam the leak in my own eyes. Satoshi poked his head into the room and, without saying anything, retreated as soon as he saw us. On the news, a fresh alert came trumpeting from breathless reporters every minute. We stopped to listen, hoping the anchors would announce the initial reports were in error—Jiji gravely injured perhaps but hanging on in the hospital. Of course, each time our hopes were dashed—Jiji was still dead.

"This wasn't an accident," Sumire said. I had no doubt she was right.

The local news in Baltimore was reporting live from the scene of the accident beside the BW Parkway. When I checked the map, I wasn't surprised to find the spot he'd died close to Ellicott City. It hadn't been snowy or icy and there were no other vehicles involved. The police were doing blood tests. A former head of the NTSB said the cause was almost certainly drugs or alcohol, a tragedy that killed thousands of Americans every year. Another congressman was cornered into admitting Jiji was known to enjoy a good whiskey. Nobody was speculating that Jiji was murdered, not even the crazy alt-right'ers retruthing the rantings of a former President saying good riddance to a traitor who'd gotten what he deserved.

When another alert popped up on the screen, I expected more of the same. I was only half-listening as a reporter announced that the FBI had uncovered video identifying Joy's killer. "Look!" Sumire pointed. I turned up the sound.

A grainy video started playing, Joy's apartment visible through a row of bare trees behind a black iron fence. It must have been taken from the next apartment complex up the block. In the dim, pre-dawn light, an old muscle car rolled across the driveway. Low-slung and menacing, quad headlights cast their cones over the black pavement. As the car drew closer, I recognized the classic grill of a 60's Mustang. As it passed under a streetlamp, its muddy color brightened to McQueen-green, the same shade as my pony, before sliding out of the frame.

The video cut to a man in surgical scrubs hopping over the fence. He strode across the lawn and climbed the wooden staircase to the door of Joy's apartment on the second-floor landing. Was that Naz? If so, what was he doing in a pony instead of his own BMW?

Another cut to the same man stomping out of Joy's apartment holding a laptop under his arm like a football. I strained to see his face as he tromped back towards the camera, but he was too far away for a clear view. Then the video stopped. The image zoomed in to show a square face with dots of stubble, narrow eyes behind wire-frame glasses. Not Afghani. Asian. Not the doctor. It was me. My hair was wild, my glasses crooked, a crazed grin across my face. A snap someone had taken at Joy's party after I'd finished annihilating the other appendages at Battle for Centaurus.

"The FBI is asking the public's help to capture and arrest this man," the reporter announced. An 800 number flashed up on the screen. "If you have any information on his whereabouts, please call the FBI tip line or 911."

Sumire gasped. "What the—?"

"Fuck, fuck, fuck, fuck, fuck," I choked out.

"What do we do?"

I fell into the depths of the couch, struggling to breathe. They'd killed Jiji. Now they were after me. How long could I hide in Satoshi's bunker before they found me? I was lucky Sumire had insisted on driving so they couldn't track my car through the highway cameras, but it wouldn't be long before someone discovered Sumire's lemon wedge in the garden parking lot and put the pieces together.

"You have to turn yourself in," she said.

"No way."

"There's no other choice."

"They'll kill me."

"You're innocent."

"So is Naz," I said. I finally understood. I didn't want to follow in his footsteps.

"We'll get a group from the garden and go out with you together so they can't shoot you. We'll prove you're innocent."

I pulled the blanket over my head to hide from the world. I didn't have her faith in the justice system. If they didn't find a way to kill me first, they'd manufacture fake evidence. Just like they did for Naz.

"Save yourself," I told Sumire from underneath the blanket. "Get out while you can."

She ripped the blanket away. "Ted Hara! You know me better than that. I'm not going anywhere. Someone killed Joy. Someone killed Jiji. We have to find out who. So get up!"

I struggled against the shapeless cushions to pull myself upright. I was pretty sure I knew who. But that didn't matter. "Everybody thinks I did it."

"The video is fake. Find out how they made it."

"It's hopeless, Bunny. Go, get out of here."

"Come on, Ted. We can figure this out. Did they start from scratch? Is it CGI? Clay models?"

Clay models? That would be stupid. And inefficient. "They had to use a real video," I said. "Then they dubbed my car into the scene."

"Who's the guy in the scrubs?"

"Not me."

"I know it's not you! We need to figure out who it is."

"How?"

"I have no idea. That's what you do. Get up! Get angry! Figure it out. You've got the truth on your side."

"The truth isn't worth much."

She stood in front of me. "You've got me."

"Thanks," I said, though I didn't see how she could save me.

"We've got Satoshi's billions at our disposal."

"He was just showing off."

"If this was one of your games, what would you do if people were shooting at you?"

"Get a shield."

"You've got a shield," she said, spreading her arms wide. "Then what?"

"I'd pick them off."

"And if that didn't work?"

"I'd be dead."

"No, you wouldn't. You'd find a way to reprogram the game. You'd steal a Kobayashi Maru."

"Sword of Muramasa," I corrected her. "Kobayashi Maru was the test in Star Trek."

"Same thing. You'd find a way to outsmart them. Because you're smarter than they are."

She yanked me to my feet, surprising me with her strength, then pushed me towards the table and sat me in front of the computer. "Figure it out," she said. "If you won't do it for yourself, then do it for me. Because after they're done with you, you know they'll be coming for me next."

She was right. They had to be stopped. If they'd killed a congressman to silence him, they'd kill anyone. But this wasn't a video game. I had no shield. I had no weapons. I was on level one, matched against the game developers.

"I'll make coffee," Sumire said. "You get started."

rhapsody in blue

I was fortunate the FBI had posted the full video on their website instead of the highlight reel, even if the point was to hang me. It was the same grainy image, but now I could follow the blue scrubs all the way back to my car and watch the pony drive away.

As the car rolled past the speed bump, something was seriously sketch. I replayed the video over and over until I realized what was wrong—the pony didn't react to the bump. It drove over the yellow-hatched protrusion as if the asphalt was flat. The car didn't slow as it approached, the tires didn't crunch when they hit the bump, the front suspension didn't jump. My car had been edited into the scene, and not by a CGI pro.

Did they think nobody would notice? That we wouldn't bring experts into court to prove the video was fake? No, they must have figured this was good enough to get me captured. Then they'd make sure I met an unfortunate accident before anyone looked too closely. I shivered in fear—they had to be planning to kill me. Whoever *they* were. Was it just the NSB, or was the FBI in on it, too?

Was it time to make a dash for Mexico? Or join Satoshi's fugitive girlfriend on her private beach in the Bahamas? I could even deliver her favorite shoes and dresses from the closet. While I considered my dwindling options, none of them attractive, Sumire handed me a bowl of matcha. "Sorry—I couldn't find any coffee."

My hands were shaking so hard it was difficult to hold the bowl. I set it on the table and jerked the mouse around until I was able to restart the video and show her what I'd found.

"Stop!" she shouted as the back wheels of my pony passed over the speed bump. She grabbed the mouse to zero in on a frame. "Can you make it larger?"

I took a screenshot and blew it up. She zoomed into the back of the car until nothing but shaded squares filled the screen.

"Look at this," she said, pointing at a halo of blueish pixels above the teal of my car. The transition from green to blue wasn't abrupt—my car had been feathered into the scene.

We moved forward one frame, back one frame. We zoomed in and out. We backed up to where my car first crossed the yellow hatches and played it until the car zoomed away. The narrow strip of blue pixels appeared only around the speed bump. It had to be an artifact of the MPEG compression as the streetlight reflected off the metal.

"It's the killer's car, Ted! It's there. Underneath. They pasted your car on top."

I looked closer. She was right. The blue halo peeked above or below my car whenever it should have reacted to the speed bump. My car hadn't. The real car had. They'd pasted my car over the real vehicle and not very well. "You're pretty good for a lawyer."

She swatted my arm. "Lawyer? I was top of my class in anime production at Princeton."

She'd been the best manga artist in high school, decorating her Converses with caricatures of her friends, but I'd figured she'd left that behind when she'd headed off to blue-blooded Princeton. "So, Miss Anime Producer—how do we see what's underneath?"

"From this? No way—it's a processed image. We'd need the original project file that contains all the layers."

"We have to break into the computer of whoever made the video?" If that was the FBI, or the NSB, that would be daunting.

She shook her head, hair swishing side to side. "We don't need to see how they made the fake. We just have to find the original video, the one with the blue car."

She was right about only needing the original. She was wrong about that being easy. The metadata didn't offer many clues—no author name or organization, not even a cryptic code like Smartgrrl's NSB-SRVR-34. The video was created with Final Cut Pro. Creation date: yesterday. Last modi-fied: yesterday. File address: 10.88.5.1. A private IP address inside an isolated corporate network, not a public address that could be traced back to the source. The address was similar to Smartgrrl's—probably the same rack of servers. It could be anywhere. Judging by the IP subnet, it was almost certainly a datacenter. A large datacenter with at least 88 racks of computers. Or 88 rows of computers. Not a little office in Ellicott City. Even a super-secret military agency ran their I.T. the same way as the smallest startup—in the cloud where everything could be backed up and secured.

Did they use MeCan's Deep Thought? Based on what Flagpin had said about the security risk of the company's Russian immigrant CEO and twenty-five thousand foreign nationals on staff, that seemed unlikely. Microsoft or Google's cloud wouldn't be any better. Had they set up a datacenter in the subbasement of the FBI building, or next to the NSA's Puzzle Palace at Fort Meade? Maybe. But my bet was on the NSB's own datacenter Jared had mentioned, somewhere in Nevada.

Using satellite images, I searched Nevada for a datacenter. That was an impossible task. It was a big state. I was looking for a single building that didn't want to be seen. It could be anywhere, buried under the desolation of the Nevada desert or hidden in plain sight as a warehouse near Las Vegas.

Checking my stolen OPM database didn't help either. With three air force bases across the state, federal courthouses in Reno, Las Vegas, and Carson, and six national parks, there was no shortage of government employees scattered across Nevada. None of them worked for the NSB. Jared had said the datacenter was new and my database ended a decade ago. This was a dead end.

Of course, knowing where the server was physically located wouldn't help anyway. It's not like I'd be able to drive up to the facility and walk in through the gate. All I needed was a way to hack into the site, wherever it was, and copy the files off the server with the IP address 10.88.5.1. I didn't have a clue where to start.

While I was trying to think of a plan, Sumire played the video over and over in a continuous loop, stopping at the least interesting point. "Look!" she said, but there was nothing to see except Joy's apartment on the other side of an iron fence. I didn't understand what she was trying to show me until she opened MeMaps and navigated to the next apartment complex up the street from Joy's. She set the two windows side-by-side to compare. The street view from the driveway showed Joy's apartment through bare trees on the left, the same as in the security video. She rotated 180 degrees and zoomed in on the red brick building. "There it is," she said. A camera mounted over the doorway of a first-floor apartment pointed outwards, straight at Joy's building. This was no RingyDing doorbell; whoever lived there had some serious home security.

I cracked my knuckles and grabbed the laptop. "Time to get started."

"Doing what?"

"Hacking in. I'll find out who lives there and break into the security system."

"How long will that take?" Sumire asked.

"A few hours. If I get lucky."

"And if not?"

I grinned. "A few days."

"There's no time."

"There's no choice," I pointed out.

"I have to go there."

"Are you crazy?" I said. "They'll call the cops."

"I'm going myself. It's my fault you're in this mess."

"No way."

She crossed her arms. "Why not?"

"It's too dangerous."

"Ted Hara! Stop being pig-headed. I can take care of myself."

She didn't know me very well if she thought I could stop being pig-headed.

"I'll be back in an hour," she said. "With the video."

Leaving the relative safety of Satoshi's walled compound to go anywhere I could be spotted would be insane. But so was knocking on doors of the type of weird people who installed serious security around their apartment. My mother's ghost would haunt me forever if I let anything happen to Sumire. "I'm going with you."

"You have to stay here."

"I'm not letting you go alone."

"I appreciate your misguided attempt at gallantry, Ted, but that's stupid. What if someone sees you?"

There was no choice but to play the techie trump card. "You don't know what I need—metadata, file formats, all that stuff." Whatever that stuff was.

She didn't look convinced. But she didn't argue either. "You'll need a disguise."

"Maybe Satoshi has a Batman costume to go with his car."

"You can be a lawyer."

Sumire led me to the well-equipped bathroom of Satoshi's former lover where she found a set of professional shears and sat me in front of the mirror. Snip, snip, snip, she cut around my neck, each cut like a jab of the scissors into my back. "Let me try to hack into the security system first," I pleaded.

Snip, snip. "No."

"Can we try calling?"

Snip, snip, snip. "No."

"Batman would be a better disguise. Nobody messes with the Batman."

She didn't laugh. "Keep your head down." She snipped around the ears. When she was done, she patted the top of my shorn head. "See! Looks great." A different person stared back at me from the other side of the mirror, a person with short, neat hair and a sharp part on the left. A person who looked like a Princeton WASP instead of an MIT geek. Exactly what my mother would have ordered if she'd dragged me to the barber herself. But even cleaned-up, I still looked like me. Same square face, same geeky glasses, same goofy expression.

"I don't look like a lawyer."

"Don't worry," she said, mussing my cropped hair. "We're not done yet."

🔒 🔒 🔒

On the way to Joy's apartment, Sumire stopped at the shopping mall, hiding me in the back seat under a sheet while she went inside. When she returned, she was dressed in a navy power suit, toting a Bloomingdale's bag. She tossed the bag over me and told me to get dressed. While she drove, I twisted and contorted my way into the new suit, my second of the week.

After crossing the Guadalupe River, she turned into a residential neighborhood behind the Tamien train station. The street was filled with single-family Craftsman houses built before the war, more rusty pickups than Prii and Teslas in this old Greek neighborhood that the techies had yet to invade. The lemon wedge rolled past the entrance to Joy's apartment complex and made a left at the next driveway.

When we stepped out of the car, she straightened my tie and clipped the tag off the sleeve. "You'll make a fine lawyer one day," she said, patting me on the lapel.

To our right, the back of Joy's building was visible through the trees on the other side of the iron fence. We walked to the speed bump we'd seen on the video and turned to the left. In front of us, the eye of a security camera stared straight ahead at us.

Sumire steeled herself and knocked on the door. From inside, we heard a dog bark. A big, angry dog. "Anybody home?" she hollered.

The dog barked louder. And angrier. Sumire knocked again.

"Go away," came the gruff voice, an old curmudgeon.

"We need to talk to you about the murder."

"I'm done talking."

"Someone's using your video to incriminate an innocent man."

"Nobody's innocent."

"We need your help."

I tried to ignore the frenzied dog on the other side of the door awaiting the chance to lunge out and rip the limbs from our bodies. "We'll pay you," I said. A cackle of derision came from above. I thought it was the curmudgeon laughing at us, but it was only a crow gawking.

"Joy Miyazaki was my best friend," Sumire shouted. "Do you hear me?"

"Keep it down," I reminded her. I didn't want the neighbors peeking out and spotting me.

But Sumire shouted at the door: "Someone killed my friend! And he didn't come in a green Mustang, did he? You know that, don't you—you've seen the video. You know it was a blue car. We need your help to prove it. Otherwise, an innocent man will be sentenced to death. And you'll have to live with that forever."

The mention of the death penalty made me shiver. But it excited the dog. He jumped around, chain jangling, claws scratching at the door. A door that remained locked.

We waited. And waited. Was he phoning the cops? Had a neighbor seen us yet? I listened for sirens, ready to make a dash over the fence in my beautiful new pinstripe suit in a futile attempt to escape. At least I was already wearing nice clothes for my funeral.

Suddenly, the dog growled, the deadbolt snapped back, and the door jerked open. A dank, musty smell wafted out through the screen door. On the other side, an old man in a dirty undershirt stood sneering at us. He was bald on top, strands of wiry hair sticking out from the side, thick white sideburns running down to his jaw.

The Doberman bashed the flat of its head against the metal grate of the screen door, the only thing that saved me from a fate worse than being shot by the cops. Sideburns jerked the dog back by the collar. "Down, Fluffy!" he shouted.

The dog growled deep in its throat as saliva dripped from bared fangs. Sideburns stabbed a finger towards Sumire. "What the hell do you want?"

She smiled at him and answered in a pleasant voice, "We'd really like to see the original video."

"Already gave it to Homeland Security."

"This is the man the police are looking for." She grabbed my arm and pulled me in front of the door. "He drives the green Mustang. Call the police if you want. But you know he didn't do it."

Sideburns squinted at me through the mesh. My heart pounding, I tried to emulate Sumire by looking friendly, like someone who wasn't a murderer. But my awkward, forced smile probably only made me look deranged. I waited for him to slam the door in our faces and call the cops. "Go away," he said. "I'm not getting involved."

I was ready to take his advice, but Sumire didn't budge. "You are involved. And we're not going anywhere. We're staying right here until you let us in. If you think Ted really killed my friend, then go ahead and call 911 right now."

His face scrunched into the next level of sourness. "What do you want?" he snarled.

"We need a copy of the video. The original. So we can prove Ted didn't do it."

"Then you're S.O.L."

"Why?"

"Because it's gone. I already told you—Homeland Security took it."

Sumire and I glanced at each other, confused. "We just want to make a copy," I said.

"And I already told you, Homeland Security took it."

He wasn't making sense. "Took what—the whole system?"

"Not the system. The hard drive. Said it was a matter of national security. Terrorism investigation. If you want it, you'll have to get it from them."

The video was gone. Someone had the original. The only copy. "You don't have a backup?"

"You're not paying attention, kid."

"Who did you give it to?" I asked again.

"Homeland Security."

"Did he show you ID?"

"Yeah. He showed me a badge. And a gun."

I guessed that was Bulldozer. "Any chance you got his name?"

"Something weird. I don't remember. I was paying more attention to the gun."

"Was it Frank Key, by any chance?"

"Bingo," he said, pointing a finger at me like a gun.

"Big guy? Jaw shaped like a shovel?"

"Yeah, that's him."

"Was there a woman with him?" I asked. "Anyone else?"

"Nope. Just the guy. And the gun."

"When was he here?"

"The day of the commotion. Right after it hit the news. In the morning. Cops came by later that afternoon, FBI in the evening. Had to tell them the same thing—you want a copy, go talk to Homeland Security."

A dead end. Sumire thanked him anyway, as if he'd done us a huge favor. He coughed an indignant reply. The Doberman growled a final warning. Sumire kneeled in front of the screen door to look into the dog's menacing black eyes. She reached her fingers though the mesh to pet the side of its face. Instead of biting her fingers off, the dog licked them, then licked her face through the screen until Sideburns yanked it away. Sumire waved and the dog whimpered a sad goodbye.

We tromped back to the car disheartened. "What now?" I asked.

"You'll think of something," she said, but she didn't really believe it, either. Driving off, she stopped at the speed bump, rolling over it slowly, then headed down the driveway back to the street. She drove in silence, not even her favorite Mozart to fill the space, until we reached the main intersection. "Stop!" I shouted.

The car jerked to a halt despite the green light. "What is it?"

I pointed up at the metal rod protruding from the light pole. "Traffic camera."

🔒 🔒 🔒

I stayed hidden in the back seat under the sheet again while Sumire grabbed supplies at Mitsuwa, the biggest Japanese market in the Valley. On the way back to Satoshi's hideout, she made a detour to pick up Higgs from her neighbor, meeting them at a park a few blocks away in case anyone was watching her building. Setting the chihuahua in the passenger seat, Higgs poked his nose around to laugh at me cramped in the back.

After crawling through the secret passage back to Satoshi's mansion, Higgs barked as he raced up the steps to Satoshi. I cringed. If Satoshi hated dogs as much as my mother, he'd kick us out for sure.

"Higgs!" Satoshi yawped, his face brightening. Satoshi kneeled down to scratch the chihuahua behind his ears. The dog danced around in a circle on hind legs. I'd forgotten Higgs had belonged to Satoshi's girlfriend before she went on the lam.

While Satoshi played with Higgs, Sumire took the groceries into the kitchen. The sound of meat sizzling on the stove and the smell of real food drifting into the living room made my mouth water. But when lunch was ready, she set the strips of steak on the floor and handed me a microwaved bento. The chihuahua dashed over and gobbled down the entire dish while Sumire petted his side, apologizing for leaving him alone. He wagged his stumpy tail. I stabbed at the plastic box of rice and fish with disposable wooden chopsticks.

When Higgs was done eating, Sumire took him for a long, romantic walk through the woods. I sat down at the computer to try to break into the San Jose traffic cameras. It'd been easy to break into the video cameras of a small county in Maryland, but would the same thing work here in the heart of Silicon Valley? I hoped so because there was no time for anything more elaborate. Fortunately, I was sure I could count on people everywhere being stupid.

LinkedIn made it easy to find the I.T. staff of the San Jose Dept. of

Transportation. It was easy to figure out their email addresses since they all used the same bureaucratic format. I scripted a personalized email to each of them supposedly from their department head, asking them to set up an appointment at their earliest convenience to review their responsibilities and accomplishments. The link installed a trojan before redirecting to Calendly to schedule a bogus convo. It was simple and crude but ought to work. I wasn't proud. If I ever had to tell anyone how I'd gotten in, I'd make up something more elaborate. But for now, all I needed was one idiot to click on my fake link.

After blasting out the email, I leaned back and waited. And waited. And waited. Not a single click. Had bureaucrats suddenly gotten smarter? No, the tracking script showed all my emails blocked by their email gateway using AI to catch spear phishing attacks like mine. Damn. I needed a better plan, and fast.

How could I trick an I.T. troll into clicking on a link? I'd have to do it the professional way—it was time to go catfishing.

I aimed the laptop's camera on Sumire returning from her walk. "Show me your tits," I said.

She narrowed her eyes and scowled her unspoken answer. Higgs growled a warning, the brown-nosed brown noser.

"I need to get a guy to click on a link," I said.

"Find another way."

Fortunately, there was no shortage of women's body parts to choose from online. I picked a particularly bouncy pair and emailed them to an old fart with hairy ears, pretending to be a new intern.

"*Hi Bob! It's Stacy here. From downstairs. I was hoping we could discuss career opportunities at DoT,*" read the message accompanied by the topless photo. Underneath was a link to a personal website. The old fart clicked on it within seconds. It held his attention with photos of the fictional Hot Stacy in various stages of undress while it installed a trojan. "Got him!"

"Who?" Sumire asked.

The old fart emailed back a snap of his bent penis. "Him," I said, showing it to Sumire.

She gagged. "Why are men so stupid?"

With the trojan installed, I had free rein to operate Bent Penis' computer remotely. But I couldn't wait until late at night when he wasn't using the machine himself.

Hot Stacy catfished another photo to close the deal. *"Go somewhere to discuss?"* She didn't even wait for him to reply. *"Meet me in the lobby,"* she said, followed by an entire row of eggplant emojis. Subtle, Hot Stacy was not, but Bent Penis didn't seem to mind. His computer was deserted within seconds.

I figured I had fifteen minutes before Bent Penis sulked back to his desk disappointed and angry. That wasn't enough time to hack a hole in the firewall to give me ongoing access. So I went straight to the storage devices and grepped for mp4s. I found the archives of street camera videos immediately. But even narrowing it down to the day of the murder, there were hundreds to choose from. With no way to identify the one I needed, I downloaded them all. The green progress bar was filled in less than halfway when the mouse moved and clicked cancel on the download. Bent Penis was back at his desk. I filled his screen with the shot of his dick before killing the connection. That would keep him busy cleaning up the evidence of his lechery before he could notify security.

Sorting through the videos I'd been able to download before the operation was cancelled, I couldn't find the one at the main intersection closest from the scene of the murder. Fortunately, there was a video at the next major street. I moved the cursor to 6:27 a.m. and set it playing from there. Within a couple of minutes, Naz's silver beemer zipped through the intersection, heading away from Joy's apartment. A few minutes later, a metallic-blue Chevy Spark buzzed through, going in the same direction, not even stopping at the red light.

for whom the ringtone tolls

WE COULD SEE the license plate on the front bumper as Blue Sparky sped through the light, but the seven letters and numbers were too grainy to read. The first number looked like a 6, or maybe an 8—it was hard to tell. The next letter could be an I, or an L. And was that an E or an F at the end? The more I zoomed in, the less I could tell. Stepping through the video frame-by-frame to try to piece together the characters was like assembling a thousand-piece jigsaw puzzle with a billion pieces. Hopeless for a human, this was exactly what computers were good at. Machine learning was perfect for the job, but it would take me weeks to train the algos.

"Isn't there some software for image enhancement?" Sumire suggested.

"Like in Blade Runner? 'Enhance two twenty-four,'" I quoted in my best Harrison Ford imitation.

"Sure. Why not?"

"Because, Bunny, that's science fiction."

Sumire rolled her eyes. "Hey, Tangy," she called to the MeCan assistant. "What's the best software to increase photo resolution?"

The ebullient orange chatbot in a hula skirt hopped onto the bottom of the screen. "Many users agree StarBase is the number one software for photographic image enhancement."

I opened the link to find some random astronomy software. A useless suggestion from a feeble-minded tangerine developed by clueless noobs like

CoDfish. I was about to prune the fruit into oblivion when Sumire pointed at the screen. "That's it!"

It was annoying having to admit she was right, but when I checked, it was exactly what we needed—an app designed to combine time-lapse images from telescopes into a single giga-resolution photo. Best of all, it was free. As soon as I fed it the video, a composite image filled the screen; the text on the license plate was suddenly as clear as the freckles on Hot Stacy's tits.

Sumire couldn't help rubbing it in. "See!"

But all I saw was seven blue characters on a white background of a California license plate. "Now what? Hack the DMV?"

"Mikey can look it up for us."

I reminded her that last time I'd asked his help with the BMW's license plate, he'd not so politely refused, saying he'd get in trouble.

Sumire shot me a grin. "Then I'll have to ask him myself."

The last thing I wanted was for Sumire to owe Mayeda a favor. One day he'd call in his *giri* and demand another date with her. Or worse. I told her to hold off while I tried to break into the DMV's database. Given the 1990's look of their website, the backend was probably running on a mainframe.

Sumire ignored me and picked up Satoshi's phone to call Mayeda anyway. I wasn't thrilled to see she had his number memorized.

"Hey, Sue Mary!" Mayeda said, sounding far too thrilled to get her call. "Heard Shrimp's skedaddled," he added with a chuckle at my predicament.

"Thank you so much for warning us, Mikey! You're such a wonderful friend." I could almost hear him blushing over the phone. "You've done so much already that I hate to ask, but I don't know where else to turn. Is there any chance you could do me a little favor?"

"Anything for you, Sue Mary."

I made a gagging sound. Sumire threw me a stinkeye, warning me to keep quiet.

"Is there any way you could look up a license plate number?"

"Well..."

"Please, Mikey? I think we found Joy's killer."

"Really? Hmmm...I'll see what I can do."

We heard him radio the dispatcher, claiming the owner of the vehicle was engaged in a 314 and possible 647b, whatever that meant. Silence.

Then the radio crackled to life. A woman said the car was registered to Handy Car Rental at 1659 Airport Blvd. "Do you require backup?"

Serious faceplant. Of course the car was a rental; nobody would voluntarily drive a blue Chevy Spark, not even a government agent. I didn't have to look it up to know that address was the rental car center at the San Jose airport. What I needed to find out was who rented it.

Handy Car was a small operation, headquartered in Toronto. A little poking around showed shockingly lax security. They hadn't even updated their MOVEit software that a Russian ransomware gang infiltrated last summer. I couldn't believe my luck—it was as if they'd posted an invite to every hacker in the world to take whatever they wanted. *"Spasibo!"* I shouted to the clueless noobs who ran their infrastructure. Sumire cocked her head. "Russian for 'thanks,'" I said, surprising her with my foreign language skills.

The SQL injection vulnerability allowed me to install a web shell. But instead of using it to steal their sensitive data, I rewrote it to create a login with full admin privileges—grabbing the keys to their kingdom. As a thank you to their I.T. team, I deleted the fake account that was forwarding all their secrets to a server somewhere in Russia and updated their MOVEit software, leaving a thank you note in Cyrillic in the log file.

Querying their database for Blue Sparky's license plate showed the vehicle had been rented the afternoon before Joy's murder and returned a few hours after the funeral. I wasn't surprised to find the name on the rental contract was Francis S. Key. Bulldozer and Laser Eye had flown back to Baltimore as soon as I'd found Joy's laptop and Naz was arrested.

A query for customer Francis Key spat out his full list of rentals. He'd been out to San Jose multiple times in the past two years, including two weeks earlier and once the previous month. Joy's murder wasn't spur of the moment—this was a carefully planned operation. He'd also rented from Handy Car a few times at the Reno-Tahoe International Airport. In Nevada.

A scan of his driver's license showed a face thinner than I remembered, sporting a thick beard and glasses. Whether he'd used an old photo or photoshopped a new one, there was no mistaking the lantern jaw and shovel-shaped chin hidden under the facial hair—Charles Henderson, a.k.a. Frank Key. He had a Nevada driver's license with an address in Sparks, NV. Nevada.

I'd never heard of Sparks, but it looked like a large suburb east of Reno that sprawled into the high desert. A search for Frank Key's address found nothing, not even a Zillow estimate or an offer to sell me a new house. Was it a fake address? The map opened to a wide, blank space with a country road meandering through the middle of nowhere. MeView showed a barren landscape of brown hills surrounded by a chain link fence topped with barbed wire. At the front gate beside the road, two guards in camouflage stood at attention brandishing machine guns. Behind them was a wide parking lot of cracked asphalt in front of three windowless white concrete buildings. Massive metal structures that resembled Transformers toys carried high voltage wires over the bare hills to an electrical substation next to one of the buildings. I zoomed in to read the red lettering on the sign bolted to the fence: "Restricted US Government Installation. Property of the General Services Administration." The NSB's datacenter. A massive secret datacenter hiding in plain sight. The datacenter where the NSB stored a copy of every text and phone call anyone sent. The datacenter with the computers Smartgrrl had used to create the fake terrorist document. The datacenter with the servers that someone had used to cover Blue Sparky with my green pony. There had to be a copy of the original video here. To prove my innocence, all I needed to do was find a way to hack into this datacenter and recover that file.

But I had no idea how. First, I'd have to find the IP addresses of the firewalls that connected this facility to the internet. Then I'd have to find a way to slip through those firewalls designed by the greatest minds in cybersecurity for the sole purpose of keeping out hackers like me. The first I was sure I could figure out; the second would be daunting. This wouldn't be like breaking into the DMV. These were the people who hacked everyone else. They knew all the security holes. If there was a known vulnerability, they'd already patched it. Which meant I needed to find an unknown vulnerability —I needed a zero-day.

Zero-day exploits were bugs in software that nobody else knew about, so nobody had a defense against them. They were incredibly valuable. Once the security hole became known, the software was patched, users were warned, and anti-virus signatures were updated. So they had to be kept secret.

Zero-days were how the NSA had disabled uranium centrifuges in Iran and listened in on German ministers' phones. A zero-day was how the

Chinese had hacked the OPM database to grab the most sensitive personnel information in the country. A zero-day was almost certainly how the North Koreans had hacked those same Chinese hackers. The Russians, Chinese, and Israelis stockpiled zero-days for future needs. I had no doubt the North Koreans stockpiled zero-days with the same vigor they stockpiled nuclear weapons. And I was willing to bet that for sufficient remuneration, the North Koreans would sell a zero-day to me.

When Satoshi had offered Sumire to put his billions at her disposal, he'd had no idea we'd use it to pay North Koreans to help us hack the government. But he owed me for whatever had happened between him and my mother that had caused her to jump off a mountain in Kyoto, or for whatever hadn't happened between them, and for hitting on my girlfriend, too. It was time to put the riches BiteCoin made from facilitating drug deals and cybercrime to good use breaking into a secret U.S. government datacenter.

But if I was going back to the North Korean pirates, I'd have to be careful this time to prevent them from pirating me. Before I navigated to their superstore of stolen booty, I installed a secure operating system on the laptop with no apps except an empty crypto wallet. The worst they could do was break into the device where they'd find nothing but a gif of laughing monkeys I left for them on the desktop.

Then I navigated to the North Korean site and asked if they had any zero-days for sale. They responded with an official statement. *"The DPRK is a thriving, peace-loving nation. It is the imperialist U.S. that does not hesitate to taint us with slanders and disgrace. Be aware your worthless and worn-out plots and fabrications will no longer work against us."*

I ignored the bullshit and offered ten BiteCoins—nearly five hundred thousand dollars—for a zero-day that could get me through an enemy firewall of the imperialist United States government.

Instead of more propaganda, they countered, *"100 Bites."* Five million dollars. A hefty sum for a peace-loving exploit of an imperialist nation.

"20 Bites," I tried.

"100 Bites. You want or no?"

I upped my offer. *"25 Bites."*

"100 Bites. You want or no?"

They really didn't understand how negotiations were supposed to work. And I didn't have time to teach them the basics of capitalism. While leering at Sumire, Satoshi transferred the crypto to my wallet. Five million dollars without even blinking. I hated billionaires.

Checking out from the rickety North Korean e-commerce site, a file with the zero-day code was supposed to appear in my wallet. The currency disappeared, but nothing showed up in return.

"*Where's the zero-day?*" I asked. No answer. "*How do I get the exploit?*"

Finally, they sent me the file. As soon as I opened it, I knew I was fucked. The fans of the laptop spun up to full speed. The CPU pegged to 100%. Hundreds of copies of my own laughing monkeys popped up all over the screen.

I hit the power button as fast as I could to shut down the machine. The bastards had taken Satoshi's coin and hacked my computer in exchange. Instead of rebooting to the Linux desktop, the monitor was filled with the dreaded red screen of death—blocky white text on a painful red background declaring me the victim of ransomware. If I wanted the contents of my computer returned, the text explained, I'd have to pay another hundred Bites.

Fortunately, there was nothing I needed on the device, so I wiped the hard drive clean. But before I could reinstall the operating system, the lights in the living room flickered and went dark. The hiss of the air conditioner fell silent; the refrigerator in the kitchen stopped humming. Though the laptop kept running on battery, the blue circle in the middle of the browser chased its tail forever. The Wi-Fi was down, the routers disconnected. We were offline. WTF?

Sumire tensed. "What happened?"

The electricity was off. I didn't know how that was possible from hacking a laptop but had no idea how this high-tech home was wired. I hollered to Satoshi, asking if he had a backup generator. If I could get the network reconnected, I could figure out what happened and fix the damage.

But before he replied, a piercing metallic sound echoed off the hills. The feedback of a megaphone, somewhere outside.

"Theodore Hara!" called the amplified voice. "This is the FBI. Come out with your hands up."

twenty-five
my mother is a
psycho star

Sumire and I rushed to the hot springs room which had the only view of the street. Down below was a scene from my worst nightmare—the road barricaded by a jumble of cop cars, the entire neighborhood flashing like Christmas with blue and red lights. Using a pair of bird-watching binoculars Satoshi handed me, I could make out the insignias on the side of the vehicles: Santa Clara County Sheriff's Dept., San Jose PD, FBI, and others I didn't recognize.

Shielding behind a police car, Flagpin—the grand poobah of the local FBI office—stood with megaphone in hand, facing the ten-foot-high wall that ringed Satoshi's property. A big, black military vehicle with a battering ram for a grill maneuvered through the chaos. Behind it, a SWAT team in riot gear stood in tight formation, machine guns at the ready. What really scared me, though, were the two fire engines and an ambulance at the bottom of the hill. The cops were prepared to shoot me out or burn Satoshi's place down. Around the bend, satellite trucks readied to broadcast the scene of my capture or killing live on-air.

I grabbed Sumire by the hand and retreated to the living room. Standing in front of the floor-to-ceiling windows, I surveyed the woodlands on the other side of the property. Away from the swarm of cops, birds chirped, squirrels chased each other, sunlight streamed through the bare branches of oak trees and landed on the brown leaves that carpeted the rocky ground. The remainder of the county park that hadn't been carved out and sold to Satoshi was deserted. I could dash over a trail escape through the other side of the forest. Maybe one of the marijuana farmers in the hills would give me a lift to Santa Cruz so long as I didn't look like a cop. Or a lawyer.

"Don't even think it, Ted," Sumire said, reading my mind from behind. "You have to turn yourself in."

As I turned to face her, a flash of light caught my eye. The window shattered with a crash. Sumire screamed. I hurdled the couch and knocked her to the floor, covering her with my body. Another shot rang out and another window shattered. I pushed the wooden dining table onto its side to shield behind it. More bullets whizzed overhead. An antique Chinese vase on the wall exploded into a thousand shards.

Satoshi walked into the room cradling Higgs in his arms. "What's going—"

"Get down!" I shouted. Another bullet screamed past his head. The dog jumped to the floor and ran away to hide.

"We have to give ourselves up," Sumire said. She rolled away from me and stood up with raised hands.

I grabbed her by the waist and pulled her back to the floor. "They'll kill us."

"The police won't," she said. "Not if you give yourself up. Not with everyone watching."

"So they can send me to the electric chair."

"We'll win in court."

"Not without evidence."

"We'll subpoena it."

"From an NSB datacenter? They'll delete it. Or call it national security."

"There's no choice, Ted." She stood again.

It was hard to think with bullets flying overhead and glass crashing all around. I knew Sumire was right—I had no choice—but she was wrong about what choice I didn't have. I had to get the video, the original one showing the murderer in a blue Chevy Spark. Without that, one way or another, I was dead. I'd be okay if it protected Sumire, but she knew too much; after they were done with me, they'd come after her next. The only thing that could save us both was that video. And I knew where to get a copy: on a secure server behind a secure firewall inside a secure building.

I needed to hack into the NSB datacenter. But that was impossible with the power out, the routers down, a SWAT team on one side of us and a sniper on the other. While I tried to figure out what to do, Sumire screaming into my ear that I had to give myself up, Satoshi yelling from the hallway to call 911, Higgs next to him barking at full volume, windows continued exploding. Suddenly, a shrill siren pierced the air—Flagpin's bullhorn.

"Theodore Hara!" he called, my name bouncing off the mountains for miles around. "You have exactly one minute to come out or we're coming in."

And now I was out of time.

"How do we get out of here?" Sumire shouted to Satoshi.

"Use the tunnel."

"You must have a door. Where's the driveway?"

"All gone," he said. "Poof. Satoshi doesn't exist."

He'd truly made himself invisible, blocking off every entrance to his compound except the underground tunnel to the garden.

I heard the crunch of steel against concrete, felt the floor of the building shake under us. The police hadn't found an entrance either. They were preparing to batter the wall down.

"Thirty seconds, Hara," Flagpin announced.

"I'm making a run for it," I told Sumire. "As soon as I'm gone, give yourself up."

"They'll shoot you, Ted."

"Better that than the electric chair."

"You can't hide from a manhunt."

"I only need a few hours."

"For what?"

"To get to Sparks, Nevada."

I'd have to go to the site and find a way in. I had no idea how. But I'd have plenty of time to figure out a plan during the long drive there.

Satoshi slid a phone across the wood floor, coming to rest at my feet. "My wallet," he said, pointing at the phone. "Hanae was psycho star."

My mother—Hanae—the love of his life. Even he knew she was psycho, something I wished he'd warned about before it was too late. "Yeah, my mother was batshit crazy," I yelled back, not hiding the bitterness in my voice.

"You try it!"

"Try what?"

"Password."

"What password?"

"BiteCoin wallet."

I finally understood. I opened the BiteCoin app on the phone and entered the password: "Hanae was psycho star." The phone beeped an error. Two tries remaining before the app locked me out. I tried again without spaces. It beeped another error and warned me I had one try left. "Doesn't work!" I hollered back.

He spelled it out: "HanaeWaSaikou*"—Japanese for "Hanae is the best". It was Satoshi who was psycho. I didn't get what he'd seen in my crazy mother. Or why he hadn't changed the password to her crypto wallet after she'd thrown herself off the mountain.

"Not a very good password," I told him.

"Test account. Your mother was helping me check BiteCoin."

I typed in the password carefully, spelling out each character. This time it unlocked. I looked at the balance and gasped.

"What is it?" Sumire asked.

I read the digits again, checked the decimal point, the commas, the unit of currency. There were exactly twenty thousand Bites in the account. "It's nearly a billion dollars." It was Sumire's turn to gasp.

"Is it enough?" Satoshi asked.

"Yeah, that's plenty for gas," I said. "But I need a car. Something fast. Can I take the Ferrari? Or the Batmobile? How do I get out?" There had to be an exit to drive the Batmobile through a secret bat cave onto the mountain road.

"Driveway gone," Satoshi said. "Poof." Then he disappeared down the hallway.

The bullhorn announced, "Time's up, Hara!"

"We'll take my car," Sumire said. "The police won't be looking for us in the garden."

"We? You're staying here."

"I'm going with you."

"It's dangerous."

"That's why I'm going with you."

"There's no reason for both of us to get killed. Hold them off while I get away, then turn yourself in."

"Ted," she said. "I'm coming and that's final."

I continued explaining why it wasn't safe, why I needed to go alone. She continued ignoring me. "Teddybear," she said. "I appreciate your concern. But I can take care of myself. Better than you. So shut up already and let's get the hell out of here."

There was no arguing with Sumire. There never was.

Satoshi returned to toss me a TJ's bag from the safety of the hallway. Inside was a Stanford cap, a blonde wig, and a fake beard. "My disguise," he said. "Nobody recognize me, even though I'm the most famous person in the world. No problem for you."

As an MIT grad, the only thing worse than getting caught in Harvard crimson was the humiliation of Stanford cardinal. It was a proven scientific fact that if I put on a Stanford hat, my head would spontaneously explode. I dropped it back in the bag. I didn't see how the wig and fake beard would do anything but make me look sketch, but I donned them anyway.

Sumire laughed. "Cute!"

Flagpin announced through the bullhorn that they were coming in now, and they didn't waste any time. The armored truck began battering the wall down, one violent crunch after another. It was now or never. I powered down the phone so they couldn't track it.

"Come, Higgs!" Sumire called. The dog padded over, wagging its tail, oblivious to the danger.

"You can't take the dog," I said. Higgs growled at me.

"I can't leave him here."

Nobody ever fled from the cops *and* the FBI toting a chihuahua.

"Let's go, Ted!"

I hollered to Satoshi, "Can you hold them off while we escape?"

"I try."

I shielded Sumire with my body as another shot whizzed past. We crawled across the floor until we reached the steps and dashed down to the basement. Three more shots rang out, followed by a scream. Sumire started back up the stairs. "There's nothing we can do for him," I said. She wanted to try anyway, but we had to bounce. I held her hand and pulled her down into the narrow, pitch-black tunnel.

billion bite banknote

"SLOW DOWN!" Sumire screamed as I wove the lemon wedge through dense traffic on 880. From her lap, the chihuahua yapped his order to do what Sumire commanded.

"I'm only going seventy-five," I protested even as I pressed my foot to the floor to get around a semi. This was my first time driving her car, or any hybrid, and I was surprised how zippy it was for such a silly-looking vehicle.

"You're going faster than the other cars."

"That's the point."

"The police will spot us."

It would be hard to be more inconspicuous on 880 in a yellow Prius unless we were driving a black Prius or a white Tesla instead. The police were too busy watching the Maseratis and Ferraris race past at over a hundred to take a second glance at us.

"Stay in the middle lane."

This was worse than working for a boss who didn't know how to program. I regretted grabbing Sumire's keys and jumping into the driver's seat. "We need to get far away before the cops realize we're gone."

"We need to get to wherever we're going safely."

"My driving is completely safe."

"Please, Ted?"

I grumbled but eased off the pedal and merged behind a white

Mercedes going the speed limit. She caressed my arm in thanks. "Are you okay?" she asked.

"Never better," I lied. "You?"

"Scared out of my mind."

I tightened my hand around hers. "It'll be okay," I said, but my attempt to sound reassuring failed miserably.

"How will it be okay? They're trying to kill us, Ted! They shot Satoshi. They killed Joy. Just to get a law passed. Our own government. That's not how it's supposed to work."

"Guess the crazy QAnon'ers were right about the deep state thing all along."

"QAnon?" Sumire scoffed. "There's no QAnon. No deep state. There's the NSB."

I didn't see the difference.

"The difference? One's a mythical conspiracy made up by people who watch too much TV, the other's a murderer with a misplaced idea of patriotism."

"Don't forget Laser-Eye. She's in on it, too."

"That's only two people."

"And Grinning Amramson, the guy who hijacked the million dollars."

"Okay, three."

An operation like this was not the work of three people. At a minimum, the dozen or so NSB employees in Ellicott City had to be involved. And I was sure the FBI, at least part of it, was in on the scheme, too, since this operation seemed to be for their benefit.

"Admit it, Ted. There's no huge conspiracy. Just a handful of bad people."

"Sure, Bunny," I answered. There was no point in arguing.

"Say it like you mean it."

"Why does it matter?"

"Because the man I love has to understand reality. Not weird conspiracies like QAnon or Area 52."

Love? The word hit me like a hammer to my chest. Was she saying she loved me? After she nearly dumped me a day ago? I had no idea how to reply. "Uh, Bunny?"

"Yes, Teddybear?"

"It's Area 51."

"What is?"

"Where the government keeps the aliens. Not Area 52."

She rolled her eyes. "You don't actually believe that, do you?"

"No. But wouldn't it be great if it were true?"

"There's no government conspiracy to hide aliens, either." She was so serious about the aliens I couldn't help laughing.

"What?" she said, poking me in annoyance.

"I love you, too, Bunny."

"My name's Sumire, Teddybear."

"I love you, Sumire."

She rested her head against me. "I love you, too, Ted. I always have. Even if you do believe in aliens and Area 52." I caught her nervous smile in the rear-view mirror. When I turned to kiss her, she screamed, "Look out!"

I swerved around the car in front that had hit the brakes for no reason.

"Keep your eyes on the road!" The yes-dog yapped his agreement. "I don't want to escape from a sniper only to die in a stupid car accident."

I said no more and drove like a robot, eyes straight ahead, one hand on the wheel, the other holding Sumire's hand, her love a warm glow surrounding me even as I was scared shitless.

The highway snaked through industrial Fremont and past the giant Tesla factory that used to be Toyota. As we descended the hill into Unpleasanton, Sumire scanned through the stations on the radio, searching for a traffic report. Now that we were out of the Valley, though, the road was mostly empty. I suggested Spotifying some driving music instead. She shushed me and pointed at the clock. When it rolled over to 10:00 a.m., the radio beeped, and the hourly news began.

"In another shocking development in the murder of Joy Miyazaki," the announcer started, "police outside of San Francisco are on an intensive manhunt for a person identified as Theodore Hara. He's suspected of murdering Miyazaki out of jealousy after learning she was getting married. Hara is currently at large and believed to be armed and dangerous. Police throughout the Bay Area are on the lookout for a late-model yellow Prius."

I slammed my hand against the steering wheel. "Shit!"

"Calm down," she yelled. "And don't break my car."

Calm? How could I stay calm? I glanced in the mirrors, expecting to see a line of cops behind me, helicopters overhead. But out here near Concord, there was nothing but ugly minivans and old Hondas patched together with duct tape. The green highway sign said 2 ¾ miles until the toll plaza before the bridge. There'd be cameras scanning license plates and cops in their cars sipping coffee, ready to chase after us. I swerved across all four lanes to get off at the next exit.

"Where are you going?"

"No idea."

I fought back the panic as I drove around downtown Concord while trying to think of a plan. Every sharp noise sounded like a helicopter flying towards us; every flash of sunlight looked like a police car's spotlight. I needed to get to Nevada, and I needed to get there alive. Without a phone, without a map, I had no idea how far we had to go. All I knew was we wouldn't get there in a yellow Prius.

If this was a movie, I'd steal a car. In real life, I could hack a website within minutes and even reprogram a video game. But a simple car lock stumped me. I had no idea how to hot wire an ignition. And a rental car was out of the question—if my credit card didn't set off alarms, my driver's license would. There was a chance they weren't tracking Sumire, but if they were looking for a yellow Prius registered in her name, the odds were not in our favor.

Then I saw it, across the street, a beat-up taxi pulling up at the lobby of a Motel 6. I swerved in front of an onrushing car, ignoring Sumire's screams, and parked in the lot behind the motel. Hand in hand, we dashed for the taxi, Higgs chasing after us on his little legs.

At the entrance to the hotel, a businessman with a large coffee in one hand struggled to pull his oversized suitcase through the door. I jumped into his taxi. "Hurry," I yelled to Sumire. She picked up Higgs and slid into the back seat beside me.

"Let's go!" I told the driver.

"Where to?"

"Just drive," I said.

"Gotta know your destination."

"Sparks," I told him.

"Where's that?"

"Near Reno."

"Reno?" he coughed, incredulous. "Like Tahoe, Reno?"

"Yeah, there. Let's go."

He laughed. "That's a long ways away."

"And we're in a hurry."

"How you gonna pay?"

"How much is it?"

He looked me over in the rear-view mirror. "More than you got."

I had a billion dollars in BiteCoin on the phone in my pocket. But he'd never believe me. And even if he did, I had no way to turn that into dollars now. The only thing I could buy with BiteCoin was other cryptocurrencies. Or drugs. Or computer hacks.

"Five thousand dollars," I offered. As soon as we returned, I could set up a BiteCoin wallet on his phone and transfer the money to him. If we were still alive. "Five thousand dollars round trip. Plus gas and tolls."

The businessman rolled his suitcase towards us and rapped on the cab's window. "That's my taxi."

"Let's go!" I told the driver.

"Let me see the money."

"I'll pay you when we get back."

He laughed. "Seems I got another fare waiting."

"I'll transfer the money to you right now." I reached two fingers through the little window in the bullet-proof plexiglass and told him to hand me his phone.

"Get out of my cab," he said. The lock popped up with a sharp snap and the businessman ripped the door open, spilling coffee over his white buttondown. We slunk away to the shouts of the businessman swearing at us as the taxi zoomed away, spewing black exhaust in our faces.

"Now what?" Sumire asked. I didn't know. A billion dollars in Bite-Coin and no way to spend it. Then I saw the Tesla pulling into the parking lot and had an idea. I dashed into the motel and asked the desk clerk for the address of the nearest Tesla showroom. Fortunately, there was one nearby in Walnut Creek, on this side of the toll bridge. But we couldn't risk getting back into the Prius the police were searching for.

Fortunately, Sumire had close to $200 in real cash in her purse. We had the guy at the front desk order another taxi. When it pulled up, it stank of cigarettes. Sumire hesitated before getting in, but we couldn't wait for another. Despite the chill, she kept the windows open the entire ride to the outdoor mall. When we arrived, Sumire took Higgs for a walk while I hid behind a dumpster to don Satoshi's blond wig and beard, even putting on his Stanford cap without my head exploding. Sumire barely recognized me, but Higgs rushed over, wagging his tail, mistaking me for Satoshi. Leaning over to pet him, he sniffed in confusion, then snarled and bit my hand. Sumire laughed and picked the mini-beast up in her arms.

At the entrance to the Tesla showroom, we were greeted by a pimply-faced boy holding a tablet as if it held the ten commandments of Tesla. I thought he'd be thrilled when I declared ourselves ready to buy a vehicle to take home.

"I'll be happy to assist you with your purchasing decision today," he said. "Do you know which model you'd like?"

"Black," I answered. I didn't care whether it was a sedan or SUV, so long as it was inconspicuous.

He asked me if I wanted the Model 3, or the X, or the Y, or the S. Or the cool as shit Cybertruck with dual-motor AWD.

"My car died," I told him. "I need a new one. With long range." Sparks was at least two hundred fifty miles away and we didn't have time to stop for recharging.

"You really ought to wait for a Cybertruck," he said, his pimples glowing red with excitement. "It's the most absolutely incredibly awesome thing you've ever seen. Here, let me show you."

I ignored the photos TruckBoi shoved in my face. "What can I get *now*?"

He frowned at my lack of fervor for the pickup and reluctantly poked at his tablet. "With our recent price incentives, we've sold out our inventory. Our next availability is a Model 3 in midnight silver scheduled for delivery tomorrow. We also have a Model X in pearl white coming in later this week. It's got a thousand horsepower—"

I couldn't wait until tomorrow. "What about that one?" I pointed at the sleek gray SUV right in front of us. "Is that one long range?" A pair of kids were jumping around on the back seat while their parents made sour faces reading the price tag.

"That's a showroom sample, sir. It's not for sale."

"Does it run?"

"Yes, but—"

"How much?"

"It's not for sale."

"Call Elon," I said. "Tell him it's Satoshi. I'm paying in BiteCoin. I want this one, right now."

"Satoshi?"

I waved him over to the corner and whispered, "I'm Satoshi Nakamoto. You know who that is?"

His eyes bugged wide. "You're not really Satoshi, are you?"

I pulled down the beard. "I'm in disguise." I took off the Stanford cap and lifted the wig up off my head. Of course, Satoshi was mostly bald. But even if I shaved my head, I'd look nothing like the tall and angular king of crypto. Fortunately, few people knew what he looked like, or knew he actually existed.

But TruckBoi was skeptical. I gestured wildly and spoke random Japanese tea ceremony phrases trying to sound angry, throwing Elon and BiteCoin into every sentence to make him think it meant something.

Sumire watched with a disapproving glower. When she stepped over to join us, I expected her to blow my cover. Instead, she pointed at me and shouted like a star-struck cryptogirl, "Satoshi Nakamoto! You're Satoshi, aren't you!"

Everyone turned to stare at us. Sumire gushed, "Oh, Mr. Nakamoto, I'm such a huge fan. You changed the world."

Sumire was a fantastic manga artist, and I had no doubt she was a brilliant lawyer, but she wasn't much of an actor. I expected everyone to laugh at her performance, but all around us people were whispering, "Is that really Satoshi?"

She handed me a sharpie and offered up a bare arm. "Can I get your autograph, Mr. Nakamoto? Pleeeeease?"

What would the real Satoshi do? The Satoshi who lusted after my girlfriend. I avoided Sumire's eyes as I unbuttoned the top of her blouse and signed my name in kanji above her bra, writing the only kanji I remembered, my own name—Hara Tatsu—not Satoshi Nakamoto, one character above each breast. Fortunately, nobody noticed her kicking my shin, or the obvious giveaway even to people who couldn't read Japanese that my name consisted of two characters and Satoshi Nakamoto was three.

A crowd gathered, men shoving Sumire aside to snap selfies beside me, women ripping open shirts to bare breasts they begged me to bless with my magic kanji.

TruckBoi went off to huddle with his manager, a young woman with long black hair, dressed in a tight mini-skirt and high heels. As the two of them discussed my situation, a crowd streamed into the showroom pointing and gawping at me. The manager made a phone call, then hung up and strode over. She stood so close I could see the drops of perspiration dotting her powdered nose.

"Mr. Nakamoto?" she asked, batting starstruck eyes. The scent of lilies wafted off her skin. "I'm Jenny. Can you please come with me?"

Jenny led me into a storage room in the back and closed the door behind her. The thin line of light seeping under the door did little to illuminate the darkness. Her heavy perfume filled the small space, making my head swim. Her arm brushed mine, sending a tingle up my spine. I was starting to enjoy my new life as a billionaire, but before I broke it to her that I had a girlfriend, she switched the lights on. The bare bulb seared my eyes. Through my squinting and blinking, I saw glossy, red lips smiling at me. "You have the BiteCoin with you?" she asked as if this were some kind of drug deal.

Was she expecting me to open a bag filled with gold coins stamped, "In Satoshi We Trust?" I held up Satoshi's darkened phone. "It's in my digital wallet."

"I see," she said, though she clearly didn't. "I've been authorized by corporate to allow you to purchase the showroom vehicle you requested."

"Thank you," I said, relieved we could get the car right away and head off to Nevada. "What do you need?"

"Just this." She grabbed the back of my neck, pulling me in to kiss her. Her lips tasted of strawberries; the tip of her tongue tickled mine. Her waist pushed against me as she wrapped a leg around me, short skirt rising high up bare thigh. I closed my eyes and did the hardest thing I've ever done—I put my hands on her shoulders and gently pushed her away, all the while praying to Buddha that when I died, I'd be reincarnated as a billionaire.

She smiled, then leaned in and kissed me once more, hard on the mouth, before straightening her skirt. I wiped at my face attempting to remove the residue of her lipstick, but my head was still dizzy. Stepping out of the storeroom, I tried to look professional, but the swelling in my jeans made me walk like a crab. With one glance, Sumire knew everything, throwing me the darkest stinkeye ever. Higgs growled and bolted over to bite my ankle.

Jenny led me to the front counter. While I installed the BiteCoin wallet on TruckBoi's tablet, Jenny stood inches behind me. With her hand brushing my butt and her breath hot on my neck, it took me three tries and all my concentration to enter the right password. After transferring two Bites—nearly $100,000—from Satoshi's account, adding a Tesla to the Batmobile in Satoshi's vehicle collection, Jenny pinched my butt.

"Keep the change," I said and scurried around to the other side of the car.

Jenny scribbled her name and number on the back of a Tesla brochure and handed it to me. "If you ever have any problems with your vehicle, Mr. Nakamoto, you can call me personally. Anytime." She blew me a kiss.

"Let's go," Sumire said, yanking my arm, her jaw set in anger.

"Mr. Nakamoto?" TruckBoi rushed over as I opened the door, raring to get out of the showroom. He shoved the tablet at me. "I just need you to fill out the vehicle registration."

Crap. I didn't have Satoshi's driver's license, or any other evidence I was him. I called over to Jenny. "I'm in a bit of a hurry—the blockchain never sleeps," I said. "Can you take care of the paperwork for me?"

Jenny's face lit up; Sumire's went dark. She shoved me into the vehicle. A crowd surrounded the car, dozens of people snapping selfies. After TruckBoi opened the front wall of the showroom, I honked the horn and started to roll forward.

"Mr. Satoshi! Mr. Satoshi!" Jenny called before we could get out, running after us in her high heels, waving a sheaf of papers over her head. "I registered the car for you in my name," she said, pulling open the door. "Now you have my address with you all the time." She leaned over to plant a wet kiss on my forehead before handing me the registration. "Come by my place to pick up the permanent plates. I'll be waiting." She licked her lips as she smoothed the tight skirt over her hips.

"Let's go," Sumire said, eyes blazing. I was anxious to get out of here, too. But we had to wait while TruckBoi affixed the temporary license plates to the front and rear bumpers. Sumire dug an alcohol swab from her purse and tried to wipe my kanji off her chest. No matter how hard she scrubbed, the permanent ink wouldn't come off. I chuckled. It gave me a thrill to see my name stamped on a hidden part of her, making it mine.

"You think that's funny, buster?" While Jenny made googly eyes at me through the window, Sumire pulled out the magic marker and drew some-thing on the spot Jenny had kissed. "There!"

I glanced up at the rearview mirror. Between the top of my glasses and the bottom of the fake yellow hair, she'd drawn a manga of her face with a text bubble that read, *Don't touch!*

I laughed hard.

"That'll stop you from being a dickhead."

Jenny licked her finger seductively and touched it to her own forehead before waving her fingers goodbye. I honked the horn again, parting the crowds to roll over the sidewalk, glad to finally escape. As we navigated through the town, Sumire harrumphed once more, but the anger started to melt away.

When we reached the highway entrance ramp, I pressed down hard on the pedal. The three electric motors of the Model X revved up, pushing us deep into our seats and sending us into hyperdrive. Within seconds, I was in the fast lane zipping past all the other cars as if they were stuck in slow motion. "Not bad," I said.

Sumire glanced around the spacious cabin, running her hands over the buttery leather. "I like my Prius better," she declared. The yappy dog did, too.

I pulled the Stanford cap low over my eyes as we passed under the cameras at the toll booth. Once we crossed the blue water and reached the brown, barren hills north of the bay, it was smooth sailing through Vacaville and into the Central Valley where farms stretched to the horizon. We raced past convoys of container trucks filled with oranges, lemons and cabbage bouncing along in the slow lane. I tossed the disguise into the backseat where Higgs ripped the fake beard to shreds.

Equipped with built-in cellular connectivity, the navigation screen on the 17" console directed me towards our destination in Sparks, Nevada. Sumire pushed random buttons on the console until the radio came alive. She navigated through hip-hop and Mexican pop until she found an all-news station.

"In today's financial news, the value of BiteCoin and Tesla are both soaring after reports that Satoshi Nakamoto purchased a Tesla using the popular cryptocurrency he invented. The purchase is believed to be intended by the reclusive Nakamoto to dispel recent rumors that he doesn't exist. According to a Santa Clara police spokesperson, Nakamoto was taken hostage earlier this morning at his mountain retreat by the fugitive,

Theodore Hara, before Hara escaped the dragnet. In other news, it was another record-breaking day on Wall Street with the Dow up...”

“They know,” I said.

“Know what?”

“Everything. If Satoshi were alive, it would've been on the news. They killed him and they're covering it up. They know he couldn't have bought this car. Which means they'll figure out it had to be us.”

“What do we do?”

I didn't have a clue. But we couldn't get to Nevada in the Tesla, either.

twenty-seven
tito's tacos

The highway was wide open. No cops. No helicopters. Nobody following us. We were safe for the moment. But the cops had a description of our car and knew we'd left Walnut Creek less than an hour ago. With the three electric motors on the Tesla delivering over a thousand horsepower, I could outrun the pokey Ford police cruisers. But there was no outrunning their radios. Out here in the middle of nowhere, it would be easy to road-block the highway. And even if we made it over the state line into Nevada, I had no idea how to get inside the NSB datacenter and grab the files I needed.

After everything that had happened today, I was having trouble thinking straight. Now that we were on the open highway with nothing and nobody around, the adrenaline rush was burning out, leaving me feeling sluggish and sleepy. Tesla's navigation said we had three more hours of driving to get to Sparks, NV. I needed coffee. I hated to stop now, but there was no sense in driving straight into a brick wall. I pulled off at the exit and headed into a truck stop, hiding the car in the back between a pair of Walmart semis.

In front of the entrance to the mini-mart, farm workers lounged on picnic benches, smoking cigarettes under the shade of yellow umbrellas. Sumire waved the smoke from her face as we walked into the store, Higgs trotting behind. At the refrigerator case, Sumire picked out a salad of wilted lettuce with a packet of salad dressing, while I filled the biggest cup they had with steaming coffee and grabbed a greasy hot dog. It looked disgusting, but better than the salad. Higgs, too, turned up his nose at the dog food selection and pulled on his leash to go.

While waiting in the slow-moving checkout line, a yellow food truck rolled past the door. When its horn trumpeted "La Cucaracha," the dusty world suddenly came alive. Higgs pricked up his ears. "Tacos!" I shouted when I saw the side of the truck. I handed Sumire the coffee and ran outside as the Tito's Tacos truck jerked to a stop blocking the air pump.

The farm workers stubbed out their cigarettes under the heels of worn cowboy boots, put on their hats, and sauntered over to the order window. I hollered over to Sumire to ask what she wanted to eat. She held up the bowl of wilted lettuce.

"Got any salads?" I asked the guy at the window.

He laughed. "Sorry, boss."

I ordered a bunch of carne asada tacos without onions, half without the carne asada, too, and asked if he could hurry. A few minutes later, a stern woman barked my name and shoved a cardboard tray through the pick-up window. I joined Sumire under an umbrella and handed her a meatless taco. She handed it back to me without even opening the foil.

After one bite of the carne asada, I understood why the entire town had been waiting for the truck to arrive. These were the best tacos I'd ever had. "These are so good, Bunny," I said. "You gotta try one."

She shook her head as she stabbed a plastic fork at her lettuce. I unwrapped a taco and pushed it in front of her. She eyed me skeptically but nibbled at the edge. Her eyes bugged out behind her glasses, and she took another bite. "Wow!" She scarfed down the remainder of the taco in two bites and held out her hand for another. Higgs yapped at her feet until she fed him one of my carne asadas.

The guy behind the order window overheard us. "Hey, Bunny lady," he hollered to Sumire. "Those are the best damn tacos in Sacramento! You know why? 'Cause my wife makes 'em from scratch. Eh, Margarita?"

The stern woman poked her head out the pick-up window and yelled, "Last order!"

With Higgs' help, we scarfed down the tray of tacos and were starting back to the Tesla when a patrol car roared up behind the taco truck and two cops jumped out. Shit! I was trapped between the truck and the building with nowhere to run or hide. All I could do was raise my hands in surrender to stop them from shooting me immediately.

A cop in mirrored sunglasses cocked his head at me and pointed a finger. "Bang," he said. The crowd of farm workers laughed.

The second cop ignored his mirrored partner and walked up to the order window. "Hey, meatball," he yelled back to Mirrors, "whaddya want to eat?"

Mirrors tipped his cap at me and joined his partner at the order window. "Hola, Margarita," he said to the woman inside. The man stuck his head out to look. "Enrique, *mi amigo!*" the cop said, reaching up to bump fists with the man who wasn't named Tito. "*Dos carnitas tacos por favor*. And a couple of adobada tacos."

His partner grunted, "Stick to English, meatball."

I took Sumire's hand. "Let's get out of here," I whispered. I was lucky the cops were looking for tacos instead of me, but I wasn't sure how long my luck would hold out, especially if they spotted the Tesla.

We tried to look casual as we stepped away, but Mirrors followed behind, aiming his gun finger at me again. "Haven't seen the two of you out this way before. Where you from?"

Sumire smiled at him. "San Jose."

"That so? You hear about all that weird shit going down this morning?"

"No, sir."

"Bunch of crazy, rich Asians shooting each other. Got an alert they might be heading this way. Highway Patrol is looking for a white Tesla. You seen one?"

Sumire shook her head. "Sorry, sir. I drive a Prius."

Mirrors thought as much of the hybrid as I did. He shrugged and bent over to pet Higgs. The dog backed away with a growl.

Margarita stuck her head out the pick-up window. "Mr. Policeman," she called, waving to the cops. "Your pig tacos are ready."

Mirrors doffed his cap to Sumire. "These really are the best damn tacos in all of Sactown."

"Come on, meatball," his partner said. They grabbed their trays of tacos and strolled back to their patrol car.

"Let's hide in the store until they leave," Sumire whispered.

I had a better idea. I stepped up to the order window. "Hey, Enrique" I called through the empty window.

"Sorry, boss," came the voice from the middle of the truck. "All finished. Come back tomorrow."

"No more tacos," I said. "I've got an offer for you."

He looked up from scraping the grill. "Yeah, boss, what's that?"

"How would you like an almost new Tesla? I'll trade you for this truck."

Enrique laughed. "You got a Tesla with a grill inside that can make tacos?"

"Sell the car," I said. "Buy another truck." I was sure the trade would net him more in one day than a year of slinging barbacoa.

"How much you think this truck costs?"

I had no idea. "Twenty thousand?"

"Hah, hah. Bet it costs more than that *rico* battery car of yours."

He probably didn't realize the fully loaded Tesla cost nearly a hundred grand. But there was no need to argue. With the jump in the value of Bite-Coin after my purchase of the Tesla, the crypto in my mother's wallet was worth a hundred million dollars more than two hours ago. "I'll give you two hundred grand for the truck. Plus the Tesla." No way he could refuse that.

But he did. "No truck, no tacos. See all those people?" He pointed to the farm workers lounging under the yellow umbrellas, enjoying a last smoke. "They come every day. They wait for me. I'm not here, everyone sad. I stay home one day, Margarita tells me we have to come." His wife paused her scrubbing to throw him a stinkeye.

Sumire pushed me aside to stand on tiptoes at the window. "Hi, Enrique," she said far more pleasantly than me.

He looked at her and looked at me and laughed. "Hey, it's the *chica* on your forehead. What can I do for you?"

"Is there any way we can rent your truck?"

"Sure, cartoon lady. You got a cartoon event? We bring the food!" He wiped his hands on a towel and pushed a glossy brochure through the window. "When you need it?"

"Uh...today? Is that possible?"

"Oh yeah, sure, no problem. Eh, Margarita?"

She didn't even look up from her scrubbing. "Two thousand minimum. Payment upfront."

I hugged Sumire. But I needed a way to pay them. "Ever heard of Bite-

Coin?" I'd have to explain cryptocurrency and walk him through exchanging crypto for dollars. And hope he had a new phone that could handle a BiteCoin wallet. And that there was a 5G network out here fast enough to download the app.

Enrique laughed. "Yeah, sure, no problem. All my friends they buy, sell Bites. You see the news today? BiteCoin up more than ten percent." He held his phone to show me the live feed of the Bite-to-dollar exchange rate updating every second. "All my friends, they're celebrating. Olé, olé, olé! One made fifteen thou today. Just because Satoshi bought a Tesla." Enrique opened his X feed to show me photos of me in a blonde wig and beard driving off with the Tesla. "Huh?" Enrique cocked his head. His eyes grew wide as he zoomed in on the photo, looking back and forth between the screen and me. "That Satoshi dude, he sure looks a lot like you, don't he? Without that fake, fake beard shit. And that *loco* cartoon on your face."

"Shhh," I said, a finger over my lips. "You can't tell anybody."

"Got it. Incognito. Respect that. Where we going, boss? BiteCoin party? Tesla factory?"

"Military base. I want to do something for the troops."

"Hop in."

Margarita opened the hatch in the back of the truck and Enrique held out a hand to help Sumire up the step. Higgs hopped up behind her. "No dogs," Margarita said.

Sumire turned to me. "I can't leave Higgs behind."

"We'll pay double," I tried.

"No dogs," she repeated. "Health regulations."

My plan to break into the secret NSB datacenter was being derailed by a smelly chihuahua. I had to do something. "Hey!" I yelled over to the table of farm workers. "Anyone want to make $170 driving a dog to Nevada?"

Sumire didn't look happy, but she didn't veto it either. One of the men raised his hand to friendly jeers and stepped over to join us. I handed him what was left of Sumire's cash and told him to follow the truck. Sumire placed Higgs in his arms. "Take good care of him," she said, rubbing noses with the whimpering dog.

We climbed into the truck and Margarita pulled the door shut. Inside, stainless steel gleamed, not a speck of grease. The smell of lemon-freshened cleaning fluids filled the air, almost covering the stink of fried onions.

Sumire ran a finger over the countertop, impressed. Margarita tossed her a Tito's apron and told her to scrub the wall.

"You, too," she said, handing me the bucket of cleaning supplies. I sprayed some cleaner on my forehead and rubbed at it with a rag. Instead of removing the manga, the patch of red, irritated skin only highlighted Sumire's drawing. She tried to hide a smirk as she tied the apron straps around her waist.

Enrique climbed into the driver's seat and cranked the engine. With a deep rumble, the truck roared to life. "Where to, boss?" he asked me, putting the transmission into gear.

"Wait! Do you have any tools?"

He told me where to find a red metal toolbox under the grill. While the motor ran, I hopped out of the truck with a handful of screwdrivers and wrenches and dashed around to the back of the building. I disassembled the Tesla's dashboard to extract the 17" touchscreen display. Its quad core, AMD processor and Navi-23 GPU for gaming was everything I'd need for hacking. But I had no way to connect the device to anything and no cash left to buy cables. I convinced Enrique to trade me $1000 in BiteCoin for $100 in green hard cash and went inside the market to buy every kind of adapter they sold.

Back on the highway, we waved to the cops eating tacos by the side of the road as we rumbled past, heading towards Nevada. I'd have an entire three-hour drive to figure out how to break into the most secure network in the world. After we finished scrubbing the grill.

taco tuesday

CLIMBING THROUGH THE SIERRA NEVADAS, ten-foot-high drifts of soot-blackened snow lined the highway as we headed towards Lake Tahoe. While Enrique drove the groaning truck through the steep hills, I worked on rooting the Tesla's console. It was different enough from a generic Android tablet to leave a lot to figure out and no time for figuring it out. Fortunately, every geek in the world owned a Tesla, and nearly every one of them had not only converted the car's screen into an Ubuntu Linux tablet, but posted a video on MeTube showing how they did it. Following their step-by-step instructions felt like cheating, but I was pretty sure the NSB wouldn't judge me on technique.

Once the cursor was blinking in a Linux command line in that warm-up exercise, I was ready to dive into the real challenges: First, I'd have to find a way to get past the guards and onto a military base. Then I'd have to find Bulldozer's files on a server somewhere in those three buildings, logon to the server somehow, grab a copy of the files I needed, and get the hell out before anyone noticed I'd been there.

This felt like a job for Mission: Impossible. How would Tom Cruise do it? He'd use silicone face peels, fingerprint overlays, and contact lenses to slip through the physical defenses. A great idea if I had an IMF crew and a van filled with spy gear, but all I had in this taco truck was marinated pork and homemade tortillas. That was Hollywood anyway—it looked slick on the screen but in real life, it was silly.

The one thing about the NSB network I could guarantee was that the routers and switches were made by Cisco. The only alternative to Cisco gear was Huawei equipment which came with backdoors for the Chinese spies pre-installed, a non-starter for any U.S. government agency, much less a secret spy organization. So that's where I'd have to begin. I thought about buying a stolen copy of the Cisco source code and finding a security hole myself. That might take a day, or it might take a month. I had two hours. Like rooting the Tesla tablet, I'd have to cheat and find a shortcut, even though that meant being labeled as a lowly skiddie if news of my accomplishments ever seeped out into the hacker community.

There was a good chance the North Koreans had exactly what I needed, but I wasn't trying them again. And no way the Chinese or Israelis would sell me anything from their stockpile of exploits. Fortunately, there were exploits available for purchase from freelancer hackers. Sometimes that was a programmer at a place like MeCan adding a backdoor to sell on the black market; sometimes it was a smart kid in Indonesia who hit a weird glitch in Windows and realized he'd stumbled into a goldmine. Often it was semi-professional hacking clubs battling each other for pfun and profit. And thanks to my mother's BiteCoin billion, I could make it profitable for one of them to sell me what I needed.

From the depths of the dark web, I messaged the hacker clubs famed for breaking into self-driving cars and voting machines, hinting I had serious coin to spend on a zero-day for an enterprise-class Cisco router. Within minutes, offers rolled in. I gasped at the ten million dollars one demanded for a Cisco Discovery Protocol hack using broken packets to trigger a stack overflow. He claimed in bad English to be a Cisco employee. Though I was sure that was bullshit, if his hack worked, it was exactly what I needed. I transferred the BiteCoins to his crypto wallet without even negotiating. "Spasibo!" he replied once the Bites hit his account. "Spasibo!" I answered when I received the code and the exploit looked legit. The Trolls from Olgino now had another $10 million to spend on Facebook ads to elect our next President.

Before getting started building the packet generator I'd need to run the exploit, I peered through the truck's windows to make sure we weren't being followed. Out here in the mountains, there weren't any cop cars on the road, hardly any cars at all except the beat-up pick-up that had followed us from Sactown, Higgs' head sticking out the passenger window, his tongue lolling around.

By the time we exited the highway in Reno and rolled past the endless rows of new stucco homes, the hack was prepped and ready. I could only hope it worked, though, because unlike the pros, I didn't have any way to test it before releasing it into the wild.

Leaving suburbia behind, the taco truck bounced over a narrow, two-lane road through barren hills until we reached a barbed wire fence that paralleled the pavement for miles. After curving around a hill, I caught sight of the three windowless concrete buildings on the open plateau.

At the entrance, Enrique pulled the truck up to the barrier arm at the guard shack. Honking the horn, the toot of "La Cucaracha" echoed off the brown hills. Two security guards in dark blue rentacop uniforms stood beside the shack, caps pulled low to shade their eyes from the burning desert sun.

"Hey, boss," Enrique called to the guards through the window. "Your tacos have arrived!"

A guard with a square face squinted at us. "No unauthorized vehicles allowed," he said. "You'll have to back up, sir."

A gust of wind blew grit and sand through the open window. Enrique turned to me. I didn't have a plan.

"Back away from the entrance, sir," Square Face repeated, putting his hand on the holstered gun like a gunslinger in an old Clint Eastwood movie. "Now!"

Before Enrique could put the truck in gear, the second guard sauntered over. His sleeve was decorated with a police-like badge in blue and gold marked Federal Protective Service. With his face and arms dotted with freckles, he looked straight off an Iowa cornfield. Farmboi poked his head through the window and peered inside the truck. "You got any carne asada?"

Enrique smiled. "*Sí, sí.* Best carne asada in all of...wherever the hell this is."

"How much?"

"Dollar each."

"Cool, man. Gimme four."

"No, no," I said. "Free tacos today! Satoshi Nakamoto is paying. A gift for everyone defending our country to celebrate the Joy Miyazaki Act."

"No idea what you're talking about, man, but cool, in that case, give me ten." He turned to Square Face. "Hear that, Bobby? Free tacos!"

"Gnarly," Square Face said, relaxing his grip on the gun.

"You gonna let us in?" I pointed at the logo of the Tito's Tacos apron I was wearing over the T-shirt.

Farmboi squinted at me. "Sorry, can't do that, sir. You'll have to park out there." He pointed towards the cracked pavement of the shoulder outside the gate.

While Enrique backed the truck out, Square Face typed a message into his phone. A horde of scraggly I.T. trolls, all male, all in flannel shirts and windbreakers, started streaming out from the building, marching towards the truck. With their hands held out in front of them, shielding their eyes from the sun, it looked like a zombie invasion.

Margarita fired up the grill as Enrique parked on the side of the road, blasting another chorus of "La Cucaracha" to summon the remainder of the zombie army. Soon, there was a line snaking past the guard shack and across the parking lot, nearly all the way to the building. Sumire asked Margarita to start making tacos, as many as she could.

"What kind?"

"Whatever's fastest."

Margarita rolled up her sleeves and donned a hairnet, ready for the challenge. She covered half the grill with tortillas, the other half with marinated fish and chopped onions. When the tacos were ready, she wrapped them in aluminum foil and stacked them onto cardboard trays.

Sumire tied her apron and grabbed two trays, handing one to me. "Come on," she said, opening the hatch at the back.

"Where are you going?"

"Into the building."

That was crazy. "You stay here," I said. "There's no sense in both of us getting killed."

"Theodore Hara! Will you stop trying to protect me?" She clambered down the metal step to the street and waved for me to follow.

Margarita shook her spatula in my face. "You listen to her, son. That's one smart *chica*."

She was right. I grabbed the Tesla tablet and followed Sumire into danger.

Higgs bounded through the window of the pickup and raced over to

Sumire trailing his leash behind him. She scooped him up and rubbed his nose as he licked her cheek.

"Get down!" I whispered, worried the guards might shoot us right here. Sumire laughed and lowered Higgs to the pavement where he licked her ankles.

I peered around the side of the truck to scope out the scene on the other side. Farmboi stood at the front of the line at the order window while his partner, Square Face, kept a watchful eye at the guard shack, hand gripped on his pistol.

I was trying to think of a way to sneak past the two guards when Sumire strode out from behind the truck. Before I could stop her, she marched straight towards the gate, a tray of tacos in one hand, Higgs' leash in the other. Holding up the tray to the salivating zombies, she hollered, "Someone named O'Connor order twelve fish tacos?"

Farmboi swiveled around, hand on his gun. "Hey!" he yelled at Sumire. Before I could bullrush him to knock the gun away and protect Sumire from getting shot, he lifted his hands up in a plea. "I was here first," he whined. "Where's my carne asada?"

"A couple more minutes," Sumire said with a smile. "Right now, I got fish tacos for someone named O'Connor, called in an order." She held the tray over her head as she followed the line of zombies past the barrier. At the guard shack, Square Face tipped his cap to her as she strode past.

"Is there an O'Connor here? Sandy O'Connor? Anyone know where to find him?" She continued down the line through the parking lot, a steady cry for someone named O'Connor. The zombies shook their scraggly beards as they salivated, though I wasn't sure if it was over the tacos or the sight of a woman in their midst. I followed close behind, toting the second tray of tacos, trying to look like her assistant.

By the time we reached the end of the line, Farmboi and Square Face were scarfing tacos beside the guard shack. We strolled past muddy pick-up trucks and minivans parked in front of the building and strode up to the heavy steel door. A sign said authorized personnel only.

Sumire pulled the handle, but the door wouldn't budge. Next to it, the fisheye lens of a retina scanner stared out at us. We were stuck. As I pondered how to hack the retina scanner wishing the Mission: Impossible crew was here with fake contact lenses, the door burst open, nearly knocking over Sumire's tray of tacos. Higgs growled as a zombie emerged from the darkness into the light.

"Sorry," he said, raising a hand to shield his face from the sun. He looked back and forth between us, confused, then his eyes lit up. "Hey, where're the tacos at?"

Sumire pointed towards the truck. I grabbed the handle before the door could click shut. Once the zombie staggered off towards the scent of fresh meat, we slipped through the door and into the dimness of the datacenter.

The building looked like an airplane hangar with a concrete floor and a steel roof two stories up. The room was filled with endless rows of computer racks seven feet high. Braids of blue cables snaked from the top of each rack to the next; thick black power cords dropped down from the girders above. Fans as large as airplane engines blasted chilled, dry air. The electronic hum of thousands of computers filled the space. All around, LEDs blinked green and amber—Christmas lights for geeks. But the building was deserted, all the geeks outside in line for tacos.

"How do we get the files?" Sumire asked.

I wished I knew the answer. There were thousands of servers in this massive building, and thousands more in the building on either side. I had no idea where to find the server that held the files we needed.

I headed down the center aisle, passing one identical rack after another. Servers, storage devices, routers, and switches—they all looked similar: gray steel bezels covered with round air holes, LEDs above rectangular ports winking on and off.

Trying to look like a geek who belonged in a datacenter, I took off the apron and stuffed it behind a rack. That's when I noticed the white vinyl label stuck on the side of a server. I turned my head to read the text above the bar code:

WARNING: PROPERTY OF GSA

IP 10.28.7.x

Every computer had a similar property tag, the digits of the IP address increasing from zero on the device at the top of the rack to twenty-three at the bottom. On the next rack, all the devices had similar addresses with 29 instead of 28.

The video of my car going over the speed bump came from a server with the address of 10.88.5.1. Now I knew how to find it. I raced down the aisle until I found the rack with the .88 devices. The server with the files I needed was the fifth from the top, a 4U box with a big square hole in the center for a 10-gigabit connection. I stared at it in panic—there was nowhere to plug in any of the 1-gigabit adapters I'd bought at the truck stop. Then I looked up. At the top of the rack was what I needed—a Cisco router with every kind of port. I placed the tacos on the keyboard tray. Running a thin, white cable from the tablet's USB port, I plugged it into the router and set the zero-day hack running.

Broken packets crafted to trigger a bug streamed into the Cisco device. The router was supposed to keel over and die. But the packets kept streaming and the LEDs kept winking. Something was wrong. Or more accurately, nothing was going wrong. Despite the ten million dollars I'd burned on the zero-day, the router continued blinking happily.

While I tried to figure out why the hack wasn't working, the door buzzed and snapped open. A zombie had returned. Step, step, step. I listened to the footfall of his sneakers, hoping he'd head down a different aisle before spotting the two of us here. Sumire stood close to me, her ragged breath on my neck.

"Hide!" she whispered as the zombie turned down our aisle.

There was nowhere to hide in a datacenter. All I could do was squeeze tight against the rack so the zombie couldn't see my face or notice I had no badge. I ducked my head low and typed on the tablet trying to look busy. Sumire drifted down the aisle holding the tray of tacos in one hand, the dog in the other.

The crinkle of aluminum foil followed lip-smacking noises as the zombie approached. My body was alert, my muscles tight, my toes tensed, ready to run if he noticed I didn't belong here. I held my breath as he grew closer, then stopped behind me. Looked over my shoulder. Then without saying anything, continued down the aisle.

I took a breath again. I thought I was in the clear. Then he stopped. Turned around. "Hey, man," he called to me.

I prepared to run. Out of the corner of my eye, I spotted Sumire watching from the end of the aisle, trying not to look scared. I couldn't leave her behind, but if I went to grab her, we'd both be trapped deep in the building.

"Hey," I mumbled in reply, trying not to sound nervous. I typed a bunch of fake commands to look busy.

"You try these tacos yet? Man, they're something special. Better hurry if you want to get some—they're almost gone."

"Got a bunch," I said, pointing at the tray of tacos atop the keyboard.

"Wish that truck would come every day," the zombie said, "Sure beats the crap out of the cafeteria."

My head down, my body against the rack, I hoped he'd take the hint that I was busy and go away. He stepped closer, trying to read the tablet over my shoulder. My heart was beating so hard, I was afraid he'd be able to hear it.

"Whatcha working on?" he asked.

I pulled the tablet closer to my chest. "Nothing important."

He stared at me. Cocked his head. "Never seen a tablet in here," he said. "How did you get authorization?"

He was taller than me, and heavier, but looked slow and clumsy. I was about to push him out of my way and make a dash for Sumire when the door buzzed open again. Shit. More zombies returning. It would be hard to get past them and out the building. Even if we escaped, there were two guards with guns waiting at the gate. And if we made it past them without getting shot, then what? Without the file I needed to prove my innocence, I was dead either way. If I stayed here, at least I had a chance.

I'd have to convince the zombies I was one of them, without the flannel or a wiry beard. And I was the worst actor in the world. My only hope was the truth. I tried to calm my nerves and steady my voice as I threw the zombie a guilty grin. "Uh...this is a Tesla touchscreen."

The zombie's eyes grew wide with surprise. I was afraid he'd tackle me and yell for security, but he cocked his head, intrigued. "Tesla, huh?" he said, combing his fingers through his unkempt beard covered with taco grease. "That self-driving stuff really work?"

Greasy Beard had given me a way in. "I don't know yet," I answered. "Tesla wants $200 a month for the self-driving feature."

"Seriously? After paying a shit-ton for the car? Fuck that. I'll stick with my beater. Anything goes wrong, I can fix it myself."

"That's what I'm doing," I said. I tried winking at him. The first time in my life I'd ever winked. It probably looked like I had a twitch in my eye. I showed him the tablet. "I'm trying to hack the payment module so I can turn on self-driving myself."

"Seriously? Cool, man."

"I'm stuck, though. Want to give me a hand?"

"Sure. What's the hang-up?"

"I can't get onto the network."

"Linux kernel?"

"Yup. Already rooted."

He held out a hairy arm. "Lemme take a look." He wiped his fingers on his jeans and took the tablet from my hands. After running a command to check the ethernet status, he combed his beard until his face lit up. "Aha!" He followed the cable from the tablet to the router. "Here's your problem." He disconnected the cable from the router and plugged it into a different hole. "You were on the wrong side of the network."

He handed the tablet back to me, the screen now displaying a window to input my username and password. I didn't have either.

"You're *really* good," I said, pushing the tablet back into his hands. "I'll pay you a month of self-driving charges if you get me into Tesla's payment system."

I was offering him $200 to break into Tesla's corporate network. Not that I couldn't do that myself, but that wasn't my goal. I'd gladly pay him two thousand dollars, even two million for his username and password that would log me onto the local network.

"Two hundred for that?" He laughed. "Nah, man, just give me the rest of those tacos." He pointed at the tray of wrapped tacos by my side.

"All yours," I said, "if you can break in within five minutes."

"Ha! Piece of cake. Don't touch those tacos."

He logged the tablet onto the local network using his username and password. That was all I needed. Everything else was smokescreen. But I couldn't tell him to go away now and leave me to hack his router.

While he typed furiously, growling and swearing at Tesla, a pair of zombies ambled down the aisle. Their flannel shirts were stained with bits of tomato and ground beef that looked like gore. I huddled close to Greasy Beard, pretending to help him, the ripe smell of unwashed geek filling my nose. They chatted about the manhunt back in the Valley, the whole world on the lookout for a dangerous criminal named Theodore Hara. "The cops should've bombed the whole place," one said. "Would've put an end to all that."

"And kill Satoshi?"

"There's no Satoshi, numbnuts. He doesn't exist. It's all made up—it's a sham by the government to steal our money."

"Moron. The whole thing is the government trying to stop Satoshi from replacing fiat currency with crypto."

I wanted to tell them it had nothing to do with money or even Satoshi. It was about the ability of the government to collect a copy of every phone call, email, and WhatsApp message and put them here in this datacenter, run by these idiots, so the government agency they worked for could spy on everyone in the world. But I had to keep my mouth shut and listen to their clueless banter. When they drifted over to watch Greasy Beard, I pushed tighter against the rack of computers to make myself invisible. Greasy Beard typed furiously. A zombie tapped his shoulder. "Whatcha working on, Steve?"

"Breaking into Tesla," he said without looking up.

"Nice!" one said.

"I hate those pinkos telling everyone we have to drive electric cars," said the other.

"How much time I got left?"

I hadn't actually timed him. "One minute fifty-three seconds," I said. Nobody seemed to notice I didn't have a phone or a watch. Or that I existed.

"Didn't we already grab Tesla's entire customer database?"

"That was Fung. He says Elon's helping the Chinese government spy on everyone so he can sell his cars there."

"Cock-sucking traitor."

After another attack came up empty, Greasy Beard scrunched his face, ran his fingers through his beard, then asked the zombies, "Where's that customer database?"

"Try Fung's workspace."

"Cool." He typed a bunch of commands to navigate to another server.

While we watched, Sumire walked over with the tray of tacos, Higgs trailing behind her. "You know where I can find Sandy O'Connor?" she asked our huddle.

"Hey," one zombie said, staring at Sumire's chest as if he'd never seen a woman before. He'd probably never seen one inside this building. "You're not supposed to be here."

If Sumire was scared, she hid it well. "Someone named O'Connor ordered twelve fish tacos. You know where I can find him?"

The two zombies looked at each other. "I'll bring it to him," one said, grabbing the tray away. He patted Greasy Beard on the back and smirked as he slunk away with his friend. From the end of the row, I heard the crinkle of foil followed by the grunts of zombies snorfing tacos.

Greasy Beard hardly noticed. "Take that, motherfucker!" he yelped as his fingers banged over the touchscreen. "Ha! Eat that, fuckers!" More typing. "Aaaaand...here it is. The latest Tesla firmware. Unlocked. Downloading it now." He handed the tablet back to me. "Like I said—piece of cake. Logged into Tesla with Elon's own username and password. Now gimme those tacos."

I handed him the tray. He unwrapped a taco and stuffed it into his mouth in one bite. Grease dribbled down his cheeks into his beard. "Mmmm," he said, "much obliged." He saluted me with the tray and walked away, leaving a trail of grease on the floor.

Once he was out of sight, Sumire leaned in close. "Did you get it?"

I was only getting started. But at least I was connected to the network with Greasy Beard's password. Now I had to break into the file server. I restarted the attack and this time, the router choked on the broken packets and keeled over, exactly as the Russian promised. With the router under my control, I executed a *sudo* command to make me superuser. That allowed me to make myself administrator of the file server, giving me access to everything on the device.

A *ls* command listed all the files in the directory, but the text scrolled on forever. There were too many files and I didn't know the name. How could I find the one I needed in the middle of a million others?

"Search for fcpx," Sumire suggested—the Final Cut Pro project files.

That returned a smaller list of only a few dozen files, all in the folder */user/chenders*. Charles Henderson's workspace. "Good call," I whispered.

As I scrolled down the list, Sumire said, "Stop!" She pointed at the screen. "There!" A folder named *fuckerzaki*. That had to be Jiji Miyazaki.

"What an asshole!" Sumire said, a bit too loud.

"Everything okay over there?" a zombie hollered from the next aisle. "Shorty bothering you, missy?" Giggles from other zombies all around.

I didn't like the quip about my height from a zombie who hadn't showered in days, and I knew what Sumire thought about being called missy. But she replied pleasantly, "Everything's fine."

"You're not supposed to be here, ma'am."

"Leave 'em alone," said another zombie. "I think Shorty's got a thing for her."

"Just leaving," she announced to everyone. She leaned in and whispered to me, "How much longer?"

"Couple of minutes."

"Hurry!"

As if I could work any faster. Inside Bulldozer's workspace were thousands of files accumulated over years: Jiji's documents. Emails between congressmen. Excel lists of campaign donors. Transcripts of classified congressional hearings. And videos. Hundreds of videos. Surveillance videos of Jiji stepping into motel rooms with different women, none of them his wife. The NSB had been watching Jiji closely. I downloaded it all onto the tablet. I needed to make this public, show the world what the NSB did. But these weren't the files I needed to prove that they were murderers, not me.

Footsteps headed in our direction. Higgs barked out a warning.

"Hurry, Ted!"

"Hey, missy?" a zombie said.

"Just leaving."

"Do you think you could bring some more tacos? Some beef ones would be great if you've got any left."

"And four more fish tacos for me," called another from the next aisle.

"Two pollo and a carnitas," said someone in the back.

While I worked as fast as I could, Sumire walked around taking orders.

Listing the files by date, I found a new project named *fuckhara*. "Asshole," I muttered to myself. But inside were the videos that edited me and my pony into the scene. I ran a command to copy the entire folder onto the tablet. The progress bar started filling in with green.

"Almost got it!" I called to Sumire standing at the end of the aisle, mobbed by hungry zombies.

She hurried back, but when she got to me, the progress bar slowed to a crawl. A ring of blue chased its tail. The message, *Loading...*, flashed underneath.

"Come on!" I said, tapping my foot impatiently. "Please, please, please!"

I prayed to Buddha. I prayed to Jesus. I prayed to Linus Torvalds. Only Linus replied: *Not enough space on selected drive.* The green progress bar slid back to an empty rectangle, then disappeared in a puff. "Fuck!"

The problem was obvious—the raw video files were huge. I didn't have enough space on the tablet's small SSD drive for all of them, but it was impossible to know which ones I needed and which I could leave behind. I deleted all of Jiji's files to make room and tried again.

The progress bar filled in green until there was only a small gap at the end. Then the bar turned red. It inched forward, counting down the files remaining to copy. 5 more. 4...3...2... One last file to go. The bar turned red. Shit! The time to completion started increasing. 15 seconds. 30 seconds. 1 minute. 2 minutes. I heard footsteps down the aisle.

"Someone's coming," Sumire whispered.

One file left. And not enough room on the drive. I hit skip and pulled the cable out of the router. "Let's go!" I could only hope that wasn't the one file I needed.

Sumire gasped. "No!" she cried.

"What?"

She made a strange choking sound. As I turned my head to look, a cold circle of steel pressed against the back of my neck, sucking all the heat from my body.

Sumire raised her hands over her head. Laser-Eye stood beside her, pointing a pistol at her chest.

Bulldozer laughed, jabbing my neck with the gun. "Not bad, twerp," he said. "But not good enough."

twenty-nine
fistful of steel

"OUTSIDE," he hissed, jabbing me in the back with the business end of the pistol. I wondered why he didn't just shoot me here. Was he afraid the zombies would call the cops? Or was he worried a bullet would damage one of their computers? I considered trying to make a dash for the door, but I couldn't leave Sumire behind. I bowed my head and did what Bulldozer demanded, marching towards the exit.

The zombies stood at the end of the aisle, watching us, jaws hanging open. "Out of the way," Bulldozer ordered.

"Where are you taking Shorty?" Greasy Beard asked.

Bulldozer lifted the bright orange badge from his neck and held it up high. The zombies who all wore blue badges stamped "contractor" in big letters, cowered as if Bulldozer was holding a glowing tube of plutonium. "If you want to keep your jobs," he shouted, "get the fuck out of my way."

The zombies scurried away in a hurry.

Bulldozer jabbed me in the back with the gun again. "I'll give you this, twerp," he said. "You got balls coming here."

"How did you find us?" I asked, hoping to distract him.

Under his scorn he was cocky. "You made it really fucking easy. Half the world lights up every time Satoshi makes a BiteCoin transaction. All we had to do was follow that wetback's phone. Thought you were making a run for Canada until you got off the highway. Nearly laughed my ass off when I saw you heading here. Surprised you got in through the gate. Looks like we'll need to replace those fucking GSA twerps with real soldiers who know how to put a bullet through the head of unauthorized visitors."

Laser-Eye pushed the door open and Bulldozer shoved me hard, nearly knocking the tablet out of my hands as I stumbled through the doorway. Emerging from the dimness inside, the sunlight hit my face like a million-watt spotlight, blinding me. Lifting the tablet to shield my eyes, I realized this was my chance. I jumped forward, ducking my head, to let the sunlight hit Bulldozer full force.

When he lifted his hands to shade his face, I swung around and reached for his gun. My fist closed around the barrel, pushing his arm to the side. With every bit of strength I had, I tried to pull the gun away. We tussled back and forth, but he was taller. And stronger. I kicked him in the shin, causing him to grunt, but that only made him angry. He ripped the gun out of my grasp, then slammed me across the jaw with a fistful of steel.

Pain exploded in my face; a burst of red filled my vision. I staggered backwards and collapsed to the pavement, twisting to prevent the tablet from smashing into the ground. I had to protect the files inside or else I was doomed. Though I was probably doomed anyway. Bulldozer kicked me in the ribs with a steel-toed boot. I howled as the bones cracked and the air exploded from my lungs.

"No!" Sumire screamed from the doorway.

Bulldozer wound up to kick me again, even harder this time. Straining with pain, I tried to roll away. He stepped in front of me and looked down to sneer. The gun was pointed straight at my chest. "Bad idea, twerp."

He lifted his foot to stamp on the tablet cradled in my arms. I cringed, waiting for another burst of pain. But as his foot started down, a hand reached out to grab his collar, pulling him off balance. Sumire.

"Stop!" Laser-Eye barked at her.

Instead of lifting her hands in surrender, Sumire placed her hands at her sides in an aikido stance, bending her front knee, holding her back leg straight. Bulldozer reached out and grabbed her shoulder. Despite years of training to defend herself against a bigger, stronger attacker, when Sumire attempted to use Bulldozer's momentum to toss him to the ground, he held her shoulder with a meaty hand. "Jiu-jitsu wipes aikido's ass any fucking day," he laughed. Then he shoved her at Laser-Eye as if she weighed nothing.

Despite Laser-Eye's pistol jammed into her back, Sumire leaned over to look at me, moaning in pain on the ground. Behind the glasses that hung crooked off one ear, I saw panic in those dark, wide eyes. "Let her go!" I grunted through collapsed lungs.

"You don't give the orders here, twerp," Bulldozer said, pointing his gun at my chest.

"I surrender." Pain exploded as I lifted my hands over my head. "Let Sumire go. She has nothing to do with it."

Laser-Eye kept her gun trained on Sumire's back as she looked over to Bulldozer.

He shook his head. "She's the brains of the operation," Bulldozer said. "You think this fuckwit knows what he's doing? She set up the Miyazaki woman, pretending to be her friend, then seduced this twerp into doing the wet work for her."

Huh? That made no sense. He'd killed Joy—Laser-Eye had to know that—she was part of the operation. Did I have everything backwards? Could Sumire have killed Joy, planted the file, and suckered me into discovering it? No! She was stubborn and bossy, and I had no doubt she could kill if that's what it took to protect someone she loved. But she wasn't a murderer. Unlike Bulldozer standing over me with a gun and a twitchy finger.

Bulldozer kicked me in the ribs again. Another sickening crunch as fireworks burst behind my eyes. My vision started to dim. Holding my breath against the pain, I counted prime numbers to keep from blacking out.

"Get up, twerp," Bulldozer ordered, grabbing my arm to yank me to my feet. I wobbled. Only his grip on my shoulder kept me from crumbling back to the ground. "Why the fuck don't you do what you're supposed to do?" he said as he shoved me towards the side of the building.

I didn't understand. "What was I supposed to do?" He shoved me again, even harder this time. I stumbled forward and fell to the pavement.

"Why me?" I asked, looking up into the killer's angry face. "Why did you want *me* to find the email on Joy's computer?"

He yanked me to my feet again and jabbed the gun into my spine. "You're a moron," he hissed. "The cops were supposed to find the damn message. You fucked up an operation we'd been planning for months. And now it's time to pay."

I craned my neck to look behind me, my ribs screaming in pain. Sumire and Laser-Eye were too far away to hear what he'd told me. "You killed hundreds of people just to pass a law?" I grunted through the pain as loud as I could so they would hear.

"We didn't kill anyone," he yelled over my head towards Laser-Eye. "That was YOU who murdered the girl."

This was crazy. Did Laser-Eye not know Bulldozer had killed Joy? Did he convince her I was the killer, and she was helping him catch me? She was in the NSB, had been at Joy's funeral, so if she didn't know Bulldozer had murdered Joy, it must've been his own rogue operation.

"Arrest me," I said, raising my hands over my head. "Call the cops. Take me in."

"Move," Bulldozer ordered, pushing me towards the back of the building.

I stood my ground. Kind of. Hunched over, one arm clutching my ribs. "I'm not going anywhere."

He pressed the gun against my forehead. "Now!"

I couldn't let him take me behind the building. With no witnesses, he'd shoot me there and claim I'd attacked him or tried to escape.

On the other side of the parking lot, a few zombies were still dallying around the taco truck. The two guards stood at the gate, horsing around. I had to get their attention. Getting arrested would at least let me live another day. Now that I had the original videos, I could try to tell my story, even if nobody believed me.

"Help!!!" I croaked as loud as my crushed lungs would allow, which wasn't loud enough. "Call the police!" I cried, waving one arm overhead. The dry wind blew grit in my face, dissipating my pleas into the ether. One zombie waved back to me; the others were too busy snorfing tacos to notice anything.

Bulldozer cocked his pistol. The loudest, sharpest click I'd ever heard. My body froze, my heart beat so fast I was afraid it would explode and kill me before a bullet could do the job.

"March, twerp."

If he wanted me somewhere else, that was reason enough to stay here. "Not going anywhere."

As Sumire and Laser-Eye approached, Bulldozer jabbed the gun at me and ordered me to march again. I stood my ground. If he was going to shoot me anyway, it might as well be here. His finger on the trigger, the barrel vibrated against my forehead. I wondered if I'd hear the gunshot before I was dead.

Instead, he wheeled around and grabbed Sumire by the hair. She screamed. He yanked her against his chest and jammed the gun against her cheek. She struggled, trying to kick his leg and bite his arm. With a thick forearm wrapped around her neck, he lifted her off the ground.

"I'm choking," she gagged, trying to pull him away.

"March," he said to me. "Or I put a bullet in cutie's brain."

Higgs rushed at Bulldozer, yapping loudly. He scratched at Bulldozer's legs and tried to bite his ankle but couldn't sink his teeth through the boots. Bulldozer lifted one leg and sent Higgs flying through the air. He landed at Laser-Eye's feet with a painful yelp. Whimpering in pain, the chihuahua struggled back to his tiny feet. On three legs, he limped towards Bulldozer, growling with every step. His forearm still wrapped around Sumire's neck, Bulldozer reared back to kick the dog even harder.

"What are you doing?" Laser-Eye screamed.

"I'm getting this stupid dog out of the way."

Laser-Eye reached down to pet the chihuahua. The dog snarled at her. "Nice doggy," she cooed, scratching him behind his ears. Higgs licked her hand. Laser-Eye's new best friend. Stupid traitor dog.

"See," she said to Bulldozer, rubbing Higgs' side. "He's just a harmless little doggie."

"Then keep him the fuck out of my way."

Laser-Eye scooped Higgs up and cradled him in one arm, pointing her gun at me with the other. Still choking, Sumire's eyes were closed, her resistance growing weaker.

"Let her go, Chuck," Laser-Eye said.

"She's the ringleader."

"We'll take her in." She shifted her gun to point at Sumire instead of me. "I've got her covered. You can put her down."

Bulldozer grumbled but removed his arm from her throat, then shoved her hard in the back, knocking her to the pavement. Before I could rush over, Bulldozer grabbed me by the collar and jammed his gun into my neck. Sumire lay sprawled on the ground, rubbing her throat, trying to catch her breath. Higgs leapt out of Laser-Eye's arms and hobbled over to guard her.

Laser-eye looked down at Sumire. "Are you okay?" she asked.

Sumire smiled at Laser-Eye, an open, friendly smile. What was she doing—had she banged her head on the ground? "What's your name?" Sumire asked, as if the pair were at a party.

Bulldozer stomped a heavy boot. "Don't answer her."

"You're not really Liz Ross, are you?"

A guilty grin. She tapped the orange badge hanging around her neck. "No. I'm Lanny."

"Hi, Lanny, I'm Sumire. But you know that already." Sumire struggled to sit up. She held out a hand to Lanny. "You can call me Suzie."

Bulldozer reached down and grabbed Sumire's hair, pulling her to her feet. He shoved her towards the side of the building.

"Stop it, Chuck," Laser-Eye said, her voice soft but insistent.

"Come on, Lanny, it's time to stop fucking around."

Sumire ignored the gun pointed at her and approached Laser-Eye. "Lanny? Can I ask you something?"

"Let's go!" Bulldozer yelled.

"You seem like a smart woman. Why are you helping this killer? He murdered my best friend."

Lanny glanced over at Bulldozer, a question mark bubble over her head.

"Come on already," Bulldozer said, snorting like a bull. "They're the killers—the two of them. I know it. You know it. He killed the girl."

She looked me over, unimpressed. "Really, Chuck? A terrorist? With a cartoon on his forehead?"

"Come on, Lanny, remember your training. It's part of their disinformation warfare. Don't let them confuse you. We're the good guys here."

Laser-Eye squinted at the manga on my forehead then turned to Sumire. "That's you!"

Sumire nodded. "Can we show you something else, Lanny?" Without waiting for her to answer, Sumire said, "Play the video, Ted."

I had a hard drive full of videos and no way to know which was the one that showed the killer arriving in the blue Chevy Spark. I sorted them by date, hoping the earliest version was the original.

Bulldozer jabbed the gun at me. "Don't you dare or I'll shoot you right here."

I pressed the button anyway to set the video running. I held my breath as cones of light split the pre-dawn darkness, then a car rolled across the pavement. Under the streetlamp, a boxy blue Chevy Spark came into view.

The tires hit the speed bump and the car jerked up and down. A real car. I hit pause and turned the tablet to show Lanny.

"Do you recognize that car?" Sumire asked. Lanny nodded, her eyes unblinking as she squinted through the glare of the sun. I slid the pointer forward until I found a big man in scrubs walking out of Joy's apartment, a laptop under his arm. "Do you recognize that man?"

Bulldozer lunged for the tablet. I pulled it away, my side screaming in pain.

"Shut that off!" Bulldozer yelled.

It was my turn to laugh.

"Shut it off now or I'll fucking kill you."

"It's up to you, Lanny," Sumire said. "Should Ted play the rest of the video? Or do you want your friend to kill my boyfriend?"

Laser-Eye nodded slowly, lowering the gun in her hand. "I reckon I should see this."

"It's fake!" Bulldozer barked. "Come on, Lanny, you're not going to listen to these terrorists, are you? They're trying to confuse you. Remember your training. Stay focused. You know me, Lanny."

"Do you really know him?"

"Of course. We—"

"Do you know he's married?"

"Separated!"

Sumire raised an eyebrow. "Does a separated man go home to his wife and son? Walk the dog? Shovel the snow?" I felt a surge of pride for Sumire. She'd be the greatest lawyer ever. If we somehow got out of here alive.

"Is this true, Chuck?"

"Lies!"

"Show her the video, Ted. The one from his neighbor's doorbell."

Bulldozer waved his gun. "What video?"

I didn't have the RingyDing video on the tablet showing Bulldozer's domestic life. Or any way to get it from here. "I don't—"

"Play it, Ted."

Bulldozer pointed the gun at me. "Don't you fucking dare, or I'll break every fucking bone in your hands."

"Cool it, Chuck," Lanny said, suddenly far cooler to him. "I'd like to see it."

"Don't do it, twerp."

"I want to see it, Chuck."

I looked at Sumire. "I don't—"

"Show Lanny the video," she repeated, saying each word carefully. With Bulldozer and Laser-Eye watching me, behind their back she mouthed, "Anything."

I pressed the button to play one of the videos on the tablet. Bulldozer jabbed his gun at my head. I heard an ear-shattering bang, felt the whiz of a bullet. But there was no pain. Was I dead? That quickly? Then I heard the scream of an enraged Bulldozer, heard the metal of his pistol skittering across the pavement. Lanny had shot it out of his hand, missing my head by microns. Either she was the best shot in the world, or I was the luckiest person alive.

I dove for the gun. Before I could reach it, Bulldozer tackled me from behind, driving me face-down to the asphalt and crushing my broken ribs into my lungs. I screamed in pain, but nothing came out of my throat. I struggled to breathe as I squirmed to try to get out of Bulldozer's grasp. He punched me in the kidneys, then punched me in the ribs. Pain shot through my body. My vision blurred. I had to concentrate not to black out. He climbed over my back, his boot stomping on the top of my head as he lunged for the gun. I wrapped a hand around one leg trying to stop him. The boot reared backwards, kicking my arm away.

Higgs darted over and nosed the gun away from Bulldozer's outstretched arm. Bulldozer pushed the dog out of the way and reached for the gun again. Higgs leapt at Bulldozer's throat, sinking his fangs into the skin. While Bulldozer twisted around to pull the dog away, I grabbed his ankles and tripped him. The heel of a boot smashed into my face. My nose crunched. Blood spurted everywhere. But I held on to his legs, knowing my life depended on it. He dragged me behind him as he crawled towards the gun.

Through the red haze, I saw Sumire grab Lanny's wrist to knock her gun away. As Lanny and Sumire struggled, Bulldozer picked up his pistol. "Stop!" he shouted, pointing the gun at Sumire.

Sumire let go of Lanny's arm.

"Hands up!"

She raised her hands in surrender.

I heard the click of Bulldozer cocking his gun. He was about to shoot her. I had to stop him—I had to save Sumire.

I gathered every ounce of my remaining strength and charged at him, arms outstretched in front of me. I heard the shot, saw the explosion from the muzzle. Red hot pain ripped through my shoulder as I thudded to the ground.

"Fucking twerp," he yelled. He aimed the gun at me and cocked it again. A second shot exploded. This time I was sure I was dead. Then I saw Bulldozer's head jerk to one side and bounce back, gore spattering over the asphalt. A gurgle, then he collapsed to the pavement.

Wisps of black smoke trailed from the barrel of Lanny's gun. The laser focus of her pale blue eyes misted over. She looked sadder than anyone I'd ever seen. "Why, Chuck?" she mumbled. She raised her gun and cocked it, preparing to shoot again.

"No!" I screamed. I had to stop her from shooting Sumire. But my body wouldn't move. I was glued to the ground. The helplessness was far worse than the pain in my shoulder, more horrible than the throbbing in my ribs. I struggled to move my arms and crawl towards Lanny.

She stared into the distance as she lifted the gun past Sumire to lodge the barrel under her own throat.

Sumire wrapped her arms around Lanny and pushed the pistol aside. "It's okay," she whispered into Lanny's ear. "It's okay. It's okay," she repeated, stroking Lanny's head. "You stopped the killer."

"I helped him," she choked out, tears rolling down her face. "Chuck. I loved him. I didn't know. I helped him. God forgive me. Let me end it now."

She tried to lift the gun again, but Sumire held her tight, not letting her move. "We need you, Lanny," Sumire whispered. "Your country needs you. You have to tell the world what happened. You have to end this."

As she sat there rocking in Sumire's arms, the two guards raced over from the gate, pointing their pistols back and forth between the three of us. "Hands up!" they ordered us all.

Sumire ignored them, holding Lanny tight. "Call an ambulance," she said. "Now!"

That was the last thing I heard.

ashes to ashes, bitecoin to bits

IN THE DARKNESS of the forest in the deep of the night, an elephant stood over me, his enormous honey-brown eyes watching, the shimmering light of the full moon turning his dusty, gray hide to silver. He set his trunk on my shoulder as gently as he could, but the press of its weight caused my body to groan in pain. I tried pushing away the heavy appendage, but I couldn't move my arms.

He spoke in a low-pitched elephant language that I somehow understood. "Thank god he'll survive," he said in the gentle tone of my father.

A harsh trumpeting from a second elephant sounded like the strident voice of my mother. "God had nothing to do with it," she scoffed in elephant language. "It was that girl who saved him. I never liked her, but she's grown up wise and kind. I have no idea what she sees in our little Tatsu-kun, but I'm thankful she's watching out for him."

"Wasn't that your responsibility?" A dig at my mother.

"Weren't you supposed to take care of our family?" My mother's bitter retort.

Even the spirits of my dead parents couldn't help bickering. "Stop it, you guys," I pleaded as if I was still ten years old. "Please?"

My father put his trunk on my forehead. My mother kissed my hand. "You found a good one," she said. "You'd better take care of her, Tatsu-kun."

I didn't bother to point out that Sumire didn't need me to take care of her. Elephants were very old fashioned that way. "I promise to support her every way I can."

They waved their trunks goodbye as the vivid scene dissolved to dim gray mist. My eyes fluttered open to a burning fluorescent brightness, causing me to squint. The entire room was painted white. This wasn't the forest, but it wasn't my apartment either.

Shivering from the cold, my whole body felt frozen except for a warm glow radiating from my hand. Fingers were wrapped around mine, squeezing softly. "Teddybear?" a voice said. "Are you awake?"

I raised my eyes to see Sumire looking down from above, concern etched into her face. "Where am I?" I croaked out through dry, cracked lips.

"In the hospital. You're safe now."

White walls, tile floors, a pair of pastel blue chairs—the room came into view. Flowers by the window, shiny balloons in the corner. Behind me, an electronic device beeped out the time. An IV dripped clear liquid into my arm. I tried to reach out to Sumire, but my body wouldn't move. Was I paralyzed? Had a bullet severed my spine, leaving me trapped in bed forever? Panic rose in my chest. I tried harder to move.

"Don't, don't, don't," Sumire said, patting my hand. "It's okay, Ted. You're in a cast."

The weight on my chest was the plaster holding my body together. I could move my hands; I could wiggle my toes; I could talk. I started to relax. But my throat was dry, my tongue stuck to the roof of my mouth. My head throbbed—I needed a coffee IV.

Sumire pressed a magic button and a man in blue scrubs with a stethoscope hanging from his neck strode in. "Awake?" he asked Sumire. She nodded. He reviewed the chart, checked the monitor, then stepped over to shine a light into my eyes. After making a note on the chart, he said to Sumire, "He'll be groggy for a while from the Nembutal, but all his signs look good."

The doctor had curly hair and hooded eyes, stubble peeking out from around the blue mask. He reminded me of the guy from the funeral. And from the jail. It was—

"Naz is here," Sumire said.

"I owe you thanks," he said, placing a hand on my cast.

A pang of guilt stabbed my chest. "I'm sorry," I said. "I thought you murdered Joy." Everything I was certain about only days ago now seemed absurd. I'd assumed he was connected to terrorists simply because his family was Afghani. Exactly what the truly evil people—Bulldozer and Laser-Eye—had counted on.

"And I'm sorry I thought you were framing me. I couldn't imagine our own government was out to get me."

Naz was out of jail, but what was he doing in Nevada? If that's where this was. Through the window all I could see was deep blue skies, a few clouds poking over the mountains. "Where are we?"

"We're at Regional Medical Center," Naz said.

I must have looked confused. "You're back in San Jose," Sumire added, which didn't help. "You've been in a coma. After the surgery, they flew you here in a helicopter."

My only chance to ride in a helicopter and I hadn't even been conscious. I didn't remember anything after being shot. "Bulldozer?" I coughed out. Had he been arrested or was he still after me?

Sumire patted my hand. "Charles Henderson is dead."

"Laser-Eye?"

"Lanny. Her name is Lanny, Ted."

"How did you know?"

"Know what?"

"Laser...Lanny...didn't...everything?"

"Does she look like a killer to you?"

I nodded.

"Seriously, Ted? Why can't you look past her face and see her heart?"

I didn't need to see her heart when I'd looked into those laser eyes locked, loaded, and set to kill. But before I could answer, the door cracked open. "Can I come in?" a woman asked, a nurse, I thought.

Sumire waved and the door swung open. Lanny the Laser-Eye walked in.

"No, no, no!" I writhed in the bed. She was here to kill us! I had to get up and stop her.

"It's okay," Sumire said, caressing my arm. "Relax, Teddybear. Relax..."

Lanny stood beside Sumire. "How is he?" she asked. Her blue eyes remained as bright as lasers, but the intensity of their focus had softened. With her shoulders hunched, she looked smaller than I remembered.

"So-so," Sumire said. "He's making less sense than usual."

"He'll be fine eventually," Naz said. "There was considerable damage to the brachial plexus nerve, but I expect him to regain full mobility."

I choked out, "You helped Bulldozer!"

She turned to Sumire. "What's a 'bulldozer'?"

Sumire shrugged an apology. "That's his weird nickname for Charles."

"Oh," Lanny said with an uncomfortable laugh. "I guess he was kind of a bulldozer, wasn't he? I loved him, though. At least the person I thought he was. I thought he was a patriot who loved his country. He convinced me we had to do everything to protect freedom. I believed him. Everything he said. Until I saw that cartoon on your forehead and nothing made any sense. I've seen a lot of militants in Afghanistan and none had cartoons on their face."

"You killed Joy!"

"No, sir, I didn't," she said. "You have to believe me. Do you think I could've gone to Ms. Miyazaki's funeral if I thought I was responsible for that poor girl's death? Chuck told everyone the terrorist did it. We were only taking advantage of the situation to give politicians cover to do what was needed."

Naz looked up from the chart. "Terrorist?"

"That Afghani doctor. He was part of ISIS."

"Uh...no," he said. "The American doctor of Afghani descent is right here. And I assure you he has nothing to do with ISIS."

She stared at the doctor. Dressed in his scrubs with his face covered, it took her a moment to realize who he was. "Oh my god, you're him! You're the terr...the doctor. Sir. I'm so sorry." She bowed her head in shame. "I'm sorry for everything."

I expected Naz to push her away—the accomplice to his girlfriend's murder. But he reached out and placed a gloved hand on hers.

"Lanny?" Sumire asked in a quiet voice.

"Yes, ma'am?"

"We need your help. We have to continue Jiji's work."

"Ma'am?"

"Jiji's friends in Congress are rewriting the Joy Miyazaki Act to guarantee everyone's privacy. No secret back doors for spies. No more NSB. As you can imagine, the FBI, Justice Department, and Homeland Security are fighting it. We need you to testify to Congress and tell everyone what really happened. Can you do that?"

She looked at Naz, then at Sumire, then at me. The killer laser eyes were gone. "Yes, ma'am," she said. "That's my new mission."

I had to know. "What was in the file on Joy's computer?"

She shook her head. "I don't know. Chuck said it came from the terrorists. I reckon old Aaron made it. Same as he made the replacement file that he got me to upload."

"You're Smartgrrl?"

An uncomfortable grimace. "Yes, sir. That's what old Aaron always called me. I was helping with your decryption project. Then the terrorists attacked and we knew the decryption would stop. Aaron said we had to do something or the terrorists would go free."

Naz glared at her. "So you framed me?"

"Yes, sir. I'm truly sorry for that. Aaron said they had field intel that you were an ISIS operative. Aaron ran all the operations."

"An operation that killed hundreds of innocent people in Pakistan?"

"No, sir. You have to believe me. We had nothing to do with that. We only reacted after real terrorists attacked by planting that file we could open."

She apologized once more to Naz and hugged Sumire before departing. Sumire stood at the edge of the bed and looked at me, eyes downcast, lips an anxious frown. She put her hand on mine. "There's something I need to tell you, Teddybear."

This didn't sound good. "What?"

"Satoshi died," she said, biting her lip. "The police recovered the body. The FBI admitted firing the shots. They claim it was an accident. They said it was supposed to be a warning shot to get you to surrender."

More lies. It would take Lannie's help and a congressional investigation to find out who had been at Satoshi's mansion shooting to kill us.

Sumire squeezed my fingers. "I know the two of you were close."

Close was hardly how I'd describe my relationship with Satoshi. He was my mother's friend—my married mother—her devoted tea ceremony disciple who followed her around like a puppy. Though it was hard to forgive him for his relationship with my mother, whatever it had been, I was sad that someone who'd been a presence my entire life had died, killed by a bullet intended for me. All I could think to ask was, "When's the funeral?"

As one of the richest men in the world, a recluse nobody believed existed, his funeral would be a media circus. I hoped it was finished already, his body cremated, his ashes spread over the wisteria and cherry trees in his beloved garden, so I wouldn't have to attend. I'd already filled my lifetime quota of funerals and had no need for another.

Sumire ran her fingers through my hair. "Well, Ted, that's up to you."

"Me?"

"His will left everything to your mother."

My mother was in his will? My dead mother? I wasn't sure whether to feel angry or thrilled. When she'd died, the only thing she'd left behind was a cabinet filled with tea ceremony implements and her precious collection of vacuums. But I was her only heir. Did that mean I inherited it all—$17 billion? Me? Was I now the seventh richest person in the world?

A billion ideas flooded my brain with all the good I could do: replant the prune and apricot orchards that had covered San Jose before the tech invasion; build a social media platform safe from trolls and assholes; open free coding schools in inner cities to train people for high-paying tech jobs. I had $17 billion at my disposal to use however I wanted.

Then reality smacked me in the face. All of Satoshi's riches were in Bite-Coin and the only person who knew the password to Satoshi's crypto wallet was Satoshi, and he was dead. Unless??? Had he used the same password as my mother? "Where's Satoshi's phone?"

Sumire found the phone inside my bag of personal effects in the closet. I powered it up and clicked on Satoshi's crypto wallet. With my arms in a cast, I had to dictate my mother's password to Sumire. It beeped an error. My excitement came crashing back to earth. Unless I could guess his unbreakable password, Satoshi's money was locked away on the blockchain, lost forever. Ashes to ashes; BiteCoin to bits. I hoped I wasn't stuck paying inheritance tax on all that money I didn't have.

At least I'd get his Batmobile. And the hot springs bath. And I still had the crypto in my mother's wallet we'd used to buy the Tesla. Wait! Did that mean I was a billionaire? For real? It wasn't $17 billion, but $1 billion was still serious coin. Maybe it wasn't enough to return all the office parks in San Jose to prune orchards, but I'd be able to open the coding schools and make a real difference in the world.

"What are you smiling about?" Sumire asked.

"I'll show you." I told her to click on my mother's crypto wallet and enter the same password. I cheered when I heard the ding of the app opening the account. "What's it say?"

Sumire lifted her glasses to squint at the small text. I waited for her to gasp. And waited. Finally, she cocked her head. "What am I supposed to see?"

"There's twenty thousand Bites in the account—a billion dollars. Plus or minus a few million depending on the exchange rate."

"Where?"

"Right there."

Sumire was still confused. "I don't see it."

She showed me the dashboard. The balance had 0 BiteCoin. 0 Eth. 0 Tether. 0 everything. Not even a single Dogecoin or a bark of Shibu Inu. Where did all the currency go? There'd been 20,000 Bites in my mother's crypto wallet when Satoshi had given us the phone. I'd bought the Tesla for two Bites, gotten cash from Enrique for 0.02 Bites, paid two hundred to the Russians, and been scammed out of a hundred by the North Koreans. That should've left 19,697.98 Bites remaining.

The trading history showed three transactions while I'd been in a coma: the first for 12,152 Bites; the second for 6,841 Bites; the last one taking the remaining 704.98 Bites. Which left exactly 0.000 Bites. Fuckers! My mother's billion dollars. My billion dollars. Every Bite of it stolen.

I pushed the blanket aside. Struggling to slide to the edge of the bed, I winced with the pain in my jaw, the throbbing in my shoulder, the explosion in my ribs.

"Theodore Hara! Where do you think you're going?"

I needed to get home. I needed to get back to my computer. I needed to track the hackers and recover the billion in BiteCoin before they could convert it all to dollars and siphon it off the blockchain. "Where's my clothes?"

Looking towards the closet, I saw the pink overnight bag overflowing with Sumire's clothes, noticed her pillow and blanket sitting on the chair. She must've stayed by my side for days while I'd been out with the elephants.

As I looked into those eyes overflowing with love, saw the worry tinged with frustration, I realized there was somewhere else I needed to be even more—here with Sumire. She was worth more than a billion dollars. The hackers would have to wait.

"Thanks for taking care of me," I said as she eased me back into bed. But after everything that had happened to both of us, she had to be suffering, too. I tightened my fingers around her hand. "What do you need, Bunny?" I asked.

She kissed me on my broken nose. "The only thing I need right now is for you to recover and make me laugh again."

I hummed her favorite song, even more out of tune than usual. That brought a smile to her lips. And a dour nurse into the room who adjusted the IV. Cold seeped up my arm. The world grew hazy as the light dimmed and my brain grew fuzzy again. I tried counting backwards from one billion to stay awake. I didn't even make it through the first digit before drifting into that strange netherworld that existed between this world and the next. The two elephants were shimmering in the silver moonlight, waiting for my return.

"Don't go," I called out through the fog to Sumire, wherever she was. "My parents are here. I have to introduce you."

I felt a warm caress on my hands. "Don't worry, Teddybear," came the soft voice. "I'm right here with you."

acknowledgments

A very different version of this novel was completed long ago, in late 2001. At the time, I'd been working at a startup selling computer networking equipment to customers that included the NSA, DISA, and other national security agencies.

A major controversy within the I.T. industry then was the balance between personal privacy and the needs of law enforcement. Who would have access to our emails and texts and see phone records and GPS history, and what limitations would be placed on them? The FBI led the charge on behalf of police forces across the country, arguing they needed the data for criminal investigations, but it was the NSA's indiscriminate hoovering of data that concerned everyone about privacy.

After abuses by the NSA were uncovered, Congress placed strict limits on the agency's authority to spy on U.S. citizens. But at the same time, to prevent the holy trinity of bogeymen—murderers, child pornographers, and terrorists—from covering their tracks with encryption, the federal government ordered every phone and computer to include a special chip from the NSA to give law enforcement access to all communications. Encryption software was designated a military-grade weapon subject to export restrictions so that non-Americans couldn't hide from our spies. However, with the explosion of internet usage, this effort proved unworkable and the federal government was forced to retreat.

Then, in September 2001, just as I was finishing the novel, 9/11 changed everything. The pendulum swung hard in the other direction. The public demanded the government do more to protect them from terrorists. The security community was given everything they wanted. Only a month after 9/11, Congress passed the Patriot Act, authorizing the NSA to eaves-drop on communications everywhere in the world, including on U.S. citizens. Soon, the NSA was collecting so much data, they had to build a huge datacenter in Utah to store all of it.

It's hard to remember those days now, but anyone questioning the heroes of law enforcement was considered unpatriotic. My novel languished on a floppy disk while I was busy selling I.T. equipment to those same agencies.

It was more than ten years later when Edward Snowden dropped his bombshell, revealing the NSA's illegal activities to expand their SIGINT capabilities. Though the headlines focused on the NSA's spying on allied leaders, it was their hidden activities that were corrupting the foundations of the internet. The NSA's cryptologists helped to standardize a broken encryption algorithm that the world depended on for everything from bank transfers to online shopping. To attack Iran, they built an ingenious virus which became the template thieves now use to infect our computers and steal our money. The NSA installed special chips on the Cisco routers running China's internet backbone to give themselves access to all communications in the country. The public paid little attention.

But with Snowden's revelations that the NSA had compromised Apple and Google datacenters to spy on all their users, the two companies updated their security infrastructure so that only users could decrypt their own data. For law enforcement, the world went dark. Suddenly, even a warrant meant nothing if the subject of the investigation wouldn't turn over their passwords.

Law enforcement was desperate to convince the keepers of our digital lives to reverse their policies. Their attempts culminated in 2016 with a very public spat between the FBI and Apple. After a mass shooting in California, the FBI was unable to open the dead gunman's iPhone. A court ordered Apple to assist the FBI in viewing the contents, even if that required rewriting the operating system. Apple refused, stating it would compromise security for all users. Despite the FBI's ongoing attempts to shame Apple into cooperating with murder and child pornography investigations, the company has stood firm in protecting data and privacy. That battle isn't over, though, with the industry expecting a renewed push by law enforcement to change the law once they find a case the public will get behind. But would they manufacture a situation to get what they want? Maybe.

Personally, I'm not a believer in conspiracies. Nobody can keep a secret. But a small group of zealots who see themselves on a mission where the ends justify the means? Yes, absolutely that could happen.

This was the backdrop percolating in my head for years. I attempted revising the original novel a few times, but always hit a wall. The world of 2001, before smartphones, before GPS, before security checks at airports, no longer existed. Minor tweaks to the plot wouldn't work. I threw away the floppy drive. That story was dead.

However, after completing a different novel, *To Kill a Unicorn*, I had to decide on Ted Hara's next adventure. As a hacker and programmer working at a competitor to Google and Apple, Ted would be in the middle of that trade-off between privacy and security, the story I'd been waiting to write.

Different characters, different location, different world. Almost nothing of that original story survived except for an encrypted file found on a dead woman's computer. But with *Countdown to Decryption*, I'm glad to have finally accomplished what I had set out long ago to write. Thank you for reading it. Without you, the reader, this story is nothing but a bag of words in a document.

Writing a novel is the most solitary activity I know of, staring at a computer screen for months on end alone in a corner of a room. But in what seems like a contradiction, publishing a novel requires the efforts of a team.

This novel wouldn't exist without the great folks at Pandamoon who turned an (unencrypted) Word document into this book and did all the work required to get it into your hands. I'd like to give special thanks to Elgon Williams and Christine Gabriel for leading the charge at Pandamoon, and to Rachel Schoenbauer, editor extraordinaire, who along with Tylee Ertel, found the many details, both big and small, that needed improvement.

I'd also like to thank my many beta readers, especially Tony Ollivier, Chloe Duckworth, David Joiner, and Yuko Tamura, who gave me the feedback needed to refine a rough draft into a polished novel.

But most of all, I have to thank my wife and partner, Satsuki, who patiently endured my screaming at the computer, cursing at the keyboard, banging my head against the wall, and demanding silence every day while I wrangled these words into submission.

I hope you enjoyed Countdown To Decryption. I would be grateful if you took a moment right now to post a quick review wherever you bought your copy, and/or on Goodreads if you have an account there.
Also visit my website to learn more about my other books and to sign up for my newsletter at https://dcpalter.com/.

about the author

DC Palter is an award-winning novelist and entrepreneur who has built and led tech startups for twenty-five years. His weekly articles on business strategy and venture capital are followed by tens of thousands of startup founders around the world.

After beginning his career as a research engineer in the defense industry, he escaped to Japan. There he developed a deep appreciation for Japanese culture and became fluent in the language. He is the author of *Colloquial Kansai Japanese*, a popular guide to the Osaka-Kyoto dialect, and editor of *Japonica*, a journal of Japanese culture.

His first novel, *To Kill a Unicorn*, was named an American Fiction Awards finalist for Best Mystery and Best Debut Novel and National Indy Excellence Awards finalist for Best Suspense Novel. He is the two-time winner of the Little Tokyo fiction contest for short stories in both English and Japanese. His stories have been published in literary journals in the U.S. and Japan, while his articles on technology and investing have appeared in over a hundred publications.

DC holds an MFA in creative writing along with degrees in engineering, marketing, and law. Together with his wife, an ikebana artist and tea ceremony teacher, he splits his time between Los Angeles and Kobe, Japan.

www.ingramcontent.com/pod-product-compliance
Lightning Source LLC
Chambersburg PA
CBHW070456300726
48975CB00007B/2192